Elaine Spires

Singles' Holiday

To Melanie

My best ever creation.

Author's Note

In spite of my experience leading groups of single travellers to worldwide destinations over the course of many years, this book remains a work of fiction. My sincerest thanks go to all the people that made up those groups – many of whom have become dear personal friends - for the good times and the bad, the ups and downs I experienced with and through them. The best careers advice I ever received was *Find what you love doing and get someone to pay you for it,* so thank you everyone for allowing me to put that into practice.

Thanks, too, go to Simon Drake for his creativity with the cover; to Keith Spires for his expertise and technical input; to Baerbel Pfeiffer and Curtis Bird for their hospitality and support in providing the best, most scenic writing studio ever; and to Kathie Philp, tour manager extraordinaire for a life-time of friendship, stories, laughs and experiences shared.

Day One

Geri jumped up and looked at the alarm clock in a panic, convinced she'd overslept. 01:55 glowed at her in the darkness.

Not even two o'clock yet!

Just twenty-two bloody minutes since the last time she'd sprung awake and looked at the clock. She tutted to herself and turned over, billowing up the duvet with her legs in an attempt to get it to fit around her comfortably, like a big puffy sleeping bag. Just the way she liked it. Since she no longer shared a bed with anyone wrapping herself in the duvet made her feel safe. But feeling safe was one thing, she needed to get back to sleep because if she didn't, if she couldn't get any sleep, she'd look like a wreck in the morning and she so wanted to make a good impression. She HAD TO make a good impression.

Just stay positive!

Why wouldn't she make a good impression? She'd spent a fortune, far more than she could afford, on face packs, creams and serums since she'd booked her holiday. And she'd deprived herself of all her favourite foods and spent endless hours in the gym trying to get her body into some sort of bikini-fit shape in spite of the obvious toll of two pregnancies in the form of stretch marks and droopy boobs. She'd even considered Botox on the wrinkles that had slowly, stubbornly taken up residence around her eyes and mouth over the last two years but had been afraid it might leave her unable to raise her eyebrows or smile properly. All she needed was a good few hours' sleep. Then, with the help of her Eye Dew and some Touche Éclat she'd look as good as any woman of forty-three could expect to.

She picked up the alarm clock and studied it again, making sure for the umpteenth time it was set for 4.30am.

Christ! I'm getting OCD!

She lay back down again working out that she could still get two and a half hours sleep if she went off at this moment. All she had to do was relax. She started to breathe in and out slowly and rhythmically, clearing her mind of all thoughts and worries, just like the lifestyle-improvement CD said she should. Then a blood-curdling screech pierced the silence, making her jump out of her skin.

Those bloody foxes!

They had muscled their way into the neighbourhood over the last couple of years and now a turf war was going on between them and the local cat population. It wasn't helped by her neighbours, Andy and Ian, who thought that drinking Fair Trade coffee made them eco-warriors, leaving out food for them. The foxes were becoming a real nuisance, and a noisy one, too. More screeches reached her from the alley way between her block of flats and the doctor's surgery next door. It sounded like there was a serious scrap going on.

That's all I need!

Geri tried again. Resettling herself on her back, she pulled the pillows up tight around her ears and started to breathe slowly, relaxing her feet, her legs, her body and then her arms and shoulders in the vain hope she'd drift off to sleep.

Ten minutes of slow, heavy breathing later she decided to get up and have a cup of tea.

***

Eve closed the front door quietly behind her so as not to wake the neighbours and shivered, surprised, because it was July, by the chill in the air.

What do you expect? It's only four o'clock!

Walking on tiptoe she wheeled her suitcase down the path and winced at the noise it made rolling over the gravel, which seemed so much louder in the night-time silence. She clicked the remote control to open the boot of her car, breathed in, bent her knees a bit and braced herself before lifting the case and swinging it up and round into the boot. Panting slightly from the effort, she tried to close the boot without slamming it. She didn't want to give Mr Peyton any cause to complain again. He'd waylaid her when she got back from a trip to Thailand earlier in the year.

"It might be time to go to work for you, but it's the middle of the night for the rest of us," he'd said, "and Sheila's a very light sleeper. Once she's awake she can't go back to sleep again. You woke her up when you slammed your front door. Then you slammed the boot of your car and finally you slammed the car door before revving up and driving off with the music blaring. It's inconsiderate." Rheumy eyes glared at her through thick glass edged with tortoiseshell as he shoved both hands into the pockets of his faded grey cardigan in what could only be considered a belligerent manner.

"Sorry about that, Mr Peyton. It wasn't intentional."

"Noise travels at night."

"Yes, as I said, I'm sorry and I'll try to keep it down in future."

"Well, just make sure you do!"

Miserable old git!

She had begun to get irritated by his attitude so it was just as well he marched back into his own garden and closed the gate firmly behind him. What did he want? Sackcloth and ashes?

Eve put the car into reverse and slowly backed off the driveway onto the road. She turned the wheel to straighten up and then, once she was out of the close and out of Mrs Peyton's hearing, she whacked up the radio. She always listened to Magic. A bit cheesy and a bit repetitive sometimes, but on the whole it was music she liked, especially at this time of the morning when it wasn't spoiled by the comments of any presenters or the monotonous repetition of commercials. Barry White was telling some lucky woman that he loved her just the way she was. Eve smiled to herself. Swinging round the roundabout and down the ramp, indicating right and pulling onto the A13, she relaxed back into the seat and started singing along. The roads were usually fairly empty at that time of the morning, although she knew that at some point she'd be blinded by an idiot in a 4x4 with six headlamps and bull bars driving right on her tail. There is no record of a herd of bulls ever rampaging down the A13 in the dark, but still, the good people of Essex obviously like to be prepared should they ever decide to. Eve smiled to herself as she sat back in the seat and put her foot down. With any luck she'd be at the long stay car park before five thirty.

***

This bloody train couldn't be any fuller! Where the hell is everyone going?

Murray fumed to himself as he looked around the carriage. He glanced over to his left for the tenth time to check that nobody had gone off with his suitcase, although quite how they could have done that as the train hadn't stopped since it left Victoria station he didn't know.

You can't be too careful!

He'd heard that gangs operated on trains. Eastern Europeans most of them. He'd seen it in the papers and heard the punters in the back of his cab talk about how one distracted you while a second whipped your case and passed it to a third who jumped off the train with it.

Just sit back in your seat and relax! You were lucky to get it.

That was true. It had been the last free seat in the carriage. He'd seen the two women dressed up to the nines in almost matching outfits made of denim and bits and pieces of lace and the young one with two toddlers eyeing it up. He'd really had his work cut out to beat them to it. He'd elbowed the foreign couple blocking the doorway to one side before throwing himself into it to claim it as his own. He was glad he didn't have to stand up all the way to Gatwick because he'd get back ache if he did. He often suffered with lumbago if he worked in the garden or lifted something. "The first signs of arthritis," his doctor had told him. Sitting in the cab all day didn't help. Still, he wasn't going to be working the cab. He was going on holiday and he didn't want anything spoiling the next two weeks. It would be a shame if he had the chance to get his leg over and then his back stopped him from doing it.

The older man in the safari jacket and corduroy trousers who was sitting next to him suddenly refolded his copy of the previous day's *Telegraph*, narrowly avoiding hitting Murray in the eye with his fist.

Why can't people read a bloody tabloid on a train?

Murray gave him a filthy look. He felt like jabbing him in the ribs and pointing out that you can fold up a tabloid without risking taking someone's eye out. His mind wandered to the advice articles he'd recently read which said you should try to relax and make the journey part of the holiday. He was finding it impossible to relax with that stupid woman's handbag bashing against his knee. He didn't know why she didn't strap hang with the left hand and hold the bag with the right. That way she wouldn't annoy him. Or she could put it on top of the holdall she was clutching precariously between her calves.

Whatever happened to manners?

And then one of the two toddlers started crying. He tutted and shifted position so that he could glare at the mother, who appeared to be taking no notice of the child. Was she deaf? Couldn't she hear the little blighter? He sincerely hoped it wasn't going to grizzle and scream all the way to Gatwick. He didn't understand why a woman would travel with children when she couldn't control them. Then a really unbearable thought occurred to him:

What if they're on the same flight as me?

They could be crying all the way to Antigua. Sometimes he hated people.

***

"Going somewhere nice?" the taxi-driver asked.

Although in other circumstances Gerri would have welcomed a man talking to her, she hoped he wasn't going to be one of those who wanted to engage in meaningful conversation and put the world to rights all the way from Reading to Gatwick.

"Antigua."

"Alright for some, innit?? Jetting off to the Med."

Geri smiled, too polite to correct him.

"Not going on your own, are you?"

"No!"

Oh dear! That was too quick!

"I'm going with a group of friends. We're meeting up at the airport."

"Oh right. That's good. Cos I was gonna say that a mate of mine went away on his own a couple of months ago with some singles' company."

He paused and looked at her in the mirror, waiting for a reaction.

"Oh, really?" She obliged.

"Yes, all singles they was. I was a bit wary, you know what I mean? I said to him 'you wanna be careful' I said. You don't know who'll be in a group like that, do you? I mean, they could all be a bit funny, couldn't they? People who haven't got no one to go away with.... well, I mean, like they could all be weirdoes or anoraks, you know what I mean?"

Oh thank you very much!

Just as she'd started to feel a bit more positive about it all that wasn't what she wanted to hear. It had taken all her courage to book herself on a singles' holiday. How could he have known she was going on one? Had he seen the label on her case? No! He couldn't have done because she'd tucked it inside the zip pocket.

Have I got 'I am a poor, lonely, single woman who hasn't got anyone to go on holiday with so she's going with a bunch of strangers' embroidered on my Country Casuals Weekend Holdall?

Gerri realised that he was still looking at her in the mirror, waiting for her reply.

"Oh, err, yes," she said weakly.

"As it turned out he had a great time. Said they was all normal. Well, on the whole. It was Easter week so they was nearly all teachers. They can be a bit funny, can't they, teachers? But he said they was up for a laugh. Told me some right old stories. Had a couple of shags as well. Nice girls. But gagging for it he said."

She began to sink further and further into the seat and her heart with it as the miles sped past. She hadn't thought of that. This was the first week of the school summer holidays so the chances were that there would be lots of teachers on the trip. Perhaps there would even be someone she knew. She felt her stomach churn at the thought.

Will they all be gagging for it? Will they all think that I am?

Well, if the truth be known, she was gagging for it. Well, not *gagging* exactly but she had been hoping that someone in the group or in the resort even, would find her attractive and that sex would be on the agenda somewhere. But she felt sick at the thought she might be the subject of gossip or speculation.   God alone knew there'd been enough gossip about her in the last couple of years to last a lifetime.

"Stop the taxi!"

She couldn't do that. She'd paid her money; she needed a break. And besides, the taxi-driver was already looking at her through the mirror as if she was a half-wit. She attempted a smile and fielded the barrage of questions he threw at her -

"You bin there before?"

"Did you need injections?"

"You ever bin to Ibeefa?"

"Did you like it?"

"Who you flying with?"

-   with one-word answers and gradually he got the hint and they drifted into silence for the final few miles of the journey. Hoobloodyray!

***

Eve had never really understood the phrase "face like a slapped arse" until she saw the check-in agent at Desk 62 that morning: an unsmiling ice-queen with walnut-whip make-up trowelled on and a badge announcing her as IVANA.

"Good morning!" Eve said approaching the desk.

"Your boarding pass, ticket and passport."

Eve produced all three from inside the orange Travel Together wallet.

"I wanted an aisle seat near the front of the aircraft, please. I tried to move myself forward when I did the on-line check-in, but your system wouldn't let me."

With a sigh that was as deep as it was dramatic Ivana snatched the documents and flapped open the e-ticket. She tapped at the keyboard and fixed her gaze on the screen.

"You are a large party. Where are the rest?"

"Well, I'm a tour manager actually, so I am with a group of people, yes. But we usually all check-in separately."

"You are on same locator."

"Yes but that hasn't been a problem when I've flown with you before."

6

"Same locator means sitting together."

"But I need to be near the front of the aircraft. I need to get off first, ahead of the group. Going through Immigration takes forever in Antigua and I have to be in the arrivals hall waiting for my group, not fifteen minutes behind them in the queue."

Another of the deep dramatic sighs. Still no eye contact.

"Groups always sit together."

"But I've just explained why I need to sit near the front, why I need to be moved."

No reply. Ivana continued to prod the odd key and look at the screen. Eve, who always tried to be nice to everyone because she knew from experience that working with the public could be the pits sometimes, was beginning to get a bit fed up with Ivana and her attitude and she particularly objected to being ignored. Last month she'd travelled from Gatwick with the same airline and moving hadn't been a problem at all. In fact, the agent, an amiable young girl called Lucinda, couldn't have been more helpful. Unlike Ivana, who was now, she decided, getting on her tits.

"If you can't move me then I want to speak to a supervisor."

The sigh went deeper and was accompanied by a tut and a shrug and some furious tapping on the keyboard.

"Twelve H."

"Thank you."

"How many cases you have?"

"Just the one."

"Put it on the scale."

Is the word 'please' nowhere in your bloody vocabulary?"

Eve lifted the case onto the scale.

"Is overweight."

Eve looked at the scale in disbelief. Years in the job had taught her just how much she could pack without going over the limit. In fact, the basic contents of her case never varied much; underwear, trainers, nightdress, toiletries' bag, two paperbacks, telescopic umbrella, lightweight cagoule, torch, paperwork, jeans, two t-shirts and then the clothes and shoes she would need, depending on whether she was on a beach trip, tour, walking or activity holiday or a cruise. She'd been to The Mango Tree Resort before and knew that she could get her clothes laundered

7

quickly and very cheaply so there was no need to take loads, and she always bought sunscreen and insect repellent locally, if and when she needed it to keep the weight down. As soon as she'd got back from a cruise through the Norwegian Fjords ten days earlier she'd washed her clothes and repacked her case ready for her next trip. She'd taken out the long jeans and replaced them with summer-weight cut-offs. If the case hadn't been overweight ten days ago then it couldn't be now. Eve glanced at the reading.

"It says twenty-four kilos."

"Weight limit is twenty-three."

"Oh! Come on!"

"You must pay thirty-five pounds."

"You cannot be serious!" Eve's voice went up an octave and increased by a couple of hundred decibels.

Christ! I've morphed into John McEnroe! And everyone's looking at me.

Indeed, the middle-aged couple at Desk 61 and the smartly-dressed woman at Desk 63 were openly watching the drama unfold. And the people at the front of the queue, which zigzagged through the check-in zone now formed an appreciative audience; grateful for the unexpected entertainment which was now brightening their very early morning.

"The limit is twenty-three kilos, Madame. You must take one kilo of items from the case or pay thirty-five pounds excess."

Eve saw red.

"Thirty-five pounds a kilo?" she screamed. "Would you pay thirty-five pounds to go to work?"

"Overweight is overweight." She finally looked at Eve as she said this. Eve unconsciously pulled her stomach in at this veiled insult and was immediately angry with herself for doing so. She released it again.

"The tariff is fixed. You pay the same if you have one kilo extra or twenty."

She looked at Eve again. Pointedly.

"Your scales are wrong! I insist you weigh this case on another scale!"

"I cannot do that."

"No? Well, I bloody well can."

Eve lifted the suitcase back off the scale and was just turning to Desk 61 when a young man with bright ginger hair appeared by Ivana's side, looking a little flustered. His badge announced him as: John McCormack, SHIFT SUPERVISOR.

"Is there a problem, Ivana?" he asked.

"Yes, there is!" Eve interrupted. "First of all, this scale must be wrong. There is no way that my case, which weighed nineteen kilos when I weighed it at home gained five kilos on the journey here this morning."

She hadn't weighed it at home but she really didn't care now. It had weighed nineteen kilos on the flight to Bergen and she knew there was no way it could now weigh twenty-four.

"I assure you that our scales are rigorously checked on a regular basis, madam. It would be illegal for us not to do so." His face was by now a vivid scarlet, which, unfortunately, clashed terribly with his hair.

John McCormack, Shift Supervisor, lifted Eve's case back onto the scale of Desk 62, where, to Eve's not-so-great surprise, the reading was now twenty kilos. They both turned to look at Ivana. She shrugged as she stared back at her boss.

"You must have put your foot on the scale!" Eve shouted at her. "That's what you did! You put your foot on the scale to make it weigh more so that I'd have to pay excess baggage."

"Come now, madam, you have no grounds to make these accusations," John McCormack said.

"Then how do you explain it?" Eve rounded on him. "Hmm? How do you explain it? You can't, can you?"

"I'll make sure someone looks at this scale immediately," he said. "Please accept our apologies."

Eve just couldn't let it go. She turned on him.

"Even if it were one kilo too heavy, how on earth could you justify charging me thirty-five pounds? And don't tell me that all the airlines are doing it. I'm not travelling with any other airline, I'm travelling with yours and I am a very frequent flyer. You might like to tell your company, Mr John McCormack, Shift Supervisor, that there can be no justification for it. There's a recession on and people will soon get wise to this sort of sharp practice. And I shall certainly make sure that *my* company is told about it, and I'll make sure they lodge a complaint about the way your staff members treat the public."

Ivana wrapped the baggage tag around Eve's suitcase handle and with a look of absolute distain and not an iota of shame and slapped the baggage receipt, new boarding pass, e-ticket and passport on top of the desk.

"Boarding is at eight thirty; look at the board for the gate number."

"You have a nice day!" Eve shot back as she snatched her documents, picked up her holdall and marched off, suddenly aware that she'd had an audience as a cheer went up from the people at the front of the queue.

"Sorry to have held you all up," she said to them.

What am I apologising for?

From the corner of her eye she noticed a young, athletic-looking man in the queue watching her. She looked at his suitcase and winced as she saw the orange label and T2G, the Travel Together logo, emblazoned across it in black.

Oh shit! One of the groups.

He smiled at her, black eyes laughing, braids dancing as he shook his head in amusement and held out his hand.

"Nice one," he said, nodding his head towards Ivana who was now putting up a CLOSED sign on Desk 62.

"I'm Michael Brown. I think we're travelling companions, I saw your label."

"Nice to meet you, Michael. Actually, I'm Eve, the tour manager. I'm sorry you had to witness that. Not very professional of me to lose it like that."

"Not very professional of her either, was it? Cheeky cow! Trying to make you pay excess baggage. It's nice to know we've got a tour manager that can take care of herself."

"Sometimes I'm a bit over-assertive."

"Better than letting people walk all over you, believe me!"

"Yes, but in my job you're supposed to be diplomatic." Eve thought she'd better change the subject; put her tour manager's hat back on. "Do you know where to go from here, once you've dropped your case?"

"Yes, I've flown from Gatwick several times in the last year or so." Michael kicked his case along in front of him as he moved to the head of the queue.

"Great! Well, I'll see you upstairs in the Executive Lounge, then."

"Yep! See you in a while. And try to stay out of trouble, yeah?" he teased her as Eve walked off towards UK Borders Agency, grinning to herself. Well, at least Michael seemed pleasant.

Please God, the rest of them are!

***

What the bloody hell's going on now? What's the hold up?

Murray fumed in the queue. He hated this Disney-style 'line', just as he hated the way Britain adopted everything American. He asked himself just what was wrong with a good old-fashioned queue at each desk. Craning his neck, he peered through the gap in the bunch of heads in front of him. Some woman had been causing a song and dance about the scales, apparently. Just typical! Packs everything but the kitchen sink and then complains the case is overweight. There was no fear of his case being overweight. He'd checked very carefully with his bathroom scales the previous evening. Fourteen kilos. He'd packed two pairs of underpants, his sandals, a pair of swimming trunks, two pairs of shorts and two plain t-shirts for the day and two pairs of summer trousers – one black one beige – and three proper short-sleeved shirts in various, neutral masculine colours for the evenings. He could use the shower gel the hotels always gave you to wash out his underpants, the socks he was wearing for the journey and the t-shirts and shorts in the washbasin. He always did that. He'd also packed some suntan lotion, his razor, shaving cream, toothbrush, toothpaste and deodorant. And that was it. That was the way it should be done. Fourteen kilos. He tutted and sighed and switched his weight from his right to his left foot.

How much bloody longer?

Looking again towards the front of the queue, he saw a young black man step up to Desk 60. Because they were that bloody awful bright orange he could see the T2G label. Strange; he'd thought the tour manager was a woman.

***

"There she is!"

Seven seconds. Eve always had a little bet with herself how long she could be inside the Executive Lounge before someone spotted her. It amused her, too, that when a group was returning home, it didn't matter where in the world they were leaving from, someone always complained they were being taken to the airport too early. *'All that sitting around.'* *'Nothing to do'* they'd grumble. Yet when it came to UK airports people didn't seem to mind how early they got there. On their information sheets the group members were asked to make contact with the tour manager in the Executive Lounge, no later than one and a half hours before departure time. Eve always got to the lounge early as she liked to gather her thoughts, not to mention comb her hair, fix her make-up, have a coffee and brace herself before meeting them. Yet there was always someone, like today, shouting out 'There she is!' as if she was late when, in fact, she was almost an hour early. She quickly admonished herself remembering that this was a trip for first-timers, those who had never been on a T2G holiday before, so it was normal that they'd be nervous.

11

Even I'm nervous and I've done it a thousand times!

Putting on her professional face, Eve smiled, turned round to see two women and a man sitting together over by the windows. The older of the two women was waving at her frantically and the man looked slightly relieved to see her. Eve smiled an acknowledgement at them before giving her Executive Lounge voucher to Vicky the attendant.

"Back again?" Vicky smiled as she took the voucher from her.

"Yes, indeed, off we go again," Eve replied.

"You've got those three," Vicky said nodding her head in the direction of the window. "And one sitting on her own over there," she added nodding her head backwards to indicate the area behind her beyond the drinks and snacks.

"Thanks," Eve said, picking up her bag and walking over to meet the three clients by the window.

"I'm Stewart!" The man jumped up and offered a hand.

"Eve," she replied as her arm was pumped up and down by Stewart, a smiling, slightly overweight, slightly balding man who looked as if he'd been dressed by Clown, at Primark. A horizontal-striped yellow and green tank top partially covered a blue shirt. His trainers were such a bright white they had to be worn for the first time that morning. Eve had often noticed when she travelled that half the people on the plane wore brand new trainers and she'd wondered why; did people buy new trainers just to wear to go away on holiday? Were they part of a secret club? Was it the travellers' version of the Masons?

"Here!" Stewart grabbed an armchair from the neighbouring table and turned it round for Eve.

"Thanks." She dropped her bag on the floor and sat down.

"I'm Frances," said the older of the two women, who by now had stopped waving.

"And I'm Jo," said the younger one, an impressive redhead with a voluptuous hour-glass figure and striking green eyes. "We haven't given you time to get in yet, have we?"

"That's ok," Eve lied. "I'll just give you your welcome letters and then I'll get myself a coffee." She reached into her bag and pulled out her orange clipboard, opened it up and extracted a pile of letters wrapped in a large elastic band. She sorted through them and gave Frances, Jo and Stewart theirs.

"Oh, what's this?" Stewart asked.

Didn't I just say it's a welcome letter? Stop it, Eve!

"It's just a letter from me welcoming you on the holiday and explaining the procedure once we get to Antigua. Things take a while sometimes at the airport, and the transport set up isn't as straightforward as it is in other places."

"Oh, right." Stewart tore the envelope open and began to read the letter with an intensity and concentration usually reserved for compensation lawyers reading insurance documents.

Eve excused herself for a moment and went into the ladies to comb her hair and touch up her makeup. She looked at her reflection in the mirror. Her eyes looked a bit puffy.

That's too many early mornings. Perhaps I'm getting too old for this job!

On the way back to the others she stopped to grab a cup of coffee and a Danish pastry. When she reached the table the group had been joined by three more people; two women who were dressed in very similar clothing, which appeared to be made up of denim and lace, and another man who didn't look terribly happy and who was also wearing brand new trainers. The women introduced themselves as Dawn and Donna. They obviously knew each other. Eve had never understood why those who had a friend or friends to go on holiday with chose to go with T2G, which was supposed to be for people who didn't have anyone to travel with. But dressing the same was a new one, even for Eve. Didn't you usually stop doing that at about thirteen? Wear what your best friend wears? Very strange!

Smiling, Eve shook hands with Donna and Dawn and gave them their letters.

"I hope this hotel's going to be nice," Donna said. "Only my chiropractor told me that he's been there twice and it's not very good, didn't he Dawn?"

"Yes." Dawn nodded vigorously.

"So how come he's stayed there twice if he didn't like it?" Eve couldn't resist asking.

"Well he said the first time was fantastic but when he went back the following Christmas, that's like not this Christmas just gone but the one before that, well it had really gone downhill. He went with Travel Together as well. He knows you. He said you were the rep on both trips."

Eve thought for a moment; a chiropractor at Christmas started ringing a bell and then she realised who it must be.

"Is his name Carl?" she asked Donna.

"Yes."

"I do remember him, yes," Eve said. She remembered Carl very well and she also remembered Lindsay, a woman in the group he'd had a fling with during the first stay at the Mango Tree Resort. They had both booked to return on the Christmas trip, but Lindsay had made it obvious from the first night, when he'd expected to pick up where they'd left off the previous holiday, that she wanted nothing to do with Carl this time around as she'd set her sights on Alistair, a fireman from Huddersfield. From then on Carl had done nothing but grumble, complain and find fault with everything. What he'd praised and acclaimed as 'the best holiday in the T2G brochure' soon became 'this dump'. Amazing how getting the brush off and not getting the sex you were expecting can cloud your vision. But Eve could hardly say that to Donna.

"Well, I think you should judge for yourself. It's a beautiful spot, the location is just amazing, the food's good. All the ingredients are there for having a great time. In groups that aren't for first-timers, like this one, we always have lots of repeat clients and I think that's always a good gauge, isn't it? Don't worry about what Carl's told you. Approach it with a positive attitude and you'll have a fantastic holiday."

"Well, we would hope so, after all, we've paid enough for the privilege," a voice at her elbow said.

Eve turned to the man who'd also joined the group, holding out her hand, which he shook with a degree of reluctance.

"Good morning! I'm Eve, the tour manager," she said.

"Murray Sneddon."

Eve gave him his letter.

"What's this?" he asked gruffly.

Why don't you read it and see?

"It's my welcome letter which also explains the procedures at the other end."

"Why? Is Antigua different from everywhere else? You go through passport control, grab your bag and go out and get on tae a coach."

"Well, yes, it is different. Last time I was there it took two hours to do all that."

"Hmm! They dinnae tell you that in the brochure, do they?"

Eve smiled. She knew from experience that Murray Sneddon was going to be the sort of client that you could never please regardless of what you did for him and who'd always see the glass as seven-eighths empty. Excusing herself, she turned her attention to the other member of the group; the woman who was sitting alone behind the drinks and snacks bar. As she approached the woman she noticed that she seemed to deliberately sink further behind her copy of the Guardian.

"Good morning! Are you travelling with us to Antigua today?"

The newspaper was begrudgingly moved down an inch and a half and a pair of tired-looking eyes slowly looked up over it. There was a silence.

"I'm Eve. Are you travelling with us to Antigua today?"

There was a very faint nod.

"Could I have your name, please?" Eve ventured again.

"Ursula Marshall," the woman mumbled.

Eve sorted through the letters in her hand and finding Ursula's, handed it to her.

"This is your welcome letter, Ursula. It explains the procedure at the other end." Eve felt as if she were shouting, the way people sometimes do when speaking to a foreigner.

Suddenly a claw-like hand reached round the paper and grabbed the letter.

"We're sitting over there if you'd like to join us."

There was no reply. The paper went back up. And that was that.

***

In the Flying Horse, Geri looked round the bar furtively yet again, and then downed the rest of her Bacardi and Coke in one go. For the hundredth time that morning she asked herself why she was doing it; why she was putting herself through it. But then she knew the answer; if she didn't go away with a group she wouldn't have a holiday at all.

She was angry with herself for feeling so nervous. Nobody was forcing her to go on this holiday; she'd decided to go and had booked it all by herself. There was nothing stopping her from pulling out now; she could turn round and go home if she wanted to. Except that she couldn't. She was now air-side and that probably meant she had to board the aircraft no matter what. She'd been fine until that bloody taxi-driver had started going on about his friend's singles' holiday. That had unnerved her, especially the bit about them all being teachers. She looked around the pub again. Her eyes came to rest on a man of Mediterranean appearance who was leaning against the far end of the bar. He was looking back at her, returning her gaze. Geri looked away quickly, but not before registering his turquoise eyes; unusual for a man of his colouring. Although she knew it was empty, she self-consciously lifted the glass to her lips in the vague hope there might still be a drop or two left in it. She placed it back on the table and looking back towards the man at the bar she saw to her disappointment that he was now chatting to the barmaid. She felt the rejection as a physical blow; as if he'd walked across the pub and slapped her face. She scolded herself for her reaction. After all he was only a man in the pub who'd happened to look her way. Then a wave of nausea swept over her.

For God's sake, get a grip!

She took a deep breath, then bent and picked up her hand luggage and made her way towards the Executive Lounge to meet the rest of her group of single holiday-makers.

***

They look a right bunch!

Murray sat sneering to himself as he looked round the group, finding something to criticise about everyone. What was the old bloke doing here? Who did he expect to find on a singles' holiday? And the one in the gaudy clothes who kept on smiling and talking to anyone who looked his way? And it went without saying that he'd have little in common with the young black man that he'd thought was the tour manager. The Welsh one seemed okay so far, but he looked like he was already getting on with the other younger bloke; they were talking sports. That left the cocky Cockney geezer. He hated types like that; Cockney wankers he called them. They always thought they were Del Boy; ducking and diving, wheeling and dealing. He met them all the time. Half the other cabbies he knew fell into that category and he was going on holiday to get away from them not to spend time with them. There didn't seem to be any men he was going to be able to bond with or hang out with. Well, not from what he'd seen so far anyway. He sipped his coffee as the door to the Executive Lounge crashed open.

She's got to be joking!

A rather harassed-looking obese woman with unruly fair hair carrying three or four brightly-coloured carrier bags containing duty-free perfumes, cosmetics and gadgets was joining them. He watched as she introduced herself to the rep, who gave her a sweet professional smile, shook hands with her and pulled a chair for her to join the group.

No wonder she's single!

He looked round at the other women. Not much to choose from so far, although the ginger one wasn't bad, if you liked them with big arses. He was more of a tits man himself. He gave a sly glance to the ginger girl's chest. Not bad! He could easily lose himself in that bosom. He looked up again as two women came in together. One was a twitchy-looking blonde, who he immediately dismissed because she had to be at least forty-five. But the other one looked more promising; a sassy, petite brunette with blonde highlights and a gorgeous smile and probably not a day over twenty-five. And then another woman, a stunningly-beautiful Eurasian, came and joined the group. He liked Oriental women, although she was a bit older than he usually liked. They reminded him of his holidays to Thailand and the Philippines.

That's more like it! You'll end up being spoilt for choice, Murray, if you play your cards right.

16

He suddenly perked up, thinking that the giant box of condoms in his case might not go to waste after all. He downed his coffee and suddenly felt like something stronger. And why not? He was on holiday and things looked like they might not turn out so bad after all.

***

Eve stood up, precariously stepped over and around the various items of hand luggage that were littering the legs of the chairs and table they were sitting at and went over to the information board to check the flight status because announcements weren't made in the Executive Lounge. Just as she got there Gate 19 started to flash against their flight number. She strolled back over to the group to give them the news. They had plenty of time because they usually put the gate up at least fifteen or twenty minutes before boarding started so there was no need to rush off. She was still holding two letters; Grace Harrison and Robert Dean hadn't come to join them. She wished they'd just come along and say hallo as they were asked to do in the information Travel Together sent them. There was always someone who didn't show up to meet her; either they hadn't read the instructions, couldn't be bothered to meet her or refused outright to do so. It wasn't much to ask of people. If someone didn't make themselves known to her, she didn't know if they were sitting in a traffic jam on M23 and so missed the flight, they'd changed their mind about travelling or were simply being stand-offish. And the ones who complained that arriving at the destination airport, resort or hotel was a shambles because they didn't know what to do were always the ones that hadn't picked up their welcome letters. She sighed and put them into the side pocket of her hand luggage.

"It's Gate nineteen for us," she told everyone, "but please take a few minutes to finish your drinks or go to the loo. We've got time, there's no need to rush."

There was a synchronised scrapping of chairs as everyone stood up and either started to drain their drinks, gather their belongings or head over to the toilets. Eve remembered Ursula Marshall and went round the drinks pergolas to give her the gate number but the seat was empty; she had already gone, which was very strange.

Still, she put Ursula to the back of her mind; she had another seventeen group members to think about. Ursula wasn't the first recluse Eve had had to deal with and undoubtedly, she wouldn't be the last.

***

Geri stumbled her way down the aisle to seat forty-nine C. She would have preferred a window seat but there had been none left when she checked in. Still, as most of the journey would be over the ocean there wouldn't be much to see although a first glimpse of Antigua from the air would have been nice. But being in the aisle was more comfortable if she'd want to get in and out, which she probably would as the flight was over eight hours and she'd need to stretch and go to the loo a few times. Arriving at her seat she slipped her hand into her bag, took out her book and put it in the seat pocket in front, then zipped the bag up and lifted it into the overhead locker. She sat down, smiling at the young couple in the seats next to her and fastened her seat belt. She felt better now that she had met most of the others. They seemed like nice people, except for that stupid Dave who made a comment about her being Old Spice, when all she was doing was pointing out to Eve how she spelled her name the same way as Geri Halliwell. She hadn't even been talking to him. He obviously thought he was life and soul of the party and she disliked him already. She wasn't sure if she had much in common with the women in the group, though. The oriental one had chatted to her a bit and the redhead had smiled and said hallo when she sat down. The fat one had tried to engage her in conversation, saying how excited she was at her first long-haul holiday. Geri had answered her politely, of course, but she didn't envisage spending much time with her. Not just because she was fat, although Geri didn't want the rest of the group to think she would associate with someone who didn't care about their appearance, but also because Suzanne, as she was called, had already tried to give Geri her whole life story in five minutes flat.

Suddenly Geri's heart lurched. The man with the turquoise eyes from the Flying Horse was coming down the aisle towards her. He stopped at row forty-eight and put his bag above seat D. Before he took his seat he turned and looked right at her; he must have felt her stare. Then he gave her a slight nod and the beginnings of a smile and turned his back and sat down.

Geri felt herself go red. But she was pleased that he had obviously noticed her in the pub and remembered her just now. He was certainly attractive; much better looking than the other men in the group, none of whom could be called handsome, or good-looking, except for the black guy. He was a dish. But he might think she was a bit old for him and already he'd seemed to be getting on with the young girl, Natalie. She'd noticed they were sitting together in row thirty-eight as she'd made her way down the plane.

> *They'll probably be at it like rabbits for the next twelve days!*

A wave of jealousy and resentment swept over her. This last year had made her realise that she'd never be thirty again, and although forty-three wasn't old, most men of her age wanted women of thirty-three. And there was no way she wanted an old man. She knew there were women who didn't mind older men, those with moobs and chests and backs covered in grey hair; those with varicose veins and beer bellies, but she'd always gone for the young athletic type. When she'd first met Malcolm he was a member of the rowing club and ran five miles every morning.

> *Why am I thinking of him? He's already ruined my life; he's not going to spoil my holiday! Try to be positive; don't think about the past at all. Think about this holiday and all the great experiences it's going to bring.*

Feeling her mood lift, Geri paid attention to the safety video that was just starting on the little screen in front of her.

***

Eve settled comfortably against the window blind and curled her feet up to the side. She'd been lucky; the video system wasn't working in row twelve so the couple who'd been sitting next to her in the middle and window seats had asked to move, leaving her with a row all to herself. She didn't mind at all that there was no video as she rarely watched films on aircraft as there were too many interruptions. If the Captain wasn't giving the weather forecast then the crew were pushing duty-free sales or talking about their latest charity appeal. She'd lost count of the times she'd been into a film and then missed a vital bit of dialogue because of an announcement. Some planes now had stop/start buttons, which was great, but this one didn't. Anyway, she preferred to read, listen to music on her iPod or sleep. Sometimes she liked to just sit quietly and get lost in her own thoughts. Now that the meal service was over she was going to take the opportunity to go through her paperwork. Her eyes ran down the list in front of her.

NAME	AGE	COMMENTS
Donna Ashton	35	Room next to D Potter
Suzanne Bates	37	
Frances Dawson	50	
Grace Harrison	54	
Deborah Martin	49	
Ursula Marshal	51	Vegetarian – full sea view
Dawn Potter	38	Room next to D Ashton
Natalie Sharp	27	
Geraldine Simpson	43	
Joanne Walsh	35	
Michael Brown	30	
Robert Dean	42	Request double bed
Huw Jones	37	
Stewart Matteson	39	
Jason Peacock	34	
Trevor Owen	60	
Murray Sneddon	52	Request king-size bed

She smiled at the double and king-size bed requests; they were almost always from men who confused the term singles' holiday with leg-over. She knew everyone had turned up; Grace Harrison had come up to her while they were waiting at Gate Nineteen to board. She'd flown down from Manchester and the flight had got in twenty minutes late and, as she hadn't been able to check her luggage in all the way through, she'd had to wait for it then sprint from North Terminal to South Terminal.

"By the time I got through passport control and security the gate was already showing on the board," she'd explained.

Eve had liked Grace instantly. She was pleasant, hugely apologetic and her lovely smile stretched all the way up to her dark brown eyes. Looking at the list she realised that Grace's looks belied her age. She was dressed in jeans and a black blazer, with a striped t-shirt underneath with flat, silver pumps on her feet. Her sleek dark hair was in a shiny bob and although she could have passed for at least ten years younger than she actually was, there was nothing mutton-dressed-as-lamb about her. Once on board Eve had paged Robert Dean and the Cabin Supervisor had taken the letter to him, returning to tell her that Mr Dean was, in fact, sitting in seat forty-eight D. She'd gone down to introduce herself to him, but seeing that he was asleep decided against waking him up.

She thought she had everyone's name by now; the rest would come over the next day or so.

Donna - friends with Dawn – the two who dress alike – but which one was which?

Suzanne – overweight, loads of shopping, hair everywhere, friendly and excited.

Frances – brown hair – the one who was already in the lounge when I got there together with Jo, the redhead and Stewart in the lairy clothes.

Grace – came late because of the Manchester flight connection.

Deborah – the Eurasian lady in the expensive cream linen trouser suit who wasn't to be called Deb or Debbie under any circumstances.

Ursula – the recluse. Well bloody rude recluse, actually.

Natalie – the young girl – lively and looks like fun.

Geraldine – to be called Geri, spelt like Geri Halliwell. Shouldn't that be Ger-eye then? The shaven-headed Londoner – her eyes scanned down the sheet again – David Wright - that was it – made a comment about her being Old Spice which she hadn't taken too well. I'll remember him!

Michael is the black guy; Robert I still have to meet once he wakes up; Huw the Welsh guy who hadn't had much to say to me because he'd spent his time talking sports to the other youngish guy – Jason.

Trevor was the older man. Seemed a bit quiet and subdued. Probably worried because he's a bit older than the others.

And Murray the guy with the Scottish accent who spoke to me with a mixture of contempt and condescension. Bless! I'll enjoy working with him!

Smiling and pleased with herself that she did, indeed, have all the names, Eve started folding her paperwork away.

"Perk of the job is it?"

She jumped out of her skin. Looking up she found Murray Sneddon's face about two inches from hers, his breath, a mixture of poor dentistry and lunchtime wine fumes forcing her to move her head back away from him.

"Oh you made me jump!"

"I was just asking if it's a perk of the job."

"What?"

"Having three seats tae yourself. I'm stuck up against the window with the fat woman wedging me in. I mean, fancy putting her in a middle seat! And there are two kids sitting behind me that havnae stopped shouting since we got on board. And here you are with all the room in the world tae yourself."

She decided to let the "fat woman" comment go for now; she'd have the opportunity to pull him about that and more before the holiday was over of that she was sure. But poor Suzanne, it couldn't be very comfortable for her, especially with Mr Nice Guy in the next seat.

"Just the way it worked out. The screens don't work in this row so the people who were sitting here moved."

"Load of rubbish on anyway. All silly so-called chick flicks."

"Never mind, we're almost halfway there now."

"Do they feed us again?"

Why didn't you listen to the announcements at the beginning? They made it quite, quite clear.

"Yes, they do. About an hour and a half before landing."

"Well I hope it's a bit better than the lunch. They said it was beef stew. Beef stew? I don't know where the beef was. I wouldn't have fed that tae my dog!"

"Well, I hope you'll enjoy the afternoon snack more. Food's such a personal thing, isn't it?"

"I like plain food myself. Or a good curry. I dinnae suppose there's much chance of that in Antigua, is there?"

"I've enjoyed some really good curries in the resort."

"Nah, they'll be a cocked up Caribbean version, I expect. Like in Cuba. It was supposed tae be paella. No prawns and just two tiny little bits of bone and gristle. That's not paella."

Fortunately, at that moment the toilet, which was behind Eve's row, became vacant and Murray went in. She shook her head at his ignorance. Attitudes like that always annoyed her. People chose to go to Cuba, a country where everything is scarce and tourists get the best of what there is, and then they moan about it. Scooping her paperwork into her folder and putting it into her bag, which she left, together with her newspaper and book strewn over the three seats, Eve stood up and went in search of Suzanne. She found her in seat thirty-one B with Jo next to her in the aisle-seat, both women concentrating on the TV screens in front of them, lost in the film. Eve smiled at them both.

"Sorry to interrupt but there are two empty seats next to me. The video system doesn't work, but would either of you like to take the aisle seat to give you both a bit more room?" Eve asked.

"No, thanks!" they both chorused loudly. "But thanks for offering," Jo added.

Eve went back to her seat. She put her MP3 headphones in, lifted her feet up onto the middle seat, wriggled herself comfortable against the window blind and closed her eyes, feigning sleep in the hope that Murray wouldn't need any more deep and meaningful conversation when he came out of the loo. But she was so tired from her early morning start that before the first song had even played the opening bars, she was already drifting off.

***

Geri felt very happy now. The three glasses of red wine were making her feel mellow, but the real reason for her joy was that Mr Forty-eight D was actually part of the Travel Together group! Earlier in the flight she'd seen one of the cabin crew give him a letter, identical to the one that Eve had been giving out in the Executive Lounge. Then, after the meal service, Eve herself had come to talk to him, but seeing he was asleep had walked back down the front. Things were looking up! Perhaps that's why he had been looking at her in the pub, because he'd seen the T2G label on her hand luggage. She wondered why he hadn't come over and said something to her. But then again, he hadn't gone to the lounge, either. Geri thought he might

22

be shy, although he had smiled at her when he'd taken his seat. She wondered if she should strike up a conversation with him when he woke up then thought better of it. It would be difficult to talk across the aisle with him being in the row in front of her without everyone hearing what they were saying. She'd have to wait to get to know him at the resort. He could be just what she needed. Smiling to herself she tapped the arm of a passing steward and ordered a large gin and tonic.

***

For God's sake!

Murray fumed to himself as he shoved the sleeping fat woman whose head had slid onto his shoulder into the upright position. Her eyes sprung open, startled. She turned to look at him, slowly registering why she had woken up.

"Sorry! I was trying so hard to stay awake, but it was a really early start this morning. Was I snoring?" she giggled.

"No, but you were squashing me up against the window."

"Sorry. There's not much room here, is there?"

Well there is for normal people, just not for people like you!

The ginger one then butted in.

"Tell you what," she said, standing up, "I'll go and take that seat Eve offered earlier and then you can move into my seat, Suzanne, and that way you'll both have a bit more room."

"But she said the TVs don't work in her row," Suzanne said.

"That's not a problem. I've seen all I want to see now, I'm happy to read." She picked up her book and got her handbag from the overhead rack, put her shoes on and walked towards Eve. The fat one then heaved herself across into the aisle seat and finally Murray had some room.

That rep must have come down and offered the two women one of the seats next to her but hadn't offer it to him. Murray decided there and then he was going to make a complaint about her as soon as he got back.

He looked at his watch and counted forward. Two hours until landing. Perhaps he could spend them resting and relaxing.

On the way back I'm going tae make sure I sit next tae the oriental one or the young one. Someone else can put up with Fatty.

***

The 747-400 series slowly and seductively swirled its way from the runway onto the tarmac to park up. As Eve listened to the Cabin Services Supervisor asking people to sit down and re-fasten their seatbelts until the plane had come to a complete stop and the seatbelts signs had been switched off, she looked through the window at the familiar pastel-coloured houses of Coolidge and Fitches Creek, nestling in the hills that surround VC Bird International Airport and gave a great big smile. Antigua was one of her favourite places; she'd been here eight times before, but the last trip had been almost nine months earlier in the previous October. Since then, her company seeing group numbers drop off due to the recession had reduced the number of trips to the Mango Tree Resort. This group was a fair size, though; eighteen was enough to cope with, especially as they were all first-timers.

Cars and minibuses seemed to race along the roadways adjacent to the airport like busy beetles and as the big plane performed a final pirouette Eve could see a large catamaran, its sails straining against the breeze, skimming over the sea in Parham Bay. Finally, the engines became silent and the seatbelt sign went out and everyone jumped to their feet like greyhounds out of the traps. Overhead lockers flew open, bags were dragged down and passports taken from zipped pockets. Everyone was ready for the off. Everyone wanted to be the first one in the Immigration queue. Everyone was eager to start their holiday or to meet their loved-ones and get home. As Eve stepped out of the plane and onto the stairway the heat and humidity were all-enveloping. She always forgot just how hot the Caribbean could be, especially in July. The walk to the terminal building was a long one past posters announcing the upcoming Carnival, which was in two weeks time. Eve thought it was a shame that they'd miss it. She'd been here once before for Carnival and had the time of her life, especially on J'Ouvert morning when she drank and danced along with the crowd from four until ten. Then, exhausted, she'd had a ling fish and chop-up breakfast before going back to the hotel to sleep for the rest of the day. But flights and hotel prices rocketed over the Carnival period so it put it out of the range of most tour operators and of course, T2G had the additional cost of twin or double rooms for single occupancy. Still, she was sure that there would be plenty of atmosphere and pre-Carnival events for those in the group who wanted them. The sounds of the welcoming steel band reached her and she smiled to herself; a steel band always made her want to dance and she noticed that the people in front of her had all started to walk in time with the music as she had done herself.

Irresistible!

Jo came up alongside her.

"Isn't it fabulous to hear that band?" Jo said, shuffling her feet, wiggling her hips and giving a broad smile.

"I was just thinking that myself. I never get tired of hearing it," Eve said.

"Rum punch! Rum punch!" A man in a bright green pineapple-print shirt beckoned to all the arriving passengers to help themselves to drinks from his tray. Jo grabbed two and gave one to Eve.

"Here you are! Cheers!"

"Cheers!" Eve was sure she was going to like Jo. They sipped their drinks as they joined the queue inside, grateful that the air conditioning was working.

***

Geri was practically running to keep up with Mr Forty-eight D. She had been pleased when she had seen that the plane was parked a long way from the terminal because she thought it would give her a good opportunity to walk alongside him and casually start up a conversation. But as soon as he got down the stairs he'd gone striding ahead of her. She was trying to keep her pace up but found she was falling further and further behind him because the two bottles of duty free she'd bought on the plane - one gin and one vodka – were weighing her down. With hindsight she wondered what on earth had possessed her to buy them; she'd completely forgotten for a moment that the resort was all-inclusive. Sweat ran in rivulets down her face and down her back but she wouldn't – couldn't – slow down. She could see the back of his head moving further away from her but there was still a possibility that she could catch him up in the queue for Immigration. And then her jaw dropped open wide in surprise at what she saw happening up ahead.

***

Suzanne had never felt happier. She loved the feeling of the heat even though it was hotter than she could have ever imagined. And she could hear a steel band playing somewhere ahead. If she hadn't been carrying so much stuff she'd have pinched herself to check she really was in the Caribbean. She decided to take her time, not just because her feet were really hurting her because they had swollen up during the flight and now her shoes felt tight, but because she really wanted to savour every single minute. And besides with all that she was carrying she couldn't rush.

"Need a hand?"

Suzanne jumped as the voice brought her out of her thoughts. A man with an olive complexion and turquoise eyes had come alongside her.

"Pardon?"

"Do you need a hand with your bags? They look heavy."

Suzanne hesitated.

"I'm travelling with the same group as you," he said. "I recognised your luggage labels."

25

"Oh, well, yes, thank you very much," she said, relinquishing her vanity case to him with obvious relief. His arm jerked downwards with the unexpected weight. Recovering, he fell into step beside her and gave her a wide grin.

"Did you think I might make off with it?" he asked.

"Well.............," Suzanne hesitated, not wanting to offend him.

"It's alright if you did," he said. "You can't be too careful in airports and with strangers. But since that last spell in Strangeways I've stopped nicking things."

Suzanne turned her head and looked at him in alarm.

"Joke!" he said and they both burst out laughing.

"What have you got in all these bags, anyway?"

"Well, my holdall's got the things I couldn't fit into my case, like my hair tongs and some sandals and my books and in the vanity case are all my toiletries. I bought them in the airport because I couldn't take them through security."

"Couldn't you have bought them here?"

"Oh! I hadn't thought of that! I suppose I could have but then I like to buy my usual shampoo and conditioner. I've got wavy hair that goes frizzy if I'm not careful."

"Such a problem!" He bent his wrist and they burst out laughing again, just as they drew level with the man handing out the rum punches.

"Thanks, mate" He took two glasses in one hand. "I'll hold onto yours 'til we get inside, shall I?"

"Oh thanks. Ooh that's better! Air conditioning!" They went into the airport building and joined the snaking queue. Suzanne put her bags down on the floor and then took the drink from his hand.

"I'm Deano, by the way," he said.

"Suzanne. Are you Italian?"

"No, I'm as English as fish and chips. My surname's Dean and my mates have always called me Deano. My first name's Robert, but I never answer to that. It's only ever my mum who calls me Robert and usually when I'm in trouble."

They laughed and again and shuffled forward in the queue.

***

The Immigration Hall was cool and although the queue was long it was moving fairly quickly. The Immigration Officers sat on pergolas of four and all the positions were manned. But it wasn't moving fast enough for Murray, who was annoyed to find himself in yet another Disney-style queue. He kept coming face-to-face with other members of the group as they went up and down following the lines. The rep and the ginger one, the fat one who was now talking to a bloke he hadn't seen before, the Welsh bloke and the sporty one he'd been talking to in the lounge, the two women who dressed alike and the short blonde woman. The oriental woman and the young one were talking to the black guy just a little way behind him in the queue. He'd have to try and get into conversation with them once they were at the hotel. If they ever got to the bloody hotel!

"They couldnae organise a piss up in a brewery, could they?" he tutted to the rep as they came alongside each other.

"Who couldn't?"

"This lot! Look at the queue! It's going to take forever at this rate. This never happens at Gatwick," he complained.

"It does happen at Gatwick," she replied, "but only if you're travelling on non-EU passports. Non-EU nationals have to queue up for ages at Gatwick and Heathrow. It's the same here; if you're a non-Caricom national the queue is slower and usually longer. Most people on our flight have British passports so they're non-Caricom nationals." She smiled as she moved away from him to find herself the next person in line.

Smug bitch!

***

Forty-five minutes later the last of the group were getting into taxis. Eve felt hot and just a little bothered. It wasn't just the heat that made her feel that way; it was the system at VC Bird International Airport. Everywhere else she'd ever been in the whole wide world provided a coach for the group, which was waiting with its Travel Together sign clearly displayed and its engine revving, waiting to set off. In Antigua they operated a next-taxi-on-the-stand system, which meant that tour operators couldn't pre-allocate transport for clients. As people came out they were put into the next available taxi – which is always a minibus – and sent off to the resorts. Travel Together's local agent, Palm Tree Tours, always did their best to enable the group to travel in the same minibuses to the resort. As group-members came through they were asked to wait to one side until there were enough of them to fill a minibus and then they were sent off. Palm Tree Tours' representative Sunny, a beautiful Antiguan woman in her early thirties, who lived up to her name because she never stopped smiling, then telephoned the resort to let them know that the group was on its way and Eve, or whoever the tour manager was, went in the final bus, after making sure that everyone and their luggage had come through. Eve saw

Sunny waiting by the Tour Operators' desk holding up the big black and orange T2G sign. The two women hugged warmly. Eve was very fond of Sunny and loved working alongside her.

"It's so good to see you, Eve! Welcome back! Welcome back!"

"Thanks. It's lovely to be here again and to see you again, of course. I think that's everyone now, isn't it?"

"Yes, one taxi just left with six in it and the others are just waiting for you over here," she said, leading Eve over to where the remaining members of the group stood.

Finally the door swung shut on the third and final minibus and Eve heaved a sigh of relief.

"Right performance that was, wasn't it? I hope the rest of the holiday's going to be a bit more organised than that."

Eve turned in her seat to face Huw Jones, grateful that Murray Sneddon had gone ahead in one of the other two taxis or she'd be getting the complaint in stereo.

"The rest of the holiday will run like clockwork," she said, mentally touching wood at the same time.

"We were standing there for about half an hour waiting for you. Aren't you supposed to be the first one out?"

"Well, in my welcome letter I did ask everyone to check with me once they'd got their luggage, but not everyone did and so I had to waste time looking for them inside the Arrivals Hall," Eve said, knowing that Huw had been one of the three who had gone straight outside and hadn't checked his name off.

"Well we could hardly get lost, could we? If we weren't inside we were outside."

Just what I need! Two smart-arses in the group!

"But there were over two hundred people inside from the Liat and Air Canada flights and I had to walk round and check that the three people who hadn't checked with me weren't standing waiting for luggage that hadn't arrived. So I'm sorry if you were kept waiting."

From the back seat of the minibus Grace piped up.

"It would make Eve's job a lot easier if everyone who came on the trip could read," she said. "Her letter was clear and helpful. If you didn't do what you were asked to you can't moan you were kept waiting. End of."

"Well, I wasn't the only one," Huw retorted, crossing his arms and frowning like a petulant little boy. "I'm supposed to be on holiday I can do what I like. I don't have to read any bloody letter."

"Don't complain if you don't know what to do then!" Grace came back at him.

Eve turned to face the front again smiling to herself as she did. That had put him in his place! The more she saw of Grace, the more she liked her.

***

The Mango Tree Resort is on Antigua's west coast; that's to say on the Caribbean Sea side. A horseshoe-shaped, three-storey building houses the accommodation east of the beach, which is half a kilometre of silver sand. Nestling within the centre of the horseshoe is the restaurant, which leads out to the main swimming pool, bar and entertainment area. To the south is the Crazy Conch, the hotel's seafood restaurant and to the north, where an hour and a half later Eve found herself having afternoon tea, is the hotel's Paradise Spa – an adults- only area with a small pool, swim-up bar, Jacuzzi and massage and treatment garden. It was a delightful little spot, surrounded by simple but effective landscaped gardens with a splendid array of all types of palms, bright bougainvillea and hibiscus bushes, which often attracted the most beautiful little humming birds, and exotic flowers. She was going to have her reviving cup of peppermint tea with some shortbread and then take a stroll round the grounds to re-familiarise herself with a few things and then go and talk to Osbert, the head waiter, about the group's seating arrangements for meals.

"Mind if I join you?" The voice at her elbow startled Eve almost making her spill her tea. She looked up to see Deborah standing beside her, looking very cool, calm and collected in a pink vest and beautifully-cut Bermudas.

"Oh, please do. Pull up a chair."

Deborah took a chair from a neighbouring table, where a young couple who were tanned to the colour of mahogany, were holding hands over a plate of sandwiches, placed it opposite Eve's chair and went to get herself some tea. She came back a couple of minutes later with Frances and Trevor in tow.

"We just met up getting our tea," Trevor said, as if he were trying to explain his presence. At that moment the couple got up to leave so Trevor got a chair for himself and one for Frances. They sat down and everyone looked round the table and smiled at everyone else, almost as if they were embarrassed. Eve broke the ice.

"Well, isn't this nice? Warm enough for everyone?"

"Oh, yes!" was the chorused reply.

"I think it might be a bit too hot for me," Trevor said, wiping his face with the iced towels that a waitress was offering the guests.

"Is it your first time in the Caribbean?" Eve asked.

"Yes, it is," Trevor replied. "I usually go to Malaga. Well, I've been taking Spanish night classes and I like to practise, but I just fancied going somewhere further afield for once."

"First time for me, too," said Frances. "I've treated myself for my fiftieth birthday. I didn't really want a party, although my son offered to throw one for me, but I didn't think I knew that many people to invite. And besides, I didn't want to draw attention to the fact that I'm now officially middle-aged."

The others laughed.

"I think it's a lovely idea!" Eve said. "We'll make sure you have a holiday to remember." She turned to Deborah.

"How about you, Deborah? Have you been to the Caribbean before?"

"Several times; but not to Antigua and not at this time of year." She pulled a scrunchy out of her shorts pocket as she spoke and expertly pulled her beautiful, thick, dark hair back into a ponytail. "I've never been anywhere where they want you to wear a tag, either," she said, scornfully pointing to the bright blue plastic identity bracelet everyone was wearing.

"The bracelet's for identification purposes," Eve said. "It's for security so that the hotel staff know you belong here."

"It's like being branded. Awful."

"Well, you are at liberty to take it off if you wish, but the bar and restaurant staff have instructions not to serve anyone who isn't wearing a band," Eve explained.

Deborah sniffed.

"I've been to Barbados at Christmas time before. And, I have to say it, to a much better class of hotel than this. The rooms are a bit basic, aren't they? I wanted to ask you if I could change mine," she turned to Eve with the quick change of subject. "It's really not a very nice room that I'm in."

Eve raised her eyebrows in surprise.

"What's wrong?

"Well, it's supposed to be a double room, but it's a bit small. There aren't any drawers at all, so there's nowhere to put any underwear. There fridge is tiny and there's a tree outside, which is blocking the view."

"Well all the rooms are the same size; they are double rooms for single occupancy, so any room you changed to would be the same size and wouldn't have a bigger fridge, unless you pay for an upgrade, which is a hundred eastern Caribbean dollars a night. An upgraded room would have a full chest of drawers instead of the shelves in the cupboard that the basic room has."

"How much is a hundred dollars a night in sterling?"

"About twenty-five pounds."

"That's a lot to pay for a few drawers."

"Yes, I agree, it is. But if you want another basic room with a better view, I'll talk to the front desk and see if they can put you somewhere else."

"Would you?"

"Yes, of course." Eve finished her tea with a gulp. "They're usually very helpful and don't want people to be unhappy. In fact, I'll go and see about it now. Do you want to wait here for me?"

"Yes, thank you, I will," Deborah smiled as Eve walked away.

"She's lovely," Frances said, nodding towards Eve's retreating figure. "Her job can't be easy at times."

"Well, it's what she's paid to do," said Deborah, sipping her tea. Trevor and Frances looked at each other and raised their eyebrows. Just then Deborah's mobile phone trilled loudly. She snatched it, stood up and walked away from Trevor and Frances, answering it as she spoke.

"I was just going to ring you. We've only just got to the hotel," they heard her say.

"I've sent my son a text to say I'm here," Frances said. "Just so he doesn't worry."

"I told my son if he didn't hear from me he knew I was fine," Trevor said. "No news is good news. Can I get you another cup of tea?"

***

Geri stepped out onto the balcony to take in the view. It was beautiful; her room, towards the south end of the horseshoe, was overlooking part of the pool and then an avenue of beautiful palm trees, which ran parallel with the beach and beyond that the sea. She looked round taking everything in, her initial disappointment at the size of the room disappeared as she did so. She could see three of the group talking together and having a drink at the bar; the young girl, the redhead and the black guy. She hadn't been in the same minibus as them or they'd have asked her to join them, she thought. They seemed nice and they were laughing and joking together. Perhaps they already knew each other before the holiday. She hadn't travelled with Mr Forty-eight D, either. She giggled as her name for him. It made him sound like a bra size. But she was very disappointed because apart from a fleeting moment at the airport when it looked they might be in the same minibus but then the Scottish man had pushed in front, she'd hardly seen him. She'd stood and watched as he helped the fat girl into the other taxi and shared a joke with her, then got in next to her. Deep in her thoughts, it took her a moment to realise that Mr Forty-eight D had joined the others at the bar. This was her chance! She rushed back into the room and started taking off her clothes and throwing them on the bed. She'd shower and change into her shorts and race down to the bar and "casually" bump into them.

***

"Oh my God!"

Natalie looked up and down the beach and took another sip of her cocktail.

"Where is everyone?" Jo asked. "So much sand, so much room!"

The two girls, together with Michael and Deano, had got their cocktails and walked through the palm trees onto the beach.

"It's like a film set," Natalie said. "Or the back-drop for a play."

"Yes," Deano agreed. "The am-dram group are doing South Pacific and the vicar's wife's painted the scenery."

"Except it's the Caribbean not the Pacific!" Michael said and they all laughed.

"Yes, well, same difference. Paradise by any other name," Deano said.

"It just feels so good having the sun on my back again," Michael said, taking off his t-shirt to reveal a muscular torso, broad shoulders and a narrow waist; the obvious product of a daily visit to the gym.

Natalie kicked off her flip-flops and started to run towards the water.

"I'm going for a paddle! I don't care if I get my shorts wet! I'm in Antigua! Woo hoo!" she shouted as she splashed into the sea, quickly followed by the others. They stood in the thigh-deep water, sipping their drinks, grinning at each other, four strangers who suddenly felt very comfortable in each other's company.

"Oi! Don't leave me out!"

They turned to see Dave Wright, the bald Cockney, bare-chested and in long white shorts covered with red flowers, running into the water to join them, kicking up the surf as he did so and wetting Jo.

"You did that on purpose!" she laughed.

"Me?"

"Yes, you! And don't start what you can't finish!" She gave a huge kick sending water all over him. Within thirty seconds all five of them were kicking up the foam, soaking each other, laughing their heads off as they tried to stop their drinks from falling from their hands.

Back at the bar, Geri came along to find that nobody from the group was there. She looked around, surprised and dismayed. She ordered herself a gin and tonic and sat at a table to drink it. She felt a bit conspicuous on her own. Looking round she couldn't see anyone who even looked familiar. Everyone else was a couple, or so it seemed. Feeling uncomfortable she finished her drink quickly.

"Can I get you another, ma'am?" A waiter stood at her elbow picking up the empty glass.

"What? Yes. Yes, thank you."

He appeared back in less than a minute with another large gin and tonic and placed it on the table next to her, smiled and walked away. Geri picked up the glass and walked past the bar onto the pathway that led through the palm trees to the beach. She started to walk along when she stopped short, seeing five of the group coming out from the water together laughing and carrying on as if they were old friends. Mr forty-eight D was among them. She ducked behind a tree before they could see her. For some reason she couldn't explain, she felt out of it; excluded. She knocked back what was left in her glass and almost ran back to the sanctity and safety of her first-floor room.

***

Eve opened her eyes and jumped up quickly afraid she'd overslept but her watch reassured her it was only 6.10pm. She yawned and stretched and got up to go to the shower. The table arrangements had been sorted out with Osbert and she'd got Deborah a room change to one without a tree outside. Eve smiled to herself as she remembered Carlo's remark.

"Carlo, the lady in room three-o-six wants to move because she's hasn't got a good view."

"What do you mean? Three-o-six looks right over the pool and the gardens towards the beach."

"But there's a tree in the way blocking the view."

"A blind man would be glad to see it," he said, looking at his computer screen and tapping the keys.

Eve had burst out laughing. It did seem trivial but then again so did most of the complaints she received in her job. She sometimes wondered if people made a list before they came away of

33

things they could complain about. Deborah had been offered three twenty-six, but had declined it as it was next to the maid's pantry, and had finally settled on two forty-four. As she let the cool water run over her she wondered what might be waiting for her at pre-dinner drinks. She gave a mental shrug. Whatever it was she would deal with it. All the ingredients were there for a wonderful holiday. If people didn't make the most of it they only had themselves to blame. She towelled herself dry and then slipped into a cream maxi-dress with cap sleeves. She liked maxi-dresses; they were cool to wear and always looked elegant. She put on some eye-liner and a good coat of mascara before painting her lips, grabbing her bag and heading out the door. Her room was on the ground floor, north side near the centre, because she always liked to be near the reception and the view was of little consequence to her. She slipped behind the stairwell and through the lobby heading towards the garden and beyond it, the bar. There was a grand piano in the lobby and at this time every day Elton, the resort's resident pianist, entertained for the cocktail hour. He was playing *Every Time We Say Goodbye* as she went through, and sang

"Eve, baby, welcome back you're looking finer" changing the lyrics as she walked by him. Eve waved and blew him a kiss. It was lovely to come back to Mango Tree Resort. People always remembered her. She smiled to herself as she went past the restaurant and then stopped and did a double take as she saw Ursula Marshall, still wearing the heavy clothes she'd travelled in, tucking into a hearty meal. Deciding that perhaps Ursula had forgotten that the group was meeting up in the bar at seven, Eve weaved her way across the dining area to Ursula's table.

"Good evening. Everything okay?"

The tired eyes reluctantly looked up without registering the slightest recognition.

"Enjoying dinner?" Eve continued.

Ursula's gaze didn't move from Eve's face as she kept on chewing.

Good God, woman! Meet me half way!

"Have you decided not to meet up with us tonight?"

Ursula nodded.

"But you're okay?"

Ursula nodded.

"Well, we'll be in the bar for about half an hour or so if you change your mind. If not, I'll see you in the morning at breakfast or at the information meeting on the terrace through the bar at half nine."

Ursula looked back at her plate and continued cutting up her food.

34

"Good night!"

Ursula popped a forkful of food into her mouth and began to chew.

She's not normal.

Eve shook her head as she walked out of the restaurant. It took all sorts!

Although it was only five to seven most of the group were already there, drinks in hand. Eve joined them smiling and asking if everyone had settled in and enjoyed what had been left of the afternoon.

"Well, we're not settled in, actually," Murray said. "We were just saying how small the rooms are." He was standing with Huw and Jason and Donna and Dawn.

"Yes, you'd never get two in there, would you?" This from Huw.

"But you haven't got to get two in there, have you?" Eve said.

Dawn and Donna giggled. Huw sniffed.

"You'd have more room with a single bed in there. I can get the hotel to take out the queen-size bed and put in a single if you want," Eve offered, knowing full-well what the answer would be.

"No! No! That's fine. I suppose you don't spend much time in your room, do you?" Huw said.

"Why would you want to with all this?" Donna motioned the whole bar and pool area with her hand. "It's beautiful."

By her side, Dawn, who was also wearing a short, cocktail dress but in a darker shade of blue, nodded her agreement. Excusing herself, Eve walked a little further down the bar making a note as she went of who was missing.

Just the woman with the short blonde hair. Geri.

Eve thought she'd give her another five minutes and then give her a ring. She never wanted to be thought of as a mother hen, but part of the job was checking to see everyone was fine. That's why a lot of people, women especially, travelled with Travel Together, for the security being in a group offered.

"Why aren't you drinking?" a voice said in her ear as an arm went round her waist.

"I was just about to order a Diet Coke," Eve said to Stewart, who was dressed in a blue and red floral beach shirt with black and white striped Bermuda shorts, belly popping over the top.

35

"That all? You don't want a drop of something in it?"

"No thanks. Not while I'm on duty."

"Okay. I'll get it for you," he said, lifting up his hand to attract the barman's attention.

"Have you settled in okay?" Eve asked him as they waited to be served.

"Oh, have I! I think it's a great place. What's not to like here? Beach, pool, booze – everything I've come for! Cheers!" He cracked a tall glass with a garish green liquid, lots of ice, a cherry, piece of lime and an umbrella in it against Eve's Diet Coke. "I must admit, I was a bit apprehensive after I'd read a couple of the things people had written on Trip Advisor about this place," he continued. Eve laughed.

"The first thing any tour leader will tell you is that you can't trust Trip Advisor because it's too easy to manipulate."

"Really?"

"Yes. There are too many people pretending to be someone else writing on it; too many hidden agendas. I sometimes read things about hotels I've stayed at and wondered at how differently the alleged guest who's writing the report has seen the facilities, staff and service compared to what I experienced."

"You're right, you know. Someone had written that the staff were rude and the service poor, yet I don't think the staff here could be nicer. Everyone's got a smile on their face," Stewart agreed.

"Is there any chance of eating tonight?" Murray, who had been left alone at the end of the bar because Dawn and Donna had got into conversation with Suzanne and Frances, and Jason and Huw were now hovering on the edge of the group formed by Jo, Natalie, Michael, Deano and Dave, stomped over to Eve and Stewart.

"Of course! I was just waiting for the last person to join us. Geri."

"What if she doesnae come?. We could be waiting all night."

"Right! Excuse me, everyone!" Eve raised her voice so that the group could hear her. "We're just one person missing so I'm going to check that she's actually coming to dinner, but in the meantime, if people are hungry, please go right on into the dining-room. Tell Osbert, the Head Waiter, at the reception podium you're Eve's group and he'll take you to our tables. I'll join you in a moment."

A stampede towards the dining-room started.

"I take it people are hungry then?" Eve said at the group of retreating backs.

***

Geri was in a deep, dreamless sleep; the kind of sleep only brought on by exhaustion and booze. Through it she could hear the phone ringing but felt unable to move. As she slowly drifted up into consciousness the phone seemed louder and more insistent. For a moment, disorientated, she couldn't work out where it was. She opened her eyes but the room was in complete darkness; just a red light flashed on her right indicating where the phone was located. She reached out and grabbed it wondering who on earth it could be; nobody knew where she was.

"Hello"

"Geri?"

"Yes."

"Oh, sorry I've woken you up, haven't I? It's Eve, the tour manager."

"What time is it?"

"It's twenty to eight. The others have just gone into dinner and as we didn't see you at pre-dinner drinks I was just wondering if you're well."

"Yes. Oh, sorry!"

"It's alright. You don't have to join us if you don't want to. It's just a courtesy call, as I say, to check that nothing's happened to you. A lot of people fall asleep on the first night, after all it is twenty to one in the morning in the UK."

"But I wanted to join you all. As you said, it is the first night after all." Geri sounded a bit upset.

"Get ready then and I'll wait for you and we can go in together," Eve said.

"I'll be down in five minutes."

And five minutes later Geri came rushing into the bar, where Eve was sitting waiting for her. She'd washed her face and put on some make-up, cleaned her teeth thoroughly because her mouth felt dry and stale, and then got into a black and white spotted halter-neck dress. Some deodorant and a spray of perfume took care of everything else. She thanked God her hair was short and only ever needed a quick brush. She was annoyed with herself. Tonight was the First Night; tonight she was supposed to make An Entrance. Now she'd blown it! Coming in late with the tour manager looking after her made her look like an idiot. Still, the alternative was staying in her room and missing out on whatever might be going on and she didn't want that. She'd come away to be part of it all and that wasn't going to happen if she sat in her room. She'd already missed out on the paddling and fun the others had had this afternoon. She wasn't going to miss out on any more. Mr Forty-eight D was going to be hers, come hell or high water!

Eve looked at her and smiled.

"Would you like a drink before we go in?"

"No, thanks." She'd had enough this afternoon and besides she assumed there would be wine at the table.

"Let's go then." Eve slipped off the bar stool, turned and said "Thanks, Elvis!" to the smiling barman, who called "You're welcome, baby!" in reply, and the two women headed towards the restaurant.

Inside the conversation at the long table where the Travel Together group were sitting was animated. Eve smiled. She always found it fascinating that people who hadn't known each other a couple of hours earlier were now sharing jokes and opinions and exchanging personal information. There were two empty seats at the far end of the table and Eve and Geri made their way there. Geri took the seat at the end of the line next to Trevor leaving Eve to sit at the head of the table.

"You all know Geri, I think?" Eve said by way of introducing her to the group. There were nods and smiles. Glenda, the wine waitress appeared like magic.

"Are you having wine or can I get you anything else?"

"I'll have a glass of white," Geri said.

"And your usual?" Glenda asked Eve.

"You remembered?" Eve was amazed.

"Of course I did! One white wine, one Diet Coke coming up!"

Trevor was sitting on Geri's right.

"Don't you drink at all?" he asked Eve across Geri.

"Not while I'm working," she said. "You never know what might happen and I need to keep a cool head!"

He laughed. He seemed more relaxed now than he had at afternoon tea.

"Grub's good!" Dave said to Eve as he munched away. "There's a beau'iful bit a pork on the carvery."

"I had the chicken curry," Stewart offered from further down the table. "Smashing!"

Eve and Geri went to the buffet. On her first trip to the Mango Tree Resort Eve had been very apprehensive; a large resort offering an all-inclusive programme sometimes meant one thing – food like school dinners. But it certainly wasn't the case here. The food was amazing; so much choice, beautifully presented and tasting wonderful. She helped herself to some smoked salmon and some mussels from the seafood bar and added some potato salad, tomato, carrot and beetroot from the salad stall. That was quite enough. She wasn't really hungry; on a day like this with early breakfast, two meals on the plane and afternoon tea on arrival, it was hard to work out what meal it was you were eating next.

She returned to the table to see that Geri was already there with a very small salad. Eve put her plate of food on the table and sat down. No soon as her backside hit the chair the questions started.

"So, how long have you been working for Travel Together, then? Geri asked.

"Twelve years."

"Really?"

"Blimey! What a job, eh? All this sun, sand and booze and gettin' paid fer it!" Dave said.

"Don't you get paid for going to work?" Eve asked him.

"Yeh, but I ain't got a job like this!"

"What do you do?"

"I've got a second-hand motor business."

Quelle surprise!

"So, how did you get a job like this then?" Geri said.

"Oh, I've always worked in travel and tourism," Eve said, not wanting to go into details. She knew she'd answer the same question at least another ten times before tonight and tomorrow were over. As she ate Eve let her gaze wander down the table. At the far end Jo was facing her and they caught each other's eye at the same time. Jo raised her glass.

"Cheers, old thing!" she said in a faux upper-class accent. "Haven't been at a table like this since the last time I was at Balmoral, what?" Eve burst out laughing and raised her glass back. "Cheers!" she called down the table, "Happy holiday!"

"Happy holiday!" The reply rippled down the table followed by much clinking of glasses.

"Here!"

Eve looked down the table towards Murray who was sitting between Jason and Grace.

Are you addressing me?

"Someone's missing, are they not?" he asked. "There was an old dear in our taxi who didn't say a word tae anyone. Is she with our group or did she just get in the wrong cab?"

"Some old dear?" Eve mimicked, knowing full well who he meant, but she wanted to cut any rudeness to other group members right in the bud, especially from such a PC specimen as Murray.

"Aye. She was sort of thin and pale and tired looking. Specs. Grey hair."

"There is one member of the group not having dinner with us tonight," Eve explained. "Ursula. I think she was tired; she ate earlier."

"That seems a bit funny, doesn't it?"

"She probably didn't like the look of us," Stewart piped up producing chuckles all round.

Half way down the table a phone started ringing. Deborah jumped up and walked away from the table, talking animatedly. At Jo's end of the table, Natalie was coming to the end of an anecdote that had involved much arm-waving and resulted in those around her, Grace, Michael, Jo and Deano collapsing with laughter. She herself laughed, drained her glass and then announced "Anyone else for pudding?" as she stood up. The other four stood up, too.

"Might be something to tempt me," Michael said.

"You don't look like a pudding boy," Grace said as she walked alongside him over to the mouth-watering desserts on display.

"Don't be fooled by appearances. My tooth is a sweet as they come."

"Mine, too! Oh, God! That chocolate mousse looks amazing."

"Coconut and rum rice pudding for me!" Natalie sang out, ladling it into a bowl. "I don't give a toss about the calorie counting now, I'm on holiday!"

"Mmmmmmm! Irresistible!" Deano said, standing beside her.

"I know. And it smells divine."

"I meant you, not the rice pudding," he said.

"Oh, please! I haven't had that many rum punches yet to be taken in by you," Natalie retorted. "And believe me; you'll get much more from the pud than you would from me!" And with that she smiled sweetly, grabbed a spoon from the stack and sashayed back to the table. Michael, who witnessed the whole exchange, grinned at Deano.

"Nice try, mate."

"Perhaps just a bit too soon," Deano said and they both laughed.

At the table Deborah yawned.

"Oh, don't!" Frances said. "You'll start me off." And with that she yawned long, hard and wide. "You see!"

"Well, it's been a long day, hasn't it?" Deborah said. "I'm going to go up, I think. I want to finish unpacking and I'm shattered."

"Me, too. You don't think people will think we're unsociable, do you?"

"What if they do?" Deborah flicked her sleek bob back over her shoulder and stood up.

"Off to bed?" Eve asked. "I don't blame you. I'm not going to have a late one either."

Seeing that nobody seemed to mind Frances stood up, too, followed by Trevor.

"Good night, everyone!" Frances called. "What time is it in the morning, Eve?"

"Breakfast is from seven and there will be two large tables on the terrace reserved for us, and then my information briefing will be in the bar at nine."

"Nine o'clock!" said Dave, looking genuinely shocked.

"You'll be awake really early," Eve reassured him. "It'll take you a couple of days to get onto Caribbean time. And if you come and see me at nine then the rest of the day is yours. I used to do it at ten or half ten, but then people found they'd just got settled on the beach and had to come back again, or that they were hanging around wasting the morning. So nine o'clock's proved more convenient."

"Don't expect me at that time," Deborah said. "I want to go to the gym first thing. I'm not interested in any trips, anyway, and I know that's what these get-togethers are usually about."

Suit yourself!

The remaining group members finished at the table and went back into the bar. A dance band was playing popular songs and a few people were on the dance floor. As they broke into their next number, *Achy-Breaky Heart*, there were squeals from Dawn and Donna.

"Oooh! Come on, everyone!" Dawn said, putting her drink down, "We can't miss this one."

But the others felt they could. Dawn and Donna scurried onto the dance floor followed only by Geri and started an intricate line-dance, which involved much rocking back and forth and an intertwining of grapevines.

"They're like the bleedin' Dolly Sisters, them two," Dave said, voicing what most people were thinking. "I bet they're teachers."

"Yes, well there's teachers and there's teachers," Huw said.

"What do you teach then, mate?" Dave asked.

"PE"

"Oh, right. You a teacher an' all, Jason?"

"Yes. Business and Economics."

"Do you already know one anuvva, then? You mates from home, like?"

"No, we just met in the lounge at Gatwick," Huw said. "There's bound to be a lot of teachers here at this time of year. It's the first week of the holidays."

"Fuck! I ope that don't mean loads of kids," Dave said. "Oh, sorry fer me language!" He apologised to Eve as she joined the three men.

"She must have heard a lot worse than that!" Huw said.

"She has." Eve replied.

"So how long have you been working for Travel Together?" Jason asked.

"Twelve years."

"Do you like it?"

"Who wouldn't like it?" Huw interrupted before Eve could answer. "What a job! It must be like being on permanent holiday."

"A bit like bein' a teacher!" Dave said. Eve and Jason laughed. Huw gave a smile that didn't quite reach his eyes and took a long swig of his drink.

Suzanne, Jo and Grace had been discussing Country and Western music when all three decided they were ready for bed.

"I'm just going to have a last nightcap and then it's me off, too," Natalie said as they said their goodnights.

"Rum punch?" asked Michael, already on his way to the bar.

"Yes, please."

Dawn, Donna and Geri rejoined the group. Geri had felt a little foolish being the only one to join the two women on the dance floor. She thought that everyone was going to dance. Still, now she was back in the group she had the chance to mingle a bit and wangle herself a place next to Mr forty-eight D, whose name she still didn't know. She picked up her drink and turned to join him and the man in the lairy clothes at the bar when he downed his drink and called "Goodnight!" to everyone.

"Goodnight, Deano!" Eve said.

Geri went over to Eve.

"I'm trying to get everyone's name," she said. "Did you call him Deano?"

"Yes," Eve said.

"Is he Italian? He looks sort of Mediterranean."

"I don't think so. He just likes to be called it." It wasn't her job to explain everyone's little foibles to the rest of the group besides which, she actually thought that Deano's *Mediterranean complexion* came from a bottle. Anyway, Geri would have plenty of time to chat to Deano in the days that followed. He could tell her about his name. Too often an innocent comment made got back to a group member starting with "Well, Eve said...." She always made a point of not entering into any gossip with any member of the group or of passing on personal information. One of the first things she'd learned in the job was that people would be prepared to tell someone they've only just meant things they probably wouldn't discuss with their closest friends. Sometimes she felt like a mother-confessor. Let Geri do her own chasing!

Eve suddenly felt a wave of tiredness hit her. Looking at her watch she saw it was almost eleven; four in the morning for her body clock. She was going to her room. She still had her paperwork for the day to complete and wanted to get everything ready for the information briefing the following morning. Looking round she could see that everyone seemed to be chatting; even Geri was now talking to Huw and Jason.

"Goodnight, all!" Eve said. "See you in the morning. Sleep well!"

***

Murray cursed as he dropped his room card for the second time. Tiredness and alcohol were taking their toll.

"Bloody stupid thing!" he muttered to himself wondering why they couldn't just give everyone a normal key instead of this malfunctioning piece of technology.

"Shall I try that for you, sir?" The voice from behind made him jump out of his skin. "It sometimes needs a special knack," said the uniformed security guard with a smile.

"It's obviously faulty," Murray said tutting with impatience and running the card up and down in the slot. "I've already tried it several times."

"You're doing it too fast, sir," the guard said. "Let me show you."

He took the card from Murray's hand and slowly placed it in the top of the slot.

"You never get it going if you do it too fast. You have to approach using the room key the same way you approach a woman; slow, firm and confident." Murray, a graduate of the Wham Bam Thank You, Ma'am School of Seduction, whose idea of foreplay was to put on a *Now* CD, looked at him blankly.

"You hold the card firmly in your hand; you guide it into the slot and when you're sure you've made a connection you proceed. Slow, confident and firm, just like you're wooing your lady." he said smiling as he passed the card down the slot and the red light on the handle turned to green and the door clicked open.

In spite of himself, Murray smiled.

"Good night, sir" the guard said, moving off.

"Good night!" Murray called to the retreating back. "Hmm! Slow, confident and firm," he said to himself.

Once inside he looked round the room, that somehow didn't seem as small now as it had earlier, and as his gaze came to rest on the bed he was suddenly overcome with tiredness. He sat on it and then fell back onto the deep, comfortable mattress. Within seconds he was snoring gently and he stayed like that until the early light of sunrise poked underneath the curtains.

***

DAY TWO

Breakfast was underway as Eve bustled into the dining-room at seven thirty.

"Eve, baby!" Osbert said, by way of a greeting, taking her hand and kissing it. "You've already got some of your people at the table." He walked with her to the terrace section of the restaurant, where two large, round tables bore signs identifying them as *'Reserved for Eve's Group'*. "You're looking good, baby, you're looking younger every time you come see us," Osbert said as they reached the table. Eve laughed.

"You're such a flatterer!"

"I mean every word!" he said, giving her hand a squeeze before walking back to the podium, smiling at and greeting those guests having breakfast on the way.

"You weren't wrong abaht waking up early," Dave greeted Eve. "We've all bin awake fer hours," he said, indicating those sitting at the table.

"Since half past four!" Suzanne said. "I just couldn't get back to sleep so I sat on my balcony and watched the sun come up. I've never done that before, it was magic. So exciting!" She shimmered in a turquoise kaftan, edged in a rainbow of rhinestones.

"And I had a swim in the sea as soon as it was light," said Trevor. "It was wonderful, just like a warm bath."

"Weren't you afraid of sharks?" Suzanne asked, wide-eyed.

"I didn't think of them to be honest. Are there sharks in these waters, Eve?"

"There are, but not usually close to shore. They stay out on the reef. There are a lot more interesting things for them to eat out there."

"Is that what that roped off area's for? Is it a net to keep the sharks out?" asked Suzanne.

"No, that's to mark the safe swimming area. If you stay inside the roped-off section you won't get in the way of a jet-ski or a windsurfer or a catamaran."

"I won't go past it. I'm not a very strong swimmer really," Suzanne continued, pausing to wipe a slither of strawberry jam that had slid from her slice of toast onto her cleavage.

Dave, who was fighting to take his gaze from Suzanne's majestic bosom but finding it a losing battle, nodded his head.

"I'm not too confident in deep water. I like swimmin', but I don't like bein' out of me depth. And I ate feeling seaweed against me legs."

"Oh, yes!" Frances said. "It's all slimy and it makes you jump."

Michael joined the group at the table holding a plate full of cooked breakfast.

"What a spread! I've got a fresh cheese and mushroom omelette, bacon and beans, just right to set me up for the day." He smothered the omelette in tomato ketchup and asked Suzanne to pass him the salt. "I can't believe I'm eating all this so early in the morning. You can't get any complaints about the food here, Eve. It's really good."

"You'd be surprised!"

"And the fruit!" said Frances. "Melon, papaya, mango, banana, pineapple. They'd cost you a fortune back home. Well, not the banana perhaps, but the rest would."

"Just enjoy," Eve said, pouring some more coffee into her cup. She looked up and suddenly felt bilious; she put her sunglasses on. Stewart was approaching the table wearing a lime green t-shirt bearing the words *'beach bum'* in lemon-yellow lettering and orange knee-length swimming shorts.

"Blimey! What's the matter, mate? You frightened of gettin' run over?" Dave said.

"What?" Stewart seemed a little bewildered.

"He thinks you're a bit colourful this morning," Michael said, by way of explanation.

"Oh I like bright colours," Stewart said, "especially in a place like this."

"You're blending in," said Suzanne. "I think you look very nice. Like an Opal Fruit."

"Oh, thank you."

Eve was sure that Stewart had blushed. She looked at her watch and saw it was already twenty past eight. She'd arranged to meet Sunny at half past so that she could up-date her on what had changed since her last visit to Antigua and for the two of them to work out a programme for the group. She drained her last drops of coffee from her cup and wiped her mouth with her napkin.

"Enjoy breakfast, everyone! I'll see you in the bar at nine," she said as she stood up and gathered her bag and clipboard and paperwork together.

"Do we have to bring anything?" Suzanne asked.

"Pen and paper if you want, but I usually have a supply of that in case you want to jot anything down."

"I've got a notebook," Suzanne said, "I'll write my notes in that and that way I won't lose them."

As Eve left the table, Natalie, Grace and Deano arrived and sat on the adjacent one.

"Isn't it beautiful?" Natalie called across to the others. "I still can't believe it. Look! Not a cloud in the sky."

"And fabulous food," Stewart called out to her raising his fork and waving a lump of pancake around.

"And no washing up afterwards!" added Grace and they all laughed.

***

Geri had also been awake for hours. After tossing and turning from four until six she had peered through her curtains to be greeted by a clear blue sky and decided to go for a walk along the beach. It was a beautiful time of day; peaceful and quiet and it felt as if she had the whole world to herself. She walked along the water's edge gently splashing in the ankle-deep, warm water and looked out to sea. A cruise ship slowly, gracefully floated by on its way to St John's to dock for the day. She noticed a large rock just ahead of her and sat on it to watch the cruise ship pass. Back down the beach she could see somebody wading into the water. It looked like the older guy in their group; she couldn't remember his name, well, she hadn't been interested in finding it out really. Deano was the one she wanted to engage in meaningful conversation. She had to find a way to get him to herself today!

The water looked tempting. She would have liked a swim but hadn't put on her swimsuit. She must make a point of doing it another morning. Tomorrow perhaps.

'Stay in the now!' she admonished herself. She was always way back in the past reliving what had-been or ahead in the future fantasising about what might-be. There was no point in going to therapy if she wasn't going to improve her behaviour. The sun had fully appeared over the hills in the east beyond the resort now and Geri could feel the rise in temperature. The older man had finished his dip and was nowhere to be seen. She looked at her watch. It was eight o'clock. She couldn't believe she'd been sitting on the rock gazing out to sea for more than an hour. She stood up and started walking back towards the resort.

'Today is where I am! Today is what matters and today I'm going to enjoy myself,' was her mantra all the way back to breakfast.

***

Sunny walked into the reception area at half past eight exactly to find Eve was already sitting at a table waiting for her. They exchanged another warm hug and sat down.

"Girl, it's so good to see you again!" Sunny said.

"It's lovely being back. Antigua always feels like home," Eve said. "So what's new since my last visit?"

"Well, in the hotel nothing much, I don't think. The Crazy Conch still opens six evenings a week and each guest is allowed to visit three times during their stay. Was Pasta Pazzazz open last time you were here?"

Eve shook her head.

"It's up where the Conference Room used to be, beyond reception going back towards the main gate."

"I remember," Eve said.

"Well, they finished the new Conference Suite now, at the north of the resort, past the Jacuzzi and Adults' Pool so the old Conference Room is now being used as a pasta and pizza place. It opens from half past six until nine every evening and you have to reserve like you do for the Crazy Conch and once again it's three visits per guest per stay. Everything else is the same, and don't forget that tonight it's the Manager's Welcome Cocktail Party."

"Oh, yes! I'm looking forward to seeing Mr Samuel again. I've haven't seen him yet."

"He left! Didn't you know?"

"No!"

"Yes, he had a big, big, win on the Caribbean Lotto and decided to enjoy himself while he still can. Bought a big house over past Johnson's Point, got himself a boat and spends all his time fishing."

"I'm really pleased for him. I liked Mr Samuel. So, who's taken over?"

"A new man; Mr McGrass. Nice guy. Very hands-on, I'm surprised you haven't seen him, he's always around. Anyway, the reception tonight is at seven o'clock down in the Hammock Room by the beach."

Eve scribbled a hasty note to herself.

"The airline still offers the Courtesy Check-In Service. We need to have the request form back three days before departure. It's the usual thing, name, passport number and date of issue, number of items to be checked in and meal and seat requests."

She handed Eve a pile of forms for each person to record their information on.

"All the excursions are the same; no price increases, although they keep on threatening to raise them. I think they'd shoot themselves in the foot if they did. I've pencilled in a catamaran for Tuesday, they should all be a bit used to the sun by then. I did ask for Wednesday or

Thursday but they're big cruise ship days and there were none free. They'll do it for the usual price and you still get seven percent. Not much, but there you go!"

"Better than a poke in the eye with a stick," said Eve.

"And warn them about the beach vendors," Sunny raised her hand as Eve went to interrupt her. "I know you always do, but the situation's not good. They'll tell them anything to make a sale and then we both know who picks up the pieces! Shirley Heights is tomorrow, as always, Jeep Island Tour on Monday, Wednesday and Friday, Stingrays and Montserrat Helicopter every day except Saturdays and Sundays and you have to ring for availability and Barbuda is Thursday and Saturday and you still have to be a good sailor! All the days and prices are on here and we'll confirm the times when I write out the tickets."

Sunny handed Eve a pile of Excursion Booking Forms.

"Anything else you need?"

"I don't think so, but if there is I'll ring you."

"Yes, call me anytime. I'm going to Jolly Beach now. I've got about ten in there, that's all; once I've seen them I'm going into the office. Call me with your numbers."

***

By five to nine only two empty seats remained in the large semi-circle that Eve had set out in the bar area. Looking round she could see that Ursula and Deborah were the two who were missing.

No surprises there, then!

There was a buzz going around the group as they exchanged conversation and some read out loud items on the Excursion Booking Form and the Courtesy Check-In Service Form. Suzanne put her hand up.

"Eve!"

"Yes?"

"Deborah said she'll be over when she's finished her breakfast. She arrived just before we all started leaving to come over here."

"OK, thanks. If she's not here by nine we'll make a start and she can catch up when she joins us. Has anyone seen Ursula?"

"Who's Ursula? The old dear?" Murray asked smirking.

"She's the lady who didn't come to dinner last night," Jo said, looking at them all sternly. "I haven't seen her at all."

Nobody else thought they'd seen her, either. Eve realised that Ursula was probably going to spend the whole duration of the holiday avoiding the group. Oh well, there wasn't much she could do if that were the case. Eve place a fistful of pens on the table in front of her and some sheets of paper.

"If anyone thinks they may be overcome with the need to make copious notes, here are some pens and paper," she said.

Everyone smiled and several of the group got up and helped themselves. Eve then gave out a sheet of A5 to everyone, which gave her room number in the resort and her contact telephone number. The local agent always supplied a mobile for the tour manager to use and then charged Travel Together for the calls made. It made sense; the company could always contact her and so could the group.

"This ain't a come-on, is it?" Dave asked, cheekily.

"No it isn't!" Eve came back at him.

"In your dreams, Dave!" Natalie called out, and everyone laughed.

"OK, everyone, it's nine o'clock so let's make a start. Thanks for coming along this morning; it makes it much easier to see everyone together on the first morning so that I can give you all the information you need now that you've rested and can take it all in. Welcome to the Mango Tree Resort, on behalf of Travel Together, or T2G as our friends call us. We all hope that you're going to have a really great time. I've given you my room number, and as I've already said it's not a come-on!" – there was another outburst of laughter – "and as it's an all-inclusive resort I don't mind you having my room number, because you can't put your wine on it as there's no charge!"

Once again laughter rippled round the semi-circle.

"Is that why we're sittin' in a circle?" Dave asked, "Cos you fink we're a bunch of alcoholics? It's like an AA meetin'."

"Speak for yourself!" Jo retorted and everyone chuckled.

"Stop interrupting! We're here to listen to Eve!" admonished Suzanne, and the group fell quiet.

"Please do feel that you can contact me at any time," Eve continued. "I'm around most of the time and every morning I'll be sitting here on the bar terrace from half eight until half ten so you know you can always find me here. And I'm at pre-dinner drinks at seven every evening. We usually have drinks and then go into dinner between half seven and eight o'clock.

All I want is for you to have the best possible holiday while staying safe and without getting ripped-off. Now this is a holiday for first-time Travel Together clients so I'd like to point out that there's no right way of doing this. Some people prefer to be with the group all the time, that's why they've come; for company. Others are quite happy with their own company during the day but like to have someone to have a drink and dinner with in the evening, and that's fine, too. It's your holiday, so you can do whatever you like. But please, if there's anything you want to do, just ask and I'll see if I can arrange it for you. Our meals are taken in the main dining-room where we ate last night and had our breakfast this morning. There are always two large round tables reserved for us for breakfast and lunch and a long table for dinner in the evening. Breakfast is from seven until ten thirty, lunch is from twelve to two. If you don't want to have lunch in the restaurant, there's a diner on the beach that serves salads, jerk chicken and fish and burgers from half past eleven until four o'clock. Afternoon tea is served by the Spa bar from half past four until half past five and dinner is in the main restaurant from six thirty until ten, although we usually eat about eight, having met up in the bar from seven-ish for pre-dinner drinks as I've already said."

"We won't go ungry then!" Dave said and everyone laughed.

"We certainly won't!" Eve agreed, before continuing. "On Sundays there's a big brunch from half eleven until three, with a steel band and I've taken the liberty of booking us all in for it. If you don't want to come just let me know by tomorrow morning, please. And the same goes for the two a-la-carte restaurants – the Crazy Conch, which is mainly seafood and the Pasta Pazzazz, which is pastas and pizzas. I've booked the Crazy Conch for Monday evening and the Pasta Pazzazz for Wednesday. If you enjoy eating there, let me know and I can make further reservations for later in the week."

Suzanne's hand shot up.

"How much does that cost?"

"Nothing, Suzanne. It's all part of the all-inclusive package."

"That's very good, isn't it?"

"Yes, it is, I agree. Oh, hi! Come and join us, Deborah. There's a seat there."

Eve indicated a seat about a third of the way round the semi-circle between Geri and Trevor.

"I wanted to ask you about the coffee," Deborah said to Eve as she sat down and Eve gave her the paperwork. "Is it decaf?"

"One of the machines at the hot drinks' station serves decaf, yes. And if you ask the waiters at breakfast they'll make sure they bring decaf for you."

"Only I have an allergy to caffeine, you see. I can only drink decaf."

Jo and Natalie exchanged glances and raised their eyebrows.

"Did you drink it this mornin'?" Dave asked.

"Yes."

"And ow do you feel?"

"Fine."

"Well, it must be decaf then, mustn't it? Or you'd be feelin' allergic now, wouldn't you?"

There were stifled guffaws and grins all around the group.

"We're being very rude, interrupting Eve," Suzanne said.

"Sorry!" Dave said.

"No, it wasn't you!" Suzanne said, looking pointedly at Deborah.

"Right, well that's the eating arrangements," Eve continued, moving swiftly on, "and, of course, if anyone wants to go out to eat any night then please talk to me about it and I can recommend some restaurants to you. Now, don't forget that all the entertainment and all the water sport activities are included in your holiday so I hope that you'll take part and make the most of them. There are Hobie Cats on the beach and if you want to take one out there are free lessons every morning at half past ten, there's no need to book, just turn up. There's also windsurfing, kayaking and they have pedalos, too. The water-sports centre is down on the beach just before you draw level with the Crazy Conch and that's also where you get your beach towel from. They will have given you a ticket when you checked in yesterday; you exchange that for your beach towel as often as you need a clean one and then on the final day you get the card back and hand it to the receptionist when you check out. The motorised sports on the beach are nothing to do with the resort; all beaches in Antigua are public beaches and people are free to come onto the beach and run their businesses. Please be careful. I speak from experience when I tell you that many of them do not have public liability insurance, so please check your own insurance details before you jump on a jet ski or go off on a speedboat ride. If things go wrong there's nothing I can do to help you there, and I had someone with three cracked ribs who came off a jet ski and they ended up having a miserable holiday and were unable to claim a penny back. So please take my advice and do be careful. The same goes with buying trips from beach vendors. I can't tell you how to spend your money but it's buyer beware. If it all goes wrong, for example if you buy a boat ticket and it rains then you won't see your money again, so think before you do anything silly. And talking about the beach, remember to put on lots of sun block. The sun here is very strong and it's really easy to get burned, especially if you're not used to it or you're fair-skinned. And I'd also recommend you using insect repellent, too."

Eve paused to take a sip from her water, hoping that nobody would jump in again. Fearing Suzanne's wrath, nobody did.

"The village is just a five minute walk away, you'll find it if you turn right as you come out of the hotel and follow the road for a couple of hundred yards. There's a bank, a pharmacy and a supermarket there if there's anything you need to buy. You can change money at the front desk if you like. The rate of exchange is the same as the bank and you will be given Eastern Caribbean Dollars. Be careful when you're out and about and buying things because usually in the world of tourism when they say dollars they'll be talking about US dollars. Now, the Eastern Caribbean Dollar is tied to the US dollar at approximately two point six, so that won't change, you can't get ripped off. But, make sure you know which dollar you're talking about because that's more than two and a half times difference."

"Will the ATMs give you US?" asked Stewart.

"No, just EC," Eve replied. "If you especially want US you'll have to go to the bank. But most places will take US for payment; some will give you your change in US and others only in EC."

Eve saw a few puzzled faces.

"It's not complicated really. If you've brought US you can use it; if you've brought EC you can use that. Most shops, bars and restaurants show their prices in EC and US and have tills that print a receipt in both currencies."

"Bloody Yanks, that is!" Murray said. "It's the same in London; they cannae work in any currency but their own. They're forever offering me dollars for their fares."

"Are you a bus driver?" Jo asked.

Murray gave her a filthy look.

"A bus driver!" he said, with venom. "I drive a black cab."

"Nothing wrong with being a bus driver," Jo snapped back. "My dad was on the buses for thirty years. It's an honest job."

"Okay, then!" Eve brought the meeting back to some sort of order. "So, as I've just said the village is nearby, but if you want to do some proper shopping then it's best to go into St John's, the capital. It's not a huge place, but it's worth going for a look-round and there are some good bargains to be had; rum, of course, cigarettes and cigars, perfumes and jewellery. Although I wouldn't normally recommend you walking around with your passports and tickets on you, I hope they're safely locked away in your safety deposit boxes, but you will need to produce them if you want to save yourself the twelve and a half per cent VAT on those goods. I usually organise a very informal trip into St John's one morning for shopping and sightseeing.

I'll let you know when I'm going and if you want to come please join me. We'll go on a day when there are no cruise ships in and we'll go on the local bus. It's only three dollars EC each way, and it's usually fun if a bit hair-raising. If you want to go in without me, then you catch the bus one hundred yards past the hotel on the right. The bus route ends under the big tamarind tree. Please remember that here in Antigua the buses and the taxis are all minibuses, like the ones we came from the airport in, and should you jump in a taxi by mistake then it will be twelve US dollars each. The taxis here charge per person not per ride. You will know if you're in a taxi or a bus by looking at the number plate. All buses have a registration that begins with the letters B U S. So there's a bit of a clue there."

Everyone laughed.

"What does that stand for?" Deano asked, prompting further laughter.

"I haven't the faintest idea!"

Eve held up the Courtesy Check-In Forms and everyone shuffled their paperwork and brought theirs to the top.

"Now, we're very lucky here because the airline offers a service whereby they come to the resort on departure day and do the check-in and issue the boarding passes and take your departure tax, which is seventy EC dollars or twenty-seven US and your luggage. All this means that when we get to the airport all we have to do is go through security and Immigration and wait in the departure lounge for our flight to be called. Sometimes it takes a little while here, because people like us who check in one at a time hold everyone else up, but it means that you can then have lunch and a final wash and brush up and leave for the airport without struggling with luggage and queuing up to check-in at the airport. You don't have to do this, but I recommend that you do, and if you want to then you must complete the form and give it back to me by breakfast time next Friday at the very latest."

There were lots of nods and murmurs of assent around the group as everyone seemed to agree that it was a good idea.

"But how do we manage for the last three days, then?" asked Deborah.

"What do you mean?"

"Well, if our case goes on Friday, how do we manage until Monday?"

A chorus of groans and a couple of cries of "Oh, my God!" greeted this. Eve felt embarrassed for Deborah, who had completely misunderstood.

"No, your luggage doesn't go on Friday; you have to let me know you want to use the service by giving me back the form by Friday. Your luggage goes at half past twelve on departure day and we leave at half past two."

"Oh, I see!" Deborah blushed.

"Two days before we leave I will give everyone a departure letter, which will explain how it all works and where you have to be when on our final day, which is Monday week. Now, you'll have all seen in the general information pack that Travel Together sent you, that we have a policy of having a whip-round for the hotel staff. It covers everyone, because so many people look after us in a resort like this. As it's all-inclusive you don't get the chance to leave a tip after a round of drinks or in the dining room, so our collection allows you to do so. I'll give out envelopes for that near the end. Okay? Are there any general questions that I haven't covered so far?"

Eve looked around the group. Stewart put his hand up.

"How much do people usually put in for the tip?" he asked.

"We suggest between twenty and twenty-five pounds for a holiday of this duration, and that works out at only about two pounds a day, but, of course, you can put in as much as you want. It's your choice, although most people think that the members of staff here are well worth twenty-five pounds."

"Does it have to be in pounds?"

"Not at all! Pounds, US or EC; whatever you have."

"I've got a complaint," Frances said. "There's something near my room that kept me awake all night. It's squeaking. Like an alarm. It really got on my nerves. Can anything be done about it?"

Eve grinned to herself.

"I think you'll find that's the tree frogs."

"Tree frogs? No. It's definitely a fan or an alarm or something. Didn't anyone else hear it?"

"I did!" Donna said. "I told Dawn at breakfast, didn't I, Dawn? I said I'd heard a sort of squeaking noise when I got up to go to the bathroom. I thought it was the battery in the smoke alarm wearing out. I was going to mention it to the reception desk this morning, wasn't I, Dawn?"

"I don't think it's the smoke alarm, either. They're tiny little creatures that look like a child's drawing of a frog, you know, really big eyes. But for something so small they make a lot of noise. If you stand under the trees and listen hard you can hear it's a creature and not something mechanical."

Frances didn't look very convinced.

"Nothing we can do about them, I'm afraid. We have to learn to live with them. It's just another sound of the Caribbean."

"Why don cha wear the ear plugs they give us on the plane?" Dave asked.

"That's an idea," Frances said.

"Okay!" Eve called to get everyone's attention again. "To end up with I'll talk about the trips and excursions on offer to us and things we can do together."

There was more shuffling of papers as everyone moved the Excursion Booking Form to the top of the pile.

"Before we look at organised trips, I want to let you know that we are invited to the Manager's Cocktail Party at seven tonight. It's in the Hammock Room, which is down on the beach. We'll do pre-dinner drinks there, just turn up and we'll all find each other. I'll be there a few minutes early so you can look for me if you want to."

"What's the point of a cocktail party when drinks are free anyway? They're nae exactly giving us anything, are they?" Murray said.

Grace shook her head and Natalie muttered "For God's sake!" under her breath.

"It's a gesture," Eve replied. "A courtesy the manager affords the guests in the way of appreciation for being here. It's not just drinks, there are canapés, too. It's not compulsory; you don't have to come if you don't want to. It's your holiday and you do as you please. For those who do want to go I'll see you there at seven and for those who don't we'll meet you in the bar just before eight so that we can eat together. How does that sound?"

There were nods of approval all round, with most of the group agreeing with their neighbour that they would be going to the party. Murray sat back looking annoyed.

Fucking smart-arse, stuck up, toffee-nosed bitch of a rep. Who the fuck does she think she is? He seethed to himself. He didn't need to be ticked off in front of the group by the likes of her. He'd show her. She could stick her Manager's Cocktail Party up her arse. He wouldn't go to it. Namby-pamby cocktails! He'd rather have a beer, or a short; a proper drink. In the bar. On his own. He dinnae care!

"OK, so, we'll move onto excursions now. There's quite an extensive excursion programme available here, but I'll just tell you about those that have proved most popular with our groups, and then if there's anything else you see or you want to ask about please do. First of all, tomorrow night, Sunday, is the usual sunset bash at Shirley Heights. Shirley Heights is one of the many fortresses built here during colonial times and it overlooks English and Falmouth Harbours. The view is spectacular, especially for sunset and then as it gets dark and both harbours light up below you. There's a steel band, which plays until seven followed by a local band which plays until nine. We leave here at five and leave there about quarter to nine and then that gets us back to the resort in time for dinner. Now, I'll be honest with you, most people love Shirley Heights; some, though, come back saying *'What was that all about?'* but like most things, it's a question of attitude. If you stand there with your arms folded, looking glum, then you probably won't enjoy yourself. But if you have a couple of rum punches and get down with the band you'll have a great time."

"Is it mainly for young people?" Trevor asked.

"Not at all! It's for everyone. I think it's a pity to be in Antigua and not go to Shirley Heights, but as I've said, not everyone likes it – it's a case of suck it and see, if you'll pardon the expression. If you don't like people and music and drinking and dancing then don't come!"

Most of the group laughed at this.

"Just remember to wear comfortable shoes because the original cobblestones are there and even if you don't want to dance and go and sit in the picnic area to listen to the music you have to walk across the grass, so no stilettos."

Eve took another sip of her water before continuing.

"Probably the most popular trip we do here is our own private charter on the catamaran. What's great about it is that it's only us; we have a catamaran that holds forty-five people for just us, and that means that we can go where we like. If the weather's not good in one place the skipper will take us somewhere else and we don't have to put up with other people or their children, either."

A murmur of approval went around the group.

"The skipper and crew know and understand our groups really well and they give us a great day out; snorkelling, swimming, deserted beaches, lunch and a full bar. We've pencilled it in for Tuesday and we need at least ten for it to go. And it's a great opportunity for the group to be together for the day."

"What if you're not a very good swimmer?" Suzanne asked. "I've never snorkelled before and I don't like deep water."

"Nobody has to snorkel," Eve explained, "and you only ever go in deep water if you want to. Usually we pull up on a deserted beach, somewhere like Rendezvous Bay, so you can walk into the water."

"Oh, that's good."

"If you want to see the island by land then there's a Jeep Tour, which takes in the whole of Antigua, except St John's. Remember this is a small island and you can easily get round in a day. You'll see Betty's Hope, an old sugar mill which has been turned into a museum; have a guided tour of Nelson's Dockyard down in English Harbour; enjoy a delicious local lunch of barbecue chicken and rice and peas and have a swim at Half Moon Bay, a beautiful beach on the Atlantic Side and a ride through the rain forest. That trip goes on Mondays, Wednesdays and Fridays."

"Isn't it cheaper to hire a car?" Huw said, frowning. "It's ninety-nine US a person according to this, but I saw car hire advertised at fifty US a day."

"Well, from experience I don't get involved in car hire," Eve said, mentally shuddering at the memory of the accident two of her clients were involved in the last time she had been on Antigua. "You saw what the roads were like on the way from the airport; pot holes a-go-go. Also half the cars are right hand drive and the other left hand drive. This means that people pull out without seeing what's ahead of them and there are lots of head-on collisions. It happened to two of my group last time I was here."

"Well, I've been driving for twenty years without a bash and I've driven on several Greek Islands and even round Barcelona."

Bully for you!

"If you're sure you want to hire a car then you'll need to go to the Police Station in Coolidge to get a temporary Antiguan Driver's Licence, which will cost you fifty EC. I'm sure the car hire company will take you there, and my advice would be to always take out the fully comprehensive policy, but be aware of how much the waiver is. It's usually more than five hundred dollars US."

Huw looked at Jason and they nodded to each other. Dawn and Donna whispered together.

"I'd be interested in joining you, if you do decide tae hire," Murray called across the semi-circle to Huw.

"Why doesn't that surprise me?" muttered Grace under her breath.

"OK, moving on," continued Eve, "we offer a forty-five minute helicopter ride over to Montserrat to see primarily the lava flows following the huge eruption of the volcano in the nineteen nineties. It really is like a modern day Pompeii. If any of you are keen photographers you can get some wonderful shots and it's all really quite poignant. If you want to do the helicopter ride I need you to put your weight on the form, please, when you hand it to me."

A groan went round the group.

"You'll have to add on a couple of pounds for each day we're here," Natalie said, making everyone laugh.

"I usually do! But don't worry about putting down your weight; I don't look like a woman who's concerned with counting calories now, do I?" Eve grinned indicating her shapely size sixteen figure. "Then just one more trip you might like to do and that's to Stingray City to swim with the stingrays. The taxi fare is extra, fifteen US per person for a minimum of four, so if we can have at least four it'll work out the best price for you. They are really wonderful creatures. They feel like fishy velvet and you'll be perfectly safe with them. The trip takes about two and a half hours and you'll be in the water with the rays for about an hour. So, that's the most popular of the trips. If you can have a think about what you want to do; tick the box next to your choices and hand the forms back to me, then I'll make all the bookings this morning and will let you know by this afternoon when you can go."

"Don't we have any choice as far as what day we go where?" asked Deano.

"We have to fit in around the cruise ship passengers who block book trips weeks ahead. There's limited availability, that's why it's important for me to know how many we've got for everything today so that I can book the places. Then you can pay tomorrow morning. The prices on your forms are in US dollars, but, of course, you can pay in EC or in sterling or with a credit card, although if you pay by card there's a five per cent charge."

The group members spent the next ten minutes in deep discussion with each other over what they planned to do while Eve got herself another cup of coffee.

"I'm nae spending nearly a hundred dollars for a jeep trip when we could get five of us in a car for ten dollars each," Murray said.

"Well I'm happy to pay for the trip," Jo said. "You've been told quite clearly that driving here is dicey and if you go on the trip, your lunch is included and you know that you get to see everything and the driver or the guide will explain everything to you; all the little anecdotes and local history and stories."

"She'll be saying she doesn't get involved in car hire because she probably doesnae get any commission on it," Murray said.

"That's a bit harsh," Michael said. "Would you deliberately not do something, then, so that you could do Eve out of some commission?"

"No, but her job is tae get the best deal for us, not tae line her own pockets."

"Who says she's lining her pockets? If she earns a commission, what's that to us as long as we enjoy ourselves? When you sell your house the estate agent gets a commission; when you book a holiday the travel agent gets a commission. Even if you shop at Waitrose the assistants get commission! And I'm sure that if you take any of your foreign passengers to bars or restaurants in London you get something for it! What's the difference with your tour manager getting a commission?"

"All I'm saying is that she should look out for us and not try tae put us off things just because she's not getting a cut!" Murray replied hotly.

"And who says she isn't?" chorused Michael, Natalie and Grace.

At that moment Eve returned with her mug of coffee and the group fell silent. Gradually one at a time they put their Excursion Booking Forms onto a pile in front of Eve; all except Murray, who folded his in his pocket and walked off.

"Thanks, Eve, that was great," Grace said, picking up her beach bag.

"Yes, thanks, thanks Eve!" echoed round the group as they all went off in threes and fours chatting animatedly about their choice of excursions or whether they were going to the pool, the beach or to the bar for the first beer or rum cocktail of the day. Eve gathered the forms together and started to collate them so that she could phone Sunny as quickly as possible with the numbers. Then she was going to have a quick swim before grabbing some lunch and then spending the afternoon filling out the Booking Confirmation Forms. But before she did any of that she had to try to find the illusive Ursula, whom nobody had seen the whole morning.

***

Soaring through the clear blue sky over the Caribbean Sea with the man of her dreams! What could be more romantic? Geri had had no intention of going on the helicopter ride, but seeing Deano tick it she'd decided to go on it, too.

"So, where are we all going?" Deano had asked as they walked away from the bar. "Pool or beach?"

"Beach!" Natalie, Jo and Michael had all chorused.

"I'm beaching as well," Dave added, coming alongside them. "I've got me stuff already. Shall I get us a few sun beds?"

"Yes, great, six or seven," Michael said. "Anyone else coming to the beach?" He turned and asked several of the others who were coming up behind them.

"I'd like to," said Suzanne, "if you don't mind, that is."

"Why would we mind?" Jo turned and linked arms with her, walking on ahead.

"Me, too," said Stewart.

"And me," said Trevor.

"And me," said Grace. "The pool's nice but it seems a shame to waste such a beautiful beach, doesn't it?"

"Well, I'm going to the Adults' Pool," Deborah announced drawing level with them. "I've got the latest Lee Childs' and I just want some peace and quiet." And she set off through the gardens towards the Jacuzzi and Spa Pool.

Geri was annoyed. She thought she was beginning to get somewhere with Deano; she thought she'd have him to herself on the beach, but then that stupid Michael had invited everyone else. She'd have to hurry up and put her swimsuit on and grab her beach things so that she could wangle it and get herself on the sun bed next to his. As she hurried along the corridor she could see the door to her room was open and the maid's cart was outside. *Bugger! Bugger! Bugger!*

"Can you leave my room, please?" she asked the maid, who looked at her as if she was crazy. "Just leave it!"

"But I'm only halfway through making the bed," the maid said, indicating the bedspread and top sheet that were on the floor as she smoothed the bottom sheet and plumped up the pillows. "And I haven't started the bathroom yet."

Geri dived into her handbag and brought out a twenty EC dollar bill.

"Thank you!" She said, thrusting the money into the startled maid's hand and edging her towards the door. "Not today. Come back tomorrow and do it all." And she slammed the door well and truly shut. Grabbing her swimsuit with one hand she pulled off her halter top with the other and then wiggled out of her shorts. Sweat ran in rivulets down her back and face. It was so hot and clammy. Then she realised the maid had turned off the air conditioning unit. Geri grabbed the remote control and pointed it at the unit and CNN came on the television set. She tutted and threw the remote on the bed and grabbed for the other remote control which was on the bedside table. This time she had more luck; as she pressed the *on* button the air conditioning unit clunked into action. She stood in front of it for a moment or two, mindful that she was losing precious moments in her race to get the sun bed next to Deano, but she was so hot she couldn't get her swimsuit on; it kept sticking to her as she tried to roll it up her legs and over her bottom. Then a fabulous idea came to her; she'd get him to rub her suntan lotion in. Then it wouldn't matter whether she was actually on the sun bed next to his or not. She smiled at her own ingenuity. In just a few minutes Deano would be moving his hands all over her back and shoulders; massaging and caressing her. The sudden moistness and tingle that she felt between her legs at that thought took her by surprise. But then she wondered why it should. She was a woman with needs and she would see to it that very soon those needs would be met by none other than Deano himself.

***

Frances had decided not to go to the beach. It wasn't that she didn't like it, but she felt a bit self-conscious in her swimsuit. Her thighs were turning to flab, and, if she was honest, she had the start of bingo wings. And she still wasn't completely confident about her breasts. Still, she was fifty and that was to be expected, she supposed. The others, apart from Suzanne, all had lovely figures. Jo wasn't slim, probably somewhere between a fourteen and a sixteen with a prominent bum, but being tall she could carry her weight off resulting in her voluptuous hour-glass figure. And besides, she was probably only about thirty-three or so. Grace had a fabulous body for a woman in her fifties. Frances hadn't believed it when Grace had let slip the previous evening that she was fifty-four. Frances thought she must spend all her life in the gym. And then there was Deborah. It was really difficult to tell how old she was; Frances thought she could be anything from mid-thirties to late-forties because Oriental woman always had lovely, smooth, porcelain skins and exquisitely slim figures. Added to which, Deborah admitted she did go to the gym for two hours every day. Frances thought that was a bit obsessive.

She looked at herself in the mirror in her jade green swimsuit. Actually, she didn't look that bad considering all she'd been through.

"I'm lucky to be here. I'm lucky to be alive," she said out loud to her reflection in the mirror. She grabbed her matching sarong and tied it around her waist and plonked her sunhat on top of her unruly curly hair, so that it sat alluringly over her forehead, shielding her eyes and gave herself a beaming smile. Grabbing her towel and beach bag, she left the room to go down to the Spa Pool to enjoy some quality relaxation time.

***

Eve thumped the house phone back on the receiver in frustration. She'd walked all over the resort, been to both pools, the bar and along the beach but Ursula was nowhere to be seen. She'd just phoned her room, but nobody picked up and it had gone to voicemail.

"Hi, Ursula, this is Eve from Travel Together. I was sorry not to have seen you this morning at the information briefing; I hope that nothing's wrong and that you've settled in and are enjoying yourself. I'm sending the paperwork I gave out at the briefing to your room so that you can take a look at it. It includes my mobile phone number and room number and the information on the excursions that the group are going on. We're going to the Manager's Cocktail Party at seven this evening down in the Hammock Room and we hope you'll join us there. I'd appreciate it if you'd just let me know you're okay. Thanks, Ursula. Enjoy your day!"

What she'd really wanted to say was *'How about showing some manners, you rude woman!'* Why did someone choose to come in a group and then take off on their own? Eve didn't have the answer. She folded the paperwork into an A5 envelope, wrote *Ursula MarshallRoom221* on it and put it in the messages book to be delivered to the room later. She turned left and walked through the reception area, past the grand piano and stepped onto the path to go to her room when her mobile phone rang.

"Eve Mitchell" she answered as she walked towards her room.

"Hey! What's up, Eve?" Sunny said. "I've got all your reservations for you. They're towards the beginning of the week, which will probably cause some of them to complain, but there's a storm warning for Thursday and Friday so helicopters and jeeps aren't taking bookings for either of those two days, okay?"

"Yes, sure. There's nothing we can do about that. Give me a sec to grab a pen," Eve said, going in and kicking the door closed behind her, "and I'll write it all down."

***

Donna and Dawn were side-by-side on their sun beds, both wearing pink tankinis; Dawn's was checked and Donna's was striped. Their headgear was also very similar, in the form of white baseball caps; Dawn's had a WTA logo on it and Donna's said *Tenerife* with a dolphin frolicking next to it.

"Don't think we're being unsociable," Donna had called out to Dave as they came onto the beach, walking past him and the seven sun beds he was guarding with his life, to sit down on four that had been covered in towels and doubled over under a palm tree several yards away.

"It's just that we have to have the shade. I really burn, don't I, Donna?" Dawn said. "I have to be really careful with the sun, so we came down early and saved these for us and for Huw and Jason."

"No worries," Dave called back, waving as he did so, and thinking they'd all had a lucky escape. Dave got on with most people. He always went out of his way to be nice and to have a laugh and be friendly. He could never understand miserable gits. Like that bleedin' Scotch bloke. Right little ray of sunshine he was. But already he was beginning to find the Dolly Sisters, as he had named them, heavy going. And he wasn't overly keen on the two teachers, Huw and Jason; he thought they were a bit arrogant. Still, it was early days and he wasn't going to let anything or anyone spoil his holiday. He'd smile and get on with everyone and enjoy himself, just like he always did. A peal of laughter and the sound of voices announced the arrival of Suzanne and Jo, who had discovered they were in a-joining rooms and so had walked down to the beach together and hot on their heels he could see Natalie and Trevor deep in conversation. He jumped up and helped Suzanne to sort herself out on the sun bed that was right under the sun umbrella.

Within ten minutes, Michael, Deano, Stewart and Grace had joined them. To a casual observer they were a group of people who had known each other a lifetime.

***

Murray finished his beer and pointed at the glass to let the barman know he wanted a refill. These bloody glasses were ridiculous. Poof measures. Two sips and it had gone. Why couldn't they serve beer in a proper pint glass?

"There you go, sir!" Elvis placed a fresh glass of beer in front of him with a flourish and removed the empty one.

"Why don't you serve it in a proper glass?" Murray asked him.

"Because if we serve it in a big glass the beer gets warm before you get the chance to finish it."

"Not the way I drink it doesnae!"

Both men laughed.

"Oh, I know, you English sure love your beer."

Murray looked at him aghast.

"I'm not bloody English! I'm a Scot. From Scotland"

"Oh, yes. Scotland. That's in the north of England, isn't it?"

"No! It's a completely separate country."

A couple who were sitting along the bar from Murray grinned to each other at his complete lack of awareness that Elvis was having a laugh at his expense.

"So where in Scotland do you live?"

"I'm from halfway between Glasgow and Edinburgh; a place called Penicuick."

"You live there?"

"No. I've nae lived there for a number of years."

"So where do you live now?"

"In Purfleet."

"Where's that?"

"London. East London."

"Isn't that in England?" Elvis asked innocently.

The couple at the bar roared out laughing.

"He's got you there, mate!" the man called out.

Murray couldn't avoid smiling.

"OK, you got me there. But just because I live among them doesn't mean I have tae like it. Or them."

"Fucking cheek!" The couple gave him a filthy look. "You're happy enough to live in England but you can't stop slagging it off. That's typical of you fucking Scots. If you hate England so much why don't you fuck off home?"

Oblivious of the insulting nature of his comments, Murray was a bit startled by the way the conversation had suddenly taken a nasty turn. He wasn't a stupid man; he could see that the Englishman he'd insulted had twenty years and two stone on him and in spite of the fact it still wasn't noon, was experiencing a great adrenaline rush due to the alcohol he'd already consumed. His girlfriend looked like she could probably defend herself, too.

"Look, no offence meant," he said. "Just a wee bit of banter, you know. We've always had a bit of good natured rivalry between us, between our two countries haven't we?"

The couple stared at him long and hard. And then burst out laughing.

"Ha! Gotcha!" the man said. "I'm from Aberdeen originally. My family left Scotland when I was four and moved to Nottingham." He offered Murray his hand. "Andrew McGregor," he said. "Now you can't get much more Scottish than that!"

Murray allowed his hand to be pumped up and down as he beamed at Andrew and his girlfriend. "Murray Sneddon," he said. "Pleased tae meet you." He turned and looked down the bar where Elvis was now enjoying himself talking to two young American girls. "Elvis! Another round of drinks, please!"

***

Frances had found a nice spot by the Spa pool. It was very peaceful there; relaxing tropical music was playing quietly in the background and the adults who were there were all lost in their books, Kindles, I-pods or dreams. She eased herself into the water, which was almost body temperature. Turning onto her back and closing her eyes against the sun, Frances floated peacefully for several minutes until she felt the sun starting to heat up her skin, in spite of the water. Reluctantly she got out and patted herself dry. She put on her sun block, adjusted the back of her sun lounger and settled down comfortably to read one of the three Maeve Binchy books she'd brought with her. She loved the way Maeve Binchy could really weave a great tale. She had wondered if three books for a nine-night holiday was a bit excessive, but she'd wanted to make sure that she would have something to do if she couldn't get on with the others in the group. Not that there seemed much possibility of that, so far; they seemed a very nice bunch on the whole. But today, she just wanted some space, some me-time. Eve had made it clear that some people preferred to be alone during the day and that it was fine if you did. Out of the corner of her eye she saw movement and a vision in royal blue fluttered into view and took the sun lounger next but one to her; Deborah.

Oh dear!

She'd wanted to be alone, away from the svelte group members and now she had Deborah close by. She decided to keep her eyes on her book for the time being in the hope that Deborah wouldn't recognise her.

***

Damn!

Deborah hadn't realised that Frances was alongside her until she'd already made herself comfortable on the sun lounger. It was too late to move away. Keeping her head forward she swivelled her eyes to the right behind her sunglasses to see exactly what Frances was doing. She hadn't appeared to notice her. That was good. Not that she thought Frances wasn't a nice woman; she seemed pleasant enough, but she didn't want to get stuck with anyone. No lame ducks. And she certainly didn't want Frances to think that they were going to be pool buddies every day. She had particularly come to the Spa pool for peace and quiet away from the group. Those two silly women who dressed alike and referred to each other for everything were already getting on her nerves and she found some of the men quite surly. She glanced to the right again. Frances was deep into her book.

Good!

 That meant she could get deep into hers. With any luck Frances might never notice she was there at all.

***

"Am I the only one that's ungry?"

Dave sat up and looked round at the rest of the group. He was already beginning to look a bit pink. Fortunately he'd taken the precaution of tying a bandana round his head. He'd seen Andre Agassi wear one once when he'd gone to Wimbledon for the day and had thought it looked pretty cool. And he had landed Steffi Graff so it must work. It beat a knotted hankie, anyway.

"What time is it?" Natalie groped in her beach bag for her watch. "Ten past one," she announced, looking at it. "No wonder my stomach's rumbling."

"Yes, we haven't eaten for a whole four hours!" Jo laughed. "But I'm ready for something. Shall we go to the main restaurant or the diner?"

"Diner!" chorused Grace, Natalie and Michael.

"I fancied the restaurant," said Deano.

"Yes, I was thinking restaurant," said Geri.

Deano was aware that a look had passed between the other women.

"I can't be arsed to get dressed," Natalie said. "At the diner we can sit outside as we are. It's more casual."

"You're right!" Deano said.

"Yes. It is more casual," Geri agreed.

They all started to get up and brush sand from various parts of their anatomy.

"Are you coming with us?" Stewart turned and nudged Murray who had come along and joined them about half an hour earlier. He didn't stir.

"What a vision of loveliness!" Grace said, looking at him as he lay on his back in his Fred Perry shirt, old-fashioned shorts with socks and sandals and with his mouth wide open, snoring gently. "I think he's had a few. Probably best to let him sleep it off. They serve lunch until four o'clock I think it is, so he won't go hungry."

"We're going for lunch," Deano called over to Donna and Dawn. "You coming?"

"We're going to the restaurant," Donna said. "In about ten minutes. We're waiting for Jason and Huw to come back from kayaking. We're looking after their stuff."

"That was a near miss!" Dave said as they walked en-masse along the beach.

"Well, I had to offer," said Deano. "They were watching us."

"They're doing my bleeding 'ead in already and they're not even wiv us," Dave said. "Talk about rabbit! They haven't stopped."

They found two empty tables on the terrace and pulled them together and arranged the seats.

"Shall I get the drinks?" Stewart asked. "And someone can get my food."

"Good idea," said Deano. "I'll give you a hand. Can someone get me jerk chicken and chips?"

"I will!" said Geri. "And can you get me a beer with lime juice?"

"Coming up!"

Within ten minutes they were all sitting happily tucking into their lunches.

"Blimey!" This jerk chicken's hot!" Deano said. "My mouth feels like it's on fire!"

"Good stuff! Puts hairs on your chest, mate!" Michael said.

"Do you always eat Caribbean food?" Suzanne asked him, pushing her hair from her face with the back of her hand.

"Not always. But I like to eat it here. No point in being in the West Indies and eating cod and chips or pie and mash, is there?"

"I suppose not!" she giggled. Made brave by the shandy in front of her she continued. "Can I ask you something, Michael?"

He nodded.

"Do you go brown? Browner I mean? Like, do you get sunburnt?"

There was a gasp from one of two of the group that Suzanne could ask him a question like that but Michael burst out laughing.

"Of course I do. Didn't you see me putting on suntan lotion this morning? Just like you, Suzanne. In fact, when I get back to my room tonight I'll probably have a mark where my shorts have been." He turned and looked directly at her. "In fact, if you play your cards right, you can see it if you like!"

Suzanne went scarlet and then joined in the general laughter that went round the table.

"Oi oi! You show me yours and I'll show ya mine!" Dave said to more raucous laughter just as Murray appeared, kicking the sand from his sandals and socks against the wooden decking.

"We didn't wake you up because you were snoring peacefully," Natalie said, pulling a chair out for him.

"I wasnae snoring!"

"You so were! And anyway, we thought Palinda might come along again and offer to take care of you." Everyone howled with laughter at the memory of Palinda, the well-rounded beach seller had spent an hour squatting on the end of Murray's sun bed telling him how she was looking for a *'usband'*. He'd been flattered by the attention until he finally realised what the others had cottoned onto a soon as she sat down, that she was chatting him up to make a sale.

"What's the food like?" He squinted across at the menu, ignoring their mickey-taking, turning up his nose as he did so. "Bloody burgers, I suppose."

Grace gave him a filthy look.

"It's a diner; a fast food restaurant, Murray. They're not going to serve roast beef, Yorkshire pudding and two veg or haggis with neeps!"

"Try the jerk chicken!" Michael said. "It's great!"

"No, perhaps I'll just have a burger," he said begrudgingly, as he stood up and went over to order his food.

"He's such a little ray of sunshine!" Deano said and Geri laughed.

"He's starting to get on my tits," Grace said. "He's done nothing but moan since he got here. Some people don't realise that others have paid a lot of money to come away and they don't want to sit listening to non-stop complaining."

"You're right," Deano said and Geri nodded in agreement.

"I don't think he's very happy in himself," said Jo.

"Well, we've all got our problems, even me," Dave said, "but I'm ere to av a good time."

"What problems can you possibly have?" Natalie asked.

"Oh, we ain't got long enough fer me to tell ya!" Dave joked.

"Sorry, I didn't mean that to be as abrupt as it sounded. You just seem a very happy sort of person."

"Even the happiest person has problems sometimes," Jo said.

"Yes, but it's all in the mind, I fink. No point in bein' negative, it's just as easy to be positive, innit?" Dave said.

"That's very deep and philosophical!" Michael said.

"And anyway, we don't want him crying into his beer!" Deano said and everyone laughed. Geri laughed loudest.

***

Eve threw down her pen as she finished the final Booking Confirmation Form, stretched and looked at her watch. Four o'clock. Her back ached. It had taken her two hours to write them up and check that she hadn't overlooked anybody's form and that nobody had a booking clash. She knew that one or two would complain that the jeep tour was on Wednesday right after the catamaran trip, but Friday's jeep was cancelled and the following Monday was too late as that was the day they left. The helicopter rides had been booked for Saturday, which was unusual as it was usually the pilots' day off, but with a storm warning for Thursday and Friday they would have a couple of days off midweek and hopefully by Saturday the weather would have stabilised. People weren't going to be happy if the weather turned, either, but there again, that was the price you paid for booking a holiday to the Caribbean during Hurricane Season.

Eve's stomach rumbled. She'd had a very light lunch, just some salad with a piece of grilled marlin, and she thought she might go to Afternoon Tea. Then she remembered the Cocktail Party at seven o'clock. She knew from experience the canapés would be delicious and plentiful. She'd just grab a cup of coffee from the drinks station and would wait until seven and enjoy the food then. There had been nothing from Ursula. Eve was beginning to get annoyed. It wouldn't take the woman a moment to leave her a message saying she was fine and didn't want to be disturbed. For all Eve knew, she could have fallen under a bus. It was so ill-mannered. Still, it took all sorts to make up a Travel Together group and if Ursula was the worst of the bunch then she wouldn't complain. Smiling to herself, she collected up the forms, which she had addressed to each of the group and left her room to take them to the front desk for delivery

***

Frances and Deborah had spent the day politely ignoring each other. There had been a slightly awkward moment when they had both got up to go into the pool at the same time, but had managed to just smile and say "hallo" to each other and carry on as they were. Deborah seemed to have spent a large part of the day talking on her mobile phone. But she'd kept her voice down and Frances hadn't been able to hear anything she'd said. Not that she was listening! Frances looked at her watch. It was half past four; tea was being laid out on long trestle tables next to the Spa bar. She liked the idea of afternoon tea and so thought she'd have some. She'd had her fill of the sun for the first day, so she started packing up her things. Just at that moment Deborah started doing the same and both women stood up, facing each other at the same time.

"Are you going to your room?" Deborah asked, folding her towel over her arm.

"No. I thought I'd go to tea," Frances said, mirroring her actions.

"Me, too. Shall we go together?"

"That would be nice."

'I've had a nice time on my own today but now I want some company,' both women thought as they smiled at each other and walked into tea together.

***

Huw and Jason were sitting at the bar each nursing a beer.

"It's like GBH of the ear-drums," Jason complained. "I mean, I like a woman who makes conversation and who doesn't just sit there dumb, but after the first ten minutes, I just wanted the pair of them to shut up. If I'd heard one more thing about fucking line-dancing or Whitley Street Comprehensive I'd have topped myself!"

"You're not kidding! It's like being at work. The fucking staff room with sunshine. How many times did they talk about Inspection?"

"I've come on holiday to get away from all that. They're just like every bloody woman teacher I've ever worked with. Talk, talk, talk! I thought they'd never shut the fuck up. And what's with all that dressing the same? It's like being with a pair of Year Eights."

"And now we're bloody stuck with them in a hire car all day Thursday. They seemed alright yesterday, but I can't put up with them all holiday and especially not shut up in a car. Can't we say we're not going?"

"Not really. I mean it's difficult, isn't it? If we go off on our own they're sure to find out. And anyway, they'll see we're not around."

"Perhaps if we give them a wide berth for a couple of days they won't seem so bad on Thursday."

"Yeah, that sounds about right. Let's give them a wide berth. And I've just seen two little darlings down the other end of the bar who look like they're much more our type," said Jason, indicating the two American girls Elvis had been in conversation with earlier in the day.

Huw squinted down the bar and a wide grin spread across his face.

"Now you're talking, my son," he said.

***

At that moment Natalie, Jo and Grace took seats at the other side of the bar. Suzanne, having declared she was *'all sunned out'* had gone up to her room for a shower, and the men, Michael, Deano, Dave, Trevor and Stewart had decided, along with Geri, to take part in the beach volleyball, which was a regular sundown feature at the resort.

"I want a rum punch," Natalie said, crossing her arms and leaning on the bar. "That'll just go down nicely."

"What can I get you beautiful ladies?" Elvis asked coming to a halt in front of them.

"A rum punch for me, please."

"And me!"

"Make that three!"

"Three rum punches coming up!" he said giving them a smile as wide as the Caribbean Sea.

"Elvis?" Jo queried, having read his name badge. "Do you think that's his real name?"

"Why not?" Grace said. "We've got a kid in our street called Beyonce and I've recently met a Cowell. Perhaps his mum liked Elvis."

"I'm going to ask him," Natalie said.

"Doing a Suzanne, are you?" Jo teased, referring to Suzanne's cross-examination of Michael's skin type earlier. "She takes forthright to another level."

"No malice in her, though," Grace said. "She's a thoroughly decent person. She's just a bit naive."

Elvis came back to the bar and expertly slid the three rum punches one after the other bringing them to an exact halt in front of the three women.

"Are you really called Elvis?" Natalie asked.

Elvis looked at his name badge.

"I was the last time I looked. I bet they told you I was dead, didn't they?"

The women burst out laughing.

"Mommy was a big fan," Elvis said, "so Daddy didn't get any say in the matter. A-huh-huh!" And with that he quivered his lip, shook his hips and struck a pose.

"Ah, but can you sing?" Jo asked him.

"Baby, I can sing. But I can't sing well. I burst into song and people start making for the exits in an orderly manner." His loud laughter echoed round the bar and the women joined in with him. "Oh, excuse me." Elvis moved off down to the far end where Huw was waving to get his attention.

"Well, what do you think? How many out of ten?" Natalie asked her eyes on his disappearing backside as she sipped her drink.

"I'd say eight," Jo said.

"Nine from me," said Grace.

"Yes and from me. He's got a great personality and although he's not drop dead gorgeous there's definitely something about him that I find very attractive." Natalie gazed into her rum punch and stirred the ice around with the straw.

"Do you like black men?" Grace asked her.

Natalie didn't look up; she continued to look into her drink.

"Some black men. It's like some white men, isn't it? Some you'd give your right arm for and others you wouldn't look twice at."

"Only I think there might be a black man in the group who's got his eye on you."

"Who?"

"How many bloody black men do you see in our group, Natalie?"

"Well, Michael do you mean?"

"Of course I meant Michael. He's been giving you the eye all day."

"He's nice. I think he'd make a lovely friend but I wouldn't want to get involved with anyone in the group. I think that's what nice about a holiday like this, it's not a dating club. I feel like I can talk to most of the men and not feel like they think I'm coming onto them."

"Except Murray," Grace said. "I get the distinct feeling he thinks it's a shagathon."

"I know what you mean about him," Natalie said, "but I think you're wrong about Michael. I don't think he's interested in finding a girlfriend."

"What? You mean he's gay?" Jo asked, slurping her drink through the straw.

"No! I just think he's happy on his own. He's joined in the banter and the conversation and jokes like the rest of us today. I don't think he's looking for anyone. But I'm sure that Stewart's got the hots for Suzanne," she added, eager to turn the attention away from herself.

"Yes, so do I. I think they'd be sweet together," Jo said.

"Is Deano Italian?" Grace asked.

"No, apparently Dean's his surname and so he's always been called Deano. But he could be. I mean he looks Mediterranean, doesn't he? Or perhaps even Middle Eastern." Jo said.

Natalie burst out laughing. Jo looked at her puzzled.

"That colour's fake!"

"No!"

"I'm telling you it is. I mean, it's not exactly East End and Essex Orange; it's a good tan, probably from an expensive spray-on booth, but it's definitely not natural. And his hair's dyed."

"So you reckon he's not foreign?" Jo asked when they'd both stopped laughing at Natalie's comments.

"Why don't we just ask him?" Natalie suggested. "While we're sitting here discussing him we might as well find out. We can ask him later."

"Or ask Geri," Grace suggested. "I bet she knows all about him she's completely monopolised him all day. Talk about make it obvious!"

"She tries too hard, I think," Natalie said. "She's so intense and in-your-face; almost as if she's desperate."

"Perhaps she is," Grace laughed. "Perhaps she's been without it as long as I have!"

"And how long's that?" Jo laughed as she choked on her rum punch.

"Too bloody long!" Grace replied. She downed the remains of her rum punch.

"So, are you looking to meet someone here, then?" Jo asked her.

"I'm not actively looking, no. But, hey! It's a holiday! If it happens it happens!"

"Have you been married?" Jo asked her.

"No. I was in a relationship for a long time; fifteen years all told. But it didn't work out."

"Married man?"

"Yes. But I knew that from the beginning. He was my boss and it suited both of us really, until four years ago, when I suddenly woke up one morning and wanted out. I've had a couple of dates since then, but to be honest I quite like my own company. What about you?"

"I'm a widow."

Grace and Natalie both gaped at her in surprise.

"Bloody hell, Jo," Natalie said, resting her hand on Jo's arm. "I'd never have thought that."

Jo shrugged.

"I've been a widow for almost eight years."

"Was he a lot older than you, then?"

"No. He was twenty-eight."

There was a silence as Grace and Natalie stared at Jo, not wanting to ask for more details, but wanting to know what happened. Jo waited a moment or two before haltingly continuing.

"Someone set fire to our shop. I was lucky; I was having a bath and the bathroom was at the back of the house. He'd been putting our little boy to bed in his bedroom at the front, telling him a story." She took a deep breath, her eyes misty with unshed tears. "The firemen found them curled up together on the bed."

"Oh, Jo!" Grace said.

74

"For a long time I wished I'd gone with them. I'd wake up at night convinced I could hear them shouting and screaming, although the fire brigade told me they'd have been overcome by smoke; that's what would have killed them rather than the burning.

"But why would anyone want to set fire to your shop?" Natalie asked.

"No reason. Other than he was an Indian. We had an off licence; we worked hard and opened all hours to make a success of the business. We were still known as *'the Paki shop and the Pakis'* even me, although I look as much like a Pakistani as an elephant looks like a lion. We'd been having hate graffiti written on the shop shutters for about three months before the fire, you know, *'go back where you came from'* and *'Muslims out!'* that kind of thing. The irony is he wasn't even a Muslim. He'd been brought up by Nuns because he was an orphan, so he was a Christian. He was a good, kind, gentle man. But even if he'd been wicked and cruel nobody deserved that. Our son certainly didn't; he was only just three."

The women sat in silence for a few moments; two steeped in disbelief and one visiting a place deep in her heart that it still hurt to go to too often. Natalie shuddered and gave Jo a hug.

"Come on! Let's have one more before we go up to get ready for cocktails! Elvis! We want one for the road!" Natalie called down the bar.

"One for the footpath, you mean!" he called back, grinning widely at them.

"One for wherever!" Natalie said. "Just as long as they're good and strong!"

***

Eve brushed her hair and pulled it back into a high ponytail; a Basildon facelift, she thought. It amused her to watch her features go up and see the Eve of twenty years ago appear. The one problem with being in the tropics was that her hair took on a life of its own and started to curl up. She wouldn't have minded if it had been a nice curl but it was more of a frizzy wave. So the best was always to put it up off her neck and at least she always looked neat and tidy that way. She slipped her feet into her silver sandals, her dressiest pair and smoothed her hand over her plum coloured cocktail dress. She must have had it at least seven or eight years, but she hadn't had that much wear out of it really. Still, the group had never seen it and she was sure the staff were all too busy living their lives to remember whether they'd seen her dress before. She picked up her evening bag, turned the light off and left the room. She was a few minutes earlier than she'd planned but it didn't matter. You could never be too early for an appointment, only too late. And besides, she didn't want any of the group to get there first and feel awkward if they were on their own.

She reached the end of the corridor and turned underneath the stairwell which led into the reception area. Carlo was behind the front desk. He saw her and waved a cheery greeting. Eve waved back and continued through the poolside area, through the bar and followed the path down past the Spa Pool towards the Hammock Room. She heard footsteps behind her and then a voice called her name. Turning she saw Michael increasing his pace to catch her up. He looked amazingly handsome in his pale blue shirt and navy blue chinos.

"Want a handsome guy to escort you to a party?" he asked.

Eve laughed and lightly placed her hand on his proffered arm.

"That's very kind of you, sir," she said as they walked along together.

"Well, I know you don't mix very well and so I wouldn't like to think that you're left out of it," he joked.

"You cheeky devil!" Eve liked Michael; she felt comfortable in his company as if she'd already known him from somewhere. "Have you had a nice first day?"

"Magic! Just what the doctor ordered. What a beautiful beach! It's just like a travel poster, isn't it? And the others are great people. I can't believe we've only just met up, we had a right laugh today."

"Have you been to Antigua before?"

"No, I haven't."

"Where's your family from?"

"St Vincent. But I've got tired of going there. I mean it's nice, you know, a beautiful island but you always get roped in to visit family that you don't know but who will get right offended if you don't go and see them, so it's just easier not to go. Antigua will do me nicely."

Eve let go of his arm as they arrived at the bottom of the short flight of steps leading into the Hammock Room; a large gazebo which had been cleared of its hammocks in preparation for the party. High circular tables were dotted around the area, each holding a bowl of nuts. At the far end a well-stocked bar stood, beautifully decorated, to attend to the needs of the guests. Over to the right was a long table covered in various dishes and hot plates with pale blue flames licking away at their bases. As Eve and Michael went up the steps Donna and Dawn appeared behind them and Eve could see Dave and Deano coming along the path. They walked the length of the gazebo to the bar and were quickly served from a list of six of the resorts most popular cocktails that were on offer that evening.

"Any chance of a beer, mate?" Dave asked one of the barmen. "I'm not really a cocktail kind of bloke."

"No problem, sir. Wadadli or Red Stripe?" he asked opening up the fridge and holding up one of each.

"Bottles?" Dave couldn't believe his eyes.

"Yeh, mon!"

"I'll have a Red Stripe, please, cos I can't say the other one."

"Wadadli," the barman said slowly. "It means *Antigua.* It was what the indigenous people called this place before the Spanish arrived and decided it was gonna be called Antigua."

"Well, there you go! Wadiddly," Dave said, deliberately mispronouncing it to get a laugh.

"I'd better try one of those, as well, then," Deano said. "It'd be rude not to."

The barman smiled and handed over the beers to the men together with two half-pint glasses.

"Gentlemen, enjoy!" he said as the two men strolled off grinning like mad.

Suzanne arrived in a flurry. She was wearing a very pretty brown and orange maxi dress with a matching headband, but the effect was rather spoilt by her cream rubber flip flops. She bustled over to join the others, looking a bit hot and bothered.

"Oh, Eve! How do you get on with this heat? I've never been so hot in my life. I mean, it's much hotter than Majorca, isn't it? That's where we usually go to visit my auntie. My dress feels like it's sticking to me. And look!" She lifted her dress up to her knees revealing swollen burned shins and ankles and flip flops that appeared to be digging into her flesh. "My feet are so swollen I can't get my shoes on."

"When you go back to your room tonight take some ice with you from the ice machine by the drinks dispenser or ask behind the bar for some. Wrap it in a towel and put your feet up on the bed and place the ice across your shins and ankles and leave it for about ten or fifteen minutes. Then lie down on the bed and put your feet up the wall for another ten or fifteen minutes or so. Make sure you drink plenty of water tonight and a large glass before you go to bed. Then tomorrow, continue with the water, keep your legs out of the sun and you should be fine."

"Oh, thank you. Eve! I'll do that. I feel terrible in these shoes, I feel like everyone's looking at me."

"They're only looking at you because you look lovely," Eve said, smiling. "Your dress is long and it covers them up. Don't worry!"

By ten past seven the whole Travel Together group were there, except Ursula, of course, who had managed to avoid Eve for the whole day and hadn't replied to her phone message either, together with about a hundred and fifty or so of the rest of the hotel guests. Waiters were moving among them offering platters of exquisite canapés that melted in the mouth.

"I won't want any dinner if I eat any more of these," Trevor said, through a mouthful of chicken drumstick in coconut and pineapple sauce. "I had a huge breakfast and an even bigger lunch. At home I usually just have a corned beef sandwich at lunch time."

"Every day?" Grace asked, raising her eyebrows.

"Yes. I tend to live quite frugally. I buy a loaf of bread and two tins of corned beef at the weekend and that gives me lunch all through the week. So it's been a shock having so much food and so much choice here. I feel like I couldn't eat another thing."

"You don't know what you can do until you try," Grace said, wryly. "Eat it up and enjoy yourself."

"I am enjoying myself. More than I ever thought I would. And it's only the first day! People are so nice and friendly and they've made me feel very welcome. Who'd have thought they'd have wanted an old fuddy-duddy like me playing volleyball with them?" He beamed and a little trickle of sauce squeezed onto his bottom lip.

"And why wouldn't they?" Grace said. "We're all going to have a smashing time, you'll see."

Murray, who had decided to turn up after all, looked through the crowd of people for his new best friends Andrew and Fiona, but couldn't see them. That was a bit odd, because they'd told him they were going to come along tonight. Not that it bothered him; he still had members of the group to talk to. He let his gaze run round and he saw Huw and Jason deep in conversation with two girls who had spent most of the afternoon at the bar. Loud, they were. Americans. He saw most of the rest of the group standing near each other and chatting. He thought he'd wait for a bit longer and then go and get into conversation with Deborah. He'd decided not to bother with Natalie or Jo; they were too full of themselves by half. He watched as the two women chatted animatedly with Trevor and Grace. No! He wouldn't waste his time on them. Deborah was far more his type. She might be getting on a bit, but she had a certain class about her.

Suddenly, conversation throughout the gazebo was brought to an abrupt halt by the screech of feedback through the sound system, which pre-empted the introduction speech from Shivonne, the Entertainment's Manager.

"Sorry! Sorry, everyone!" She said, adjusting her microphone, with fingers that displayed nails that were over two inches long, until the feedback was no longer an issue and the sound at a perfect level. Then she continued.

"A pleasant good evening, ladies and gentlemen, welcome to Antigua, the island with a beach for every day of the year, and an especially warm welcome to the Mango Tree Resort. My name's Shivonne and I am the Entertainment's Manager. We have a great programme of daytime and night-time entertainment awaiting you during your stay with us and we really hope

78

that you are going to take part and enjoy yourselves to the full. Tonight it gives me great pleasure to introduce you to the person whose guests you are at this evening's beautiful cocktail reception. Please give a warm welcome and show your appreciation to the General Manager of the Mango Tree Resort, Mr Melvyn McGrass!"

A very tall, very dark-skinned, elegant man, wearing a superbly tailored pale green shirt and black trousers with creases like a knife edge, stepped forward, smiling at the crowd and acknowledging their appreciation. He took the microphone from Shivonne and started to speak.

Eve suddenly felt an icy wave crash over her. Her legs started to shake and buckle and she felt her glass slipping through her fingers. She grabbed it with her other hand and set it down on the high table in front of her. Turning, she stared hard at Melvyn McGrass, saw his eyes shining as he looked around the group, his lips moving as he spoke, soundless words that she couldn't hear. The ice was replaced by an intense heat; one that started to suffocate her. She couldn't breathe; she needed air. She needed to get out for a few moments before she made a fool of herself in front of everyone. If she didn't sit down she'd fall down. Walking slowly backwards and trying not to draw attention to herself, Eve felt her way down the steps and then turned and sat on the wall which divided the resort from the beach. For one awful moment she thought she was going to vomit.

   Get a grip!

She closed her eyes and concentrated hard on her breathing; slow, deep breaths that she counted in and out. She told herself not to think about the nausea; just to concentrate on her breathing. The noise of the cocktail party mingled with the crash of the sea until they blended and she couldn't separate one from the other.

   Just keep on breathing deeply!

After a few minutes, the nausea began to pass. Eve opened her eyes and was pleased to see that everything was in its place; nothing was spinning. She'd stay here, sitting on the wall until she was back to normal, although at that moment, she didn't think she'd ever feel normal again.

                              ***

Back inside the Hammock Room Melvyn McGrass was coming to the end of his welcoming speech.

   "And please remember that if there is any little thing that I or any member of my staff can do to make your vacation a more enjoyable one in any possible way, my door is always open. Thank you for coming along this evening, and enjoy your stay with us."

The crowd broke into a spontaneous round of applause and then he and the senior members of his staff began to circulate and talk to the guests. Deborah found herself in conversation with Hazel, the Housekeeper.

"Of course, I always love the flower arrangements in the tropics," Deborah said. "Especially in Barbados. The Sandy Lane has such amazing floral displays in such wonderful colours. These are lovely, too." She indicated a large display sitting at the end of the buffet table, almost as an afterthought.

"The only problem we have," Hazel said, inspecting the tall vase and the rainbow of colours in it, "is that tropical flowers die very quickly once they're picked."

"So I understand."

"Yes. It's a problem we have with weddings. Brides always want tropical flowers in their bouquet or decorating the wedding arbour, but if they're getting married late in the day the flowers start to wilt before the photos are finished."

"Ere! Deborah! Over ere!" Dave interrupted, pulling on her arm. "We're gonna av a group photo."

"We're not!" Deborah disentangled herself from Dave's grasp. He looked taken aback.

"But we're all ere togevva."

"I don't care. I do not want to be in anyone's photo. End of!"

"Alright! Please yourself."

Dave shuffled off, rebuffed.

"The Ice Maiden don't want her photo took," he said. "Don't know what all the fuss is abaht, it's only a bloody photo."

The others had all grouped themselves by the entrance to the Hammock Room at the top of the stairs. Suzanne was wielding her camera.

"But if you take it, you won't be in it," Stewart said. "Can't someone else take it?"

"Where's Eve?" Frances said. "I'm sure she wouldn't mind taking the group photo."

Everyone swivelled their heads around but nobody could see Eve.

"Grab that bloke!" Murray said, referring to the General Manager. "And give him my camera, as well."

"Would you mind taking a group photo for us, please?" Suzanne asked Melvyn, smiling sweetly.

"Not at all, it would be my pleasure."

Suzanne showed him which button to press, and then Murray, Frances, Donna, Natalie and Trevor all produced cameras, too. Melvyn was obviously an old hand at this. He dangled all the cameras from his right arm and then as he took each picture transferred the camera, until they were all hanging from his left arm.

"There you are! Now, we just need everyone to remember which is their own," he joked as the group members claimed their cameras. "What are you? A family wedding group?"

"No, we're with Travel Together," Stewart volunteered.

"Oh, yes! The singles' group. How are you all enjoying yourselves?"

"Great!"

"Fab!"

"Brilliant!"

"Well, that's what I like to hear. Don't forget, my name's Melvyn; people call me Melv. If there's anything you want just let me know."

He smiled and shook hands with each member of the group, personally welcoming them and wishing them the happiest of holidays at the Mango Tree Resort and reminding them he and his staff were there for them for whatever it was they needed.

Eve got to the top of the stairs and saw that the group were standing talking together in a circle.

"You just missed the group photo," Suzanne said.

"Oh, never mind. I... um... had to go and see to something for a moment. Is everyone ready for dinner? This seems to be over now, shall we move back to the bar?"

There was general assent for dinner and the group moved down the steps and back along the path past the Spa bar and through the gardens to the restaurant where their long table was waiting for them. Eve knew she wouldn't be able to eat a thing, but she'd at least put a small portion of something on her plate and push it around a bit so that nobody noticed she was off-colour. Fortunately, she could say that she'd eaten more than her fair share of canapés and wasn't very hungry. On her way into the dining room she stopped at the podium.

"You haven't seen the lady from my group who was dining alone last night, have you? Ms Marshall?"

"She just left. She came in alone and sat and ate alone and she just left. She went towards the reception area."

"Thanks, Osbert."

Eve checked everyone had a seat and excused herself while she went to see if she could find the illusive Ursula. As she went past the grand piano she saw her heading for the north corridor and quickened her pace to catch up with her. As Eve turned into the north corridor at room 135 Ursula was walking up the stair to the first floor.

"Ursula!" Eve called out. "Ursula! Ms Marshall!"

Ursula didn't stop or even acknowledge the fact that she was being called. She just kept on walking up the stairs. Eve ran up behind her, calling again.

"Ursula!" She pulled alongside her as they reached the first floor.

"Good evening," Eve said. "I've been trying to find you all day. I wondered if anything was wrong as none of us had seen you."

Ursula peered at Eve as if she were seeing her for the first time. And then she curled back her lip and glared at her.

"I'm aware you've been trying to contact me from your note and your phone messages. When, or rather if, I need you I know exactly where and how to find you. Until then, please stop hounding me!" She made to walk past Eve down the corridor towards her room. Eve stepped smartly to her left blocking the way.

"If you had had the manners to turn up to my information briefing this morning, or to have answered my note or either of my telephone calls then perhaps you wouldn't feel hounded. You have chosen to come away with a singles' group and it is my job as tour manager to check and make sure that everyone in my group is safe and getting the holiday they paid for. However, now that I know you have decided for reasons of your own that you don't want anything to do with the group or myself, rest assured that I won't bother you again until I send you the departure information, which everyone gets two days before we leave. Thank you and goodnight!"

Eve turned on her heel and made her way back towards the stairs.

"I'm sorry!"

The words stopped Eve in her tracks and then she slowly turned round.

"I'm sorry if I was rude to you." The tired, rheumy eyes blinked several times behind the glasses. "I've had a very stressful time recently and just needed to get away. I thought that being in a group was what I wanted but I realised as soon as I got to the airport that I'd made a big mistake." She paused and gulped and her eyes filled with tears.

"Do you want to come downstairs to the lounge and talk?" Eve asked her.

"No, I want to go back to my room. But, I owe you an apology. I was inexcusably rude and I'm really sorry."

"That's alright. Apology accepted," Eve said. "Sometimes being in a group of strangers can be a bit overwhelming."

Ursula nodded.

"I don't mix well with people, really. I've always been a bit of a loner; I enjoy my own company. Perhaps I'd have been better off on my own somewhere quiet. My job's really stressful and it's been a horrid year." A tear ran down her cheek. Eve laid a hand on her arm and waited for her to continue.

"I'm a teacher; I teach Physics in a failing school and I lost my temper with a boy who'd been fooling around throughout the whole lesson. He kept on interrupting and calling out and being silly and then he turned an equation I'd written on the board into something obscene and I just saw red. Before I realised it I'd hit him across the face." By now she was sobbing quite openly. "I have been suspended and have to face a disciplinary before the new school year starts."

"I am so sorry," Eve said, feeling helpless in front of her obvious distress.

"No! I'm sorry," Ursula said, drying her eyes on the back of her hand. "I don't know why I'm telling you all this. Whatever has happened to me it's not an excuse for rudeness. I know you're just doing your job and my behaviour was totally unacceptable."

"Would you like me to get you a cup of herbal tea, or something stronger perhaps?"

"No, thank you. I just want to go to my room. But thank you for your concern. I'm perfectly okay on my own. And anyway, the group has probably all made friends with each other now and I don't want to have to give explanations for why I've been alone."

"The group would welcome you!" Eve reassured her. "They're a great, friendly bunch of people. But, just remember, your holiday is your own and you can spend it however you like. If you want to be on your own that's fine, but we meet up in the bar every evening just after seven for pre-dinner drinks. You'd be made very welcome if you decided to join us one evening. And it's always nicer to have a bit of company for dinner, isn't it?"

"Thank you, my dear. Thank you." Ursula gave Eve a brave smile and slowly walked along the corridor to room 221.

***

Dinner was over and the band was playing an Abba medley. The mood was mellow and most of the group were sitting around a large table on the bar terrace, quietly chatting and enjoying the music and their drinks. A loud, drunken hen-party had taken over the dance floor. The bride, wearing a veil made from a net curtain, adorned with a colourful assortment of condoms, was trying to drag Steve, one of the entertainments team, into a clinch. He was trying, not altogether successfully, to keep her at arm's length.

Michael had gone off for a walk before turning in. He said he felt really tired; knocked out.

"I can't believe it. I haven't done anything all day," he said, before excusing himself.

"It's all that turning over on the sun bed," Jo said, "and walking backwards and forwards to the bar for drinks."

"You're not wrong! See you all in the morning!" he called as he strolled off.

Natalie had also gone to bed. She'd taken umbrage at the hen-party for some reason.

"Silly, cows! What must local people think of us when they see behaviour like that? It's all too Essex."

"You have a problem with Essex?" Eve teased her. "Let's have no Essex bashing, please."

Natalie blushed as she realised someone had told her Eve was from Essex.

"No! Not everyone from Essex. I don't mean you, obviously."

"Where in Essex are you from?" Jo asked.

"Horndon-on-the-Hill. Do you know it?"

"Is it near Brentwood? I've got an old friend who lives in Brentwood."

"Not far at all."

"Well, excuse me if I was rude, Eve, I'm not going to sit and watch them get even drunker and make complete prats of themselves. I'm off to bed. Nighty-night!" And with that Natalie had gone off to her room, clutching a rum punch nightcap.

Murray was deep in conversation with Dave about London traffic and the Congestion Charge and Frances, Jo, Grace, Suzanne, Stewart and Deano were discussing their favourite Abba songs, as the band swung from Mamma Mia into Dancing Queen. Donna and Dawn were once again on the dance floor, doing another complicated line dance. Geri was sitting next to Deano but was a bit miffed that he seemed to be ignoring her and talking to the other women. Trevor was sitting on her other side.

"Not taking to the dance floor tonight?" Trevor asked her."

"No! Geri replied, a little too quickly. "I like dancing, but line dancing isn't really my thing."

"What kind of dancing do you like, then?"

"Most ballroom or Latin dances."

"Really?" Trevor looked at her, smiling.

"Why? Do you dance?"

"Oh, yes, I do. I go to Latin classes twice a week."

Geri jumped up.

"Come on, then!" Grabbing a beaming, if somewhat surprised Trevor by the hand, she led him onto the dance floor, as far from the hen-party as was possible. Trevor raised his right hand onto her shoulder and took her right hand in his left and off they went. Geri was amazed.

"You can really dance, Trevor," she said.

"Yes, I've got my gold medal," Trevor said. "How come you dance so well?"

"I used to teach PE and leisure activities,"

Shit! She hadn't planned on making that public knowledge. It was too late now she'd let it out. Then Geri suddenly realised that everyone was looking at them, including Deano. Good! He was taking notice of her. He'd seemed distant on the beach that morning. Her plans to have him apply her suntan lotion had got messed up when Grace saw her holding the bottle and offered to do it for her. She could hardly say that she didn't want her to because she was waiting for Deano to do it. And after that, every time she offered to get him a drink or to rub his suntan lotion in or get him a fresh beach towel, she felt he'd been a bit abrupt with her. Well, this would show him. She was the group's own Dancing Queen and she was dancing with another man! She'd treat him mean and keep him keen!

"Thank Christ for that!" Deano said to the others as they watched Geri and Trevor on the dance floor.

"Don't you dance then?" Frances asked him.

"Oh yes, I do, but I have to be in the mood."

"She got tired of waiting for you to ask her to dance," Grace said.

"Well, she'll wait a long time," Deano replied. "No offence, but she's not my type and she's a bit too clingy."

Eve came up to the table at that moment.

"No more takers for the dance floor?" She asked, looking round the group and smiling.

"I love dancing," Frances said.

"Come on, then!"

Frances stood up to join Eve and much to her delight everyone else got up except Deborah and Murray. Frances wasn't surprised. Deborah had already told her that she didn't dance. She didn't do a lot of things, apparently. Although Frances quite liked her, she found her a bit scathing, especially of other members of the group. And she refused point blank to have her photo taken. She'd got quite short with Frances when she'd asked the waiter to snap them both at afternoon tea. What was that all about? And tonight she'd been missing from dinner for about twenty minutes talking on her phone.

Abba gave way to Bob Marley and the group continued to bob and jiggle more or less in time to the music. Stewart sang along in a loud voice in Suzanne's ear as they held onto each other and shrugged their shoulders up and down and their feet back and forth. Back at the tables Deborah yawned and then excused herself and Murray sat at the table alone, watching the others. His little chat with Deborah hadn't gone exactly to plan. She'd made it quite clear she was in Antigua to relax and take it easy. He'd have to reconsider his approach. But he hadn't forgotten that she'd said she wasn't going to do any excursions because neither was he. Everyone else was going out on the catamaran on Tuesday, apparently. So it would be just the two of them left behind in the resort. He gave a little grin to himself. He'd have her to himself for the whole day.

"Show time!" the bandleader announced as No Woman No Cry came to an end with the group all singing a rousing chorus from the dance floor. They returned to their tables with Geri making sure nobody else got the seat next to Deano. As the lights dimmed for the cabaret to begin Eve made her exit. She felt exhausted. The day had been tiring enough, without the shock she'd had at the cocktail party. And besides, she liked to give the group a bit of privacy; they didn't want the tour manager with them the whole time.

"Good night, everyone! Enjoy the show!" she said.

There was a chorus of "Good night, Eve!" as she left them to their own devices.

***

Bugger!

In room 274 Geri slapped on her night cream feeling really annoyed with herself and had managed to get some in her eye. She reached for a tissue and gently wiped the corner of it then blinked rapidly. She'd done absolutely everything she could to get Deano interested in her, but it didn't seem to be working. She'd stayed up with the last of them – Deano, Jo, Grace, Dave and Murray – and had actually been enjoying herself. Although she didn't like the way that Deano kept looking at Jo and directing all his comments at her, Geri had to admit she was a lovely woman. And so was Grace, even though she was a bit of a feminist in Geri's opinion.

86

She didn't seem to mind if the men disagreed with what she said; in fact, she seemed to relish arguing with them. And in the end, both Deano and Dave had agreed with her when she'd said that there was no possible argument, moral or ethical for paying women less than men for doing the same job.

"But I still say I'd wanna be rescued by a burly bloke an' not a skinny woman if I was in a burning building," Dave had said. "It'd be the only time I'd rather be in a man's arms than a girl's." They'd all laughed at that, Grace included. At that point Geri had gone to the ladies. She'd begun to feel a bit light-headed and had decided she'd better have a soft drink next round instead of another rum punch. But when she got back to the table only Dave, Trevor and Murray were left.

"Where are the others?" she asked. "Not gone to bed, surely?"

"Yep! All tired out. Me an' all." Dave downed what was left of his beer and put the empty glass back on the table. "I'll see you all at breakfast. You comin' Trev?

"|I think I'm going to get a rum and take it back to my room and drink it on the balcony," Trevor said, slurring slightly and getting unsteadily to his feet.

"I'll wait fer yer," Dave told him, realising that he'd had one too many. "Night," he said to Geri and Murray, who realising they were left with each other both stood up at the same time.

"I'll be off."

"Yes. Good night."

Then they both started walking in the same direction. Geri had found it a bit embarrassing, so she'd veered off and walked through the gardens only to come face to face with Murray again at the stairwell. It felt like they were going to the same room, especially when they both climbed the stairs to the first floor, but Murray stopped at room 266, just four doors before hers, 274. She hadn't been able to find out Deano's room number, but she knew he was on the other side, in the northern half of the horse shoe the rooms formed. Still, there was plenty of time. Jo might think she'd won, but tonight was only the first round. Tomorrow night they were going to Shirley Heights. Eve had said it was a party with lots of rum and good music. She'd wear her Vivien of Holloway dress that had cost a fortune but really made her look rather fantastic. Deano wouldn't be able to resist her.

***

In room 311, Natalie put her book down and checked the time on her watch. Quarter to midnight. She was annoyed with herself for leaving early but the sight of those awful, loud women and their chav hen-party had upset her so much it had taken her by surprise.

I'm still vulnerable. Much more vulnerable than I thought.

Her thoughts turned to Michael and she thought about what Jo and Grace had said. She wasn't stupid, she knew he liked her and she quite fancied him, but probably only because he reminded her of Andy.

Stop thinking about Andy!

She screwed her eyes up tightly as if trying to remove his image from her mind and then opened them wide and gave a great big sigh. Deciding not to be too hard on herself, she turned the light off, bashed the pillow into shape and quickly drifted off into a fitful sleep where she dreamt of a drunken hen party trying to drag her along to join them.

***

In room 320 Suzanne hugged herself as she snuggled under the sheet. People were so nice. Especially Stewart. He was extra nice. He'd been really interested and quite sympathetic when she'd talked about Mum and how difficult it was sometimes running the corner shop with her now that she was getting older. He even offered to walk her back to her room. She'd got cold feet at that, though. But now she wished she'd accepted his offer. And then she realised that she didn't really know anything about him. She hadn't asked him as she'd been so busy talking about herself. She hoped he didn't think her rude. It was a new feeling for Suzanne to have someone to talk to, apart from her mother. And she couldn't remember ever talking to a man like that. She went over their whole conversation again and relived their time on the dance floor. She gave a huge smile in the darkness and hugged herself again.

This is what happiness feels like.

***

Michael sat on the balcony of room 356, staring into space; staring at the thousand stars that twinkled above him in the cloudless sky, but without seeing any of them. His thoughts were racing, reliving those special moments over and over again still unable to identify or put a name to what he had felt; amazed that there hadn't been a clap of thunder or a shower of fireworks. And there had been no recognition or feeling of relief or accomplishment, just a feeling of anti-climax was almost too much to bear. Without warning he felt his shoulders heave and he found himself sobbing as if his heart would break.

***

In room 266 Murray pulled the sheet over his belly and burped loudly. He went over the conversation with Deborah again and this time he felt more confident. She'd only said she wanted to relax and take it easy, she hadn't said she didn't want sex. At the thought of sex with Deborah he felt a stirring underneath his hands. He smiled to himself as he realised he wouldn't have to engage in his usual ten minutes of fiddling. He closed his eyes and yielded to the image of a naked Deborah climbing on top of him; smiling at him through her curtain of heavy black hair as she leaned forward and started to kiss his body and that brought him relief faster than he'd ever thought possible.

***

Eve knew that getting into bed would be a waste of time because there was no way that she was going to sleep. She stood at the patio doors looking out into the garden waiting in vain for the knot in her stomach to untie itself, numb, dazed and in shock.

***

Day Three

Eve hadn't slept a wink. Her stomach was still churning, her mind going over and over the events of the cocktail party. At three o'clock she had finally turned away from the windows and had climbed into bed, but in spite of having the a/c unit going, it had felt hot and clammy, with the sheet sticking to her and at almost four o'clock she'd turned the light on and started reading her book. Her thoughts, though, were in grasshopper mode and after realising she'd read five pages and hadn't taken in a single thing, she'd given up. Sleep had finally come at some time after five, and when the alarm sounded at seven to snatch her from a dream where she was bobbing about on the ocean, alone in a tiny kayak, she felt like she'd had no sleep at all. Remembering that she had to collect all the excursion money this morning and so really needed her wits about her, Eve turned the shower to cold and let the water run over her for the longest time possible, hoping that its therapeutic pounding would help to bring her back to the land of the living.

***

Deano walked towards the breakfast terrace with his sunglasses on. This enabled him to check out where everyone was sitting without them knowing he was doing it. He spotted Jo first, probably because she was the one he was looking for, sitting on one of the round tables facing the sea. Trevor was sitting on her right, deep in conversation with Frances, who was on his right. There was a space where someone had been on Frances's right and then Natalie next to Suzanne, then two spaces to Jo's left. And no sign of Geri. He had been flattered at first when he'd realised she was making a play for him, but it had quickly turned to embarrassment when she'd made it so obvious that the others could see what was going on, too. In other circumstances he'd have probably gone along with it, after all, he thought, that was part of the reason he'd come away. If it was there before him on the next sun bed, why should he refuse?

But there was something about Jo. He'd never gone for redheads before, usually preferring small blondes. Like Geri. That was ironic; physically, Geri was just his type, although he liked them younger than she was. But taking it all into account, he'd have probably gone along with it with Geri if it hadn't been for Jo. He'd surprised himself when he'd suddenly realised half way through the previous evening that he really liked her. He looked towards the second table and saw that Donna and Dawn were alone on it, both talking without drawing breath. He wasn't up to having breakfast with the two of them and besides there were too many empty seats on their table. Beyond them he could see Jason and Huw on a table for four with the two American girls. Seizing the opportunity, he slid onto the empty chair next to Jo.

"Morning!" he said to the whole table.

"Morning, Deano!" Geri said, appearing behind him and taking the place on his left.

***

"So quarter to five in reception and don't forget to wear comfortable shoes."

Eve's head was spinning as she said it for the fifteenth time in the space of an hour. Deborah smiled, thanked her, picked up her beach bag and set off towards the Spa Pool where Frances had promised to save her a sun bed. Eve had been surprised to get any bookings from Deborah given that she'd been so vocal on the first evening about not wanting to do any trips, but she was pleased to see she was going to join the group for Shirley Heights that evening and on the catamaran trip on Tuesday. That meant the whole group was going to both except Murray and, of course, Ursula. She'd seen Ursula as she'd made her way through reception earlier and she'd given Eve a shy little wave and had almost smiled. Eve hoped that she'd be able to persuade her to join them for at least a couple of evenings. Although she accepted that being alone was Ursula's choice, she always took it as a personal failure if someone didn't gel with the group. Her back and shoulders were stiff from leaning forward. Thank God for calculators, she'd thought more than once this morning. Most of the group had paid in US dollars, which was straightforward, and even those who had paid in EC caused no trouble as all she had to do was multiply the US by two point six. But Deano and Trevor and Grace had wanted to pay with credit cards, which had to be converted into EC and then carried a five percent surcharge, and Huw had insisted on paying in sterling. And to crown it all, Donna had brought Euros.

"They're left over from our holiday in Zakynthos last year. I thought they'd take them here."

"Well, yes, they do, but I don't know the rate of exchange," said Eve, frantically dialling Sunny's number and eliciting impatient tuts from Huw and Jason who were next in the queue.

Looking across to the main pool area, where aquarobics was just starting, Eve saw Murray jump up from a sun bed as Deborah walked past and start to engage her in conversation. Deborah barely slowed her pace calling the answers to his questions over her shoulder as she tip-tapped purposefully on in her heeled mules. Eve grimaced as she took the final swig of her now-cold coffee and started to pack away her calculator and pens when she saw Murray rushing across the bar towards her.

"I want tae go on that thing tonight," he said.

Good morning, Eve! And how are you today?

"Good Morning! Do you mean Shirley Heights?"

"Yes. I, er, forgot tae tell ya yesterday. I wanted tae sort myself out first and I nearly forgot this morning. It is alright is it? I mean, there is room?"

"Yes, there is. I don't have to confirm numbers with the taxi drivers until about half past three, so there's plenty of time.

"How much is it?"

"Twenty-five US plus eight US entrance fee, which you pay when you get there. Drinks are then extra."

"It's nae cheap, is it?"

Eve shrugged. She didn't have to defend the price of the taxi ride to Shirley Heights to Murray, even though she did personally think that there should be a group rate.

"I'll just go and change a traveller's cheque. I'll not be a minute."

Eve sighed and sat down again. She looked at her watch and saw it was already almost half past eleven. As soon as Murray came back she was going back to her room to count and check the money, put it in the safe, grab a sandwich from the beachside diner and then she was going to get back into bed for a couple of hours siesta before getting ready to go off to Shirley Heights. Part of her felt it was a shame to spend daylight hours in bed when the beach was so beautiful. But she knew she needed to sleep, if her thoughts would let her. Then she remembered she'd booked brunch for everyone at one o'clock. She had to turn up; there were no two ways about it. She gave a mental shrug. If she ate quickly and then excused herself, she'd just have time enough to grab a quick siesta for an hour or so before she had to be ready for Shirley Heights. There was nothing else for it. She yawned as a wave of tiredness hit her. She wished Murray would hurry up.

***

"No thank you!"

Natalie smiled sweetly at the elderly man who was waving a large machete in his right hand and a coconut in his left.

"It's good. It helps you make beautiful babies," he said, nodding his head towards Michael, who had his earphones in and his eyes closed and was oblivious to the laughter that went round the sun beds at his expense.

"He's not my husband!" Natalie said quickly, surprising herself and everyone else by blushing.

"He doesn't have to be your husband for you to make beautiful babies together," the coconut-seller said, to more laughter.

"We got no money," Dave explained to him, slowly and loudly as if the man wasn't a native English-speaker. "We are all-inclusive. All food and drink included. No money necessary." He mimed eating and drinking and then pulled out the pocket of his shorts to show it was empty.

"I come in peace," said Stewart, raising his right arm from the elbow and mimicking Dave's tone of voice. The roar of laughter was loud and spontaneous and even Dave joined in. Sighing because he didn't make a sale, yet still managing to smile at them, the coconut-seller moved on.

"Nice one!" Deano said, still chuckling and nodding towards Stewart.

"Does anyone fancy going out in a pedalo with me?" Natalie asked. "Just for half an hour. I mean, look at that beautiful sea; it's such a shame not to be on it. And besides, I think I should do something, I spent the whole of yesterday and all this morning on this sun bed."

"Are you usually active then?" Suzanne asked her.

"I'm a dancing teacher. I teach tap, ballet and jazz."

"Oh that's good, working for yourself," Suzanne said. "Is it your own school? Is it big?"

"I've got about ninety children and thirty adults. I have a singing teacher and drama teacher, too, so we offer proper stage school training."

"What's it called?"

"The Natalie Noakes Performing Arts Academy and Theatrical Agency."

"Blimey, that sounds posh," Dave said.

"Natalie Noakes? Didn't you used to be an actress?" Jo asked, sitting up and looking at her.

"Yes. I'm really Natalie Sharpe, Noakes was my stage name. I was in a children's television series called County High for five years. That's probably where you know me from."

"It is! I thought you looked familiar. Well, well well!" Jo lay back down again.

"Do you still perform?" Suzanne asked.

"I occasionally do the odd thing. I was in a couple of West End shows, in the chorus mainly, and I was in those adverts a year or so ago where people were dancing at Liverpool Street Station. I loved acting and performing professionally but it's a hard business to get on in. So much depends on luck, really. And besides, I really enjoy teaching and some of my kids are doing well. You know, adverts, parts in things like Silent Witness and Law and Order UK and I've got one in Billy Elliot at the moment. I run classes three evenings a week and on Saturday mornings, so I do something physical most days."

"Oi oi!" shouted Dave.

"I'll ignore that, but as punishment you can be the one to come out on the pedalo with me. Come on!" she ordered, pulling him to his feet. "And for being mouthy you can do all the pedalling." They ran off laughing down the beach towards the water-sports centre.

"I'd quite like to go in a pedalo," Geri said. There was a silence that was almost tangible. Deano daren't take his eyes off his Kindle or move a muscle. He felt as though he was at an auction for a million pound painting. A glance at the wrong moment or a simple hand movement could be completely misconstrued.

"I'll go with you, if nobody else wants to," offered Jo, feeling a bit embarrassed at the obvious silence from Deano.

"No, it's OK. On second thoughts the sun will be very strong out there as it's almost midday," Geri said feeling her face turn scarlet and furious at Jo for being so bloody patronising. And she was angry with herself for opening her mouth. Sensing her distress Trevor sat up and brushed sand from his paperback.

"Who's for a drink?" he asked.

"Wadiddlys all round, I think," said Stewart.

***

Frances was languishing in the Spa pool. She floated on her back feeling the warmth of the sun while at the same time the water cooled her down. She sighed contentedly.

This is the life!

She didn't know how long she'd been there, in fact, she couldn't be sure she hadn't drifted off to sleep, when she felt splashing near her and opened her eyes and lowered her feet to the bottom of the pool as Deborah came up beside her.

"That bloody man. He's giving me the creeps," she said, referring to Murray who had appeared shortly after Deborah had made herself comfortable on the sun bed next to Frances. "He leers at you; talks to your boobs instead of your face. And he doesn't stop talking."

"Moaning, you mean. He hasn't stopped going on about things since he sat down."

"Quite! He's critical of everything. I know it's not the Ritz, I mean to say, I was very disappointed myself when I first arrived as it's not really what I'm used to or what I was expecting, but I'm really relaxing now and enjoying myself. The only thing spoiling it for me is him!"

Frances couldn't help looking at Deborah in amazement. What a difference a day made! For the first night Deborah had been the one who was complaining about everything.

"And I hope he doesn't turn up here every day. It's our little spot," Deborah continued.

"Perhaps if we both read our books and don't pay him any attention he'll go away," Frances suggested.

"Let's hope so. I don't want my holiday ruined by him!" Deborah said, wading towards the steps.

Both women got out and went back to their sun beds. Murray's sun bed was empty.

"Perhaps he's gone," Frances said.

"Some hopes! He's left his towel and bag behind."

No sooner the words were out of her mouth than Murray appeared, wiping the sweat from his face with the back of his hand.

"I didnae think it'd be this hot."

"Well, it's the Caribbean, isn't it?" Frances said. "Why don't you take your shirt off? You'd be cooler."

"Oh, I never take my shirt off!" he replied, shaking his head. "But you'd think they'd have a few more sun umbrellas. Not everyone likes the sun. You'd think they'd have one per sun bed."

Frances and Deborah exchanged a look. Frances had had enough. She picked up her book and opened it where she'd turned down the corner of the page.

"Do excuse me, you two. I'm at a very interesting part of my book." She buried her head in it. Taking her cue from Frances, Deborah picked up her MP3 player from her bag.

"And I'll get back to Michael Buble!" she said, putting in her earphones.

Murray looked at them both and smiled, completely oblivious as to why they had both shut him out. Completely oblivious that he had been shut out. Across the pool he saw Andy and Fiona. Holding his arms wide to encompass the two women, he smiled and winked at the couple over the water. They waved and he waved back, raising his glass in Caledonian camaraderie, unable to see Fiona muttering *'Oh, please, God, don't let him come over and join us'* under her breath.

***

Brunch had been a real success. The setting of the Crazy Conch, on the beach surrounded by a kaleidoscope of tropical flowers and tall, swaying Royal palms, gave it a really special feel. The sound of the steel band, the alluring aromas rising from the trays of food and the sight of waiters moving from table to table with wines and exotic cocktails all added to the atmosphere.

"Sunday dinner will nevva be the same agen!" Dave said, finishing off his rum and raisin ice-cream.

"It's like a dream! It's just like I imagined it but better!" Suzanne said.

"We certainly know we're in the Caribbean now!" said Natalie, swigging her glass of rose wine. She held up her glass. "Cheers, ears!" she shouted and everyone clinked glasses and joined in the toast, even Murray.

Eve, desperate for sleep and refusing all the group's attempts to foist alcohol onto her in case she fell asleep at the table or went into such a deep siesta that she failed to wake up in time for Shirley Heights, had excused herself as soon as the meal was over. Most of the group had remained at the tables to finish their drinks. Huw and Jason hadn't joined them for brunch. There had been a bit of a stand-off with Eve because she wouldn't let the American girls join the group on their tables.

"But we want them to eat with us!" Huw had said.

"The company has a very strict policy," Eve had tried to explain. "You have chosen to come away with Travel Together and that means you're in our group. Now, if you want you sit with other people then please feel free."

"We don't need your bloody permission," he interrupted.

"I'm not suggesting you do. I'm just saying that you can sit with whoever you like, but we don't allow outsiders in with us. If everyone brought someone into the group it wouldn't be Travel Together, would it?"

"You haven't heard the last of this!" was his threatening, parting shot as he and Jason headed off to a table for four with the two Americans in tow.

Jo put a hand on Eve's shoulder.

"Don't let him get to you," she said.

"If he can't see that he's in the wrong and what Travel Together's all about then he shouldn't be on the trip," Deano said, joining in.

"'E's arsehole," was Dave's contribution.

"We could all bring people in, couldn't we?" Dawn chipped in. "Me and Donna was talking to two guys from Bradford on the way to the beach this morning. We told them about the group, didn't we, Donna? But they didn't want to join us and we wouldn't have suggested it, would we Donna?"

Donna shook her head.

Eve had shrugged and smiled at them. This was a problem she often had to deal with; outsiders trying to join the group. Usually they latched on to the neediest or the most vulnerable member of the group as a way in. Inevitably it caused trouble as other group members didn't want outsiders joining them. They'd paid to be in their group and felt, rightly so, that others should do the same. She was curious to see what would happen when the time came for Shirley Heights; would Jason and Huw go with the Americans or with the group as they'd booked? She gave a sigh as she pulled the sheet over her and adjusted her eye mask. Frankly, she didn't care.

***

At four forty-five all the group had gathered in the reception area ready for Shirley Heights, except Jason and Huw and Deborah. Eve looked round the group, checking everyone's footwear with her gaze as she did so. Donna and Dawn were both wearing cut-off jeans and milkmaid-style blouses, Donna's red and Dawn's green. Eve couldn't help thinking they looked as if they were going to a barn dance. They both were wearing sandals with a fairly high heel.

"Are you going to be OK in those shoes?" Eve asked them. "You know you have to dance on grass or cobbles."

"These are our dancing sandals," Donna said. "We wear them to our line-dancing classes. They're non-slip."

"You're gonna av ter speak up. We can't ear you over Stewart's shirt," Dave said, nodding towards Stewart who was wearing the offending garment; bright turquoise with emerald and black palm trees on it.

Stewart grinned good-humouredly as the others laughed and raised his middle finger at Dave.

At that moment Jason and Huw appeared. Jason smiled round the group and said 'Hello' to everyone, while Huw stood a way off scowling. The two Americans had obviously gone to Shirley Heights with the rest of the hotel guests at four o'clock, if they were even going. Eve always took her group up a bit later so that they saw the sunset and then really appreciated the party atmosphere when the local band came on at seven and a lot of the tourists started to leave.

"Ere comes the Ice Queen," Dave said as Deborah finally made an entrance and they all scrambled into the two taxis, Geri making sure she was in the same one as Deano. She was pleased with herself because she thought she looked really good, but also because she had timed it just right. Jo was already in, and sensing that Deano would want to sit next to her, Geri had deliberately taken the empty seat by Jo, forcing Deano to sit on the back seat with Donna and Dawn. She might not be sitting next to him, but neither was Jo. She wanted a holiday fling with Deano; she had fancied him since she'd first seen him at Gatwick and a Little Miss Nice-and-Friendly like Jo wasn't going to get in her way. Of course, she now had to put up with Jo all the way there. It wasn't that she didn't like her; she just resented the fact that she came across as a really nice person and everyone liked her. At lunch, after a couple of glasses of wine had loosened her tongue, Geri had tried to suggest to Natalie that Jo was a bit too good to be true and she'd snapped her head off.

"You know nothing about her, Geri!" she'd said lowering her voice to a harsh, hushed whisper. "She's had a terrible tragedy in her life. She's a lovely person."

Geri wondered what the tragedy had been. She didn't know much about Jo and they hadn't spoken to each other much, either. The taxi trip might give her the opportunity to find out. And, anyway, Jo didn't have the exclusive rights to tragedy! As the minibus/taxi rattled its way south through the rain forest and villages beyond Geri switched off from the driver's banter and continual anecdotes and allowed herself to go over the awful events of her life three years earlier; the events that had led to her leaving a really successful teaching career; leaving before she was drummed out of the profession. Involuntarily she gave a little shudder.

"You OK?" Jo asked.

"What? Yes. Yes, I'm fine. I was just daydreaming about something I'd really prefer to forget."

"We all have moments like that, I think."

"Do you? You don't strike me as a person with things they'd rather forget," Geri said, jumping at her chance to find out something about Jo.

"Don't I?"

"No. You seem cool, calm and collected. You seem in control of your life and besides, everyone likes you and you look really good tonight in spite..." Geri came to a halt.

"In spite of having ginger hair and being a size sixteen?" Jo finished for her.

"No! I just meant... well, yes I suppose."

Jo burst out laughing.

"Being a size sixteen makes me the average British woman. Having red hair probably means that somewhere back in my ancestry there were Scots or Irish. And it's a common misconception that all red heads are fiery. The secret is that I'm content with who I am and where I am."

"But you haven't got a man or you wouldn't be on this holiday," Geri retorted.

"Just because I haven't got a partner at the moment doesn't mean I'm not happy. I've found contentment and I'm on this holiday because I wanted to come to the Caribbean and I didn't want to holiday alone. Probably just like you."

Geri nodded. She sat quietly taking in what Jo had said; thinking to herself that Jo was kidding herself she was happy. Who could be ginger, a size sixteen, have no man in her life and be happy? Yet Deano seemed to like her and find her attractive, Geri was sure.

"What have you done then to make you so content with life?" Geri asked, refusing to let the subject rest until she'd got to the bottom of Miss Ginger Perfect.

"I have my faith. I'm a practising Christian."

Geri looked at her in amazement. Her jaw wide open she took in the curvy redhead with her long hair and beautifully made up face, which made her gorgeous green eyes look even bigger, in her 50s style white dress with purple flowers, noticing for the first time the cross and chain hanging around her neck.

"But you don't......" Geri spluttered.

"What? Look like a Christian?"

Gerri nodded.

"How does a Christian look, Geri?"

"No, it's just... you don't... I mean, you don't talk about God all the time. And you drink!"

Jo laughed out loud and shook her head slightly.

"I might not talk about Him, but that doesn't mean I'm not thinking about Him, and thanking Him continually for all my blessings. And I like a drink now and then. Moderation is the key word. And even vicars have to have a break sometimes."

"You're a vicar?"

"Yes."

Geri saw this as her chance; Deano wouldn't want anything to do with a vicar. She turned to face the rest of the minibus, but directed her words to the back seat.

"Jo's a vicar! A vicar! Who would have thought that?"

She beamed round at all the other faces waiting for their comments and surprise.

"Well, she has to be something," Suzanne said, holding on to Natalie for dear life as the taxi veered round a sharp bend, while avoiding a large pot hole at the same time. Everyone carried on with their own conversations. Nobody was interested in what Geri had just said. She felt foolish. She'd expected some reaction from Deano, but he'd just looked at her sternly. And she still didn't know what Jo's tragedy was. She didn't like not knowing things.

At the back of the minibus Deano smiled inwardly to himself. He'd never dated a vicar before, but he didn't care if Jo was a vicar or a pole dancer. All he knew was that he wanted to get her between the sheets. That would be a first for him, though; sex with a lady-vicar. He couldn't stop the smile from breaking onto his face. She might be a woman of the cloth, but she was still a woman.

***

The sunset over Shirley Heights had been glorious and even now, twenty minutes after it had set the effects could still be seen in the candyfloss, pink clouds that floated across the darkening sky. Standing, looking down on English Harbour and Falmouth Harbour where fairy lights were beginning to twinkle reflecting all the stars that were now showing themselves above, Eve thought that this was one of the loveliest sights the world had to offer. Some of the group were beside her, talking, taking photos and admiring the view, while others had gone back towards the main stage area to listen to and bob along to the steel band, who were just reaching the end of their finale. For the first time since the previous night's cocktail party, she felt composed and to a degree, peaceful.

"Can I get you a drink, Eve?" Stewart asked, appearing at her side.

"Oh, thank you. A Diet Coke, please."

"Isn't it beautiful?" Grace said, joining them. "It's such a gorgeous spot."

"I just love it here," Eve said.

Murray, who had been standing alone on the edges of the group, moved towards them.

"Thank God that bloody steel band's finishing at last!"

"I think they're amazing musicians," Grace retorted. "Didn't you hear them play the classical stuff? Or the jazz? Or the Bob Marley tribute?"

"We've heard nothing but bloody steel bands since we got here!"

"We're in the Caribbean. What did you expect, the Pipes and Drums of the Grenadier Guards?" Grace snapped at him.

Eve had to turn away. Her face broke into a huge grin and her shoulders started to jig up and down. Murray, taken aback, mumbled something about getting another drink and looking for Deborah and walked away.

"I'm sorry, Eve, but he just rubs me up the wrong way!"

Dave, Geri, Deano and Jo, who had overheard Grace's remark, burst out laughing. That had put him in his place. The local band started up and Eve invited the others to go with her to the main arena and they all did. And right in the middle of the dance floor were Natalie and Trevor, leading the moves. Before long everyone was dancing. Eve caused a few raised eyebrows when she danced with Royston, who was one of a dozen or so local men who went to Shirley Heights every week to give foreign women visitors, the local experience. They danced Caribbean style, with Eve in front and Royston behind her, moving from side to side in time to the music.

"Looks like she's bein' goosed ter music," Dave observed, but before long he found himself with Grace, Deano had grabbed Jo, Stewart had grabbed Suzanne, Donna and Dawn had been grabbed by two local boys and Natalie had pulled Trevor behind her, Michael in front of her, and they were all dancing and singing along, drinks in hand, enjoying themselves to the full. Sitting a little way off from the others Geri was downing another rum punch. She watched Deano and Jo with a loathing and hatred that she didn't know she was capable of. She wanted to be with Deano, she'd seen him first! What right had this bloody fat, ginger, religious bitch got to take him? Smug cow! How dare she talk down like that to her like that, with all the self-righteous *'I'm happy because I've got God'* bollocks?

She took a long swig from her drink, emptying the glass. She could see everyone in the group enjoying themselves. Those that weren't dirty dancing were bobbing around together, smiling and singing. What was it about her that meant she was always on the outside? Clutching hold of the stone wall she'd been sitting on Geri stood up and paused while the world righted itself. She wanted another drink and lurched forward towards the bar when a pair of strong arms enveloped her and a crotch thrust itself against her backside in time to the music. She was startled at first and tried to pull away.

"Relax, baby, relax!" a voice said in her right ear. "We just dancing!"

Geri looked over her shoulder into a pair of eyes as black as polished conkers and a wide, sexy smile. Geri relaxed back against her partner. The evening was finally beginning to look up.

***

Eve had found a quiet spot on a bench in the garden at the far end of the fort and was sipping her Diet Coke deep in thought when Huw and Jason appeared in front of her.

"Oh there you are! We've been looking for you for the last half an hour," Huw said.

Eve refused to rise to the bait. Half an hour ago she'd been standing next to both of them as they sulked with long faces watching their two American friends dance drunkenly with a couple of Australian hunks who were crew on one of the largest yachts in Falmouth Harbour.

"We've had enough and we want to go back to the hotel," Huw continued in the tone of a petulant ten-year-old.

Eve looked at her watch.

"We've only got half an hour until we're due to leave. Don't you want to wait until then?"

"No, we don't! This is rubbish. It's so touristy and the music's crap."

"Well, if you want to wait a minute I'll see if there's a taxi with spaces going back to the resort before us that'll take you. I'll have to see what the charge will be."

"Charge?" Eve thought someone had grabbed Huw between the legs. "We've already paid!" he squealed.

"Yes, you paid the taxi driver that brought you for a return journey. You can't expect someone else to take you for free."

"But if he's got empty seats it's no skin off his nose, is it?" Huw retorted hotly.

"It's up to the taxi driver," Eve explained. "He might take you for free or he might ask for payment, but either way I have to first find out if anyone's leaving before us. Wait here a moment." She stood up and started to walk back towards the throng to find the taxi drivers, who usually congregated outside the front entrance.

"Well, if it's only half an hour we can wait," Jason called after her.

Eve stopped and turned to face them.

"It's up to you, but please don't let me set something up if you're not sure you want to go."

"I'm happy to stay," Jason said. "What's the point in paying when we've only got to stay for another half an hour? It'd be different if it was two hours or something."

"Yeah, I couldn't stand it if we were staying another two hours!" Huw said.

But you haven't got to, have you? I've just said we're leaving in half an hour!

"So, you're happy to stay then?"

Two heads nodded, one slightly more enthusiastically than the other.

"Not exactly happy, but we haven't got much choice, have we?" Huw had to add.

"Go and have another rum punch and let your hair down for the last half-hour and you might end up enjoying it," Eve said.

Huw marched off. Jason gave a little shrug and grimaced in apology for his friend's petulance before walking off, too. Eve thought it was a shame that Jason had palled-up with Huw so early in the holiday. He probably felt that as they were more or less the same age and both teachers they had a lot in common. That often wasn't the case, though. Travel Together holidays sometimes produced the most unlikely bedfellows.

Eve sipped her drink and looked up at the night sky. She should be feeling wonderful, yet the knot had returned to her stomach and her head was in turmoil. Uncontrolled thoughts kept on swirling round and round taking her to a place she didn't want to be.

Pull yourself together!

She stood up and wandered back towards the band to find the group. She laughed out loud as she saw them; one unsteady conga line lead by Dave and Natalie, weaving in and out of the crowd of dancers. It was just lovely to watch them; a bunch of strangers who were now having the time of their lives with each other. She noticed that Michael was standing by himself to one side with a smile on his face as he watched the rest of them. He'd been a bit quiet today, she thought. She'd seen him sitting on his own in the bar staring into space when she'd opened her curtains after her siesta. At that moment Dave brought the conga line up to him and Natalie grabbed his arm; Michael stood no chance, he was doing the conga! Further down the line, Trevor clutched Dawn's hips and Stewart held onto Suzanne like a drowning man clutching a lifebelt. Frances held onto Deborah, who in turn was holding onto Donna, who was holding onto Murray. Eve couldn't believe her eyes. Murray was actually enjoying himself. The band suddenly went into *I Gotta Feeling* and the whole place went into meltdown. Chucking her empty Coke can into the recycling bin Eve went and joined the group; it was impossible not to. Even Jason was on the dance floor, jumping up and down with all the others. Huw was nowhere to be seen.

It was with some difficulty that Eve began shepherding the group back to the taxis at nine o'clock. The music came to an end, but most of the group were still bopping to the songs in their head. Jo and Deano were slow-dancing together. Trevor was only standing up because Grace was holding his arm and Natalie and Dave were singing loudly with arms around each other for support. In the end, Eve knew the only way to get them out was to start another conga line, which led them through the bar and down the driveway to where the taxis were parked.

"We already got one!" Epson, the taxi driver shouted, pointing through the window to Huw, who was sitting inside arms folded. Getting everyone in was a challenge. Michael shoved Natalie into a window seat and then sat tightly next to her, to keep her upright. Everyone was either loud or giggly. Eve went from one taxi to the other counting heads, checking they were all there. There was one missing. She looked round the group and realised it was Geri.

"Has anyone seen Geri?" she called out, trying to make herself heard.

"Yeah! She's short wiv blond air. I've seen 'er!" Dave shouted out and the others laughed as if it had been really funny. Eve grinned to herself. The measures of rum at Shirley Heights were legendary; rarely did she take a sober group back to the resort. She hurried back up the driveway and into the bar looking for Geri. There was no sign of her. She went through the bar back into the dance area, but it was deserted apart from the band packing up their gear and the staff cleaning up.

"You looking for me, honey?" the singer called out to Eve, "'Cos I'm here if you are!" Eve grinned, but was beginning to feel a mixture of concern and annoyance at Geri. Everyone else had managed to get back to the taxis. She went back through the bar and down the driveway. Only their two taxis remained parked up.

"Has she come back?" Eve asked Epson.

"No. She's not here."

Eve went back up the driveway to the bar again. It was now empty except for the bar staff.

"I'm one missing," she said.

"Try the bathrooms," the barmaid suggested. "You go to the far ones and I'll go to the ones down the steps." Eve set off towards the far end of the grounds into the gardens only to find the toilets empty. She arrived back at the bar at the same time as the barmaid who was shaking her head.

"Nobody there," she said. "Everyone's gone. She must have left already."

Eve went back to the taxis and climbed in the front next to Epson.

"Let's go!" she said.

"You're not leaving her here, are you?" Donna asked.

"She's not here," Eve replied. "The whole place is empty. She's already left."

Deborah's phone started ringing. She ignored it.

"Your phone's ringing," Murray said.

"You're a bright boy," Deborah replied.

"Well, aren't you going tae answer it?"

Deborah ignored his question as well as the phone. She looked out of the window until the noise stopped as abruptly as it had started.

Eve switched off to the conversation that followed which speculated on what might have happened to Geri. She was concerned, of course she was. Anything could have happened to her, after all. But she felt that it would be the same old story; Geri had gone off with someone without letting her know.

"Can we stop?" Trevor suddenly shouted out. Petrified that someone might be sick in his cab, Epson slammed on the brakes. Deano and Dave had to get up from the folding seats and get out of the cab to let Trevor off. Eve jumped out with a plastic bag, but it wasn't needed.

"Call of nature! Call of nature!" Trevor shouted as he turned his back on the taxi and had the longest wee in history, during which he almost fell over three times.

"I dink Trevor's thrunk," Suzanne said from the second taxi as it sailed past the first.

"I dink he's not the only one!" said Stewart, making the rest of them laugh.

***

When they got back to the Mango Tree Resort everyone piled into the dining-room to have dinner before it closed, except Eve, who went straight to the house phone and rang Geri's room. There was no reply. She then checked with the front desk to see if there were any messages; there were none. She then joined the others in the dining-room, just in case Geri was there. There was a possibility that she hadn't enjoyed herself at Shirley Heights and had decided to come back early without letting Eve know. But she wasn't at dinner or in the bar area.

"What are you going to do about her?" Deborah asked as soon as Eve said Geri didn't appear to be in the resort. "You can't just leave it anything could have happened to her. You should call the police."

"Probably better to wait a bit to see if she turns up later," Deano said.

"You should get in touch with the British Consul." Trevor shouted down the table.

Suddenly everyone's a missing persons' investigator!

"She's also an adult and should be able to take care of herself," Natalie said. "I can't believe she just went off and didn't tell Eve she was going. That's just bad manners and rude! Just bad manners and rude! Isn't it? Michael? Grace? Isn't it rude?"

"Yes, alright, Nat, she's bad mannered and rude," Grace agreed. Natalie smiled at Grace and nudged Michael's arm.

"Oww!" he said, rubbing it.

"You didn't agree with me." Natalie said, staring at him.

"Yes she's rude and bad mannered," Michael sighed. Natalie gave a huge grin and threw her arms round him.

Eve didn't comment. Let them discuss it among themselves; none of them was making much sense. She'd wait and see if Geri turned up later and if she didn't then she'd deal with the situation. Eve picked at her food; since last night she'd lost her appetite and Geri's disappearance wasn't helping. Everyone was in the kind of deep conversation that only drink can produce and there was a lot of drunken laughter around the tables so Eve decided to go to bed. She felt shattered and the fleeting good humour of Shirley Heights had evaporated. She stood up, said her goodnights to everyone, was hit by a barrage of loud good wishes back and set off towards her room. Suddenly as she reached the piano lounge her path was blocked.

"Hello, Eve."

There he was. Standing before her. Melvyn McGrass. Her mouth went dry and as she looked into his face, a face which was older, a little more lived-in, a little more lined, but unmistakeably the one she had once loved with passion and intensity, she didn't know what to say. For some years she'd fantasised about meeting him again and in her head she'd planned and rehearsed her speech a million times. But that was then. Now, as he stood there, she couldn't remember a single word of it, and even if she could, it wouldn't have mattered because she was incapable of speech.

"I recognised you from a distance last night. I knew it was you, even though, when I checked the register this morning your name was different."

"Married," she stammered. "I was married once. Mitchell is my married name."

"Once?"

She nodded.

"No longer married?"

"No. You?"

"For twenty years with two children."

Eve bit her lip.

This is nuts!

She almost giggled nervously; here they were, two people who had once meant so much to each other standing self-consciously like two fifteen-year-olds with neither knowing what to say.

"Well, it certainly worked out for you," Eve said, indicating the resort with her hands.

"I only work here, I don't own it," he laughed nervously, too, "But I can't complain, there are worse locations."

They looked at each other awkwardly again. Melvyn coughed and then looked into the distance.

"Look, would you like a drink? Shall we go to the bar?"

No! She had enough on her hands with the missing Geri without taking a trip down memory lane. And besides, even after all this time, just seeing Melvyn again brought back the emotions that she thought she'd buried forever, deep inside her. She felt sick again; churned up and light-headed.

"No, thank you. Please excuse me. I have a problem with one of the group."

"Nothing serious, I hope?"

"Someone's missing from Shirley Heights. She wasn't there at the end and I can't find her in the hotel."

"Well, you know she's probably met a boyfriend and gone off, but if you feel really worried we can call the police."

"No. I'll wait and see what happens. I don't want to panic and involve the police if she's gone into town to the Coast or somewhere. If she hasn't turned up in the morning that's different."

"So, if you can't do anything about it, why can't you have a drink with me?"

"No! I'm really tired."

She could have added *"Because I spent the whole of last night tossing and turning after seeing you again."*

But she'd spoken harsher than she had intended. What was the point in having a drink with him? Why rake up the past?

"It's just that, the group keeps me rather busy. But it was nice to bump into you again." And with that she turned on her heel and fled back to her room, ignoring him as he called after her.

***

"Anyone else want a Wadiddly before bed? Eh? Anyone up fer a little nightcap?" Dave asked, looking round the table. "I'm going to the bar if you'd care to join me." He stood up and there was a loud crash as his chair fell to the floor behind him.

"Oops!"

Bending over to pick it up, he lost his balance and fell onto his knees, head-butting the buttocks of a waitress carrying a tray of ice-creams as he tipped forward to end up flat on his face with ice-cream plopping all around him and the poor, unfortunate girl. Members of staff rushed to help them, but the group, seeing everything through the hazy effect of too much rum, could only sit and scream with laughter.

"Dave, you're pissed!" Natalie shouted to him, not realising how loud she was.

"Is everything OK here?" Osbert asked appearing from nowhere and looking with resignation around the table. He'd worked with tourists for so long, and Sunday nights were run-of-the-mill to him.

"We're fine," Jo said, "Sorry to be making such a noise, but we've had a good night at Shirley Heights."

"Sshhhh! Everyone, sshhhh!" Suzanne yelled, putting her finger to her lips. "We're making too much noise!"

"Do you want to go for a walk, Suzanne?" Stewart asked her suddenly emboldened by their proximity in the conga line and the rum punch. "You know, get a bit of fresh air and cool down a bit."

"I'm going to bed!" she announced as Stewart's face lit up. But she grabbed her bag from the back of the chair and tottered towards her room.

"Never mind, Stew," Natalie shouted down the table, "We've still got a week to go!"

Stewart looked a bit crestfallen. He helped Dave to his feet and the two of them staggered over to the bar. Deano leaned towards Jo and whispered quietly in her ear.

"Do you want a bit of fresh air?"

"We're in the open air. We're on a terrace."

"A bit of exercise then?" He suddenly reddened, hoping she hadn't misconstrued what he'd meant. "Like, a stroll, I mean."

Jo smiled at him. She knew that he liked her; he'd made it obvious for the last two days. Perhaps it was time for her to let go. Perhaps she should go for a stroll with him. And she'd enjoyed their slow dance.

"Okay."

They got up and left the table and strolled down past the bar towards the beach.

"Go on, my son!" Dave shouted out as he watched them walk together and everyone in the bar turned to see who he was shouting at.

"I'm so sorry," Deano said.

"That's alright. You're not responsible for what Dave says."

They walked in companionable silence until they reached the sand and Jo sat on the wall.

"I haven't got any insect repellent on so I'd rather not walk on the beach," she said.

Deano sat next to her. Although he was a man who could hold his drink he knew that he'd have to watch what he did and said.

"So how long have you been vicaring?" he asked.

"Vicaring?" She laughed.

"Yeah. You know, being a vicar. How long have you been a vicar for?"

"I was ordained three years ago."

"Have you always been religious? Like, were your mum and dad Bible-bashers?"

Jo winced at the term.

"Not really. I discovered God's love for me when I was in my mid-twenties at a time when I was looking for answers."

"I sometimes go to church," Deano said. "Well, Christmas and that, you know... weddings and funerals."

"I know. Like most of the population; hatch, match and dispatch."

"Is your church big?"

"Not very. It's pretty, eighteenth century although it had extensive restoration work in the early twentieth century."

"How many does it seat?"

Jo laughed at the question.

"I suppose about two hundred at a push," she said. "We don't look at it like that. It's not the O2 or Wembley Stadium."

"Are you the only vicar there?"

"No. There are three parishes, and we work them between us. There's Tom, who's the other vicar and then Mike the young curate."

Deano moved a bit closer to her and slid his arm round her shoulders.

"So you work alongside two men! I could get jealous of that!"

"They're both married. Tom is quite difficult sometimes; very set in his ways, but I get on very well with Mike and his wife." She suddenly sat up straighter on the wall causing

109

Deano's arm to fall down from her shoulder. He jerked himself upright and put his arm across her back, resting his hand on her neck.

"Cornwall, isn't it? Where you live?"

"Yes. Near St Ives."

"I could come down and visit. I've never been to Cornwall."

Deano moved closer to her, his lips gently touched her earlobe then her cheek and then, as she turned towards him, her lips. He pulled her close to him and her arms went round his neck as they kissed each other with passion. But when Deano's hand found itself curling around one of her breasts, Jo pulled away from him and stood up.

"What's up?" he asked. "You're not leaving now, surely? We're just getting to know each other." Taking her hands in his he looked into her eyes. "I really like you, Jo. I do. And I think you like me as well."

"I think you're a nice bloke. But I also know we've both had a few to drink so let's not get into something we both might regret in the morning and which we'll probably not remember properly because we're not sober," Jo said, gently extracting her hands from his.

"Goodnight, Deano," she said. She planted a kiss on his forehead and then turned and walked back down the path.

***

Back at the bar, where the one for the road had become three, Stewart, Frances, Trevor and Dave were laughing out loud at the events of the evening.

"Well, she really put im in is place, didn't she?" Dave said.

"I missed it," Frances said. "What did she say?"

"She asked im if ee'd expected the massed bagpipes of the Cold Stream Guards!" Dave paraphrased Grace's earlier comment and the three of them burst into uncontrollable laughter, all the more exaggerated because of the drink they'd consumed.

"Priceless!" Frances spluttered, wiping tears from her eyes. "I love her sense of humour and he's so bloody pompous! Such a bloody know-all! He's really been getting on my tits today at the Spa Pool. Excuse the language," she added, slurping her drink.

"You're alright!" Dave said, raising his glass.

"But she's right, I mean, what sort of music did he expect in Antigua?" Stewart asked. "I love it. I love steel bands, I love reggae. I play a lot of it at my gigs."

"You a dee-jay?"

"Yes."

"What on the radio? You famous?"

"No, pubs and weddings, birthdays, you know. Music's my thing. I love it."

"I like music," Frances said. "Especially Lionel Richie. And Neil Diamond. I love him."

"You can't beat Frank Sinatra," Trevor said, leaning forward and looking as if he was in danger of falling off the bar stool.

"I love a bit of Loofah," Dave said.

"I've never heard of them. What sort of music do they play?" Frances asked.

"They?" He looked at her, puzzled. "Loofah. You know, Loofah Vandross."

"Oh yeah." Frances and Stewart both nodded and then their attention turned to the edge of the dance floor where Donna and Steve from Entertainments were trying to help a very wobbly Dawn to stay upright.

"Good night, all!" she shouted across to them, waving her arms around and clouting Steve at the same time.

"She's a bit tired," Donna said as Dawn toppled onto her knees, dropping her handbag and losing a shoe in the process.

"She's pissed, more like," Stewart said almost disapprovingly, as if he hadn't had a drink all night.

"Ere! Look! Over there!" Dave was pointing across the bar towards the reception where Deborah and Murray were walking side by side.

"She's spent all day saying she can't stand him!" Frances said.

"Well, they're only walking along together," Stewart said, wistfully, thinking of how he'd wanted to do that with Suzanne.

"No smoke without fire, my old sunshine!" Dave said. "You'd be surprised what a couple of drinks can do. Alcohol can thaw the frostiest of knickers!"

Frances and Stewart burst into another bout of laughter as Dave stood up unsteadily.

"One for the road?" he asked. "Go on! Have anuvva Wadiddly. It puts lead in your pencil, Stew."

"Shame I haven't got anyone to write to, then!" Stewart retorted and the three of them fell about laughing. Trevor, in a world of his own, slipped off the bar stool and sat down with a thump on the floor, which only made the others laugh all the louder.

***

Eve had a shower and jumped into bed. She just wanted to go to sleep; it was the only way she wouldn't think about Melv. She plumped her pillows and turned out the light. And just as her head hit the pillow the phone rang.

Shit!

She sat straight back up, felt for the light switch and then lifted the receiver.

"Eve speaking."

"Oh, Eve, it's Donna. Dawn's had a bit of a fall. Can you come? We're in reception. They're putting some stuff on it."

"I'm on my way."

Cursing to herself, Eve slipped on a pair of trousers and a t-shirt, not bothering with underwear and pushed her feet into flip flops and made her way to reception where she found Donna holding an ice pack to Dawn's face. Steve from Entertainments and Philip the night receptionist were standing next to them.

"It seems that the lady tripped coming through the patio and hit her face on the big flower pot with the palm tree in it," Philip said. "We're putting ice on it but perhaps she should go to the hospital as she's hit her head."

"Yes, it would probably be best," Eve agreed.

"No! I don't wanna go to hospital! Don't let them take me to hospital, Don!" Dawn, suddenly sober, begged Donna.

"Alright! Sshhhh! We're trying to stop it swelling with the ice. We won't go to hospital if you don't want to." Donna turned to Eve. Eve was surprised to see that she was crying.

"She doesn't want to go to hospital. I'll give her some paracetamol and spend the night with her. She won't be on her own."

"Well, I can't force you to go to hospital, Dawn," Eve said, looking at her. "But if you feel worse in the night or if you feel woozy you must call me and then I'll go with you. Okay?"

Dawn nodded and then winced in pain. Skipper, the security guard arrived with an accident report form which had to be completed. Eve took it from him.

"I'll see it's filled in tomorrow and get it back to you."

"Just hand it in at the front desk and I'll see the young lady gets a copy for herself," he said.

"Do you need a hand?" Eve asked Donna.

"No. I can manage her. Come on, Dawn, stand up!" Donna said, pulling her friend gently to her feet and holding her arm tightly. Eve watched as the two of them shuffled off.

"Drink's a terrible thing!" Philip said, walking back round behind the desk.

"You're not wrong! Good night!"

Eve made her way back to her room. She'd been surprised by Donna's tears and at how upset she'd been. Perhaps she was afraid that something awful might happen to her friend. She wondered if there was something more to their relationship, but then dismissed the idea from her mind. Donna had also had a skinful and the drink had probably made her tearful. Or perhaps she was just embarrassed that Dawn had made a bit of a fool of herself. She'd have a shiner in the morning that much was certain. Eve leapt back into bed and turned the light out, daring the phone to ring again. All she wanted was to be able to sleep!

***

Day Four

Unusually, the tables bearing the *Reserved for Eve's Group* signs stood empty until almost nine o'clock, when one by one the group started to appear, most of them nursing hangovers.

"I didn't realise they were so strong," Natalie said. "I only had two but my head was spinning when I got into bed."

"Two? Ten more like!" Grace retorted.

"I didn't have ten! Did I?"

"Well, perhaps not ten but you must have had at least six."

"Yes, we got four each out of the kitty," Trevor, who'd been the group's treasurer, confirmed, "and then Dave bought another round so that's five."

"And I got you one," Jo said.

"So, I'm a drunk, don't rub it in!" Natalie said. "At least I didn't fall off my chair and end up with on the floor with my arse in the air covered in ice-cream!

"Oh, Christ! I'm never gonna live that down, am I?" Dave said as he plonked himself down on an empty chair. "Can we av a truce, please? Blimey! What appened to you?" he asked Dawn as she appeared at the table with a big plaster across her nose, Donna by her side, each carrying a huge pile of toast in one hand and a bowl of yoghurt-covered mango and pineapple in the other.

"I tripped on an uneven tile as I was going back to my room," she said, very nasally. "You have to be ever so careful around here in the dark. I could have had a really nasty accident, couldn't I, Donna?"

"Yes you could," Donna agreed nodding furiously. "Has Geri turned up?" she asked in an attempt to turn the attention away from Donna, although the size of the plaster and the angle at which it was stuck across her nose drew everyone's eyes to it.

"I haven't seen her," Natalie said.

"Nor me," said Trevor. "I expect Eve's organising some kind of search at the moment. And why is everyone shouting this morning?" he added, putting his hands over his ears and cringing.

"We're not shouting," Natalie bellowed in his ear. "You're hung over. You fell off the bar stool, so I hear," she laughed.

"Well you heard wrong. I was tired so I decided to sit on the floor!" he said.

"Blimey! Do you two even eat the same fings?" Dave asked Donna, examining their breakfast plates as they both sat down.

"Just coincidence," Donna said. "We both just like the same things."

"At least we know oo's oo nah Dawn's got a plaster on er nose," Dave said pointing to Dawn's face and making her blush.

Dave looked at them, shook his head and smiled. This morning they were both dressed in knee-length denim shorts with checked shirts ready for a shopping trip into town. Donna's was blue and Dawn's yellow.

"I thought Eve said she was going to organise a shopping trip on a day there were no cruise ships in," Grace said.

"Yes, but we don't want to sit in the sun this morning, do we, Don?" Dawn said.

"And if you wait for her you could be waiting all holiday," Murray chimed in, stirring his tea with his fork.

"What are you doing, stirring it up?" Grace asked him.

"I couldnae see any spoons."

"No, I mean, what are you doing stirring up other things, about Eve? Don't you think she's got enough on her plate with the missing Geri without you putting the boot in?"

"I'm nae putting the boot in. She just doesn't seem overly efficient to me."

"For God's sake! She takes efficient to another level! Look at all the organising she's done, look at the great time we had last night! I've been on holidays where you only see the rep at the meeting and then on the day before you go home. She's with us all the time."

"Well, she's not here now!" Murray added, viciously. "Didn't she say she'd be sitting over there in the bar every morning? Well, where is she?"

"She's probably sorting out that silly cow Geri," Natalie said.

"You don't think she might have had an accident?" Trevor asked.

"If she'd have had an accident at Shirley Heights we'd have known about it."

"P'raps she fell over the cliff!" Dave said.

"Oh look on the bright side why don't you?" Donna said.

"I reckon she just went off with someone," Grace said. "I've seen people like her before. They're attention seekers. Deano gave her the brush-off and so she went off with someone. She'll turn up."

At that moment Deano appeared at the table to be greeted by an awkward silence.

"Did I hear my name?" he asked looking round the table and smiling.

"We're just speculatin' what happened to Geri after you dumped er," Dave said with a big grin, knowing that he was winding Deano up.

"I didn't dump her! Don't drag me into it! It's nothing to do with me. I don't know where she went or why."

"She'll turn up. Wait and see," Grace said. "Has anyone gone and saved the sun loungers?" she added, changing the subject.

"Michael might have," Natalie said. "We haven't seen him yet this morning. I'll go down and check." She downed the rest of her orange juice and stood up. "How many am I getting if he hasn't done it?"

Five hands shot up in the air.

"Plus Stewart and Suzanne," Jo said, "and, of course, Michael, if he's not down there, and one for yourself."

"I can't manage nine!" Natalie protested.

"I'll come and give you an and," Dave said. "You want one, Murray?"

Murray had been the only one apart from Donna and Dawn not to put his hand up.

"No. I'm going round the Spa Pool. It's much quieter and more peaceful round there."

"And not to mention it's got the added attraction of the delightful Deborah," Natalie said, bursting into laughter as she and Dave set off for the beach.

"We saw em going off togevva last night, him an' Deborah," Dave said.

"Well, at least they don't spoil another couple!" Natalie said. "Morning!" she waved to Michael, who was on his way to the dining-room. "Did you get the sun beds?"

"No!"

"Alright! Don't bite my head off! I was only asking."

"Sorry, Nat. I've just got up; I didn't sleep very well. I haven't had time to get them."

116

"So, do you want one?" Natalie's tone was also sharp.

"Yes, please. I'll grab a coffee and see you in a bit."

Michael walked on to the restaurant with his beach bag and towel over his shoulder as Natalie and Dave continued down the path to the beach.

"'E's got out of bed the wrong side this morning, inn'e?" Dave said.

"He's probably hung over like the rest of us!" Natalie said, grinning.

***

Eve had woken up in a foul mood. It had almost been morning before she'd finally fallen asleep after hours of her head spinning from thoughts of Melv and reliving the events of thirty years ago then going over the many possible scenarios involving Geri's disappearance.

I could slap the bloody woman for being so inconsiderate!

Rolling over in bed she rang Geri's room number but hung up when the voicemail kicked in. There was nothing for it; if Geri wasn't around by the time Eve had showered and dressed she'd have to call in the police, although she knew that unless someone was missing for at least forty-eight hours they probably wouldn't get involved. In the shower it occurred to Eve that Geri might be in her room and not answering the phone. She decided to go and knock on the door and if there was no answer she'd ask for a pass key so at least she'd be able to see if Geri's bed had been slept in and reassure herself that she wasn't unconscious on the floor. Crossing the bar area she could see some of the group having breakfast on the dining-room terrace. She waved at them but carried on towards Geri's room; she didn't want them to start asking questions that she couldn't answer just yet. Tired from her lack of sleep, Eve huffed and puffed up the stairs and along the corridor. Stopping outside room 274 she put her ear up against the door. She thought she heard shuffling in the room so she hammered loudly and when there was no response put her ear up against the door again. It was quiet, but she just felt sure someone was inside.

"Geri! Geri! It's Eve. Please open the door."

Nothing happened; the only sound was silence. Eve hammered again.

"Geri, if you don't open the door I'm going for a pass key. I need to know you're okay. Please open the door."

Eve heard muffled steps and then the door inched open and Geri's face, red and puffy, appeared from behind it.

117

"You've seen me now. Okay? Please leave me alone."

Eve put her foot in the door to stop Geri closing it.

"Whoa! Whoa! Just a minute! I think you owe me some sort of explanation, don't you?"

"Why? Who are you? My mother?"

"No, I'm not your mother. I'm someone who's trying to do her job. And you're not making it any easier for me. I spent a long time looking for you last night. You kept everyone waiting until I'd checked that everyone had gone and the place was completely empty. Didn't it occur to you to let me know you weren't coming back with us? What happened to you?"

"I made friends with someone and he took me for a drink in English Harbour and then brought me back here. Sorry if I didn't ask your permission."

"Geri, please don't take an attitude with me. I would have thought you'd have had the manners to let me know you were leaving without us. I've been very worried in case something had happened to you."

"Well, you don't need to worry about me. I'm fine as you can see. Thank you for your concern." And with that she closed the door in Eve's face.

Geri waited until she heard Eve's footsteps retreating down the corridor before she threw herself down on the bed and started to cry.

You stupid, stupid woman!

Her anger was aimed at herself, not at Eve. The previous evening had been a complete nightmare and she had nobody to blame but herself. Richie, the man she'd met, had danced several dances with her and then asked her to buy him a beer, which she had. He then suggested going to English Harbour. Geri hadn't realised this meant hitching a lift with another couple; Cleveland and Rosie. Rosie, tall, big-boned and blonde, was, she said, a paralegal from Harrogate. She'd only just met Cleveland but they were going back to the villa she was renting in Jolly Harbour. They had dropped Geri and Richie at a small bar in English Harbour that had no other clients apart from the two of them.

"Sunday's always quiet," Richie had explained as Geri brought their drinks back to the table. "Everyone goes to Shirley Heights."

He took a big, shaggy-looking cigarette from the ashtray and inhaled deeply on it, then offered it to her. Geri shook her head.

"I don't smoke," she said, before the smell hit her and she realised what it was. Richie sucked his teeth as much as to say *'Your loss!'*

They'd talked a bit about their lives and Richie, who said he was a lawyer, although Geri somehow felt he wasn't, finished his drink quickly and his spliff a lot slower. He then suggested they have dinner somewhere before taking a taxi back to the Mango Tree Resort. In spite of the amount she'd drunk and feeling woozy from his smoke, Geri felt apprehensive. She didn't want to go back to the resort. Or rather, she wanted to go back to the resort, but not with Richie. She'd felt she was doing something daring, exciting and different when she'd gone off with him, but now she wasn't so sure. She felt uneasy and all she really wanted to do was have a shower, sober up and have dinner with the rest of the group. She wanted to find Deano. She remembered telling Richie that and then he'd started kissing her and he'd pushed his hand down her top and started to massage her nipple. She liked the feel of his rough thumb and fingers on her bare flesh, but as drunk as she was, a voice inside her head had kept on telling Geri she should leave.

The next thing she remembered was standing by the side of the road while Richie peed into a bush and then he asked her for some money for the taxi.

"We'll go halves," he'd said.

When she opened her evening bag, he'd put his hand inside and pulled out the rest of her money. She'd protested and then found herself on the ground as he'd shoved her hard, pushing her over before running off as a car had pulled up and she heard loud voices, speaking in what she assumed was a local dialect and Richie had disappeared into the night, taking her money with him. A young girl and two young men from the car had asked her if she was okay and had helped her up onto her feet and given her a lift back to the resort.

"Do you want us to take you to the police station to report this?" the girl had asked, but Geri had refused.

"You need to be careful here, Miss," the man in the front passenger seat had turned to her and said. "We're good, honest people on the whole, but you can't trust someone you just met like that."

She'd turned away and looked out of the window into the darkness while that familiar feeling of making a mess of things brewed up inside her.

She knew it had to be Eve when she'd heard the phone in her room ringing last night but she didn't want to talk to her about it. She sniffed loudly and pulled a tissue from the box on the dressing table to wipe her eyes and nose. She'd already decided that she'd tell the group she'd had a wild night with a group of local people. There was no way that she was going to tell anyone what really happened. It was none of their business. Let them think she'd had a great time! That should make Deano realise what he was missing!

**

Frances had saved a sun bed for Deborah, who hadn't appeared until after ten o'clock. She was quite put out to see Murray lurking nearby again.

Wretched man!

After seeing them together the previous evening, Frances hoped she wasn't going to be playing gooseberry to the two of them. She didn't think it likely. Deborah had made it quite clear that she wasn't interested in Murray at all. Quite the contrary! She'd said he was getting on her nerves and that she couldn't stand him.

When Deborah finally appeared she was wearing yet another matching swimsuit and sarong, this time purple and mauve silk with butterflies on. She opened her towel and put it over the sun lounger and then collapsed on top of it.

"I feel dreadful! Those bloody rum punches! My head's thumping." She opened her beach bag and took out two paracetamol and downed them with water from her bottle. "I missed the gym again this morning. You drank as much as I did, so how come you're not hung over?"

"Who says I'm not? I've got a bit of a headache, too, but I made sure I drank a huge glass of water before I got into bed last night."

"Did you go straight up after dinner?"

"No. I sat in the bar with Stewart, Trevor and Dave until almost one o'clock. We had quite a laugh. Trevor was so pissed he fell of the bar stool. Well, just sort of slid off it, really, straight down onto the floor. I saw you go up."

Deborah went scarlet. But before she could say anything her phone started ringing. Snatching it from inside her bag, Deborah leapt up and walked over to the far side of the pool where she couldn't be overheard. Frances thought about the fact that Deborah had had quite a few phone calls in the last couple of days. After texting her son Darren on the first night to confirm she'd arrived in one piece and again this morning to tell him she was enjoying herself and to remind him to eat properly, she'd switched her mobile off and put it away in her safe. It was almost twenty minutes before Deborah came back to join her. She made no reference to the call, slipping her phone back into her bag, straightening her towel and then collapsing again back onto the sun lounger.

Murray appeared half dragging, half carrying a lounger, which he managed to manoeuvre between Deborah's and the small table, placing it just inches away from Deborah's prone body.

"Good morning! Another beautiful day!" he sang out.

Both women grunted at him. He appeared not to notice as he started applying suntan lotion to his forehead, face, forearms and legs.

120

"I've been tae see about the hire car," he said to Deborah, who jumped visibly.

"Hire car?" she said, as if he'd suggested hiring a steam train or a space rocket.

"Aye. I've provisionally booked it for Thursday. I thought that would give us a day tae get over the boat trip."

"I thought you weren't going on the boat trip."

"I've changed my mind. Everyone else is going and I thought I'd go and make up the numbers."

"But isn't the weather going to be bad on Thursday?" Frances butted in.

Murray gave her a poisonous look.

"If the weather's poor that's even more reason tae go out for the day in a car."

"I think it's going to be a bit more than just overcast from what Eve was saying. She said there's a tropical storm on the way."

"What does she know? She's nae a weather forecaster, and anyway, I always find that people scaremonger and exaggerate these things."

"But think of the roads! I mean, they're not in very good condition, are they? Look what it was like going to Shirley Heights last night!" Deborah said.

"You'll be in good hands, won't you? I've been driving the streets of London for almost twenty years. There's nothing I havnae dealt with. Driving round Antigua will be like a trip through the park for me."

"Well, you could always drive if you feel safer," Frances said to Deborah, thinking she was helping but not realising she was making it worse. "I always feel better when I'm the one that's driving. I'd much rather drive than be a passenger."

Deborah gave Frances a venomous look.

"I drive an Alfa at home. I'm hardly likely to take to a Twingo, am I?" she said, hotly. "And anyway, I didn't say I was definitely going, Murray."

"Oh, I thought you did," Murray said. "I asked if you wanted tae come and you said you'd rather that than go on an organised tour."

"Well, I've changed my mind!"

Frances almost felt sorry for Murray. His shoulders drooped and his bottom lip pouted and quivered.

"I'll go and cancel it then, will I?"

"Perhaps one of the others will want to go with you," Frances suggested. Looking at her as if she were mad, Murray stood up, slipped his feet into his sandals and slouched off to cancel the hire car. As soon as he was out of earshot Frances and Deborah burst out laughing.

"Poor man! I feel quite sorry for him. Have you been leading him on?" Frances asked.

"I have not! And before you get any more ideas, nothing happened between us last night. Nothing at all. We chatted for a bit at the table after dinner then he walked me back to my room and I might have had a few drinks, but I managed to get in and get the door shut firmly behind me before he had the chance to try anything."

"What, not even a goodnight kiss?"

"Not even a handshake!"

They burst out laughing again.

"God! The thought of being stuck in a car all day with him, the Knight of the Road, would just about finish me off! Do me a favour, would you, Frances?"

"What?"

"If I show any more signs of being nice to him or of encouraging him give me a smack right on the nose, would you?"

***

Geri decided to have breakfast on a table inside the restaurant thus avoiding the rest of the group. She'd seen some of them sitting outside and had just managed to duck her head in time when Donna and Dawn walked by on their way to reception. They looked as if they were going out somewhere. She saw that Dawn had a large plaster over her nose. Something must have happened to Dawn that she didn't know about! She'd have to chat to them later and find out what it was. She didn't really like Dawn and Donna. She found them a bit twee and old fashioned; quite pathetic, really. They must be forty if they were a day, yet here they were dressed like two silly schoolgirls. She felt the same about men who couldn't grow up. At her last school there had been a bunch of male teachers who really thought they were *it*. They'd all given each other silly nicknames, like Smithy, Mazza, and Robbo. How sad was that? Grown men still calling themselves the nicknames their mates had given them when they were twelve.

A bit like Deano.....

She shook her head. Deano was different. She'd decided to have her breakfast and then take care with her appearance and go down to the beach to join the others as if nothing had happened. That way they were sure to ask her where she'd been last night and she could tell them the story she'd invented about an Antiguan hunk and the beautiful people on the yachts in Falmouth Harbour.

***

Grace was in a little world of her own as she lay in the dappled shade of a palm tree, listening intermittently to the others' conversation and then drifting off for a few moments into a pleasant, tranquil twilight zone of almost-sleep. But when she felt the moist, cool hand start to work its way up her thigh her reaction was automatic. She flicked her wrist and Zebedee, the wizened, toothless aloe vera seller, found himself face down in the sand with his arm in a lock up his back in two seconds flat.

"Wa! Wa! I ain't done nothing, Lady, I ain't done nothing!" he protested, spitting sand from his mouth and grimacing in pain at the same time.

"Fucking hell, Grace!" Stewart spilt his drink in surprise. It dribbled onto his shorts, which were fortunately an array of green, blue and orange swirls so the stain didn't show.

"I was only trying to sell you some aloe vera for your skin," Zebedee continued to protest.

The others looked on in silent amazement as Grace pulled him to his feet with one swift tug. She held him by the front of his t-shirt just six short inches away from her face.

"The next time, try selling it without touching the buyer. 'Cos if you touch me again you won't only end up face down in the sand, but you'll have your aloe vera plant stuck up your arse at the same time. Do I make myself clear?" She shook him a little. Zebedee nodded. Grace released her hold on him.

"Now, piss off!" she said.

There was a cacophony of laughter, howls and comments from the other beach vendors who had seen what happened as Zebedee stumbled up the beach putting as much space between himself and Grace as quickly as he could. When he thought he was at a safe distance he turned and started to yell abuse at her, telling her she was a crazy woman and that he was going to inform the *po-lees*. Murray, who was on his way back from cancelling the hire car and had been a spectator to what had happened, made a beeline for the group to find out what was going on.

"What are yer? A bouncer?" Dave, the first to regain his voice, asked her.

"No. I'm a police officer."

"Oi oi! I love a woman in uniform!"

"Dave, shut up!" Natalie said. "You're so predictable!"

"It's alright, Natalie," Grace said. "It's the usual reaction and it's why I never tell people what I do."

"So it's WPC Grace, is it?" Murray joined in. "We'll have tae watch ourselves with you, won't we?" Murray held his arms out in front of him. "It would never do if you had tae handcuff me and punish me, would it?"

Natalie looked at him for a moment then mimed sticking two fingers in her mouth and vomiting. Grace sighed. She'd avoided talking about work for four days and now she'd dropped herself in it.

"I haven't been in uniform and I haven't been a PC for quite some years now."

"Oooh! Sergeant Grace!"

"Actually, it's Detective Chief Superintendant."

The silence was tangible.

"It must be very exciting being a Detective Chief Superintendant," Suzanne said, suddenly. "You must see and do a lot of really interesting things."

"Yes, I suppose *interesting* is one word you could use to describe it."

"You're better lookin' than Morse an' Frost!" Dave said. "And that bird in Taggart. I can't understand what she says, except 'murrrrderrrr'. I fink they should show it wiv subtitles. No offence, Murray!" he added quickly.

Grace laughed.

"Well, now you all know!"

"Excuse me, the girls are waiting for me," Murray said, backing away. He loved being the bearer of news. Like Geri he thought it gave him a certain authority or kudos with other people. Wait until Deborah heard this!

"The ladies have such exciting jobs," Trevor said. "Natalie's a dancing teacher, Jo's a vicar, Grace is a senior police officer, but I just work in a bank. That's boring, isn't it?"

"Bankin's where the money is!" Dave said.

"How long have you worked in the bank for?" Natalie asked him.

"Since I left school and that is a long time ago! I could have taken retirement by now but I don't know what I'd do if I didn't go to work. I mean, I try to keep busy all the time; since Pearl died I've kept up the garden and I go to Spanish classes and Latin American dancing twice a week."

"You're a sly orse!" Dave said. "Latin American dancing and learning Spanish, eh? You ad oliday romance or sumfink? Got some señorita on the go?"

"No! Although I wouldn't mind one!" he said, making them all laugh. "It just gets me out of the house a few evenings a week, if not I'd go crazy just watching television."

"Haven't you got any family?" Suzanne asked him.

"Yes, but I don't see them that much. My son lives in Yorkshire. He went to university at York and met a girl and stayed on. He's the editor of a small regional newspaper. And Rose, my daughter, lives in Birmingham. She's a social worker."

"Haven't you got any grandchildren?" Suzanne went on.

"Only one grandson: Joe. He's seventeen and off to university himself next year."

"Is that your son's son or your daughter's?"

"My son's."

"Isn't your daughter married?"

"No. She has a long-term partner. Sonia."

"Oh, I see," Suzanne said. "Oh! A woman!" she added as the penny dropped.

"Now she really does see!" Deano said,

Trevor nodded.

"It's not a lifestyle I'd have chosen for her, but she seems happy enough," he sighed.

"Wouldn't you rather she was happy with a woman who loves and takes care of her, as opposed to a man who mistreats her?" Jo asked him.

"Yes, If you put it like that, I suppose I would," he nodded.

"Well I think you must have a lovely life," Natalie jumped in. "And I bet all the women fight over you at dancing class."

"I should be so lucky! There are some very pleasant women there, but most of them have a regular dance partner."

"No widows showing an interest in going round the floor with you? You're a real catch, Trevor," Natalie insisted.

"Not at dancing there aren't. But I've had to be careful with a couple of them from Church. One woman, Mrs Patterson, was very friendly and always offering to do things for me.

I met her when I stayed behind after the service on Sunday mornings, you know, they serve tea and biscuits and it's quite nice to chat and meet people. Well, I found Mrs Patterson to be very friendly and chatty, and after she'd made me some chicken stew and brought it round when I was poorly with the flu, I invited her to the pictures as a thank you."

"And what happened?"

"We went to the pictures and the next week, as a thank you for taking her to the pictures, she invited me to see the local drama society's version of Anything Goes."

"And did anything go?" Natalie giggled.

"No, but it wasn't for want of her trying! I was really embarrassed. I took her home and she invited me in for a drink and just outright asked me to stay the night!"

Everyone laughed.

"You old rascal!" Dave said.

"Woo hoo!" Natalie laughed, slapping her thigh.

"And did you?" Deano asked.

"No I didn't! I got out as quickly as I could and I've avoided her ever since. I didn't like her, you know, in that way. I mean, I liked her but I didn't fancy her. I could have gone to bed with her but I might not have enjoyed it and I didn't want to start something I couldn't finish."

Everyone burst out laughing at that, but Trevor, oblivious to what he'd said just carried on.

"I'd just thought we were friends. And, besides, you can never be sure if someone isn't after your money."

"Are you worth a few bob then, Trevor?" Natalie asked.

"I'm not a rich man, but I've got my own house and a good pension," he said earnestly, making everyone laugh again.

"Well, I think it's a lovely story," Suzanne said, and Dave nudged Stewart hard in the ribs.

"What about the rest of the men, then?" Grace said. "We know what Trevor does; what about the rest of you?"

"I'm a car dealer and Stew's a dee-jay." Dave said.

"You're a dee-jay? Are you on the radio?" Suzanne asked him.

"No. Pubs and clubs and weddings mostly."

"That must be so exciting!"

Dave nudged Stewart again.

"What do you do, Suzanne?" Jo asked.

"I run a corner shop and general store in the small village, in Norfolk, where we live."

"That sounds like hard work."

"Not really although it is long hours. Well, it's fine most of the time. Busy, you know. But we get up really early to do the papers and we don't close until seven in the evening and to be honest it's getting a lot for Mum to do so I'm doing more and more."

"You need a man abaht the place." Dave winked at Stewart who moved out of the way before Dave could nudge him for a third time.

"We have a good security system installed. We're connected to the local police by an alarm under the counter. We had that put in after someone tried to rob us last year."

"Surely your mum's not on her own in the shop now, is she?" Jo asked.

"My Auntie, the one who lives in Majorca's come over to help out for a few weeks so that I could get away. With her husband Pedro. That was nice of them, wasn't it?" Suzanne looked at her watch. "We'd be watching Jeremy Kyle now if I was at home."

"Oh, God! Britain's underclass gets its fifteen minutes of fame!" Deano said. "Spotty drug-addict seventeen-year-old has kid with fourteen-year-old neighbour who then finds out he's also shagging her mum who he's also got pregnant, which is a surprise to her lesbian lover who didn't know and who the shallow youth stole two hundred pounds benefits money from!"

"Yeah, that abaht sums it up. You ain't gotta av no teef ter go on it," Dave said. "You noticed? Nobody on there eva as any teef."

"And he's right up his own arse, I can't stand Kyle," Deano added.

"How do you watch Jeremy Kyle if you're busy in the shop?" Stewart asked her.

It goes a bit quiet about ten o'clock. The school run's over and that's when we have a coffee. We've got a little TV set behind the counter so we can watch the programmes we like if it's quiet."

"What do you do, Deano?" Grace asked bringing the subject back to jobs.

"I work in the import business."

"Importing what?"

"Pottery, paintings, statues."

"Where from?"

"Developing countries mainly; Latin America and sub-Saharan Africa. What's this line of questioning? Am I under arrest, Chief Superintendant?"

Everyone laughed, Grace loudest of all.

"No! I was just interested, that's all!"

"I've got my import licences and the whole business is bona fide."

"What does Michael do?" Suzanne asked. Everyone turned to look at him. He was fast asleep, earphones in, untroubled by the noise and completely unaware of the drama that had just unfolded next to him.

"He works for a mobile phone company. T-mobile I think, he said," Natalie said. "What about Geri? Anyone know what she does?"

"She said she used to be a PE teacher," Trevor said, "but she didn't say what she does now."

"Well, we can ask her," Stewart said looking back towards the low brick wall. "Here she comes."

A growl went round the group as Deano grabbed his Kindle and became immersed in it. Several of the others put their ear phones back into their ears and lay down. Geri sashayed up to them.

"Morning, everyone! Another beautiful day!"

She seemed oblivious to the silence that greeted her as she dropped her beach bag onto the sand and pulled a sun bed as close as she possibly could to Deano's, which wasn't too close as he had deliberately boxed himself in with Jo on the right, Dave on the left and Michael just in front of him. Geri took off her sun dress, folded it up and placed it in her bag and then put her towel on the sun bed before sitting down. She reached into her bag again and pulled out her suntan lotion, put a splodge of it into her hand and then tried to reach behind her.

"Shall I do that for you?" Grace asked, standing up. "I know it can be difficult reaching your back."

"It's okay. I'm going to do my front today," Geri said, putting the lotion on her chest and stomach and starting to rub it in.

"Did you all enjoy yourselves last night?"

128

Grace looked around. She was the only one who appeared not to be sleeping, reading or lost in music. It would be gross rudeness to ignore the woman.

"Yes, we had a great time."

Geri waited a moment but it soon became obvious that Grace wasn't going to ask her about her evening. But then again, now wasn't the moment to tell them what a fabulous time she'd had because they weren't listening. She'd wait until later when she had their full attention.

***

Only Murray had come to see Eve during her morning surgery. After the little episode with Geri she'd realised she was late and so she'd grabbed a juice and croissant from the buffet and had gone to sit on the bar terrace where she'd told them she'd be. She knew from experience that most would be recovering from the night before; she smiled at the memory of them dancing and singing their hearts out and she'd put money on the fact that most of them probably carried on drinking until the bar closed. She saw Jason and Huw walk towards the big pool. Jason waved and called out "Morning, Eve!" but Huw didn't even acknowledge her. Eve would always do everything in her power for her group to have the best holiday possible, but she had little time for petulance and she'd met a lot of petulant people in the years she'd worked for Travel Together. She'd lost count of the so-called grown-ups who stamped their foot the moment they didn't get their own way. She looked at her watch and saw it was almost a quarter to eleven. She had to go and get the money from her safe and bank it and pick up the ticket for the catamaran trip which Sunny had arranged to leave at the reception desk. She started to gather her things when Murray came over.

"I want tae go on that boat trip. Have you put me down?"

Thinking that putting him down might solve a lot of problems; Eve told him she hadn't, at the same time resisting the temptation to add that he hadn't said he was going and she wasn't clairvoyant. And she had a sense of déjà vu. Wasn't this a replay of what had happened yesterday morning? Hadn't he appeared then just as she was going?

"Can I pay you tonight?" he asked.

"I don't usually take money in the evenings, but bring it down to dinner if you want."

"Well, either that or I can pay you in the morning before we go."

"No, tonight's fine. I'll put the money in for you, as long as you're sure you want to go because once I tell them you're going and we change the ticket you'll have to pay even if you change your mind as it's under twenty-four hours."

Murray grunted.

"I'll nae run off with your money. I'll bring it tonight." And off he went.

Thank you, Eve, for putting me on at the last minute and for trusting me about the payment.

Oh, you're welcome, Murray!

Eve put everything away in her bag and went back to her room. She smiled and waved at Carlo and April as she breezed through the reception area and then swept down the corridor to her room to pick up the money and go to the bank. When she got inside her room she had a huge surprise. One of the most enormous, beautiful floral arrangements she had ever seen was sitting on the dressing table. Next to it was a fruit basket, complete with a white linen napkin wrapped around a sharp knife and a fork. Nestling among the blooms was Melv's business card with an envelope stapled to it. Eve separated the envelope from the card and opened it up and took out the handwritten note.

Eve,

Please accept this little gift.

Seeing you was the most wonderful surprise and I'd really like to invite you to dinner or at least for a drink somewhere off-premises where we can relax, be ourselves and catch up on the last thirty years. How can it be so long? My extension is 8090. Please ring me and say 'yes'.

Melv xx

Eve sank onto the bed. Her instinct was to ignore it; ignore him. After all, their relationship had been over for thirty years, why rake up the past? Who was he, after all, except an old boyfriend? She'd had lots of them over the years. She gave a deep sigh.

Who am I kidding?

In her heart of hearts, Eve knew that Melv had been *the one*. It had taken her for ever to get over him; every man she'd ever been out with had been compared to him and had always been found wanting. And she knew that he would want to talk about the way things had ended; even after all this time he might think he deserved some answers.

Why put yourself through it, Eve? Why stir it up, all those feelings, all that emotion, after all this time?

And yet... And yet she knew that she did want to see him again and if she let this opportunity go by she might always regret it.

He's not asking you to marry him! He's already got a wife.

She picked up the phone and dialled 8090 before she could change her mind. The phone rang four times and then she heard a woman's voice;

"Good-day. Mr McGrass's phone. How may I help you?"

"I'd like to speak to Mr McGrass, please."

"He's out of office right now. Can I take a message?"

"No! No, I mean, no thank you. I'll call him back. When will he be available?"

"At around one o'clock. Who shall I say called?"

Eve hung up. There was no way she was leaving her name with a secretary. She knew she could pretend it was hotel business but she wanted to talk to Melv personally. She picked up his business card, which showed a cell phone number. Dialling 9 for an outside line, Eve rang the cell phone. Melv picked up on the second ring.

"Good day. Melvyn McGrass."

"Hi! It's me. Me. It's Eve. I... um... thank you for the beautiful flowers and for the fruit."

Christ! I sound about fourteen!

"Hi, Eve, what's up? I'm glad you liked them."

There was a pause.

"You're ringing me so I guess you'd like us to have dinner together."

"Well, not dinner. It's difficult because of the group. I've booked us all in at the Crazy Conch tonight and I really have to go with them. But if none of them wants to go out afterwards I could meet you for a drink."

"That sounds good. What time do you think you'll be through?"

"Probably not until about ten."

"That's fine. I'll pick you up outside the main gate at ten. If you get held up then just give me a call and we can rearrange."

"Okay."

"So I'll see you at ten."

"Okay."

Shit! Say something else, you stupid woman!

131

"You have a good day now." And he was gone.

In spite of the air conditioning unit, which was going like the clappers, Eve's hand was sweating so much she almost dropped the phone as she tried to put it back in its cradle. She sat, motionless, on the bed with one thought going round and round in her head.

I'm going on a date with Melv. I'm going on a date with Melv.

She suddenly snapped out of her reverie. She had things to do. Why was she making such a thing of having a drink with an old boyfriend? People did that every day. Since the advent of Friends Reunited and Facebook millions of people have got in touch with old friends. It was a surprise they hadn't done so before. Or that their paths hadn't crossed given the number of trips Eve had led, not just to Antigua but to the rest of the Caribbean.

Get on with your day!

She stood up and opened her safe. She had work to do! But she was going to give herself a little reward of a swim today, come hell or high water. She smiled at her own pun, but really yearned to get into the sea. And besides, she felt that not only she deserved it, but it would calm her nerves ready for whatever she was going to face that night.

***

"She's a police officer! A Detective Chief Superintendant!" Murray was beside himself with pleasure as he gave the gossip to Frances and Deborah.

"Well, she has to be something," Frances said. She liked Grace and she didn't want Murray to drag her into any gossip about her.

"Aye, but you'd think she was a secretary or something, would you not? Not a high ranking police officer."

"And what's wrong with being a secretary?" Frances asked, bristling.

"There's nothing wri' it. I'm just saying that that's what you'd expect a woman like her tae be, or a teacher or something a bit more mundane." Murray said, defensively.

"I disagree," Deborah said. "If you look at her she exudes an air of authority. She obviously works out because she's trim and fit, and she's very well groomed."

"But a Detective Chief Superintendant!" Murray insisted.

"So you could envisage her being a constable, is that it?" Frances asked him. "I'm not really surprised after all you wouldn't mess with her, as you've found out when you tried," she added. "She's given you your answer a couple of times."

Deborah grinned at Frances.

"Is that what you are then, Frances, a secretary?"

"Yes. I'm a legal secretary. I work for a solicitor who specialises in divorce cases."

"That must have come in handy for you then," Murray said, nastily. "You are a divorcee, I take it?"

"Good job she's not a recent widow, Mr Sensitive," Deborah threw at him.

"I mean, I expect he gave you the benefit of his expertise and probably some company discount," Murray said, unaware that he was still digging.

"She gave me the full benefit of her expertise to guide me through my divorce and refused point blank to charge me anything. She prides herself that her job is *'taking the bastards for all they've got.'* And I love working for her."

Murray's face was a picture. Already red from the sun, he now turned puce. His top lip pulled back in a snarl.

"Aye! That's typical, that is. Always blame the man for the divorce. Always say it's down tae him."

Deborah and Frances looked at him in amazement as he leapt to his feet, fists clenched, fury making his accent suddenly much more pronounced.

"You know nothing about me or the circumstances of my divorce," Frances said. She wasn't going to be bullied by the likes of Murray.

"Exactly! All cases are different and yet the scales are always weighted against the man and people like your boss make that so. You tell me I know nothing about your divorce, well let me tell you, that your boss doesnae know shite about a lot of men. Ma ex-wife walked out on me, not the other way round. I came home from work one day tae find a note telling me that she'd taken ma two wee kids tae Crete tae set up a restaurant with some slimy Greek bastard she'd met when we were on holiday the previous year. She'd been having an affair wi' him right under ma nose and I didnae have a clue. It took years of going tae court and it nearly bankrupted me trying tae get my kids back, but the court found in her favour. They said the kids were settled in Crete and didnae wanna come home tae me and if I wanted tae see them I'd have tae go to Crete because she put on a big crying act and said she feared I'd nae let them go back tae her if they came and visited me in Scotland. And then I had tae sell the house, the place that had been our family home, and give half the money tae her! So don't talk to me about bastards! What about the bitches who get everything they dinnae deserve just because they're bloody females!"

And with that he stormed off. Several people around the pool were looking over at Deborah and Frances. Most were giving them dirty looks because the Spa Pool was a quiet area. But some had amused grins on their faces. Deborah and Frances looked at each other.

"I think it's rum punch time," Deborah said.

"Double rum punch time," Frances added just as Deborah's phone rang. "I'll get them," Frances said, moving off giving Deborah some privacy to take the call.

***

Walking along the beach enjoying the feel of the sun on her shoulders and the warm sand between her toes, Eve could actually feel herself relaxing. She'd banked the money and picked up the ticket for the following day and now she could actually indulge herself for an hour or so and try not to think about her date that evening. She reprimanded herself; it wasn't a date, it was just a drink, a chat, a catch-up. Going on a date turned it into something it wasn't. And besides, Melv was married and there was no way she was going down that road again. She allowed herself a little grin, though, as she remembered Melv as an earnest, sexy twenty-two-year-old student. She'd fallen for him the moment she'd seen him; so handsome, so exciting, so different from anyone she'd ever met before. She was brought out of her daydream by the sound of someone loudly calling her name. She looked around to see a large contingent of the group sitting on the beach together. She changed track and walked over to join them, passing as she did Geri, who was having her hair braided.

"Take a seat!" Dave said, moving his legs and making room for her on his sun lounger.

Eve sat down, pulling her sarong across her legs and tucking the end under her thighs, conscious of their size compared to the likes of Natalie and Grace, who didn't have an inch of cellulite between them.

"Want a Wadiddly? I was just going to get a round in," Stewart said.

"Not a beer, but I'll have a Diet Coke if you're going, thanks."

"Same again for everyone?" Stewart asked.

"Has a rag doll got cloth tits?" Natalie asked.

"Yes, please!" the others chorused.

"Having a bit of time to yourself?" Suzanne asked Eve.

"Yes. I thought I'd go for a swim. I haven't been in the sea yet."

"Oh, it's gorgeous! Like a warm bath!" Suzanne replied. "I don't like the water much but I can't keep out of it."

Eve looked round the group. Everyone had taken out their earphones or put down their books to include her.

"She turned up, then," Dave said, nodding towards Geri. "She ain't told us nuffink abaht where she went. She told you?"

Eve shook her head. She sensed, the rest of the group didn't really take to Geri, and it didn't have all that much to do with her disappearing act of the previous evening.

"She doesn't know what to do next to get attention," Natalie said. "I mean, hair braiding? Unless you're black or seventeen you look ridiculous."

"Or Bo Derek!" Dave said. "I'll never forget seein' er fallin' out of er bikini and swingin' er air beads when I was young and impressionable. Cor!" The men all laughed as the women groaned. "I just ope the Dolly Sisters don't get it done when they see er. That'd be all we need!"

"Don't you get a day off?" Natalie asked Eve.

"Not really, but I get a few hours most days, you know, in between seeing off trips and doing paperwork, to have a swim or to relax a bit, go shopping."

"Yes but you never know what's going to happen, do you? I suppose you always have to be on call in case one of us has an accident or does something silly."

"That's true, but that's why I give everyone my mobile phone number so that if you need me and I'm out of the resort you can reach me."

"You've got a lovely job, though, haven't you?" Suzanne said.

"When it's all going right it's the best job in the world," Eve agreed. "It becomes a way of life really, more than a job."

"Well, it's more exciting than mine," Trevor said as Stewart reappeared with a beer in each hand and Noah, the waiter, in tow, carrying a tray laden with drinks.

"You work in banking, don't you, Trevor?" Eve asked.

"Yes. I live in Hertfordshire and commute to the City every day. All the days are the same, they all roll into one. At least you have a beautiful office," he said, opening his arms wide to encompass the beach.

"I don't complain," Eve said.

Everyone helped themselves to drinks from Noah and Stewart and took long swigs, enjoying the moment when their thirst began to be quenched.

135

"You know you can always come and sit with us, don't you?" Natalie said. "Don't be on your own. Well, unless you want to be, that is. But if you want some company we're here."

"Yes," agreed, Suzanne, "don't feel you can't join us. After all, you are one of the group!"

"Aw, thank you!" Eve replied, genuinely touched by their friendliness. Occasionally she'd felt like the hired help when she'd accompanied a group, so it was nice to feel included.

Suddenly, Rod Stewart's voice singing *Maggie May* disturbed the peace and quiet as a powerful motorboat roared round the headland and whooshed to a halt in the shallow waters on the edge of the beach. Everyone turned around to look at the statuesque blonde who clambered out, helped by a younger black man with waist-length braids and a body that shouted *'I work out for three hours every day!'* The woman turned and walked up the beach as the man went over and high-fived the young guy who ran the jet-ski rides before engaging him in a loud and energetic conversation. As the woman drew near to the group she smiled and called out.

"Eve? Eve? Is that you?"

Eve jumped up as she recognised the voice and ran towards her with arms outstretched.

"Georgina! How lovely to see you! What a surprise! I should have realised it was you when I heard Rod Stewart!"

The two women hugged tightly then both took a step back and looked each other up and down.

"You look great!" they both said in unison, and then burst out laughing and hugged again.

"You here with a group again?"

"Yes, and you with a hunk from what I see!"

"That's Cranleigh. I met him last time I was here, in March."

"Nice boat!"

"Yes, but it's not his. He's borrowed it from a friend for a couple of days."

"Nice friend!"

"Yes, but I don't ask too many questions, if you know what I mean!" Georgina laughed at herself.

"Where are you staying?"

"I've got an apartment in Dickinson Bay this time. It gives me a bit more privacy than staying in a hotel. You know, no security guards watching your every move in and out."

"How long are you here for?"

"Three weeks; I leave on Saturday week. You?"

"Just eleven days this time; we leave next Monday."

"Well, we'll have to meet up for a drink before then. I'll give you a call."

The two women hugged again and Georgina sashayed back down the beach where Cranleigh helped her into the boat. It roared into life and speed round the bay and out of sight to the strains of *We Are Sailing*. Eve chuckled to herself as she went back to join the group.

"That was Georgina! She was in one of my Travel Together groups about eighteen months ago and she's been back four or five times since then."

"Looks like she's found a reason for returning," Grace said. "He was quite something!"

"We could all look like that!" Dave said, "But we've got lives, ain't we, lads? We don't spend all day workin' out."

"Envy is a dreadful thing, Dave!" Natalie said. "It'll make you all bitter and twisted!"

"Rubbish!" Deano joined in. "Look at the two of them. I mean, race apart, you take off the muscle and the hair and put on fifteen years and you've got Dave!"

"Yeah!" Dave said before realising it wasn't a compliment. "Oi! You're s'posed to be on my side, Deano. Us white unks av ter stick togevva. Oh, sorry! No offence, Michael!"

"None taken," Michael laughed. "When it comes to women I can see that you two have got it all sewn up!"

The women screamed with laughter and after a couple of seconds the men joined in, too.

"How many drinks have I had?" Jo asked, suddenly.

"That's your second. Why?" Deano said.

"I thought I could hear *Here Comes the Bride*."

"You can," Eve said. "There's a wedding today."

"Oh, yes! Those girls who were in the bar the other night," Suzanne said, standing up. "Shall we go and watch?"

Dave elbowed Stewart, spilling his drink as everyone wandered along the beach towards the wedding arbour, where a nervous-looking, red-faced groom stood sweating in a three-piece suit waiting to be joined in matrimony to a girl who was laced into a tight-fitting bodice, which showed off her white swimsuit strap marks and large heart tattoo against lobster red shoulders, and was tottering along in high-heeled shoes underneath a huge meringue skirt. She was on the arm of an older man, who was dressed the same as the bridegroom; dark grey suit and waistcoat with a fuchsia cravat, with six grown up bridesmaids, wearing narrower versions of the bridal dress in fuchsia, holding the hands of five little girls wearing baby pink. Everyone was sweating profusely. Eve had never understood people who brought English Wedding to the Caribbean. Why be uncomfortable in such heavy clothes when it was 90F with eighty percent humidity? Surely they'd be better off in cotton or linen; a flowing cheesecloth dress for her and cut-offs and a beach shirt for him?

Suddenly, as the final notes of the steel band's recording faded, Natalie burst into tears, turned and ran. Grace, Jo, Michael and Eve, the only ones who noticed, looked at each other, puzzled and unsure of what to do.

"I'll go," Eve said, setting off up the beach behind her.

***

"Have you ever been married, Deborah?" Frances asked as the two women stood in the shallow end of the Spa Pool, sipping mojitos, prompted by the faint sounds of the wedding music.

"No."

There was a short silence while Frances composed her next question.

"Do you work?"

"No."

"Have you ever worked?"

"Yes."

"What did you do?"

Deborah didn't reply.

"Or is it a secret?"

Deborah took a long sip of her drink and then stirred the straw around, studying the bottom of the glass, weighing up how much of her life she wanted to reveal to Frances, knowing how it probably sounded to outsiders who wouldn't, couldn't understand.

"I used to work as a secretary, too. Well, a PA actually, for twenty-two years. Then my boss retired, so I retired, too."

"Ooh! Lucky you being able to retire so young! You must have had a really good pension, then?"

"Sort of." Deborah vigorously stirred her drink again, which was mainly just melting ice and mint now. Frances looked at her expectantly; she wasn't going to let her off the hook. Deborah knew a lot about her and now she wanted to know about Deborah. Deborah sighed.

"For the twenty-two years I worked I had an affair with my boss, Maurice. When he retired he wanted me to retire, too, so that we could spend time together."

Frances looked at her quizzically.

"So, how come you're on a singles holiday if you're spending time with your ex-boss?"

"Oh, we've never been on holiday together. Every year when he took his annual leave I had to work to keep his diary and his affairs up to scratch. Then I'd go away to the Norfolk Broads with my family or I'd just stay at home. After my parents died I'd go with my sister and brother-in-law and a group of their friends to Barbados, to the Sandy Lane every Christmas. Maurice would always pay for it, obviously."

"Obviously!" Frances said her tone deeply sarcastic.

"Well, he didn't like the idea of me spending Christmas alone and spending it with him was out of the question."

I'll bet!

"So, what happened? What changed?"

"Eight months ago he had a stroke. He didn't turn up one day. You see, his wife thought he was still working part-time, two days a week, Mondays and Wednesdays. But those days he came and spent the day with me; nine to five-thirty." Deborah smiled at her thoughts. "I'd have breakfast ready for him and then we'd spend the morning reading the papers together and then have lunch followed by a siesta, before he had afternoon tea and then left."

"That was very cosy! And how long did that you on for? You know, playing happy families?"

Deborah noticed Frances' disapproving tone.

"For seven years."

"And all this time, for the last seven years, his wife thought he was still at work?"

"Yes. Oh don't look at me like that! People don't understand; can't understand! This man was my all for twenty-two years; a whole lifetime."

"So for twenty-nine years you've been his bit on the side?"

"I was the love of his life! I still am!"

"So how come he never left his wife for you?"

"He has children, of course. His children were in their early teens when we met. It would have been too much of an upheaval for them. And besides, they would never have accepted me as their stepmother. Maurice's wife would have seen to that."

Deborah paused and Frances flipped onto her back for a moment to cool down. She ducked her head under the water, keeping her glass in the air, and then stood up, nodding at Deborah to continue.

"So what happened when he had his stroke then?"

"A few days after he had it I heard from one of his friends who'd gone to visit him in hospital. I'd been frantic with worry when he hadn't showed up and I hadn't heard from him. Maurice sent his daughter out on an errand and once he and Jim, the friend, were alone he told him to call me and tell me. I went straight to the hospital to see him and she was there. Sadie. The wife. She stood barring the entrance to the Intensive Care Unit. *'Well, I wondered how long it would be before Miss Saigon turned up,'* she said. *'I don't know how you've got the nerve to show your face, but then, what more could be expected from the likes of you? For over twenty years I had no option but to speak to you every time I phoned my husband at work even though it killed me to do so. Now I don't have to be nice and polite to you any longer. You're not wanted here. Maurice has his family around him now and we're all he needs so you can just fuck off back under the stone you crawled out from.'* And she turned and went back inside. She'd even given orders to the nurses not to tell me how he was over the phone. I was devastated, as you can imagine, not knowing what was happening to him. It was a really depressing, difficult time."

Deborah put her empty glass on the side of the pool and wiped the tear that was running down her cheek away with the heel of her hand.

"Did he die?"

"No. He's slowly recovering. He phones me whenever he can but it's impossible for him to come and see me. And the monthly allowance he's always paid me has been stopped and so have the rent cheques to the management agency. It's a good job I've got some savings put by. But I know that it's her doing! She's taken over the running of all his affairs and bank accounts and has power of attorney. She's stopped it all. How spiteful can you get?"

Frances didn't answer. She looked at Deborah in disbelief, knowing that only on one other occasion had she wanted to slap another woman so much. But Deborah was lost, wrapped up in the memory of Maurice and the life they'd shared together in a parallel universe to the real one he had with Sadie and the family.

"He was always very generous and he knew I'd given up a lot to be with him. He didn't like me going out on my own, but he paid for me to do some courses, you know, interesting things like aromatherapy, creative writing and floral art."

"Can't you earn a living from doing any of them?"

"Well, no, I've never worked at any of them. I had to be there for Maurice. I just went on the courses to give me something to do. You know, I was able to give him wonderful aromatherapy massages and the floral art meant my flat always has the most beautiful floral arrangements. He likes me, us, to surround ourselves with beautiful things."

"So did he pay for you to come on this holiday, then?"

"No. My sister did. She can be brutal at times. She said I'd spent enough time locked away and needed to get out and enjoy myself. It's alright for her, though. She married an older man, a surgeon, who she met when she was working as a nurse. She's never wanted for anything; he still treats her like a princess after all this time. And she's a very talented dress designer. She gave up nursing once they married and he set her up in her own boutique once the children were at school and she's never looked back. But because she's had the Mills and Boon novel she thinks everyone should have it. She wouldn't give up with me. She kept on sending me e-mail links to various singles' holiday companies and dating sites. In the end we quarrelled over it and we haven't spoken to each other for two months. It felt wrong coming away when we've fallen out and she's paid for the holiday but I'll go and see her when I get home. I know she means well and I know how it looks to other people. Samantha, that's my sister, is always saying that I've thrown my life away on Maurice and perhaps... well ... she might be right in a way. So, I thought about it a lot and ... hell... what's the harm? So I decided to come. Maurice wasn't happy about it, naturally."

"Is that him that keeps on ringing you?"

"Yes. Now that he's recovering he can go out into the garden or into his study or take a little walk to the local shop and so he takes advantage of that and rings me."

"What, is he checking up on you?"

"No! He just wants to talk to me."

"Well, it seems to me as if it's a control thing. He's ringing you at all hours to check up what you're doing and who you're with, making sure you're not having too much of a good time. That's why you won't have your photo done, isn't it? In case anyone in the group posts their pictures on Facebook or the Travel Together website. He might see you enjoying yourself with other men."

Deborah turned angrily and faced Frances.

"You know nothing about him! About us! Maurice loves me! If he didn't he wouldn't keep in touch. He's just living for the day he'll be strong enough to come and see me again, so that we can pick up where we left off. We both are."

"Oh get real! He's a man, isn't he? He's got a huge ego. You've been his bit on the side for years and now he can't stand the thought that someone else might be with you."

"I wasn't his bit on the side!"

"Don't make me laugh! Women like you are a disgrace. You've no qualms about taking someone else's husband. You encourage him to carry on behind the wife's back; lying to her, cheating on her, giving you what should be going to his kids."

Around the pool people, who had at first tried to pretend they weren't listening, were now putting down their books and openly looking at the two women having a slanging match in the pool.

"It wasn't like that! Our relationship has been deeper than most marriages."

"You're a stupid, selfish woman!" Frances slammed her empty glass so hard on the blue porcelain tiles edging the pool that it shattered. "Have you no conscience? Did you never once think about his wife? About that other poor woman who's also wasted her life on him?"

"She chose to stay with him. She could have left but she was too comfortable; she knew what side her bread was buttered. Maurice gave her a good home and a good lifestyle."

"No! *She* made the home for *him*! Can't you see? He was the one that was comfortable for all those years."

"Their marriage was loveless; it was practically an arranged one, sorted out by their fathers, two wealthy Jewish men who wanted their children to marry so that they could keep up appearances."

"Oh, please! Don't tell me you've swallowed the *'my wife doesn't understand me'* lie for twenty-nine years! He's had you on a piece of string. And what about all the lies he's told her when he's been with you? And how do you know what he's said to her throughout the years? When they've been alone in bed at night, two heads on the pillow, discussing dreams, and making plans? Eh? I bet he told you they haven't had sex for years, too, didn't he?"

Deborah, her face red and flustered, turned away from Frances and made for the steps to get out of the pool. A waiter hurried over with a broom and pan to sweep up the broken glass.

"Did you cut yourself, Ma'am?" he asked Frances. She shook her head and clambered out of the pool after Deborah, determined not to let her get away until she'd finished telling her just what she thought of her. Deborah grabbed her towel from the lounger and started vigorously drying herself, giving her actions her full attention. Frances sat down on her lounger.

"The trouble with women like you is that you don't realise the harm you do, or the hurt and pain that you cause."

"Women like me? What do you want me to do wear a scarlet letter? For God's sake, Frances! I'm not the only one!"

"Oh, I'm well aware of that! But because adultery's common it doesn't make it right, does it? For three years my husband had a sordid little affair with some office junior, who was eighteen years younger than him. They had sex in such classy places at the men's toilets at work until she got a flat on her own in Leeds and he'd go there every Wednesday night when he told me he was playing snooker with the lads. All the time we were planning our son's future at university and beyond and talking about how we could perhaps save up and buy a little holiday flat in Spain, he was telling her that he was just waiting for Darren to leave home so that he could move in with her. It was only when Darren went to Warwick in October 2007 and Martin didn't move straight in with her that she decided to try to hurry things along. She phoned me up, out of the blue, and told me straight that he loved her not me, gave me every detail of their three years together and told me to *do the honourable thing* and let him go. I told her she wouldn't know honour if it jumped up and bit her on the arse and neither would he. But I also told her she was welcome to him. When he came home that night, all his clothes were in bin liners sitting in the front garden and the locks were changed. He went mad; first of all he denied knowing any woman called Kylie, but then he said he did know her and she'd fancied him for ages and when he rebuffed her she'd said she'd get even with him by telling me they'd had an affair."

"And how do you know that wasn't true?" Deborah jumped in. "Something must have been really wrong in your marriage if you were just prepared to believe everything she said without giving your husband a chance to defend himself."

"Oh, I checked up, alright! She was able to give me dates, times and places. She described in detail the hotel in the Cotswolds he'd taken her to when I thought he was in Cardiff on a course. And I knew she was telling the truth because he'd taken me there the previous year when I had my first cancer scare. She described his body with a detail that only someone that'd seen him in the buff and knew every nook and cranny of it could, right down to the mole on his right bum cheek. Yet he still tried to deny it. And I just knew that I could never forgive him. Or forget. I knew that he was capable of anything; he'd told me so many lies that I could never trust him again. Darren even spoke up for him. He said his dad had had a midlife crisis; that he'd been flattered by the attention of a younger woman and that it had meant nothing. But the pain I felt went so deep, the betrayal... I knew that every time he was five minutes late home I'd be looking at the clock, wondering where he was and who he was with. I'd be questioning everything he said to me, trying to catch him out in another lie. And I knew that I didn't want to live my life like that; I knew that I deserved more. Why should I lose my peace of mind when I'd done nothing wrong? So I started divorce proceedings. And do you know something? He still hoped that I'd have him back. He wouldn't commit to her, to Kylie, in case there was a chance I'd change my mind. He told her that they couldn't get married because I wouldn't divorce him. She came to see me as I lay on the sofa at home, nauseous, weak and bald from the latest batch of chemo, insulting and upsetting me, calling me all the names under the sun because she thought I wouldn't let him go. I told her in no uncertain terms that she was welcome to him that I never wanted to see him again. And then I told her just what I thought of women who encouraged men to behave badly."

"But, surely..."

"I'm not just blaming the woman, Deborah, I'm not. After all, I don't know what he said to her to reel her in and if I'd been married to him for over twenty years and didn't know he was a lying, cheating bastard, how was she supposed to after just a few dates? But she did know he was married. She always knew he was married, and that's what I find unforgivable and despicable: deliberately causing another woman grief."

Frances stood up and wrapped her sarong around her waist and shoved on her sun hat. She slipped her feet into her sandals and grabbed her towel and bag.

"So don't expect me to be taken in by your fairytale love story. I think it's cheap and nasty and I can't believe you'd waste your life on such a selfish man."

She strode off, head held high, beach bag swinging by her side towards the main bar. Deborah watched her go, disbelieving. In the space of an hour she'd fallen out with two people. Well, she hadn't really fallen out with Murray; he'd been angry at Frances. She'd have to seek him out later and be nice to him. She didn't really like him very much, but she didn't want to be completely alone, either. She'd started to get used to company. She shrugged and leaned back against the lounger. She hoped Frances would come round. She'd become quite fond of her in the last day or so. And although she hated to admit it, she knew deep inside that Frances was telling the truth. Frances was right. Deborah felt decidedly uncomfortable.

***

Geri was puzzled. Palinda was just finishing off her braids when she'd seen the whole group get up and move down the beach out of sight. She was also slightly annoyed, after all, they could have told her where they were going and what they were doing.

"There you go, Sweetie!" Palinda said, holding up a mirror showing her reflection. "You look hot!"

"I am a bit warm. I'll probably have a swim in a minute."

Palinda's laugh exploded like a volcano deep inside her, making her whole body heave and shake with mirth as she packed up her mirror and beads.

"You look hot don't mean hot. It means hot. You know, sexy. Your husband's gonna give you good lovin' tonight when he sees you like this."

Geri smiled, secretly pleased that she looked sexy. It took the sting out of being left out of whatever was going on. She didn't bother to go into explanations that none of the men she sat with on the beach was her husband, or that she was with a singles' group. She paid Palinda the twenty-five US dollars she'd asked for and gave her another five as a tip.

"Thank you. God bless! You enjoy the rest of your day now," Palinda said as she waddled off up the beach, her hair braiding kit and her jewellery balanced easily on her head.

Geri walked back to her sun lounger, swinging her beads as she went. She sat down and tossed her head around a little. She liked the feel of the braids and the click of the beads as they touched each other.

I look hot!

She smiled to herself. She liked the idea that she was the first one in the group to get braids. Well, apart from Michael, but he was black and, of course he didn't have beads. She thought about Michael and had to admit that he was quite a hunk. He was quiet and thoughtful, too. She liked that in a man. Perhaps if she got nowhere with Deano she could move onto him. She squirmed with surprise at the sudden stab of wetness she felt thinking about Michael. Perhaps he was what she should be aiming at; perhaps he was what she needed. She'd never had sex with a man who was that much younger than she was, or with a black man of any age come to that. She pondered her options and decided she was going to have one final assault on Deano that night. She'd have to work out the details but she had the ghost of a plan stirring in her head to come between him and Jo. And if he wasn't interested then she could pull in Michael from the subs' bench. She smiled at her own ingenuity as she leaned forward to rub some suntan lotion on her face when she saw Natalie running up the beach towards her. She looked upset, but as she got to the group of sun loungers and saw Geri she gave a loud sob and ran on past down towards the far southern end of the beach, beyond the water sports station. Geri wondered what had upset her. She thought about going after her to find out and was just about to stand up and follow her when Eve came hurrying along the beach following Natalie.

"Is everything okay?" Geri called out to her, but Eve barely acknowledged her, concentrating instead on the rear view of Natalie that was now clambering over the rocks that marked the southern boundary of the resort.

Stuck up cow!

Geri felt really left out of everything now. Even her new braids and looking hot couldn't make up for that feeling that she wasn't quite part of it all; that she was on the outside looking in.

When Eve reached the rocks she couldn't see Natalie at first. Then, as she climbed over the first one she could see her sitting on the sand with her head bowed, shoulders heaving. Slowly and quietly, almost as if she were afraid of startling her and making her run off again, Eve climbed over the remaining rocks and gently eased herself down onto the sand next to Natalie. For a moment or two Natalie acted as if she wasn't there. Then, very slowly she turned and looked at Eve, her face like a small child's with her huge brown eyes red and full of tears and mascara streaks running down her face.

"I'm such a horrible person!" she said, breaking into sobs again and clutching onto Eve, who slowly wrapped her arms around Natalie's shoulders, embracing her, holding her tight against her chest, while Natalie sobbed and cried until she was all cried out.

***

"And I hereby declare that Kevin and Carly and now husband and wife. You may kiss your wife, Kevin." The Registrar, looking official in her neat navy blue suit and beaming from underneath her large navy blue and white 'church' hat led the applause as Kevin and Carly kissed and the CD player started again with an anonymous steel band's rendition of Can't Help Falling in Love. The Travel Together group joined in the applause and then turned away to make their way back down the beach, back to their usual spot under the royal palms.

"Aw, wasn't that lovely?" Suzanne said. "I love to see a wedding. It made me feel all weepy."

"I know what ya mean. I never knew why people cried at weddins then I got married meself!" Dave said, making them all laugh.

"I didn't think you'd been married, Dave" Grace said.

"I ain't! I was jus' kiddin'."

"So how come some gorgeous woman has never snapped you up, then?" Grace continued, refusing to let him off the hook and enjoying the banter.

"Jus' bin lucky I s'pose!" he retorted, to more gales of laughter.

Grace linked arms with him on one side and Jo the other as they made their way along the beach.

"I bet you'd make someone a lovely husband," Jo said to him. "You can't be Jack the Lad all your life."

"Why can't I?"

"Have you never been close to getting married?" Grace asked.

"Not really. I've got a kid. Josh. He's twenty-two, but I've never seen much of im, though."

"Oh, that's a shame!" Jo said, letting go of his arm and sinking back down onto her sun lounger.

"Not really. E don't know me. Is mum and me was only togevva for a little while. I mean, I paid for im an' that, you know, didn't wan' im to need nuffink, but she married anuvva bloke when Josh was only two so e's sort of fought of im as is dad. At least e knows abaht me and e's ad two dads, which is better n me, cos I didn't av none!"

"Were you adopted?" Michael asked.

"No. I grew up in children's omes. I was found in Stratford Bus Station, near where they're aving the Olympics, wiv a note saying *'His name's David, please look after him'*.

Everyone looked at Dave and then each other; there were one or two nervous sniggers as nobody was sure if he was joking or not.

"Usually little babies get adopted but I was ill; I ad asthma and eczema an all sorts. By the time I was stronger I was a righ' toe rag, a righ' andful and nobody wanted me. At least Josh knows oo e is."

"But didn't you feel as if part of your past was missing? That you didn't know who you were?" Michael insisted.

"It's never bovvered me. I'm jus' grateful I never belonged ter some of the families that fostered me. I mean, some of em was alrigh' and two was lovely, but some was only in it fer the money. But then agen, like I've said, I wasn't the easiest kid ter deal wiv."

"Oh, Dave, I'm so sorry," Jo jumped up and gave him a hug.

"S'alrigh'. I'm appy. Although I cud do wiv anuvva ug," he said, pulling Jo back into his arms and placing his head on her bosom. Everyone laughed, Geri shaking her head as she did so. She looked round the group, but nobody commented on her hot new hairstyle.

"Where did you all go?" she asked, in spite of herself. "Because I saw you all move off and then Natalie ran past, crying with our leader running behind her."

"We went to see a wedding," Suzanne said. "It was lovely."

"Oh that'll be Kevin and Carly, won't it? That couple from Accrington?" Geri said. The others looked at each other and raised their eyebrows; Geri was such a busybody. She just had to know everything about everyone.

147

"And her dress was really like Princess Catherine's, wasn't it?" Suzanne ploughed on, determined not to let Geri muscle in on something she hadn't even seen. She looked round the others for confirmation.

"Sort of," Grace said. "Except it didn't have lace sleeves or a train and it was bigger."

"Oh that's nice. I liked her dress," Geri said, missing Grace's point completely.

"So did I!" said Suzanne.

"I fought er sister looked a bit of alrigh'," Dave said. "When they showed 'er from be'ind when they went in the Abbey; phwoar!"

"Yes, she looked well fit," Deano agreed. "A gorgeous, slinky, sexy brunette; just how I like 'em!"

"I suppose there'll be a glut of Kate lookalike dresses now," Stewart observed.

"People need to get a life," Deano said. "Why would a woman want to get married in a dress that's already been seen by half the world? I don't understand."

"It's a girl thing!" Stewart said.

"No it isn't! It's fashion rather than copying Kate," said Grace. "She's started a trend, everywhere you look in the shops now it's all lace. Although, I have to say, I thought she looked a bit old fashioned, you know all those pleats round the waist and hips. And I thought her veil looked like a little girl dressing up in her mum's old net curtain. I thought she'd have had something a bit sexier personally. More like the one who married Albert of Monaco."

"Well, I thought she looked beautiful. We had the TV on in the shop and I was glued to it all day!" Suzanne said. "They looked so happy together."

"Let's just hope he didn't have a mistress sitting in row six of the Abbey and that he treats her a bit better than his father treated his mother!" Grace said.

"Oh, I'm sure he will! He seems like a lovely young man. And I think a lot of that's down to her, to Diana."

"That's what I mean. Growing up with the Windsors must have been like living with the Adams Family, or the Munsters; completely dysfunctional eccentrics who live in draughty old castles," Grace said. Everyone laughed.

"But he's turned out well, I think," Jo said. "And the whole world was watching to see what had become of Diana's son; of that young boy who walked behind his mother's coffin."

"Exactly! It's because of Diana that they're still interested in him. Never was anyone's presence felt so much by their absence. And I think it was a disgrace that the old trout was up the front at the wedding."

"That's a sign that the Princes accept her, isn't it? That they've all put it behind them and moved on," Jo said.

"Their mother's dead. She can't move on, can she?"

"Not a royalist then?" Trevor smiled at Grace. "Aren't you supposed to swear an oath of allegiance or something when you sign up to the police?"

Grace laughed out loud.

"I had my fingers crossed, Trevor. I used to be a royalist until they made Diana's life a misery and I think it's a poor show that in all the years she's been dead Charles has never once found one single nice thing to say about her in public. After all she was the mother of his children!"

"I watched some of the wedding," Stewart said. "I mean William and Kate seem like a nice normal couple and you wouldn't wish them ill, would you?"

"Of course you wouldn't! I like them," Geri said.

"Line them up against the wall and shoot the whole bloody lot of them!" Deano said, winking at Dave as they both registered Geri's discomfort at apparent their conflicting views.

"At least we got a day off," Trevor said.

"We didn't!" said Michael.

"I gave myself the day off, but we... I... went down the pub and had a laugh with my mates." Deano said. "It was worth a bank holiday, I'll say that."

"And we've got Zara's wedding next Saturday!" Suzanne said clapping her hands with glee. "Do you think it'll be on the telly here?"

"Who knows? Who cares?" Grace said.

"And anyway, you can't see it we're on the helicopter ride on Saturday," Stewart reminded her.

"So what was the matter with Natalie?" Geri asked, shaking her head a little again.

"We don't know, she just got a bit upset and ran off," Michael said. "Perhaps she just doesn't like weddings."

"And that one was a bit ostentatious, wasn't it?" Grace said. "Fancy having all those bridesmaids for a ceremony that lasted ten minutes! How many were there? Ten?"

"Six big ones and five flower girls," Suzanne said, not having missed a single detail.

"It did seem to involve a lot of toddlers, taffeta and tattoos," Trevor observed. "I'd have preferred to have seen the bride and bridesmaids without butterflies on their shoulder blades and Chinese symbols on their arms."

Grace laughed out loud.

"You do make me laugh, Trevor. You're so dry sometimes."

Deano looked at his watch.

"It's Wadiddly o'clock. Am I the only one who wants a drink?"

"If you insist," Dave said. "After all, we aven't ad one fer ten minutes!"

***

Frances wriggled herself comfortable on the bar stood and called out to Elvis for another mojito. That would be her third. Or was it her fourth? She didn't really care! She was footloose and fancy free! She didn't have to answer to anyone! She was on holiday! She could do what she damn-well pleased, and if that meant drinking twelve mojitos, then she would!

"There you go, ma'am" Elvis said, placing the mojito in front of her. "Are you sure you wouldn't be more comfortable over there at one of those tables on the patio?"

Frances looked over to where a dozen or so tables and chairs were attractively placed under fancy sun shades.

"Why? Don't you want me at the bar? Don't you want my company?" she asked him, coquettishly, stirring her drink and looking over her sunglasses at him.

"It's not that. It's just that it's not so far to fall from the chair as it is from the stool," he said, grinning.

Frances laughed so loudly that the other people at the bar turned to look at her.

"Oops!" she giggled. Then she raised her glass towards them all. "Cheers! Happy holiday!" she said. Elvis shook his head, giving a wry smile. He'd have to keep an eye on her. Frances, oblivious to it all, sat happily alone, sipping her mojito, glad that she was alive and spending time in such a beautiful place. Whatever else happened, she wasn't going to let the likes of Deborah and Murray ruin it for her. She'd waited too long and fought too hard to mess up this opportunity of having a bloody good time.

***

"I feel so stupid, now."

Natalie dried her eyes and blew her nose on the last of the tissues that Eve had run to get from her room. She looked at the empty box in her hand, and stuffed the used tissues inside it.

"I can't believe I used a whole box!"

"That's fine. It does us all good to have a really good boo hoo every now and again. And you certainly had your reasons," Eve said, patting her hand. "Are you ready to come back and join the others now, or do you want some time on your own?"

Natalie thought about it for a moment.

"I'll come back to the others. The sooner I face them the easier it'll be. Get it over and done with."

"You don't have to give them any explanations if you don't want to."

"I think I owe them that. They must be wondering what the bloody hell was wrong with me running off. And you know what? I really like them. I can't believe that we've become such good friends in such a short time; I feel like I've know some of them, like Jo and Dave, for years. It'll be more awkward if I don't say anything. I mean, I even feel better for talking about it to you. Thanks, Eve."

"I didn't do anything."

"But that's exactly it! You were just here and you listened. You know that's the first time I've ever talked about it. Really talked about it, I mean. And I feel better than I have for a long time; sort of happier... lighter. Does that make sense?"

Eve nodded. She knew exactly what Natalie meant. Bringing a problem out into the open seemed to somehow dilute it, as if the wind weakened it or the sky swallowed it up.

"It makes perfect sense," she said.

The two women stood up and made their way back along the beach towards the group.

"Would you like a drink, Natalie?"

"I could murder a rum punch! I know it's not lunchtime yet, but I feel like a really need one. God! Doesn't that sound awful?"

"No it doesn't! I'll get us a drink each. Do you want to wait for me and for us to go back to the group together?"

"No, it's okay. I'll walk on ahead, if you don't mind."

151

Eve cut through the palm trees and along the path towards the bar while Natalie turned, took a deep breath and walked towards the group. As Eve got to the bar Elvis headed for her with a look of consternation.

"A rum punch and a Diet Coke, please, Elvis. Is everything alright?"

"There's a lady. I think she's one of yours. She's had a few to drink and I think she needs to go back to her room for a while."

Eve looked round the bar and across at the tables but couldn't see anyone from the Travel Together gang.

"Who is it? I can't see anyone I recognise."

"She's just gone bathroom," Elvis said, mixing the rum punch. "She's been gone a while."

At that moment Eve looked across towards the Ladies and saw Frances come lurching out. Her sunhat was down over one eye, her beach bag dangled from one arm with her sarong hanging from it and her towel was falling from her left shoulder. She was barefoot but seemed to be reeling to one side and shuffling along like a demented crab. Eve stared at her trying to work out what was wrong. Then she spotted the lump of swimsuit dangling at her right thigh and realised that Frances had put two legs in one hole and was now finding walking through the bar quite difficult, if not impossible.

Oh dear God!

She hurried over to Frances as quickly as she could, while trying not to draw attention to her.

"You okay, Frances? Just going to your room?"

Frances turned round at the sound of Eve's voice and took a moment for her eyes to focus and recognise her.

"Hallo, Eve! How are you? I'm having a lovely time. Oops!" she bent to try to pick up the towel which had slid onto the ground, tangling itself round her left ankle.

"Let me get that for you." Eve grabbed the towel. "Now, shall I help you back to your room?"

"I'm not going back to my room. I'm going to have another little mojito and them I'm going for a swim."

You are not!

"Frances, you've got your swimsuit on wrong. Look! You've got two legs in one hole."

Frances roared out laughing, attracting the attention of the whole bar and those who were having early lunch on the restaurant terrace.

"Ha ha ha! No wonder I couldn't walk straight! I bet you thought I was drunk, didn't you? Eh? You thought I was drunk! And I've got two legs in one hole. Ha ha ha!"

"Well, let's go to your room and get you sorted out, shall we?" Eve said, taking her elbow and steering her towards the nearest staircase. "We'll put both legs back in their right holes and then you can have your drink and swim."

Eve propelled Frances along beside her; no easy task given the restriction of movement caused by the swimsuit malfunction and the effect of the four mojitos before lunch. As they reached the stairwell Eve got on the outside and told Frances to hold onto the banister to haul herself up.

"That Deborah's a right bitch, you know? She's got no scruples. No qualms about taking another woman's man. She's been having an affair with my husband for twenty-nine years."

Eve stopped climbing and looked at her. Surely that couldn't be right; Frances was too drunk to know what she was saying.

"Having an affair with your husband?"

Even though she knew that engaging Frances in conversation in her present condition was a complete waste of time, Eve couldn't help herself. The question was out before she could stop it.

"Who's having an affair with my husband?"

"You said that Deb... that someone was."

"Some young tart he worked with. How did you know?"

Eve ignored the question. She grabbed Frances' arm and started up the stairs again.

"She's caused me a lot of upset, she has. A lot of upset. She's welcome to him. He's not worth it. Let Deborah have him!"

Frances continued her rant all the way along the corridor until they got to Room 221.

"Where's your key card? Give me your key, Frances" Eve said, taking her beach bag and rummaging in it. Frances grabbed the bag back.

"I'll get it." She foraged around inside the bag, but couldn't seem to make contact with the key. "Here somewhere!"

Eve regained control of the beach bag, put her hand inside and pulled out a small wallet.

"Could it be in here?" she asked, waving the wallet in front of Frances's face. Frances nodded, and then struggled to open it up and get the key card out. She handed it to Eve who opened the door, pushing it wide and ushering Frances inside. The wave of cold air that greeted them was most welcome. Eve closed the door behind her and followed Frances into the main body of the room and watched as she fell face down onto the bed. Eve slipped the hat off Frances' head and put it on the dressing table, next to the beach bag and then draped the towel over the back of the chair. She looked at Frances, who already appeared to be asleep. Eve turned her head to the side and moved her shoulders so that her body twisted into the recovery position. She wasn't going to even attempt to take her swimsuit off; Frances would have to sort that out once she came to. She pulled the curtains and quietly left the room, putting the *Do Not Disturb* sign on the door as she silently closed it behind her.

***

Natalie looked round at the assembled faces and felt a wave of affection towards all of them, even Geri. They looked at her, huddled together on the edge of their sun loungers, concerned yet expectant; non-judgemental, waiting to hear what she said.

"I think I owe you all an explanation and an apology."

"You don't have to tell us anything," Jo said, quickly. "It's none of our business. You don't owe us anything at all."

Oh shut up! Geri wanted to know what was going on. Bloody do-gooding Jo could piss off if she didn't want to hear what Natalie was going to say. Geri was all ears; she loved a bit of gossip.

"No, Jo! I want to. You've all been really nice to me and I was just saying to Eve that I can't believe I've only known you a couple of days. Anyway, just over a year ago, well, twenty-second of May last year to be exact, I was supposed to be getting married. I'd been going out with Andy for four years. He was in the army and I met him when some of my kids danced at a local town show and he was there manning the Army's tent. He was in the Fifth Regiment of the Royal Artillery. Anyway we started going out and in no time I was madly in love with him. When he was away I'd look forward to his letters and his e-mails and his phone calls, when he could phone, that is. And when he asked me to marry him I was the happiest woman in the world. And so we started preparing for our wedding; the biggest, best wedding in the world to let everyone know just how we felt about each other. We both felt it was wrong to get married in church as neither of us is particularly religious, so we booked up St Cuthbert's, a stunning fourteenth century monastery that's been converted into a gorgeous little hotel. My sister Leanne and Andy's sister Fiona were going to be my bridesmaids and Leanne's little boy Matthew was going to be the pageboy. My senior dancers were going to form a guard of honour in their Forty-Second Street costumes. Andy's best friend Colin was best man."

She paused and gulped. There was no sign of Eve with the drinks. Sensing her discomfort Grace passed her a bottle of water to sip from, which she accepted, gratefully.

"Anyway, to cut a very long story short, it was all perfect. Everything about this wedding was what I'd always wanted and what I'd always dreamed about since I was a little girl. And then suddenly, I don't know why, but with a month to go I just felt that I couldn't go through with it. I loved Andy. It wasn't that I didn't love him, because I did. But, I just didn't want to marry him; I didn't want to be an army wife. I loved him and I knew that being a soldier was what he was born to be. It was what made him Andy. But I lay awake at night tossing and turning, worrying about what to do. The weight was dropping off me and everyone thought it was that I was dieting madly to get into the wedding dress but it wasn't that. I was sick with worry. I wanted to call it all off, but I didn't know how. The days were flying by and the wedding was looming. It got to my hen weekend and that was when I knew I had to put a stop to it all. I phoned Andy and told him to meet me. He was surprised that I wasn't on the hen weekend. I'd told Leanne that I was ill and for them to all go on without me, but that wasn't true. So Andy came round and I just told him; that I couldn't marry him. Of course, he was mad at first. He was sure there had to be someone else involved, was convinced I'd met another bloke. He just couldn't understand that I still loved him but didn't want to marry him. But then how could he? I didn't even understand it fully myself. And then, of course, he was heartbroken. My mum and dad tried to talk me round. His mum and dad tried to talk me round and when they couldn't they got abusive. They said that it was all down to race; that a white girl couldn't understand him and that he should have been with an Afro-Caribbean in the first place. But I wasn't having any of it. The wedding was off. And then, a few months later, in October, his regiment was deployed to Afghanistan. Two weeks later Andy was blown up by a roadside bomb."

There was a shocked silence as everyone took in what Natalie was saying. Suzanne was crying. Stewart put his arm round her and drew her head onto his shoulder.

"But you weren't to know he was going to die," Michael said.

"He didn't die. Sometimes I think it might have been better if he had. That's awful, isn't it? Thinking it might be better if someone died so that I'd feel better about myself; less guilty about what happened to him. He lost a leg and a forearm and the sight in one eye. In the space of a few months he went from doing a job he loved and thinking he was going to marry a woman who'd love and look after him, to being an invalid in a wheelchair, on his own. I felt really guilty about the accident, as if it was my fault. I know it was. I mean, what if he wasn't concentrating on what he was doing because he was thinking about us? What if we'd been married and everything had gone to plan? Would he still have trodden on the landmine? Leanne said not to flatter myself. She said he was a thorough professional and besides it was six months afterwards; she said I'd have been the last person on his mind. But I can't help wondering."

She paused again and everyone sat quietly, lost in thought, digesting what Natalie had just shared with them.

"And I'm such a silly cow! I thought I was okay, I thought I'd dealt with it. After all, I've seen brides and weddings since I called it off. But seeing the hen party the other night unsettled me and then watching that wedding today just brought it all to the surface."

"That's understandable, Natalie, you've been through a lot," Jo said.

"Thanks." She looked around the group and gave a sheepish smile. "Sorry for being such a silly cow. And thanks for listening. I feel better for getting it off my chest and if there's another wedding you'll know what's wrong with me. You won't think I've flipped if I run off again."

"I reckon you need a drink," Dave said.

"Eve was getting me one," Natalie said, looking down the beach to where Eve had disappeared along the path towards the bar. "But she seems to be taking a long time. Oh here she is!"

Eve was hurrying up the beach carrying a rum punch and a Diet Coke that she was trying hard not to spill. She looked round the group and could see at a glance that they'd heard Natalie's story and were supporting her. She gave Natalie her rum punch.

"Sorry!" she said.

"What kept ya?" Dave asked.

"You wouldn't believe it!" Eve replied, downing her Diet Coke, wishing it had a large shot of rum in it.

***

Murray felt a shadow fall across him as he sat reading yesterday's *Daily Mail* on the bar terrace. His friend Andy who was leaving today had given it to him. Murray himself certainly wouldn't have paid the equivalent of three pounds for it. Looking up, he had to shield his eyes to see who it was and to his surprise recognised Deborah, who was holding a beer in her hand. She pushed it towards him.

"Peace offering," she said. "Sorry if I upset you earlier. It wasn't intentional."

Murray looked at her in disbelief; unsure as to whether this was a wind-up or not. Deborah moved the beer closer to his hand.

"Please take it. Even if you can't forgive me at least I know I've offered the olive branch," she said, afraid she might be trying too hard.

Murray thought for a moment, and then a smile spread across his face.

"Aye, well, I've never been one tae hold a grudge," he said taking the beer from her. "Won't you sit down and join me?"

"Well, I was thinking about getting some lunch," Deborah said, pulling out one chair and placing her bag on it and then sitting on the other one, at right angles to Murray.

"Aye, that'd be nice," Murray agreed, taking a big sip and getting a foam moustache in the process. A few hours earlier Deborah would have thought that was gross, but now she found it rather endearing. She looked at his balding pate, red where he'd forgotten to put on sun block on the first day, his Fred Perry shirt, 80s style shorts and socks and sandals but instead of asking herself what she saw in him, she felt grateful she'd decided to make this man her friend.

Murray, meanwhile, couldn't believe his luck. Perhaps Deborah had been turned on by his outburst earlier that morning. Perhaps she liked a man who stood up for himself and wasn't afraid to speak his mind. Perhaps she liked him. Perhaps his giant box of condoms wouldn't go to waste after all.

***

Lunch was over and the sun was burning down relentlessly from a cobalt, cloudless sky. Most of the group had pulled their sun loungers into the shade and were snoring happily, lost in a post-lunch slumber. Suzanne had decided she'd had enough sun for the day so she went back to her room for a shower and then decided to take a walk over to the village. She felt quite drained with all the drama of the morning: Dave's story, Natalie's story and, of course, the wedding. Deano had made them laugh at lunch.

"Blimey, what a morning!" he'd joked. "We've had My Big Fat Chav Wedding; Dave's really Oliver Twist; Grace's a raving republican; Trevor's really Len Goodman; Natalie's the Runaway Bride and thanks to her new hairdo Geri looks like a tarantula on speed!"

Suzanne had laughed along with them all, but she felt she needed some space this afternoon away from any more drama. But it was much too nice a day to spend it shut away in her room. She took her umbrella from her suitcase, having decided to use it as a parasol. She was afraid of burning and she knew that tomorrow's boat trip would mean another full-on blast of sunshine. She put on a thin cotton top and a pair of cut offs in matching pink. The trousers would probably make her hotter than a skirt, but then again, a skirt would mean her legs rubbing together and she didn't want that in case it was noticeable when she wore her swimsuit. She was going to look in the village pharmacy and see if she could get some talcum powder. That should make any chaffing easier.

Approaching the village, Suzanne walked slowly. She'd noticed that all the local people she'd seen seemed to walk at a steady pace; nobody rushed around because it was too hot for that.

I'm walking like an Antiguan!

She grinned to herself as she said it. She certainly felt like an Antiguan; she'd only been here four days, well three really, she corrected herself, yet she felt so at home. She just loved it and knew that leaving next Monday would be a huge wrench. Then she reprimanded herself for thinking about next week when that was still six days away. Six superb, brilliant, breathtaking, amazing days! She saw she was approaching a man sitting under a large parasol, in front of a small table laden with mangos. He looked at her expectantly as she approached and as she drew near his serious face was transformed by a huge smile.

"Good afternoon, Miss. Would you like some mangos?"

"Good afternoon," Suzanne said in reply. She wasn't sure if she did want any mangos or not, but thought it rude not to buy, or at least to appear interested in them.

"Are they from your garden?"

"From my own trees, yes. I grow them myself. They fell from the trees this morning, you know, because you should never pick a mango. You always wait until it's ripe enough and it falls from the tree itself."

"Really? That's interesting. How much are they?"

"Five dollars for a bag. The bag has three big ones or five small ones."

Suzanne quickly converted five dollars in her head and made it one pound twenty pence. She thought that was really reasonable. After all, they couldn't buy them from the wholesaler back at home at that price. They were far more expensive.

"I'll have three big ones, please," she said, sorting through the change in her purse and handing over what looked like five fifty-pence pieces, but which she knew were, in fact, EC dollars. The man took the money and handed Suzanne the bag of mangos.

"You enjoy the rest of your day now," he said.

"Thank you. You, too."

Suzanne smiled and walked on past the man towards the centre of the village where Eve had told her earlier that she would find the pharmacy. She'd only gone about three steps when the man called out to her again.

"Miss! Can I ask you a question?"

Suzanne turned to face him and nodded.

"Do you have a Caribbean grandmother?"

"No." She shook her head, puzzled by his question. "Not as far as I know. Why?"

The mango seller looked at her and gave an even wider grin.

"Well, I ain't never seen a arse that size on a white woman before!" he declared. "From the back you look amazing! Your husband must be a very happy man!"

Suzanne was mortified. Especially as at that moment Stewart appeared behind her and overheard everything the mango-seller had said. The mango-seller turned to Stewart.

"I must congratulate you, mon!" he said, shaking his hand. "Your wife's all-woman! All-woman! What man don't love a woman with a bit of meat on her?"

"Thank you very much," Stewart said, returning the handshake and then putting his other hand under Suzanne's elbow and noting that she was scarlet, he moved her forward.

"Come along, wife! Let's go and enjoy our mangos!"

"Good afternoon!" the mango-seller called after them.

"Oh, Stewart, how embarrassing!" Suzanne disentangled her arm from Stewart's grip. "Saying things like that about... about my bottom."

"Well, that's why the Caribbean's such a great place. They don't do size zero here, do they? Everything's big and lively. And they love bright clothes and colours. That's why you and me fit in!" he said indicating his purple Bermuda shorts and turquoise polo shirt.

"But, I'm really sorry, about the rest. You know, him thinking we were... you know... a couple."

"A married couple? There are worse things I can think of! He could have thought I was your dad or your son!"

Suzanne looked at him and squirmed, thinking he was taking the mickey out of her. He faced her square on.

"I mean it, Suzanne. Why wouldn't he think we're a couple? We're both about the same age, we're both English, we know each other, we look good together..."

"Do we?"

"Course we do! Look, I knew you were coming into the village and so I thought I'd come along, too, in the hope that I'd bump into you. I'd like us to spend some time together away from the others, you know, to get to know each other a bit."

"But we're all getting to know each other together."

159

"Yes! I know we are! But I'd like us to have some time on our own. Please. Let's have a drink together. Look! There's a bar over there. Please, Suzanne. Please have a drink with me."

Suzanne suddenly felt as pleased as punch. She took Stewart's arm as they picked their way around the cars, the pot holes and the three young boys on bicycles to reach the other side of the road. She was so happy she thought she might burst. They climbed up the six deep steps and onto the wooden veranda of the bar and sat at a table overlooking the street. Suzanne looked through the trees and beyond the wooden houses dotted across the landscape and pointed her finger.

"You can see the sea from here. Look!"

"You can see the sea from everywhere. It's magic, isn't it?"

A sulky-looking young woman with hair straightened to within an inch of its life, wearing a mauve mini-dress that looked as if it had been painted onto her ample body sauntered over to them.

"Good afternoon. What you having?"

"I'd like a coffee, please," Suzanne said.

The waitress gave a sort of grimace and sucked her teeth.

"This is a rum shop. We ain't Starbucks. No coffee."

"Well, we'll just have to have two rums then!" Stewart said brightly, determined the waitress wasn't going to put a damper on his first date with Suzanne. "Do you have coke to go with it?"

The waitress nodded. He looked at Suzanne and raised his eyebrows. She nodded.

"Two rum and cokes then, please."

The waitress turned to go inside as Stewart called after her.

"Excuse me!"

She turned and looked back at him.

"And could we have a nice big smile, please?"

The waitress's face broke into a massive grin, transforming it just as the mango-seller's had.

"Smiles are ten dollars extra," she said, cheekily.

"A smile like yours is worth it!" Stewart said, surprising himself by suddenly becoming a sweet-talker. "Just call me Mr Smooth," he said to Suzanne who was looking at him in mock-horror.

"That's all that mixing with Deano and Dave," she said. "They're nice men, aren't they? Even though they've got all the chat. And Trevor and Michael, of course."

"They all are really. I find Murray hard work and I haven't said much to Huw and Jason, I suppose I haven't got much in common with them. Although, I wouldn't have thought I'd have had much in common with the other men either, yet we're all getting along."

"I suppose that's the good thing about holidays like this, singles' holidays, you know, everyone gets on together on the whole."

The waitress served the drinks, smacking the glasses of rum and the cans of Coke onto the table, then giving a great big smile, first at Stewart and then at Suzanne, before walking away laughing to herself.

"I like the women, too. I know people think that Dawn and Donna are a bit funny because they dress the same and everything, but I've got on well with them so far."

"Geri's a bit obvious, with all that chasing after Deano. Cheers!" Stewart chinked his glass against Suzanne's.

"Cheers!" she said in reply and took a sip. "Oh, look!"

She waved her hand furiously at a bus that was going by.

"Talk of the devil! That was Dawn and Donna. They must have just got back from St John's. Oh, dear, they saw us."

"Well, of course they did, you were waving at them! But so what? Do you feel uncomfortable being out with me, Suzanne?"

"No! Not at all! But I bet they'll tell everyone now."

"Everyone already knows," Stewart admitted, reddening. "The boys egged me on to come after you."

"The boys? Egged you on?"

"I don't mean that how it sounded! They've all known, Deano, Dave, Trevor and Michael, since Shirley Heights that I fancy you. And when I said *'egged me on'* I really meant to say encouraged me. You know. They all like you, Suzanne. And even Grace said she thought we made a sweet couple."

Suzanne gulped her drink. She felt embarrassed to think that the group had been speculating about her and Stewart, but at the same time she felt rather pleased. She liked Stewart. And it was a long time since she'd sat and had a drink with a man like this. Correction! She had never sat and had a drink with a man like this. Was this a date? She felt a little thrill at the thought. She looked at Stewart who was looking at her like a little puppy waiting for a word of praise from its owner for using the litter tray. Feeling bold, she put her glass down and reached across the table. Placing her hand behind Stewart's neck she gently pulled him towards her and planted a tender, rum-flavoured kiss right on his lips. When they parted they stared at each other, both surprised at what had happened. Then they were startled out of their trance.

"Way to go, lady!" the waitress shouted, laughing out loud and giving them a round of applause.

***

"I wonder ow Stew's gettin' on," Dave said, stretching his arms over his head. "E's bin gone a long while."

"That's a good sign," Michael said. "If she hadn't been interested he'd have been straight back." He looked at his watch. "Anyone coming to play table tennis? There's a tournament starting at four and it's ten to."

"I'll come!" Natalie said, jumping up and straightening her bikini top that was in danger of exposing her right breast.

"Me, too!" said Deano, taking advantage of the fact that Geri had gone into the sea for a swim with Trevor and Grace. "I used to be a fair old player at one time. I'll give you a run for your money, Michael!"

"No chance! You are looking at the 1997 Barfield School's Table Tennis Champion, I'll have you know." Michael said.

"Well, that's hardly one step down from the Olympic Team, is it?"

"Boys! Boys! Let's not start dick measuring before we've even got there," Natalie said.

"Such a nice turn of phrase, Nat!" Michael chided her, chuckling, as the three of them set off towards the games' area.

A few moments later, Trevor, Grace and Geri arrived back to join Dave and Jo, just as Dawn and Donna came along the beach looking for sun loungers.

"Hallo! Any spares here?" Donna asked.

"Yeah, these free are free," Dave said, indicating the loungers that had just been vacated by Deano, Michael and Natalie.

"Ow's yer ooter?" he asked Dawn.

"Fine, thanks," she said, a little sheepishly, her hand flying to her face to check the plaster and her nose were still there.

"Has Deano... have they all gone?" Geri asked, shaking her head to dry her braids.

"Yeah." Dave refused to give Geri any further details. She was getting on his nerves, especially the way she followed Deano around. He'd met women like her before. They were usually trouble; they did all the running then said you'd mistaken the signs. Very dangerous!

"Oh! I like your hair!" Dawn said, flopping down on one of the spare sun loungers.

"Thank you," Geri said, waving her head around again, giving Dawn and Donna the full benefit of the beaded braids, and also glad that, finally, someone had mentioned her new hairdo.

"It looks really nice, doesn't it?" Dawn asked the group in general.

"It looks like she's got a big blonde tarantula sittin' on er ed," Dave said.

There was a group titter at this. As always, Jo, who hated anyone to feel uncomfortable, jumped in.

"Ignore him! You're in Antigua and you've entered into the spirit of the holiday," she said. She felt she couldn't actually lie and say that Geri looked nice, because Jo agreed with Natalie; braids on a middle-aged white woman looked silly.

"We could get it done, Dawn," Donna said.

"I knew it!" Dave muttered under his breath. He stood up. "Wadiddly time," he announced. "I'm retirin' to the bar. I'll see yer all at beach volleyball at five. If not, see yer fer drinks later."

"I'll come with you," Trevor said, getting up and gathering his things. "I think I've had enough sun for today."

"We've just seen Suzanne and Stewart together!" Donna announced to Geri, Jo and Grace.

"Well, what's unusual about that? They do know each other," Grace said.

"Yes, but they were together, if you get my meaning." Donna made inverted commas with her fingers as she said the word 'together'.

"Where were they?" Geri asked, annoyed that she'd missed what was going on.

"Sitting in a bar down in the village, having a drink. We saw them as we went by on the bus, didn't we Dawn?"

Dawn nodded vigorously.

"Yes, Suzanne said she didn't want to spend any more time on the beach and she wanted to look round the village," Jo said.

"So Stewart must have followed her," Geri concluded.

"Hardly *followed*," Grace said. Geri reminded her of someone she once worked with; the station gossip who had to know everyone's business and thrived on being the one to pass all the news and tittle-tattle on. "Anyway, they're two grown-ups, if they want to have a drink together they're hardly breaking the law, are they? It's not earth-shattering news, is it?"

"Well, they looked sweet together, didn't they Donna?" Dawn said. She stood up. "I can't wait to get into that water. It was so hot and crowded in St John's."

"Did you buy anything?" Jo asked.

"We both bought a beach dress each with an elasticated bust and little straps; mine's red with white flowers and Dee's is black with orange flowers. And I got a carton of cigarettes for my dad for only twenty dollars. That's only about thirteen pounds. God! In England they're five times that!"

The two of them, both wearing green swimsuits this afternoon, made their way across the sand and into the water. Geri lay back down. She felt good that they'd liked her hair. Only that stupid Dave had something to say again. He seemed to have disliked her from the word go. She still hadn't forgiven him for calling her Old Spice when they'd only just met. And she felt miffed that someone like Suzanne had a man interested in her, while she, who took care of her appearance and kept herself trim, was getting nowhere fast where men were concerned. Not that she'd want Stewart! God! She'd die if she went out with someone like him, dressing the way he did. But Suzanne must feel very flattered that she'd got a man to be interested in her. Geri sighed. She'd have to try really hard with Deano tonight. She started to finalise her plan.

***

Lunch for Deborah and Murray had been a very pleasant, civilised affair, which had quite surprised both of them. It had been a leisurely meal and the staff had topped up their wine glasses several times. They had shared stories about life in London, Deborah living in Marylebone and Murray in Docklands.

"Oh, whereabouts in Docklands do you live? A friend of mine lives in St Catherine's Dock."

"Ermm, it's Purfleet, actually."

"Purfleet? Where's that?"

"Oh, it's at the eastern end of Docklands, just beyond the O2 and Canary Wharf," he lied, hoping she'd never have reason to look it up. Well, it wasn't exactly a lie; Purfleet was east of Canary Wharf; about twenty miles east of it. Murray told her he'd moved to London after his divorce to start afresh. He then told her some horror stories of other drivers and London traffic and his taxi passengers. Deborah, whose Alfa stayed in the garage as much as possible because she'd always lived in Central London and used the Tube and buses, was fascinated by his tales and found she was actually enjoying his company.

After lunch they had both gone back to the Spa Pool and found two empty sun loungers that had partial shade. There was no sign of Frances; Deborah hadn't seen her since she'd gone off in her fit of pique earlier in the day. She hadn't felt it necessary to tell Murray anything about that. Deborah suddenly felt herself jolt and realised that she'd been asleep. A noise reminiscent of a train in a tunnel had disturbed her and she realised that it was Murray snoring. She nudged him awake.

"It's nearly time for afternoon tea. I'm going to have a dip first, though."

"I don't know about tea, but it's certainly time for a drink. Would you like something? A glass of wine or a cocktail?"

"Not for me, thanks! I had enough wine at lunchtime. But you go ahead. I'll have my swim and tea and then I'll see you with the others for dinner."

"Perhaps we could meet up before pre-dinner drinks and, you know, have a drink together?"

"That sounds like a good idea. I'll see you in the piano lounge at half past six," Deborah suggested.

Murray went off for his drink and Deborah had her swim. She got out and dried herself and prepared to go over to Afternoon Tea, which was just being served. She was secretly hoping that Frances would be there. She was sure that they could share a cup of tea together and agree to disagree. But even though she drank as slowly as she could, there was no sign of Frances at Afternoon Tea, at all.

***

Frances wasn't at Afternoon Tea because at half past four she was still snoring happily, in the deep, deep sleep that only too much alcohol can produce. She'd turned over at one point and almost woken up, but was soon out of it again. When she finally did wake up, it was with a slow lifting of one eyelid and then the other. Her face was resting on her hand and she could see a plastic identity bracelet around her wrist. Her head was throbbing.

Oh, God! I've been in a terrible accident and I'm in Intensive Care!

She didn't remember being in an accident, though. She didn't remember going anywhere. Slowly her gaze lifted and took in her surroundings. No tubes or respirators; pink floral curtains, a white dressing table with her sunhat and beach bag on it.

Antigua!

That was it! She was on holiday. She was having a great time, but if that was the case why was a steel band playing just behind her eyes? She tried to sit up, but when the pounding got worse, she groaned and fell back onto the bed again. Slowly, the events of the morning – the argument with Murray – falling out with Deborah – drinking herself silly on mojitos - all came back to her. She licked her lips. Her mouth felt like the bottom of a budgie's cage. She timidly looked to see if she had any water in the room. There was none that she could see, but there might be a bottle, in fact she was sure there was, in the bathroom. But that meant getting up. She'd have to be thirsty for a couple more minutes; until the world stopped spinning and the steel band took their break. She didn't remember coming back to her room at all. Had she had lunch? What time was it? She looked towards the alarm clock, but it was flashing 15:27, which meant that the power had gone off for a while during the day.

"Oh, God, help me!" she groaned as she lay very still, trying to remember if she had any Paracetamol in her bag, hoping that the merry-go-round would soon come to a halt and let her get off. She felt sick and dehydrated and couldn't blame anyone but herself; it was all her own fault. "Never again! Never again!"

***

Eve had changed into and out of four different outfits. She was beginning to get annoyed with herself for thinking what she was going to wear was so important.

It's just a drink!

She'd told herself that a thousand times that day. Fortunately she'd been kept busy with Natalie's incident and then with Frances; that had helped to keep her mind off her date.

It's not a date, it's just a drink!

But Eve knew how she felt; she knew that in the thirty years since she and Melv had been apart she'd never met anyone who filled her heart the way he had. And Life, in its weird and wonderful way of working, had plotted and planned so that their paths would cross again. She felt like a silly teenager on a first date. Several times she'd decided she wasn't going to go and then each time changed her mind, because she wanted to see him; wanted to talk to him; wanted to tell him what had really happened at the end. But would she be brave enough? She didn't think so, and besides, that was too heavy! It was just a drink with an old friend.

She grabbed the turquoise silk, loose-fitting blouse and the white jeans. They were a bit tight but the blouse fell below her bum and would hide that. Although Melv had always liked the way her hips bulged voluptuously. "A woman should be shaped like a guitar," he'd once told her.

I'm more like a double base now!

She chided herself as she put away all the other clothes. She wouldn't think about it anymore. She knew what she was going to wear, so she'd have her shower and get ready. If she didn't get a move on she'd be late for pre-dinner drinks.

Half an hour later, she walked into the bar to see most of the group assembled, including, she was pleased to see, Frances, who looked a little red-eyed and not quite herself. She went over to her and leaned in closely so that the others couldn't hear.

"Is everything alright, Frances?"

"Yes! Yes! Why shouldn't it be?" she asked suspiciously.

"I was just wondering if you were feeling better now."

"Oh, God! Oh! How bad was I? Please don't tell me I made a fool of myself in front of everyone!"

"No, you didn't. I saw you in the bar before lunch and you were suffering from a little mojito excess. So I helped you back to your room."

"I've lost my sandals somewhere. They're my nice ones with the rhinestones on."

"You were barefoot when I saw you, but I'm sure they've been handed in to Lost Property. We need to ask at the Front Desk. But are you really okay now?"

"My head still aches a bit, but I've taken a couple of aspirins and besides, I'm starving. I missed lunch and afternoon tea, so I'm really ravenous and ready for dinner. Then I think I'll have an early night."

"Most people will, I expect, as it's the boat trip tomorrow. Nobody wants to spoil their day by being hung over."

Gradually the group all gathered; Deborah and Murray surprising everyone by arriving together from the piano lounge, obviously enjoying each other's company.

"Oi oi!" Dave had said when Stewart appeared, "Ow did it go?"

"Oh be subtle, why don't you?"

"Was it alrigh' then?"

"We had a very pleasant afternoon, thank you," Stewart said, trying to act cool, as if what had happened with Suzanne was nothing at all.

167

"So, d'yer get anywhere?"

"Dave! Behave yourself!"

"Oh, I see, you didn't this afternoon, but you migh' tonigh', is that it?"

Deano and Michael who had joined the two men laughed at what Dave was saying.

"I might!" Stewart said, trying to act as if he had romantic interludes with women as an everyday occurrence.

"Go on, my son!" Dave said bending his elbow and making a fist.

Michael took a sip of his beer and laid the glass on the top of the bar. He took Stewart's arm and pulled him nearer. The other two also closed in.

"I hope you've come prepared, Stewart," he said, winking. "You know what I mean."

"What?"

"You know; protection. It's important in this day and age to have safe sex."

Stewart snorted his beer through his nose.

"We haven't got that far yet! We only had a quick kiss this afternoon."

"Ah, but that was this afternoon," Michael said,. "Tonight's tonight."

Stewart gulped.

"Oh, fuck, I hadn't thought of that."

"What time's the chemist shut?" Dave asked.

"I don't know. I can't ask Eve."

"Yes, but going to the chemist's is no good," Michael said.

"Why not?"

"Well, you know." He looked down towards Stewart's groin and then his own. "We're not all built the same, are we?"

"Aren't we?" Stewart gulped again.

"No. There's no point in you buying condoms here because they won't fit. They're built for local men. You should have brought them from England."

Stewart looked at Deano and Dave.

"Have you got any I can have?" he asked, an edge of desperation coming into his voice. They both shook their heads, looking serious. "Well, what am I going to do?"

"You'll just have to roll it up, you know, double it over, and hope it stays on," Michael said. "Or, stuff it with something. Let's hope Suzanne's one of those women who really does believe that size doesn't matter."

Stewart nodded, looking miserable.

"I thought all that... you know... you being bigger than us... well, that it was just a bit of fun, you know, made up, not true."

"What? No way!" Michael said, feigning indignation. "Why do you think women say once you've had black you'll never go back?"

"Do they?"

"Of course they do! I've seen some of my brothers with dicks so fucking long you wonder how they can put them inside their boxers. And last year my mate Winston had his girl-friend's name, Wendy, tattooed along his dick."

"Oooh!" Stewart winced.

"Still, that must have been some size," Deano said, playing along.

"Yes, but when he went on holiday he was standing at the urinals in a club in Montego Bay when a bloke stood next to him and he had Wendy tattooed on his, too. Well, Winston looked at him and said remarked on the co-incidence of them both having the same woman's name tattooed on their dicks. The other bloke turned round to Winston, looked at his dick and said *'What you talking about?'* and he pulled his foreskin back and it actually said *Welcome to Jamaica, have a nice day!*"

Dave, Deano and Michael cracked up. Stewart, who was still unsure how much he should believe or not, smiled nervously, looking from one to the other as the three of them high-fived each other, tears rolling down their faces.

"He's pulling your plonker!" Deano said, wiping his eyes on the back of his hand. "Oh, no pun intended!" he added as they all laughed again.

"You bastard! You really had me going then!" Stewart said, slapping Michael on the shoulder and laughing with relief.

"What are you all laughing at?" Suzanne appeared next to them and they all fell silent.

"Nuffink! Just boys' talk," Dave said, quickly. "Oo wants anuvva Wadiddly?"

***

Dinner had seemed endless to Eve who had joined in the banter and answered questions on auto-pilot. The food in the Crazy Conch was as wonderful as ever, but she couldn't have told you what she'd eaten. She just wanted ten o'clock to come as quickly as possible. Everyone seemed to be enjoying dinner; not just the food, but each other's company. On another occasion Eve would have been so glad to see this but all she could think about was making an exit. Finally, as coffees were drunk and the meal drew to an end she excused herself from the group.

"Now don't forget, we've all got to be up and ready for the boat trip which leaves at half past nine, tomorrow. We'll meet on the beach by the water sports centre just before nine-thirty, okay?"

"Yes. I think I'm going to have an early night tonight," Grace said. "Some of the others are going to walk into the village to have a drink at the little bar that overlooks the street but I'm not going. I don't want to spoil the day by having too much to drink tonight and being hung over."

"That sounds sensible," Eve said, standing up. "Please excuse me. I have to make a phone call then I'm going to call it a night, too. So everyone's clear about tomorrow, then?"

"Can we go in our beach gear?" Donna asked.

"Yes, because we're stepping straight onto the boat."

"Do we need to take any money?" she asked.

How many bloody times have I said this?

"Just for a tip for the crew, because they do look after us nicely. They sell t-shirts and caps on board, so you might want to take twenty dollars or so, in case you want to buy anything. Okay? Goodnight, everyone. See you at breakfast." And with that she made her escape.

She went back to her room to check her make-up, clean her teeth and spray on a bit more *Poeme*. She looked at her watch; twenty to ten. She didn't want to seem too keen. She'd wait until it was ten o'clock before she left her room. That way, by the time she walked up to reception and then down the driveway it'd be five past. She sat on her bed and flicked the TV set on with the remote control. It slipped from her hands, which were sweaty. Ugh! She got up and washed them and then sat back on her bed. On the TV Piers Morgan was interviewing an aging American actor Eve had never heard of. She couldn't stand Piers Morgan at the best of times and especially not tonight when she was on edge. She switched channels to find only baseball. She couldn't stand that either, yet it was probably marginally more watchable than Morgan. Why was she so on edge? She was just having a drink with an old friend, she told herself for the fiftieth time that evening. She looked at her watch again. Eighteen minutes to ten. She picked up her book and decided to read a chapter, but after two sentences she knew she couldn't concentrate so she put the book down and turned the TV off. She went and sat on the armchair in the corner of the room and closed her eyes. She'd meditate for a few minutes to calm herself down. Suddenly the room phone rang. She sprang up.

Oh, please don't let there be an emergency with someone in the group tonight!

She thought about not answering it but she couldn't do that. She had to be there for them twenty-four seven. She grabbed the receiver afraid it might go to voicemail before she could get to it.

"Eve, speaking."

"Hi!"

"Oh! Hi!"

She just knew it! He was ringing to say he'd changed his mind and he couldn't make it.

"You okay?"

"Yes, thank you. You?"

"Yes. But I thought I'd just check that everything was as it should be or whether you were just running late, or something."

Running late?

Eve looked at her watch. Ten thirty-one.

Shit!

"Melv, I'm so sorry. I was here in the room, sort of killing time until ten and I must have just fallen asleep."

"So excited by the prospect of seeing me, huh?"

"No! It's not that!"

"I'm teasing you," he said, trying to calm her. "I'm sitting outside waiting for you if you'd still like to have that drink."

Eve gulped. She caught sight of herself in the mirror; her mascara had smudged and her mouth felt stale.

"Can you give me five more minutes? I promise I'll be there in five minutes."

"Take your time, baby. I'm not going anywhere."

Eve cleaned her teeth again, wiped her right eye with a cosmetic pad and reapplied her makeup. Grabbing her bag, she flew down the corridor and the driveway, reaching the main gate in just under four minutes. She hoped as she galloped along in the night-time heat that her deodorant was everything it claimed to be in the ads. She could feel a sweat breaking out across her forehead and down her back.

Just up from the main gate, parked at a discreet distance away from the prying eyes of the security staff, Melv sat in his large, white 4x4. As she approached he got out and opened the passenger door for her.

"I told you to take your time. There's no need to rush and get yourself all hot and bothered."

"I've already kept you waiting half an hour. I'm so sorry, Melv," Eve said clambering into the car, which took two attempts as it was higher than she thought. Melv started the engine, swept the car in a semi-circle and they set off.

"I've got some drinks in a cool box in the back. I thought it'd be nice to go and sit on a quiet cliff top or down on a beach. Just the two of us. Nobody else. How does that sound??"

Where nobody can see us and tell your wife!

"Yes, if you like. I'd prefer cliff top to beach. The sand flies think I'm their supper. I have to be careful what perfume I wear or it attracts them. Some people are lucky, they never seem to get bitten, do they?"

Oh, God! I'm gabbling!

Melv followed the coast road south, towards Morris Bay. An easy-listening CD was playing.

"Who's this singing?" Eve asked.

"John Holt. He's a Jamaican singer who was really popular twenty years ago or so. Still sounds just as good today."

"Yes, he does," Eve agreed as John Holt slid beautifully from *The Girl from Ipanema* into *Killing Me Softly*.

Suddenly, Melv turned the jeep right and went down a track, which lead to an opening among the trees. It wasn't exactly a cliff, but it overlooked a deserted beach, about twenty feet below, which was bathed in silver moonlight giving it an almost eerie glow.

Melv pulled the handbrake on and killed the engine. He leaned behind him onto the back seat and reached into the cool bag, bringing out a bottle of champagne and two plastic flutes. He pulled a lever and a tray opened up over the automatic gear stick. Melv placed the glasses on the mini table and opened the bottle and poured the champagne out.

***

Geri was really pleased with herself; she'd managed to sit next to Deano through dinner, and had managed to take his attention from Jo for some of that time by bombarding him with questions. Deano, on the other hand, was really pissed off with her. Every time he'd tried to talk to Jo, Geri had been squawking over his shoulder like a parrot on a perch. Jo stretched her arms above her head and wiggled her shoulders, completely unaware of the effect she was having on Deano.

"I think I might have a little leg-stretch before turning in," she said.

"I was just thinking that," Deano said. "Fancy a walk along the beach?"

"Yes, that would be nice. I've got my mozzie spray on. Wouldn't you think they'd make it in something that smelled a bit nice?" she said. "But then I suppose it wouldn't keep them away, would it?" she added, answering her own question.

Deano and Jo stood up, Deano draining his glass at the same time. Dave caught his eye and winked.

"We're just going for a little after dinner walk," Deano said. "See you all a bit later."

"I'll come! I fancy a walk." Geri jumped up, too, and scuttled along behind them.

"How thick can you be?" Natalie asked the rest of them as they watched the three of them go off. "How much clearer can Deano make it that he likes Jo? And Jo obviously likes him. Geri must get some sort of kick out of thinking she's spoiling it for them. Nasty cow!"

The trio walked through the bar area and gardens, past the avenue of huge palms and along the path to the beach. They walked in silence, each deep in his or her own thoughts. Jo was surprised as the animosity she felt towards Geri at that moment. She'd suggested a walk in the hope that Deano would come along. As the holiday had progressed and she'd spent more time with him, Jo realised that although she'd only known him a few days she was beginning to have feelings for him. She wanted them to spend a bit more time alone, getting to know each other.

Deano was fuming. He knew how to read the signs and he was sure that Jo was, in her own way, giving him a green light. And now that stupid bitch Geri was determined to spoil it. He wasn't interested in her. Well, she might have done for a quick fuck if Jo hadn't been on the holiday. But he'd been surprised to find that he really did like Jo; there was something about her that attracted him. He'd wondered if he was just curious in his own perverted little way, to get off with a woman of the cloth. But it wasn't that; he really did like her. He'd have to think of a way to get rid of Geri, even if it meant being rude to her.

Geri was beaming inside. While she was with them, Jo couldn't get Deano on his own!

After walking the length of the beach the three of them sat on the low sea wall and looked at the silver reflection of the moon slithering across the sea. Deano moved his left hand across Jo's lap and took her hand in his. She didn't resist. And when he caressed her fingers with his thumb she squeezed his hand in response. Geri, sitting on his right, had sat so close to him she was almost on his lap. Her left thigh was jammed up against his right one. He was trying hard to move away, but if he shifted any further to the left he'd shove Jo off the end of the wall.

And so that sat like that, in silence, for about ten minutes. Deano toyed with the idea of telling Geri to fuck off, but he didn't want to appear like some sort of crude bully in front of Jo. Finally, Jo let go of Deano's hand and stood up.

"Good night!" she said to both of them, and turning walked back along the path towards her room. Deano jumped up and went after her.

"Wait, Jo!" She stopped and he caught her up. "Don't go! Please!"

He grabbed her hand and held it in both of his. Jo stared at his face, the contours shaded by the moonlight and her heart flipped. Over his shoulder she could see Geri, who had stood up and was walking slowly towards them.

"I'm tired, Deano. And we're not going to be able to shake her off without being downright rude. Let's leave it for another night when I'm not so tired."

She leaned forward and kissed him on the cheek and turned and walked off just as Geri sidled up beside him. She linked her arm through his.

"Well, as it's just the two of us now, let's have a drink!" she said.

***

"It's a beautiful spot, isn't it?" Melv said, offering one of the flutes to Eve.

"Yes. Beautiful. Well, the whole island is. I've never been here before. I didn't know it existed."

Oh, shit! I'm gabbling again!

Eve took a deep breath and tried again.

"Have you been here in Antigua long?"

Melv tapped his flute against the one Eve was holding and looked into her face.

"Cheers! To old friendships! It is just amazing to meet up with you again, Eve."

"To old friendships!" Eve gulped her drink, causing the bubbles to hit the back of her throat and go up her nose, making her cough.

"Careful! You okay?"

Eve nodded, still coughing, absolutely furious with herself. She was acting like a fifteen-year-old who was only used to lemonade. Melv reached into his pocket and pulled out a pure white linen handkerchief, which he patted against Eve's cheek, where tears had formed due to her coughing fit.

"I've been in Antigua since 2001," he said, answering her earlier question as he patted. "I was working for Beachside Resorts International in Barbados. They're a large multinational concern, who have two properties on the north of Antigua and knowing I had an Antiguan connection through my wife, they offered me a transfer here managing one of those properties ten years ago. Then at the end of last year I heard that Martin Samuel was leaving Mango Tree Resort, so I applied for the job."

"Do you like it?" Eve asked, having regained her composure.

"Oh, yes. I like working for a private company and I pretty much have a free reign to do whatever I like, within reason, of course. It's early days yet, and the worldwide recession hasn't helped our situation, here in Antigua, but so far, the owner seems pleased with what I'm doing and is open to my proposals, so I feel quite positive and enthusiastic about the future. How about you? You've been to Antigua before, I understand."

"Loads of times over the last few years. It's strange... you know... you were here all the time and yet our paths never crossed."

"Strange that we didn't sense each other being so close, you mean?"

"More that we could have been in the same restaurant, or in the bank, or passed on Market Street. Perhaps we did. Perhaps we just didn't recognise each other."

"We recognised each other on Saturday night. I knew it was you the moment I saw you. You haven't changed. Not a bit."

Melv reached into the cool bag for the bottle of champagne and topped up their glasses.

"So," Eve said, "tell me about your family. You say you have children?"

"Yes. My son, Radley, is studying Law in New York and my daughter Juliette is in her last year of high school. She thinks she wants to be a primary school teacher."

"And your wife?"

Melv stared through the windscreen of the vehicle, out at the moonlight dancing over the surface of the sea.

"Mary works for ABI Bank."

"And she's Antiguan?"

175

"Yes."

"So, where did you meet?"

"In Barbados. She was there working in the same bank as a friend of mine and he introduced us."

He suddenly turned and looked at Eve and took her hand. Her first instinct was to snatch it away, but the feel of his hand, his skin against hers, familiar again after so many years, was good and she liked it.

"I tried to find you, Eve. I got in touch with Janet Morris. All she would say was that you'd gone away and she didn't know where. She said she had no contact details for you. I didn't know where to begin. I even thought about trying to find your parents but Janet said you hadn't gone home. I don't understand. I wrote and told you my father had died and I didn't hear from you again. I waited months for a letter from you. Every day I'd practically pounce on the mailman but there was never anything from you. Nothing. You just disappeared."

"What was the point of contacting you? It was a fling we had; we both knew it could never come to anything else."

"No we didn't! We'd made plans together!"

"I know we had. But they were just foolish dreams. You left, but I couldn't follow. So it was best for me to just disappear out of your life. And you seem to have got it together nicely. You didn't need me for anything."

"How can you say that?"

"Well, look at you! You've got a wife, two lovely kids, and a successful career... where would I have fitted in?"

"You would have been my lovely wife!"

Eve laughed and drained her champagne, leaning back to put the empty flute into the cool bag before Melv could top her up again. She was a lightweight where alcohol was concerned and she could already begin to feel the effects of the champagne.

"Would have, could have, might have! We'll never know, will we? We can sit here and get all poetic and nostalgic, imagining what might have been, but we don't know. We were just kids then and when we grew up we might have spent all day and night arguing and fighting and ended up killing each other!"

Melv reached for both her hands and pulled her towards him. She let herself go forward, but held firm against his grip. She wasn't going to simply melt into his arms. She couldn't believe the waves of emotion that swept over her, one after the other at being with this man again, so close, so near, so alone. She knew without a doubt that she could fall in love with him again in the twinkling of an eye. She'd never loved anyone with the intensity of the deep love she'd had for Melv. He'd been her first lover and nobody else had ever been able to match him in bed, either. Sex, since Melv, had always been an anticlimax.

"We didn't used to spend all day and night arguing if you remember. We spend all day and night in bed!" he said.

"We were eighteen-years-old! Well, I was. And you were twenty-two. Of course we spend all our time in bed, there'd have been something wrong with us if we hadn't! But that was then and this is now."

"I'm not saying we should spend all day in bed now! Well, not unless you want to!" he added, laughing to dilute his words.

"Nice try, Melv! But I don't think us having sex, even if it were just for old time's sake, would be the answer to anything, do you? And I don't like you just assuming I'll just fall back into bed with you."

"This is going all wrong! I'm not assuming anything like that! I didn't want to get you alone to try to talk you into having sex! I really, genuinely, wanted to spend time with you. I want to know everything about you, everything that's happened to you since the last time I saw you. And I simply wanted to know why you disappeared. Why you ended it."

"Melv, it's all in the past. Why dig everything up now? Just accept it. I knew it wouldn't work. I couldn't follow you to Barbados. So I got on with my life."

He looked hurt. She could see that her words had stung him.

Why am I being such a cow?

"Let's spend some time together! We can get to know each other again. Would you like to come out with me for the day? I've got a small speed boat. We could go to a nice secluded beach or down to Falmouth or English Harbour."

"I heard the weather's changing."

"Yes, Thursday there'll be a big storm. You can feel it coming; that's why it's so oppressive tonight. But we could go tomorrow, or Wednesday."

"Sorry, I'm on a catamaran tomorrow with the group and then most of them are going on a jeep excursion on Wednesday that I'll have to see off."

"Please say you'll make time for me before you leave," he implored. "Even if it's just for an hour or two."

"Perhaps, although what's the point, Melv? Why start something up again after all this time?"

"Can't we be friends?"

"But we wouldn't be friends, would we? We'd eventually become lovers. And you're married and I'm not prepared to go down that road, on a carrousel to nowhere."

"But I'm not happily married..."

"Oh, please! Credit me with some intelligence! Don't make out you and your wife just potter along next to each other in a sexless marriage while you've been waiting for me to re-appear in your life!"

"That's not so far from the truth, Eve."

John Holt started to sing *Never, Never, Never.* Melv took her hand again and spoke the words along with the artist.

"Impossible to live with you, but I know I could never live without you!"

"You've been living quite nicely without me for the last thirty years. It's getting late, Melv, I think we should go. Please take me back to the resort."

His face was a mixture of disbelief and disappointment as he looked at her. She took her hand from his and turned to face forward, waiting for him to start the engine. When he didn't she spoke without looking at him.

"I mean it, Melv. I want to go back."

He turned the key and put the car into reverse. They drove all the way back to the resort in silence.

Shit! This isn't how I wanted it to be!

But even though it wasn't how she'd wanted it to turn out, Eve couldn't think of anything she could do or say now that wouldn't make the situation worse. As they got to the Mango Tree Resort, the security guard, recognising Melv's car, lifted the barrier to let him through.

"You could have dropped me at the gate," Eve said.

"Could have, would have, might have," he said, bitterly as he raced up the driveway and pulled to a halt outside reception, throwing up gravel as he did. He leaned across her and opened the passenger door, quickly pulling back his hand and placing it on the steering wheel.

"Good night, Eve. Enjoy the rest of your stay."

"Good night."

Eve slid slowly off the seat until she felt her feet make contact with the ground as elegantly as she could under the circumstances. She turned and closed the door and before it had even clicked into place, Melv had revved up and roared off into the night. Eve stood there in disbelief that it had all gone so horribly wrong. Melv was behaving like a petulant child. But then, perhaps she'd completely misunderstood. Perhaps he really did think they could be just good friends. Was she the one spoiling it by assuming he'd want to bring sex into the equation and even that he'd want to be unfaithful to his wife? What was her name? Mary? Perhaps all he did really want was some answers as to why she'd left him.

Nice one, Eve! You've ballsed it up again!

What had really surprised her was the depth of her feelings for him after all this time. She felt her stomach tighten into a knot and a great big sob begin to form.

Fuck it! I need a drink!

Up until that moment Eve had never understood people who said they *needed* a drink. But she did need one and she was going to have one, lightweight or not. She marched through reception and out onto the terrace where just a few people were sitting. Striding up to the bar she ordered a rum and Diet Coke from Nellie, the barmaid, who was on instead of Elvis tonight, as he had done the daytime shift. The rum felt really good, somehow comforting and reassuring, as it went down. Yes she really needed this drink! In fact, when she'd finished this one, she'd order another one to take to her room. She looked around the bar and terrace lounge area to see if there was anyone she recognised. There wasn't. She was pleased about that, it probably meant they'd all taken her advice to have an early night so they'd be bright-eyed and sober for the catamaran trip the following day.

I'd better make sure I am, too!

Her gaze went over to the far side of the terrace, her attention attracted by a man's arm in the air, waving at her. He appeared to have a woman lying across him, her face buried into his neck. Eve realised that the man was Deano and it was her he was waving at.

Oh, please, God, give me a break! Not another drama tonight.

Deano's arm was now bent and his hand curved, beckoning Eve over to him. Approaching the table she recognised the blonde head covered in braids and beads. It was Geri. Eve was a bit surprised, because she thought that the signs all pointed to Deano getting it together with Jo, although she didn't really know why as Jo was lovely, and there was something about Deano, with his fake tan and his turquoise eyes and cocksure manner that Eve just didn't take to at all. Sighing, and kicking herself for coming into the bar in the first place, Eve put her empty glass down and walked towards the two of them. As she got closer she could see that Deano was mouthing *'Help!'* at her. Her day had been dramatic enough. She wasn't in the mood for this.

"What's up, Deano?" she asked loudly.

Deano beckoned her to come closer. When she did he then started to talk in a stage whisper.

"Look at the state of her! She's rat-arsed. I don't know what to do with her."

"How did she get in this state?"

"Well, she'd been sitting next to me all through dinner and then tagged along when Jo and I went for a walk then when Jo said she was going to get an early night, I said I was going to have just one, just a nightcap, at the bar with the lads. Well, before I could look round she'd joined us and she started... you know... coming onto me, pushing against me, dancing round me. The others left and she was all over me, like a rash."

"Couldn't you have just left? Gone to bed?"

"What? Leave her like this?"

"She's not your responsibility. And if you felt uncomfortable about her behaviour you should have just walked away. You should have gone to bed when the others did."

"Well, don't act as if it's my fault. I didn't do anything. I don't even like her. Everyone knows Jo's the one I like."

"So, where's Jo, then?"

"She went to bed ages ago."

"Well, I don't know what you expect me to do, Deano. You got yourself into this."

"No, I didn't"

"You encouraged her."

"Don't take that tone with me! I've already told you she was all over me."

"Yes, and you were probably loving it. Deano, I've met men like you before. You create a drama to star in. Geri's been after you all holiday; even I've been able to see that. But I can't help thinking you're playing your part; you're actually enjoying having this woman follow you around, even though you fancy someone else. You could have gone to bed two hours ago, but you didn't, you chose to sit and let her come onto you and make a fool of herself so that you'll have a story to tell the boys in the morning. Isn't that right?"

Shit! I've gone too far.

Deano, somewhat taken aback by Eve's shrewd observation of exactly what had happened, said nothing. At that moment, Geri farted long and loud. Eve and Deano looked at each other and burst out laughing, their animosity temporarily forgotten.

"I'll get security," Eve said. "Geri can wake up in the morning in the knowledge that not one, but two young handsome men took her back to her room tonight."

"Will she be alright, with two men, do you think?"

"Will they be?" Eve asked, laughing. "I'll go along, too, but they can carry her between them. I put my back out once helping a drunken Travel Together client back to his room; I'm not risking it again."

Just at that moment, Spencer, the Head of Night Security at the resort came strolling along with Skipper, doing one of their patrols.

"The very people!" Eve said, beckoning them over. "Gentlemen, we have a problem."

Spencer and Skipper, made short work of Geri. Skipper swept her up into his arms and with Spencer and Eve as the outriders took her safely back to her room.

"If only we had a picture of this to show her in the morning! Geri curled up in the arms of a hunky security guard." Deano said as they parted ways on the staircase. "You can't wait while I get my camera, can you?"

"Deano, quit while you're ahead," Eve said.

"Will do!" he said, looking suitably chastised. "And, Eve?"

"Yes?"

"I'm sorry about tonight. It wasn't what it seemed."

"Goodnight!" Eve called out as she followed Spencer and Skipper down the corridor to Geri's room. She knew it was exactly what it had seemed.

Once in her room Skipper placed Geri gently on the bed in the recovery position and left Eve to take off her shoes and put her handbag on the dressing table.

"Thanks, guys. I appreciate your help."

"No problem, Eve. We're happy to help. Goodnight," Spencer said and the two of them went off back to continue their patrol while Eve, finally, went back to her own room. Was she in the Guinness Book of Records under *The Person Who's Assisted Most Drunks Back to Their Rooms*?

She stood under the shower and let the water run right over her, washing away all the day's events, all the problems, all the drama and the evening with Melv that hadn't gone to plan. She decided to put it out of her mind and not think about it anymore. She dried herself and wrapped her wet hair in a towel. That would dry while she was asleep; it would probably cause her rheumatism at some point in the future but she was too tired to dry it now. She lay down and leaned over to the light switch.

As Scarlet O'Hara more or less said, thank Christ tomorrow is another day!

***

DAY FIVE

It seemed like only two hours later, but was in fact almost seven, when Eve woke up. She jumped out of bed and pulled the curtains open wide to see what the weather was like because today was the boat trip. It looked like a lovely day for sailing; there were a few light clouds and the palm trees were being gently rustled by the breeze.

Good!

The last thing Eve wanted was to have to deal with people who were seasick, or to have the day spoilt by rain, although that rarely happened because Amos, the captain of the catamaran, could read the weather signs like others would read the newspaper. She looked at herself in the mirror and gave herself a fright. The towel had worked its way off her head during the night and the result was a hairstyle that resembled Ken Dodd's, but wasn't quite as elegant. It was a good job she was going on the boat. She damped it down and brushed it back as hard as she could and put a band around it. She then put a dollop of conditioner into her palm and worked it through the ponytail to protect it from the sun and the salt water. She smiled to herself as she got ready. She loved the day out on the catamaran; it was the best boat trip in the world as far as she was concerned. Amos was what could only be described as a cool dude and he really understood the Travel Together groups very well and always gave them a great day. She was glad that the boat trip was today because she needed to enjoy herself and have a good time so that she could forget about her disastrous date with Melv.

Don't even think about last night! Don't even think about him!

She had a group of people to take out and look after and it was her intention to see they had the best day ever. And she could only do that if she concentrated on her job and didn't go off into Cloud Cuckoo Land about what might have been with Melv. She was jolted out of her thoughts as she was wriggling into her swimsuit by her mobile phone ringing. She grabbed it and looked at the screen, which was showing the call as coming from *Mango TR*.

"Good morning! This is Eve speaking."

"This is Ursula. Ursula Marshall."

Surprise! Surprise!

"What can I do for you, Ursula?"

"I'd like to go on the boat trip. I believe it's today, isn't it?"

"Yes, it's today."

"Is there any room left? Or is it too late to book?"

If she'd been a real cow or really wanted to play it by the book Eve could have told Ursula that it was, indeed, too late to book for the boat trip. But she was pleased that Ursula had decided she wanted to do something with the group at last and a day out on the boat would be an ideal way to break the ice and introduce her to the others. And one more wouldn't make any difference, plus it must have taken a degree of courage to pick up the phone and ask to come along.

"We can always squeeze one more in, Ursula. It's our own charter so I'll let them know there's an extra one. And I'm delighted you've decided to join us."

"Well, I think I've sat alone feeling sorry for myself for long enough. Now, how do I pay you?"

"Why don't you meet me in reception in ten minutes?"

"Yes, that'll be fine. I've got US dollars, is that okay for payment?"

"That's fine. See you in ten."

Eve hung up and gave a great big grin. Sometimes her job had lovely moments and this had just been one of them.

***

If it hadn't been boat trip day, and she'd rather bite off her own right hand than miss that, Geri would have just turned over in bed and gone back to sleep again. She felt bad, really ill. She sighed, annoyed with herself. She had to try to curb her drinking. She wasn't an alcoholic! Oh, no! Nothing like that! But she realised that she was drinking more heavily than she should, even allowing for the fact that she was on holiday. Getting drunk had got her into a mess on Sunday night at Shirley Heights and again last night. Although, what had actually happened last night she didn't have a clue. She knew that she'd been getting on well with Deano and that they'd been dancing together standing at the bar, but what happened next or how she'd got back to her room and into bed was a complete mystery. She'd obviously spent the night alone. There were no signs of anyone else having been in her room; no dent on the other pillow; no boxer shorts on the bathroom floor; no condom foils in the bin. She was still wearing her peach mini-dress. It looked like a rag now, all screwed up and with a big, brown drink stain down the front. She shuffled over to the dressing table and opened her toiletries bag and took out her Alka Seltzers. Pouring a glass of water, she downed them while they were still fizzing and then burped loudly. She looked at her watch and saw it was already eight forty-three.

Bloody hell! Get in the shower!

She wanted to turn up on time and looking as fresh as possible. She was spending the day on a catamaran with Deano. They could pick up from where they'd left off the previous evening, wherever that might have been. And short of diving overboard, he wouldn't be able to get away from her.

***

By nine twenty-five all of the group were assembled on the beach by the water-sports' centre, except Dawn and Donna, who had had to go to the ladies for one last time.

"I don't know if I'll be able to go on the boat, you know, the toilet might not be very nice. And I'm funny like that, aren't I, Dawn?" Donna had felt the need to share with them.

"You're funny alrigh'!" Dave had called after their disappearing backs. He was slightly hung-over having gone to Macy's Bar in the village with Trevor, Michael and Natalie the previous evening for 'just one' that had become five.

Dawn had decided to take off the plaster, which was a great improvement, although she had a nasty graze across her nose and cheek.

"I think I need to let the air get to it," she said.

"I see the old dear's coming then?" Murray had said to Eve five minutes earlier when he had seen Ursula walking towards them, obviously dressed for a day out on a boat in her straw hat and floral, button-through cotton dress and deck shoes.

"Yes, Ursula is joining us," Eve hissed, trying to keep her voice down so that she wouldn't overhear them. "It's not easy for her coming along today as the rest of us already know each other. It's taken her a lot of courage, so be nice, please!"

"Yes, Miss!" Murray said, in a sing-song schoolboy voice.

Oh, piss off, Murray!

Had she really said that? No! It had been Grace who was standing next to her and who made a point of greeting Ursula with an outstretched hand and the others all followed her example, except Huw who almost smiled at her from his position of leaning against the counter. The word at breakfast had been that he had crossed swords with Grace, Jo and Natalie at dinner the previous evening after Eve had left, over suggesting he could bring along Jacqui, a woman who he'd got into conversation with at the bar earlier in the day.

"He said one more wouldn't make any difference and I said it would, because she wasn't one of our group. And then he said *'but she's on her own'* and so Grace said *'well she should have come with Travel Together then. Shouldn't she'* And then he said he was going to bring her along anyway, and Jo said you wouldn't have that. Has he asked you?" Natalie was indignant.

"No, he hasn't. And, if he does the answer is *'No she can't come.'*" Eve had replied. How much clearer did she have to make it to someone like Huw?

"Good!" Natalie had said, biting into her toast as if it were Huw's ankle.

Eve smiled at the memory and then looked across the bay and saw the familiar tall, white mast with its green chevron markings as the Arawak Arrow came round the headland and headed towards the beach just in front of them.

"There's the boat!" Geri, of course, had to be the first one to see it.

An excited buzz went round the group as if they were ten-year-olds on a school outing and they moved across the beach towards the water's edge. The sea was like a millpond; it was truly a magnificent day for the boat trip. The catamaran pulled as far onto the beach as it could get and a slim, yet muscular crewman with braids tied up in a knot on his head, smart in his pristine, white shorts and green and white stripped sailor's top with intertwined AA embroidered on it, lowered the ladder from its place between the nets and then walked down it into the water.

"Good morning, everyone! Please take off your shoes. Now you all just relax and let me help you up the ladder and my co-worker will help you onto the deck at the top."

He stood firm in the sand, one hand on the ladder and the other ready to assist his passengers. Geri was the first one to board.

"There you go, young lady," he said as he gripped her arm until she was steady on the ladder.

Simpering at being the first one on and being called *'young lady'* Geri climbed the ladder and then allowed herself to be assisted by the next sailor, who was wearing a gold chain almost as wide as the one holding the anchor, with two gold teeth to match . Gradually the whole group boarded without incident, Eve, as always bringing up the rear. The group started to sort itself out, those who wanted shade grabbing it and others making for the nets and the decks to soak up as much sun as they could. Eve made her way down the catamaran to greet Amos.

"Eve, baby! You look as hot as ever!" he said, hugging her against his belly. He had changed little in the months since she'd last seen him. He wore his shaved head covered with an Arawak Arrow cap; his goatee beard neatly trimmed; a large gold sleeper in his right ear and smart wrap-around shades.

"It's good to see you, too, Amos," Eve said, returning his embrace. "We've got quite a nice group here, so there shouldn't be any problems," she reassured him.

"As you know, there's nothing we can't handle," he chuckled and then barked out work orders to the crew in local dialect as he put the catamaran into reverse and pulled away from Mango Tree Resort.

There was a rush of people and cameras as everyone moved towards the back of the boat to get an off-shore photo of the resort, which looked huge and luxurious nestled in among the luscious foliage surrounding it. Then, bags were opened, towels taken out, t-shirts, shorts and sarongs taken off as they all settled down and Amos began his PA.

"Good morning ladies and gentlemen and welcome aboard the Arawak Arrow," he said. There was a very low murmur of *'good morning'* and *'hello'* from the group. Amos sucked his teeth and tutted loudly into the microphone.

"Now that was terrible. I'm going to try again and if I don't get a proper response we're gonna turn right around and go back on the beach and drop off all the men."

This caused a laugh to ripple down the boat and people to actually turn and look at Amos as he spoke.

"So, good morning ladies and gentlemen and welcome aboard the Arawak Arrow."

"Good morning!" chorused the group, loud enough to be heard back in the resort.

"We have a beautiful day planned out ahead of us for you today. We're going to head over to Cades Reef and do a little snorkelling. Any of you want to try that? Do we have any snorkelers on board?"

About ten or eleven hands were raised.

"Good! So we're going to spend a little time on the reef so that you can take a good look around and then we're going to cruise down the southern coast and probably pull in at Rendezvous Bay, which is a beautiful spot and with any luck we will be the only people there enjoying it. From there we'll go on down the south coast and into Falmouth Harbour and show you some of the beautiful yachts inside there and then onto English Harbour Nelson's Dockyard, where we'll pull over and have our lunch and then if the wind is with us we'll put the sail up and come back to Mango Tree Resort under wind power only. So that's the plan. We're lucky to be sailing today, because from tomorrow the weather is gonna change; we're expecting a big storm on Thursday and Friday and you'll see that even tomorrow the sea conditions will be very different from today. Now, we have two toilets on board, which are both to be found on the starboard side, that's the right hand side to those of you who aren't familiar with nautical terms and are being pointed out to you now by the crew. The toilets are for human waste only and are operated by the hand pump at the side of each bowl."

The three crew members were all stationed around the catamaran pointing towards the toilets so that everyone on board could see where they were. They then picked up a life jacket each.

"In the very unlikely event that you will need to use a lifejacket you will find them under the seats in the middle section of the catamaran and in the closet on the port side of the bar, that's the left hand side. You place the lifejacket over your head the way the crew are showing you and you inflate it by pulling on the red tag. There is a light and a whistle for attracting attention."

He paused while the crew mimed blowing the whistle and waving to attract attention.

"We have a full bar service onboard today, including sodas, water, fruit juices, rum, scotch, gin, vodka and beer. However, for safety reasons the bar is not open for alcohol until after snorkelling is finished. Now at Arawak Cruises, we pride ourselves on having the best crews in the whole Caribbean, but they're on day off today, so you've got us."

There was an appreciative laugh at his joke.

"There are three crew members working with me today and they're going to go out of their way to make your cruise the best one possible. If they don't they're gonna have to swim back to St John's. First of all, we have our own Lennox Lewis lookalike, the man Neville..."

The sailor who had helped everyone up the ladder from the beach lifted his hand.

"Good morning and welcome!" he shouted.

"Morning, Neville!" the group chorused.

"Over there, struggling to get out of his lifejacket is Skinnyman..."

"Good morning to everyone!" Skinnyman said giving a little bow.

"Morning, Skinnyman!" the group said laughing, as Skinnyman was anything but. A giant of a man, at least six foot four with huge shoulders and arms, made big and strong by years of pulling rigging, and a belly that made him look like he was carrying twins.

"And over behind the bar we have Aaron."

"Good morning!" Aaron waved and gold teeth flashed and once more the group shouted a greeting.

"So, you sit back and relax, make sure you put on your sun block. You don't want to make the same mistake that we did. Just look at how we ended up!" he joked. "Ladies and gentlemen, enjoy your day and the bar is open!"

Amos's tone was just right and as Eve looked around the cat she could see everyone was relaxed and ready to enjoy the day. Ursula had taken a seat in the middle section of the catamaran, under the awning, in the shade. She was next to Suzanne who was already engaging her in deep conversation. Eve noticed that Stewart had put his bag next to Suzanne but she had her back to him and he looked a little put out. Eve liked Stewart; she hoped he and Suzanne hadn't fallen out. Deano was out on the port deck next to Dave and Jo. He'd avoided her so far this morning; perhaps he'd taken in what she'd said to him last night. Geri seemed to be ignoring him, although she was making herself comfortable on the port net just up from where Deano was sitting. Eve also noticed that Frances had gone onto the starboard net by herself. She didn't seem to be friends with Deborah any more. Deborah herself was sitting on the deck and Murray was unscrewing the top of a bottle of suntan lotion, ready to put it onto her back. As he poured the lotion into his hand he was startled by Amos calling out "Just a moment, sir!" and striding down the catamaran towards him. Everyone turned to look at them. Amos's face was stern and his fists were clenched.

"What do you think you're doing?" he demanded to know.

Murray looked at him, startled and unsure of what was going on or what he should say. Amos stared at him, eyeballing him with a look of venom.

"Don't you realise you're taking jobs from local people? Eh?"

He leaned across and took the bottle from Murray's hand.

"That's MY job!" he said and started liberally applying the lotion to Deborah's shoulders and back, in big, exaggerated, sensuous motions. The group screamed out laughing, even Murray.

"Oh, boy! I love my job!" Amos purred. Deborah was purring almost as loudly.

"You had me going there for a moment, Amos!" Murray said.

"No hard feelings," Amos said rubbing in the white cream as if his life depended on it. "And just to prove it, I'll buy you a beer as soon as snorkelling's over."

Murray laughed again and settled down on his towel, which he'd placed next to Deborah. Natalie, who was perched on the port deck near the net, looked back at him.

"I wonder if Murray'll take his shirt off today," she said. "He hasn't had it off since we got here."

"Yes but he looks as if he might later on!" Michael quipped, nodding towards Deborah.

"Ha! Ha! Ha!" Natalie screamed out laughing and high-fived Michael's hand. "Nice one!"

"Perhaps he's got a disfigurement," Trevor suggested.

"Or a fird nipple!" Dave said, causing Natalie to screech with laughter again.

"Or a really hairy back. That's such a turn off," Grace said.

"Yeah, but he could get that waxed, couldn't he?" Natalie said.

"Waxed?" Trevor and Dave looked at each other in horror and chorused their disapproval.

"Yes. Back, sac and crack. It's all the thing among men, apparently," Grace said.

"Although not the men on this trip, obviously," Natalie added.

"Yeah, well, it's probly alrigh' if you're a chorus boy or sumfink, but it's not for real men, is it, Trev?"

"Certainly not for me," Trevor agreed, with a shudder. "It sounds as if it's quite painful."

"What we men have to suffer to improve our looks!" Michael sighed dramatically as he turned to look at the sumptuous beach that they were just passing. "Look at that!"

"That's Turner's Beach, sir," Skinnyman said, appearing at their side. He offered his knuckle to Michael, who knocked it with his own. "Where you from, brother?"

"I was born in England, but my parents are from St Vincent."

"Beautiful place. You know it?"

"Oh yes, I went there a lot as a kid. Antigua takes some beating, though."

"You're not wrong. Now, what can I get you folks to drink?"

***

"Did you put on your sun block, ma'am? We don't want you burning, now do we? You heard what the captain said."

Frances, who was in a little world of her own enjoying the gentle swing of the net, opened her eyes to find herself looking into a pair of black eyes with the longest eyelashes she'd ever seen. It was Neville, the sailor who looked like the boxer, whose name she'd forgotten.

"No, I'm fine. I've put it on."

"And have you rubbed it in?"

"I've rubbed it in," she said.

"So, you don't need me for anything at the moment?"

"Not at the moment, thanks."

Frances gulped. Was he coming onto her? Surely not!

"Would you like a drink?"

"Just water, please."

"I'll be right back."

Bloody hell! Frances could feel herself blushing. He was a hunk; a young hunk, young enough to be her son. But surely he was just being nice? Wasn't he? He was back immediately with a glass of iced water. He knelt down beside her so that she only had to raise her arm to take the glass from him. She daren't raise her gaze as his groin was on a level with her head. She took a long swig of water.

"What's your name?" he asked.

"Frances."

"I'm Neville. I'll see you for snorkelling, Frances. Take it easy."

And he was gone.

Bloody hell!

***

As the morning wore on, Eve began to relax and enjoy the day; it was like having a day off for her, while being around the group at the same time. The snorkelling at Cades Reef had been a great success; in the end, most of the group had snorkelled, with only Suzanne, Murray, Deborah and Eve herself, staying on the cat. Eve was pleased to see Ursula joining in, wearing her plain navy blue racing swimsuit.

"I love the water, so relaxing!" she said as she tried on fins and allowed Aaron to fit her mask properly, before expertly flipping over the side into the beautiful, clear water.

"You betta tell the Dolly Sisters that the fins only come in black," Dave said to Aaron. "They'll be askin' yer for matching masks in a colour to go wiv their bikinis," he added.

Neville had overheard what Dave had said. He looked at Geri, Dawn and Donna, who were sitting together putting on fins.

"You three sisters, then?" he asked.

"Not me!" Geri said quickly, not wanting to be associated with the other two. "Just them!"

"No we're not!" Dawn said. "We're just friends, we work together," she explained to Neville.

"You all look alike, though, you could be sisters," he said. Dawn and Donna simpered and smiled at his words while Geri scowled and tossed her braids. Her head was actually quite sore in places, where the beads had dug into her head while she'd slept. She thought she might have to, regretfully, take them out later. They hadn't exactly been a raging success. The only time anyone had mentioned them she'd got the distinct impression they were taking the mickey out of her.

"Everything okay with you, Suzanne?" Eve asked as they stood watching the snorkelers getting off the boat.

"Oh, yes! I wish I could bottle this up and take it home with me! You have such a lovely job, Eve. You live a real champagne lifestyle."

"Champagne lifestyle, lemonade money," Eve said, thinking as she always did that she'd be ashamed for people to find out she worked for so little, as Suzanne giggled at her words. The tourism industry has always been notoriously poorly paid. "But I hope you're taking photos of all this so that at least you can look at them and relive the holiday when it's a cold, dismal UK day."

"It's not just the weather. It's the place, the people, everything!" she said flinging her arms wide.

"Yes, especially the people..." Eve smiled and looked at her. "Is everything okay with the people?"

Suzanne giggled like a little girl.

"You mean Stewart, don't you? Well, yes, we're getting on really well, but, I'll tell you this in confidence, Eve, I had to ask him to slow down a bit last night."

Eve fought to keep a straight face, not because she was laughing at Suzanne and Stewart's romance, but rather the innocent, earnest way that Suzanne was talking so openly to her about it.

"I really like him and we spent a nice afternoon yesterday in the village together, but just because we're getting on well doesn't mean I want to take it any further just yet. We danced together last night and had a little kiss and cuddle when he walked me back to my room, but that was it."

"You're a wise girl!" Eve said, thinking it was a pity other people on these holidays didn't all think like Suzanne. It would stop a lot of upset and aggravation if they did.

While the snorkelers were exploring the reef with Aaron and Neville as their guides, Skinnyman followed them in a dingy, leaving Amos on the cat.

"Okay, now that snorkelling's taking place the bar is officially fully open. What can I get you? Rum punch? Beer?"

"Oh a beer, if you insist," Murray said. Amos dived into the huge ice-packed cool box and pulled out a can of beer, which he opened with a flourish. "You happy to drink from the can, local style, or do you want a glass?"

"The can's fine."

"What's up? You had too much sun yesterday?"

"No. Why do you ask?"

"You've got your shirt on. People only usually keep their shirts on if they've got burned."

"No, no! I just like tae keep my shirt on, that's all," Murray said, a trifle, pompously. Amos turned his attention to the women.

"Ladies, three rum punches?"

"Not for me, thanks," Eve said. "Just my usual Diet Coke."

"One rum and Diet coming up!" he joked.

Eve laughed but she knew he would never serve her alcohol if she didn't want it. Like her, Amos was a thorough professional, and although to all intents and purposes it looked like he was carefree and having as good a time as his passengers, Eve knew that he didn't miss a detail and safety always came first. Her point was proved seconds later when Deborah asked if he could play some music.

"Not while we're snorkelling, darlin'" he said. "Just in case we have a problem in the water with the people, I have to be able to hear the crew callin' me. As soon as everyone's back on board we'll put the music back on and you can choose it. How about that?"

Deborah smiled sweetly and thanked him.

Eating out of his hand!

And now, as they rounded the headland into Rendezvous Bay everyone was having a great time. Eve didn't have to ask, she could see it. Even Huw had smiled at her a little earlier; his hissy fit obviously over. The beach at Rendezvous Bay is practically inaccessible by road and consequently it was deserted apart from a couple who, having secured the whole place for themselves looked up in dismay as the Arawak Arrow sailed towards them, music blaring. To make matters worse, they were on the exact part of the beach that Amos needed to pull up on. He sounded the claxon.

"Sorry, guys!" he said over the PA. The couple, both in very brief thongs, raised their hands and waved an acceptance of his apology.

As Eve floated on her back in the water, eyes closed, she felt completely relaxed. In fact, she couldn't tell where her body ended and the sea began; it was pure therapy. Eve adored the sea. She could spend hours just sitting looking at it or lying in it like now, letting herself go with the flow like a piece of driftwood. She truly believed that if everyone could float in the sea for an hour a day all the stress in the world would disappear. She suddenly realised that she hadn't thought about Melv for at least two hours.

So don't spoil it and think about him now!

She was aroused from her trance by screams of laughter coming from Dawn and Donna, who had been treading water in the shallows when Huw and Jason had swum up behind them and pulled their ankles.

"I thought I was drowning! I thought it was a frigging shark!" Donna said splashing out at Jason who was now trying to swim away but found his way blocked by Natalie and Jo.

"We've got him for you!" Natalie shouted as the two of them grabbed him and then joined by Dawn ducked him under as hard as they could.

"I ope e's be'avin'!" Dave called over to Suzanne, who was being held up in the water by Stewart. "Nunna that dirty dancin' stuff you was doin' at Shirley Ites!"

Stewart let go of Suzanne with his right arm to stick two fingers up at Dave, causing her to slip under. He hoisted her up, as she coughed and gasped.

"Sorry! That was Dave's fault."

"'Ow's it my fault? I'm ova ere!" Dave called out laughing.

There was a loud smacking noise and they all turned to see Murray surfacing from a belly-flop from the side of the catamaran.

"Ouch! I bet that hurt," Jo said.

Murray smiled manfully; he was far too macho to acknowledge the smarting that had just flashed up the front of his body. He should have done his shirt up and not just left it flapping open. If the truth be known he was hot in his shirt. But he couldn't take it off now; he'd look like a navvy, with brown forearms, face and neck and a white body.

Seeing that Jo was looking towards him as he stood on the deck and certain he'd look like Tom Daley after Murray's pathetic attempt, Deano decided to give an exhibition of his diving skills. He'd always been a good diver and he couldn't pass up the opportunity to show off. He poised on the side of the cat and then expertly dived into the water causing barely a ripple. The water passing over him felt really good. His fingertips brushed the sand and he turned them upwards to rise to the surface, but as he did so he felt a sharp pain, like a stab wound to his right elbow. He looked down to see what it was; completely forgetting he shouldn't open his eyes under the

194

water. He flapped up to the surface, fearing the worst and realising that it had happened. He swam straight back towards the ladder, climbed onto the deck and made for his bag. He put on his shades and then grabbed his towel to wipe his arm, where a graze was leaking fresh blood along the underside of his forearm.

"You cut yourself, buddy?" Amos asked, coming over and taking a look at it. "You don't want to bleed into the water. It attracts the sharks."

Deano looked at him with fear spread across his face.

"Joke!" Amos said quickly.

"I caught it on a rock," Deano answered. "I think I've got some disinfectant cream in my bag."

"I've got the very thing." Amos went below deck and then came up with a first aid kit. He opened it and took out a piece of gauze. He then went over to the bar, poured some rum into a glass and then soaked the gauze in it before applying it to Deano's wound. Deano winced, in spite of himself.

"That'll have it right in no time. The rum kills everything," Amos chuckled.

Deano chuckled along with him, although he could have cried. He could have cried even louder when he saw Geri coming up the ladder and stepping back onto the cat. She made a beeline for him.

"You okay? You got out of the water a bit sharpish. Oh! You've hurt yourself!" she said, grabbing his arm and making him wince in pain.

"Careful! I've cut my elbow on some coral or a rock, that's all. It's nothing to make a fuss over."

"I've got some cream to put on it." Geri made to get her bag.

"I said don't fuss! Amos has already put some rum on it. I'm fine."

"I just wanted to help."

Deano turned to face her. He'd just about had enough of Geri. It had been a bit of a laugh at first, the way she threw herself at him, but now it was getting beyond a joke. Not only was she ruining his chances with Jo, she'd made him give Eve a bad impression last night. He knew that what Eve had said had been the truth; he could have gone to bed at any time and he could have got rid of Geri, but he had been furious at Eve's suggestion that he'd created a drama to star in. It was all Geri's fault and looking at her now, pathetically offering him some ointment for his arm, he was overcome with a burning desire to really hurt her.

"Just do me a favour and leave me alone, will you? You made a fool of yourself last night. I'm not interested in you so piss off!" And with that he swung round and dangled his legs over the side, watching the rest of the group in the water.

Geri felt tears welling up in her eyes. What was he talking about her making a fool of herself last night? Had it been Deano who had taken her back to her room? Geri felt herself go scarlet. She turned away from him and walked over to the bar.

"What can I get you, darling'?" Aaron asked her.

"A large rum punch, please."

***

Swimming around the back of the catamaran Frances felt wonderful. She'd really enjoyed herself snorkelling and after the ride in the sun to Rendezvous Bay, she'd been ready to get back into the water again. As she kicked her legs and flipped over onto her back she felt a contentment that had eluded her for a long time. She was aware of a motion in the water and turning she saw Neville surface alongside her.

"I thought it was a mermaid," he said, his arms brushing her body as they both trod water. "You look just like one."

"You've seen a mermaid?" Frances said.

"I have now. And she's more beautiful than I ever imagined."

Neville lent in towards her and kissed her full on the mouth and to her enormous surprise Frances felt herself kissing him back. As she did so, his arms pulled her towards him and then encircling her, held her close to him, while his tongue, gradually, gently probed her mouth. He moved his hands down over her buttocks and under her legs, lifting them and wrapping them around his waist. Suddenly, Frances froze. She pulled her face away from his and kicked to lower her legs, but he held on to her.

"What's up, baby?" he whispered into her ear. "Don't you like me?"

"Of course I like you! I just don't think this is the time or place," she said, looking round to see if anyone had seen them.

"It's okay. Nobody can see us; we're hidden by the cat."

"That's not the point," Frances wriggled to free herself, but Neville still held on.

"Come out with me tonight. Promise to come out with me tonight and I'll let you go."

Frances looked at him, feeling unsure. She had surprised herself by the way she'd responded to him, returning his kisses as if she snogged young men she'd just met every day of the week.

196

Then she realised that she did want to go out with him. He was like nobody who'd ever asked her out before. He was exciting. Frances smiled and nodded.

"I'll wait for you in Macy's Bar. It's in the village, just up from the Mango Tree Resort. It's got a wooden veranda that overlooks the road. What time shall we say? Nine?"

"Nine's fine," Frances heard herself say, before Neville gave her one more kiss and then swam away.

***

"I wonder what the rich are doing today," Michael said as he floated alongside Dave, Stewart, Trevor, Huw, Murray and Jason, beer in hand. "It's just like another world, isn't it?"

"You're not wrong," Jason said, sipping from his can. "I could get used to this. I don't even want to think about leaving it all behind."

"Too fucking right! You'll be dragging me up the plane steps on Monday," Michael said. "At least you teachers have got another four weeks' holiday. Some of us have to go back in on Wednesday!"

"I can understand why people do that, you know, stay on, don't want to go home," Trevor said. "It's making me think that perhaps I should take early retirement; get out while I can."

"Well, you ear about lots of old geezers oo keel ova before they av a chance to retire, don't ya?"

"Oh, nice one, Dave! Make him feel good, why don't you?" Stewart said laughing.

"Yoo hoo! Boys!"

The men all turned round. Without them realising, all the women, except Frances, who couldn't be seen and Geri, who was on the cat, had grouped together in the water about twenty yards away. Suddenly they all jumped up in unison either waving their bikini tops or with their swimsuits around their waists, flashing and shaking boobs of all shapes and sizes at the unsuspecting men. Eve, who was sitting at the back of the cat roared with laughter at the men's faces.

"Fuckin' ell! I wasn't expectin' that!" Dave said laughing his head off.

"I've dropped me beer!" Stewart said, making them all laugh even harder.

Murray was glad he was up to his chest in water. The sight of so much female flesh was having an effect on him. Good job he had his shirt on, he'd have to pull it down over his crotch if he hadn't calmed down before they got out.

"All aboard!" Amos shouted just at that moment.

Oh fuck!

Murray would just have to make sure he was the last one out.

The women readjusted their swimsuits and swam towards the cat, laughing and chatting as they did so.

"Nice one, ladies!" Amos said, as he helped them all back up the ladder and onto the deck.

"Even the old dear joined in," Huw remarked to Jason as they finished their beers before climbing up. "And hers were in better condition than some of the others!"

"I never ever thought I'd go topless!" Suzanne said, vigorously rubbing her head with her towel.

"Well, it was hardly topless," Natalie said, "it was just a quick flash, really wasn't it? I mean, even our lady vicar flashed!" she added, turning to Jo.

"Even vicars have boobs," Jo said which made them all laugh again. She went and sat alongside Deano, who'd placed himself on the net.

"You okay?"

"Me? Yes I'm great. Just knocked my arm a bit on a rock, that's all."

"Nice dive, by the way."

"Nice tits by the way!"

Jo laughed and gave him a playful slap as he leaned over and whispered in her ear.

"Any chance I'll be seeing them a bit closer up?" he asked, his lips almost touching her ear, causing her to feel a surprisingly sexy tingle. She turned her head to face him, their lips just inches apart, the electricity between them suddenly palpable.

"Not a cat in hell's!" she said as he moved his lips towards hers, just as Amos sounded the claxon, making them both jump apart, startled out of their skins, and then collapse laughing next to each other on the net.

Watching them from further down the cat, Geri downed the rest of her rum punch in one go.

***

The day was a huge success. It passed far too quickly for everyone, except Geri, who had just wanted to get off since Deano had snubbed her at Rendezvous Bay. For the rest of the day she couldn't take her eyes off him and Jo enjoying themselves together. She'd tried to get close to the crew, but while they were friendly, they kept their distance from her.

They had eaten a great lunch of fish, chicken, macaroni cheese pie, roasted tomatoes and salad, when they'd dropped anchor near Falmouth Harbour and were now lying on the nets and the decks, drinking, chatting or sleeping as the Arawak Arrow made her way back along the south coast with her sails fully open, powered by the wind. Suzanne decided she wanted another glass of the rich red wine she'd had with her lunch and, not wanting to disturb Stewart who was enjoying his siesta and snoring gently beside her, stood up and went over to the bar to get it herself. She was just on her way back to her place in the shade when Amos suddenly shouted out, "Turtle! There's a hawksbill turtle on the starboard side. At one o'clock."

Suzanne span round to see where Amos was pointing, as the others all started to rouse themselves and as she did so she slipped and the wine shot from the glass, flew along the deck and splash landed against the back of Murray's shirt. She was too excited to apologise; she'd never seen a hawksbill turtle before and even Murray, who was also taken with the thought of the turtle, didn't realise it was red wine and so though no more about it for a few moments while everyone shaded their eyes and scanned the sea looking for the turtle.

"I can't see anything," Donna wailed, looking frantically from side to side of the cat. Skinnyman came alongside her. He took her hand and pointed her index finger forward. Then he stood behind her and moved her head until she was looking straight down her arm.

"Keep lookin' straight down your finger. There! You see?"

"Oh yes! Yes! I've seen it!" she beamed.

"Well, I couldn't see it," Grace said as she flopped back down on the deck next to Jo. "I think I need to go to Specsavers!"

One by one they all returned to their places or went to the bar for more drinks. As Murray went for another beer Deborah noticed the state of his shirt.

"Your shirt's got a huge stain on it. It looks like red wine. Here, take it off and we can rinse it out so it won't stain," she said grabbing his shirt by the lapel and pulling it off his shoulder.

"No!" Murray went to pull it back on, but it was too late. Dave and Deano who were standing next to him had already seen the large QPR shield tattooed onto his right upper arm.

"QPR? I wouldn't av ad you dahn as a QPR fan," Dave said.

Murray looked down, abashed and embarrassed, rocking from foot to foot.

"I'm not.

"Well, you don't see many of those on non-fans!" Deano quipped.

"It was a mistake."

By now a small crowd had gathered. Murray looked around the expectant faces; Dave, Deano, Jason, Dawn, Deborah, Natalie and Suzanne all looked at him, waiting to hear the story. Murray swallowed and then took a deep breath as he recalled the still-painful events leading up to the tattoo.

"Okay. I might as well tell yous the story. It was in 1992; the ninth of May tae be exact. I hadn't been living in London very long and I had a wee flat in West London, in Shepherd's Bush. Anyway, Rangers made it tae the final of the Scottish Cup that year; the first time in eleven years that we'd finally got that far. We beat Celtic in the semi and I made a promise that if we won I'd have the team's shield tattooed on tae my arm. And we did win; we beat Airdrieonians two-one. So I went along tae a tattoo parlour just off Wood Lane, near the BBC and told the bloke tae put Ranger's shield on my arm. Before I knew it, he'd put Queen's Park Rangers' shield on instead!"

Everyone fell about laughing; Dave had tears rolling down his face. Murray was still indignant.

"I mean, the stupid bastard, he could hear by my accent I wasn't a Londoner!"

"Yes, but, I live in Norfolk and I support Manchester United, so I suppose you couldn't really blame him," Suzanne said.

"An' so you ain't took ya shirt off for nearly twenty years?" Dave asked in amazement.

Murray nodded causing gales of laughter again.

"Well, I think Suzanne's done you a favour," Deborah said, slapping him on the arm. "You've finally faced your demons, your big secret is out in the open and you can take your shirt off again!" Murray looked round the group sheepishly and then started to laugh himself. "Give me the shirt," Deborah ordered. "I'll rinse it out in the sink in the loo and we can hang it up to dry so it won't stain." Murray took the shirt off.

"Now I look like a navvy," he said.

"No, you look like you're wearing a white shirt," Suzanne said in her own tell-it-as-it-is way.

The catamaran pulled onto Turner's Beach for a final swimming stop and when they all climbed back on board the crew had trays of champagne waiting for them, with cheese or tuna sandwiches and slices of rum cake.

"Nah, this is what I call afternoon tea!" Dave said, showing his appreciation by shoving a cheese sandwich into his mouth and washing it down with the champagne.

As soon as the anchor was up, Amos whacked up the music and Neville and Aaron started to limbo dance under a rope that Skinnyman had tied across the deck. They got Huw, Michael, Trevor and Jason to join in and then Dawn and Donna. And, after very little persuading from

Skinnyman, Geri also had a go. Everyone was doing fine for a couple of rounds then the rope got so low that only Neville and Aaron with a lifetime of practice could make it underneath. Then Amos changed the music and insisted that everyone come onto the main deck to join in a local dance called the Dollar Wine, which consisted of the woman standing in front of the man and the two of them swaying in time, until it got to the chorus.

"Now, everybody take a partner" Amos shouted, grabbing Eve to demonstrate.

"I wanna dance with Miss Marple," Skinnyman said, offering his hand to Ursula, who jumped up beaming. Everyone laughed at his observation; Ursula, in her straw hat and floral dress did bear a real likeness to Joan Hickson's character. Neville pulled Frances up and Aaron shimmied over to Grace. Eager to avoid Geri, Deano made a beeline for Jo, leaving Michael to be her partner. Jason danced with Donna, Trevor with Dawn, Stewart with Suzanne, Dave with Natalie and Murray with Deborah. Huw stood to one side watching, resisting all attempts to pull him into the melee.

"Now, listen up, everyone," Amos said. "The chorus goes *cent, five cents, ten cents, dollar*. On *cent* we move to the left, on *five cent* we move to the right, *on ten cents* the lady pushes her bottom back into the man and on *dollar* the man pushes forward. Now guys, we're going from ten cents all the way up to a dollar, that's ninety cents' worth, so you've got to let her know you're there, guys! Okay! So, everyone got a partner? Then let's go!"

The dance was a riot; with inhibitions down, thanks to a day of drinking rum punches, beers and wine, everyone threw themselves into it with gusto, collapsing with laughter as the music faded.

"Don't sit down!" Amos shouted running back to the wheel, "This is a party and I want you all dancin' all the way back to Mango Tree Resort."

And that's exactly what they all did.

***

Dave decided to have another drink at the bar before going back to his room for a shower before dinner.

"Anyone avin' a drink wiv me? It's only five o'clock," he said, as they turned from waving their goodbyes to Amos and the crew, as the Arawak Arrow disappeared round the headland out of sight.

"I'll join you," Michael said.

"Deano?"

"Yes, I'll just have one."

"Anyone else?" he looked round the group, holding his breath, waiting for Geri to say she'd join them. But she walked ahead of the group on her own, towards the rooms.

"Not me! I want a nice cup of tea," Natalie said.

"Oh, yes! That sounds lovely!" Jo agreed as the two of them, joined by Grace, Suzanne, Stewart, Trevor and Frances made their way towards the Spa Bar and afternoon tea. As they did so, Jo saw Ursula just ahead of them.

"Coming to afternoon tea, Ursula?" she called out. Startled at hearing her name, Ursula span round and blushing a little squinted at the sundrenched group of stragglers wandering along behind her.

"Oh, I'd love to! I've never been before. I didn't know anything about it."

"Well, you come along with us," Natalie said, taking her elbow and propelling her along in front of them. "There's nothing like Tiffin at this time of day."

***

"Free Wadiddlys is it?" Dave asked the others as they got up on the bar stools and the other two nodded their agreement.

"Free beers please, Elvis!" he called down the bar.

"What a fantastic fuckin' day!" Dave said. "When Eve said it'd be good I fought she was jus' givin' it ard sell, you know. But it was bleedin' brilliant. Cheers!" He chinked his glass against the other two and took a long swig.

"Best day of the holiday so far," Deano agreed.

"That's one of the best boat trips I've ever been on," Michael agreed. "I know that boat trips are always good, but there was something about this one. I think it's because it was just us. I had a great time."

"I fink you're righ'. It wouldn't av bin the same wiv uvva people on it, would it?" The other two shook their heads.

"An' you looked like you was gettin' on alrigh' wiv Nat," he said to Michael.

"Me? What makes you say that?"

"You was togevva a lot, sunbavin' an that."

"She dirty danced with you, not me! She's a lovely girl, very easy to talk to and I'd like to think we'll end up as friends at the end of the holiday, but I'm not looking for anyone. I haven't come away for that. I think I just remind her a bit of her ex. We get on well. She's a mate."

The three men sipped their beers, deep in thought.

"Geri seemed to give you a bit of space today," Michael said to Deano.

"Thank fuck for that! I had a bit of a problem with her last night and today I had to tell her to piss off; that I wasn't interested."

"What problem was that, then?"

"Oh, after dinner me and Jo went for a walk and she tagged along and then we sat on the wall looking at the moon on the water and she sat with us, pushing her thigh up against me. She completely ignored Jo and started coming on to me. Jo got fed up with it and said she was tired and was going to bed and left me with her. She then got gradually drunker and drunker; wanted to tell me her life story. She rambled on about her husband trading her in for a younger model. She was going on and on, it was embarrassing. And then she collapsed across my chest just as Eve came by and she accused me of encouraging her!" Deano sounded very misunderstood and hard-done-by. Dave and Michael shook their heads.

"I can't stand a woman oo can't old er drink, or oo even drinks too much," Dave said, knocking back the rest of his beer and signalling to Elvis for a refill. "Oo's fer anuvva one?" he asked Michael and Deano.

"Not for me," Deano said. "I want to go and have a shower."

"I'll have one with you," Michael said, swinging round and back again on his bar stool.

"What a laugh about Murray, though," Deano said, standing up and reaching for his towel and bag. "That just cracked me up. I wish I'd been a fly on the wall when he realised he'd had the wrong tattoo!" The three men laughed out loud and Deano was still chuckling to himself as he walked through the tables and onto the path on the way back to his room. Although he wasn't sure why he was laughing at someone else's misfortune; he had his own to sort out.

"It sounded like you had a bit of a rough time growing up," Michael said, as their second beers arrived. "You know, I mean, judging by what you were saying yesterday, about the children's homes and that."

"That's life, innit? Some kids av a rotten life wiv their real parents."

"That's true, I suppose. Have you ever tried to find your birth mother?"

"Nah! Wos the point? If she'd wanted me she wouldn't've lef' me in the bus station, would she?"

"Perhaps she couldn't cope. You have to think that she gave you up because she wanted what was best for you, don't you?"

"I s'pose so. Or what was best for er. I dunno. That's why I don't fink abaht it; it'd do me ed in if I let it."

"What about your father?"

"Not a fuckin' clue! Could've bin the Duke of Edinburgh; could've bin a dustman. Me mum didn't say nuffink abaht im in the note. She didn't say nuffink abaht erself or anyfink."

"But haven't you ever been curious about who you are or where you come from?"

"Sometimes I do fink abaht it but what's the point? You can drive yourself nuts finkin' abaht it all. Me mum decided she couldn't look afta me, for wha'ever reason. *It is what it is* as they say. An' when all's said an' done, I ain't ad a bad life, not as a grownup I ain't. An' I'm doin' well now wiv me motors. Got a nice little line goin' in personalised number plates, an' all."

"What, some of those that look like your name if you've got dyslexia or pretend a two is an s or a three is an e?" Michael laughed, ribbing him.

"That's me!" Dave laughed with him.

"Where's your showroom?"

"St Albans. I moved out that way from Forest Gate abaht ten years ago. You ever there give us a bell. *Mr Wright* me busniss is called. 'Cos me name's Dave Wright, see? I chose that meself, by deed poll. I liked the idea of bein' Mr Wright." He paused to take a look around the bar. "Nah. I ain't done bad. So, I don't know oo me parents was, but p'raps that's better'n finding aht an' bein' disappointed. An' anyway, you make your own life, don't ya? Wevver you're a good bloke or not's dahn to you not oo your mum an' dad was.'

"I'll remember that," Michael said, looking thoughtfully into his beer.

***

The group of people who gathered together for pre-dinner drinks that night looked chilled out to the maximum. There were a few red noses, some panda eyes and some deep tans forming. Nobody had bothered to dress up; the women in cotton dresses or cut offs and the men in shorts. Dinner was to be on the terrace of the main restaurant, a casual affair. Deano had phoned Eve to say he wouldn't be joining them at dinner as he was really whacked out after the boat trip and he wasn't hungry.

Ursula had had afternoon tea with some of the group, but had then scuttled back off to her room and hadn't been seen since.

"She's lovely, but it's a bit like pulling teeth," Natalie said to Eve as they sat down together, joining the others as the tables. "She'll listen and answer you if you ask her a direct question, but doesn't have any input into the conversation."

"Still, at least we got her to join in," Eve said. She looked around the group to see if anyone else was missing. "Has anyone seen Frances?"

"Here she comes!" Natalie said. "Blimey! She looks amazing!"

Frances did, indeed, look amazing. She was wearing a blue and cream dress, which was slightly off one shoulder and really brought out the golden syrup colour of her skin that the day on the boat had produced. Her curly hair was swept up at the sides and was held by a sparkly clip at the top of her head. Eve thought there was an air of something about her that she couldn't quite put her finger on. Confidence? Expectation? Excitement? Or perhaps a mix of all three?

"You've made an effort!" Jo said as she joined them. Frances smiled, showing off her glossy lips. "Thank you," she said, skirting round the table to avoid sitting next to Deborah, and pulling up a chair on the other side.

"You know we're only eating here, don't you? Pizza Pizzazz is tomorrow night," Natalie said.

"I know." She refused to be drawn on her appearance and deliberately turned to Trevor and asked him if the power in his room had gone off for a short while earlier. Eve looked at her knowingly. She had a date with someone, Eve was sure of it.

Good for her!

Eve yawned. All the fresh air had tired her out. She'd be going straight to her bed after dinner. She'd gone back to her room with trepidation, fearful that there would be a voicemail message from Melv and fearful that there wouldn't. There wasn't. Although she was glad, a part of her was disappointed. She chided herself for being so shallow and childish.

Don't play games, Eve!

She'd told Melv she wanted nothing to do with him and he'd taken her at her word, so why should she feel a bit peeved? And after all, seeing more of him, opening the Pandora's Box that was their past would do no good whatsoever. She'd made her decision thirty years ago when she'd chosen not to tell him the truth, not to follow him and not to have any further contact with him. As her old granny often said, there was no point in stirring up shit unless you wanted a nasty smell. She was aware that Jo had asked her a question.

"Sorry, Jo, I didn't quite catch that," she said to cover up what might be taken for her lack of interest.

"I was just asking if we needed to take water with us on the jeep safari tomorrow."

"No, you don't. They have a bar and it opens as soon as you set off, which is eight thirty. So those of you going, please make sure you're ready in reception at eight twenty-five."

"I know Natalie, Michael, Trevor, Grace and I are going. Who else is? How many of us are going?" Jo asked.

"Me!" Dave said.

"And me!" Frances put her hand up.

"And Deano," Natalie said.

"And me!" Geri added. She turned to Eve. "Will we all be in the one jeep?"

"Yes. There are nine of you and the jeep takes ten. Well, eleven if you count the seat next to the driver, up front."

Dawn and Donna were deep in conversation, talking quietly for once so they couldn't be overheard. Donna suddenly turned to Jason, who was sitting beside her talking football with Murray.

"Excuse me butting in, Murray, but I just wanted to say, Jason that Dee and me have decided not to go out for the day in a car. The weather's not supposed to be very nice on Thursday and we've decided to see if Eve can fit us in for tomorrow's jeep safari. Sorry to let you down."

Jason could barely conceal his glee. He'd been practising telling them that he and Huw had decided to cycle round the island instead of taking the car, but was afraid to do so in case it turned out that they were both keen cyclists. Now he didn't have to worry.

"Oh, no problem. I understand," he said, masking his secret delight at the news. "We were going to suggest taking a rain check ourselves. You know, we don't want to get stranded anywhere if there's a storm, do we?"

"No we don't. Well, that's okay then. We just didn't want to let you down." Donna then turned her attention to Eve.

"Eve! As there are two spaces in the jeep for tomorrow can Dee and me go?"

"It should be okay, unless they've put two more people in." Eve said. "I assume the jeep was just for our group." She took out the mobile phone that Sunny had given her. "Let me just ring through and see if I can get anyone."

Eve dialled the number and walked away from the group in an attempt to find a quite spot to make her call. As she edged her way through the tables on the terrace towards the path she found herself dodging right and then left to try to pass someone, who she recognised at Melv, just at the moment that jeep safari office answered the phone.

"Good night," Melv greeted her, side-stepping and walking passed her. She stood watching his retreating back with her heart hammering and her mouth dry. It took her a few seconds to realise that her call had been answered. Checking that there were, indeed, two empty places tomorrow, Eve booked them and rang off. She stopped for a moment to take a deep breath before going back to join the group. Melv, she saw, had stopped to talk to Shivonne, the Entertainments Manager and some of the group as he passed the table.

Don't let anyone ask him to join us!

She needn't have worried. As soon as she sat down and told Donna and Dawn they could go the following day, Melv gave the group a beaming smile, said, "Enjoy dinner! It's real good tonight," and walked off.

"I'm looking for volunteers for karaoke, Eve," Shivonne said, waving a couple of song books around as she teetered on five inch purple heels that matched a dress that could only have been sprayed on. "Can I count on you?"

"Only if you want your night to be a huge flop, but I'm sure we must have some singers here," she said, indicating the group.

"I like singing, but I'm not doing it on my own," Suzanne said.

"I'll do a duet with you," Jo piped up. She took a songbook from Shivonne's hand. "What shall we do? Something upbeat? A ballad?"

"Let's see what's in the book." They poured over the list of songs as Shivonne, encouraged by their enthusiasm tried to persuade more of the group to take part. "What about the rest of you? Don't let these ladies be the only ones to enjoy themselves."

"I'll have a go!" Jason said.

"I'll have a look, too." Trevor took another book. "I'm not very good but I do enjoy singing. I used to sing in a choir many years ago."

"You could all do sumfink togevva, the free of ya," Dave suggested to Suzanne and Jo. "Trev could sing and you two could be is backin' singers."

"I'll do a song with you, Trevor," Geri suddenly said, moving to crouch down beside him and look over his shoulder at the book.

"Is the world ready for this?" Murray sneered, to find himself quickly admonished by Grace, who rounded on him sharply.

"Let's wait and see how well they do before we criticise, shall we? And if you're not prepared to sing, don't poke fun at those that are."

"Unless you and Deborah want to do *I Got You, Babe,* or something," Natalie added.

"Wild horses wouldn't get me up there!" Deborah said, laughing. "If he wants to sing he's on his own."

"I have no intention of singing," Murray said, icily.

"So stop having a pop at those who are going to sing, then" Natalie said. "What are you going to do, girls?" she asked, turning back to Jo and Suzanne.

"*Sisters Are Doing It for Themselves,* and if that goes alright *It's Raining Men,*" Jo said.

"You are so not like any vicar I've ever met," Natalie said, giving her a hug.

"What? You expect me to sing *Amazing Grace* or *Jerusalem*?"

"More like *All Fings Brigh' an Beau'iful*" Dave said. "Or *Jesus Wants Me fer a Sunbeam*!"

Jo laughed at them and shook her head. "Nobody else going to join us?" she asked looking round the group.

"You're joking! Karaoke is the Japanese word for *making a prick of yourself*!" Huw said. "It's something you only do on stag nights or when you're shit-faced after a rugby match."

"I agree!" Stewart said, nodding his head vigorously, even though he'd never been to a rugby match in his life. "I've had too many gigs ruined by idiots who want to sing along and don't realise how terrible they really are."

"Being terrible is part of it, it adds to the fun," Shivonne insisted. "And besides, we have a prize for the worst singer as well as for the best."

"I'm gonna do Loofah's So Amazin'" Dave said.

"You like Luther Vandross?" Shivonne said. "He's my favourite singer."

"Mine too! I like a woman wiv taste!" Dave said winking at her. She gave him a beaming smile and his heart melted.

"You two not doing it?" Stewart asked Donna and Dawn. They shook their heads vigorously.

"We're dancers rather than singers," Dawn said seriously.

"We're doing *Something Stupid*," Geri said, although nobody had asked her.

Eve looked at Shivonne, who was beaming; the karaoke night was saved! Once she had a couple of volunteers the others usually snowballed. Eve stood up.

"Shall we eat?" she asked.

***

Frances had checked her watch at least twenty times during dinner; she was sure that the battery was running down as the hands seemed to barely move. At one point she asked Huw, who was sitting next to her, if he had the time. He did and it was the same time she had. He'd looked at her watch, pointedly.

"I just thought mine had stopped," she said, feeling the need to give him an explanation.

"What you got a hot date or something?" he asked, chuckling at the absurdity of that being the case.

"Or something," Frances replied. That shut him up for a moment.

Finally, the hands crept round to eight forty. The group had all gone back to the bar in anticipation of the karaoke. On the stage a scruffy-looking character, who'd announced himself as *'Pete from Newcastle'* was murdering *Chasing Cars*. Frances smiled to herself, glad she was missing it. She'd pass on karaoke, thank you! She went back to her room to use the loo, cleaned her teeth, retouched her make-up and had another spray of perfume and then sat down hard on the bed.

What the hell am I playing at?

She wasn't going to go. By going she'd just make a fool of herself; one of these silly women you read about in the Sunday papers, having flings with black men young enough to be their sons. And speaking of sons, what would her Darren make of it all if he ever found out? But then, he wouldn't find out, would he?

Sod it! I'm going!

Frances stood up and strode out of the room before she could talk herself out of it anymore. She walked down the hotel driveway and through the security barrier.

"Good night!" the security guard called after her. Frances thought it comical how people here said *'good night'* when she would have said *'good evening'*. But when he added "Enjoy your evening, ma'am!" she blushed uncontrollably. Surely he couldn't know where she was going?

She slowed her pace through the village; not knowing if Neville was watching her and not wanting to appear too eager. She spotted Macy's Bar and could see that Neville was already sitting at a table looking down the street at her. He waved a hand when he realised she had seen him. She waved back as she continued to walk towards him. No turning back now. Her legs felt like jelly as she climbed the steps to the veranda overlooking the street. As she got to the table Neville stood up and taking her hand, guided her into the seat next to him.

"You're looking beautiful," he said. "Hot." His eyes ran over her body. "What do you want to drink?"

Frances saw that he was nursing a beer, so she said she'd have one, too. Neville stood up and signalled towards the bar and then sat down next to her again, putting his arm around her. She felt silly. Surely the whole bar, if not the whole village, was looking at them and wondering what he was doing with her. Her beer appeared and Neville handed it to her. With his left hand he clinked his glass against hers saying "to beautiful people and beautiful love affairs!" Frances gulped her drink and said nothing. Neville then delved into the pocket of his jeans, which were sitting very low over his hips and pulled out a small tin, from which he took a joint. He lit it expertly and took a long drag, then offered it to Frances. For a second she hesitated. She'd never even smoked a cigarette before.

In for a penny! It's all part of the experience!

She took it from him and putting it in her lips, inhaled deeply. She wasn't sure what she'd expected but apart from the strange sensation of smoke caressing her mouth and throat for the first time, she didn't really feel anything. She liked the smell of it, though; sweet and rich. Neville took a deep drag himself then turned to her and kissing her hard, blew the smoke into her mouth again. Frances coughed and her eyes watered.

"Oh, sorry, baby," Neville said, leaning back from her and sipping his beer. They sat in silence for a few moments; Frances felt as if she should say something to break the silence, but didn't quite know what to say. Neville turned his head towards her again and gave her a beaming smile.

"Why you so tense? Relax. Just relax. We're here to enjoy ourselves."

Enjoy ourselves?

Frances wondered exactly what that meant.

***

"And now, next up we have Jo and Suzanne who are going to do *Sisters Are Doing It for Themselves*!" Shivonne announced, looking around the audience. "Jo and Suzanne, where are you? Oh right! I see them. Here they come."

Jo and Suzanne went onto the stage. Eve whipped the Travel Together group into a frenzy of encouragement, but after a moment or two it became more than clear that both women had fabulous voices. Eve, Natalie and Grace all stood up and started rocking in time to the music. Dawn and Donna quickly followed and then to everyone's surprise Deborah joined them.

"Blimey! You wouldn't fink a posh bird like 'er would join in, would ya?" Dave said to Stewart.

"Why not? Don't posh birds sing and dance?"

"Yeah, I s'pose they do, but she's well posh, ain't she? I mean, we was in the sea this afternoon but she got back on the boat to av a wee!"

"Now that is posh!" Stewart said.

The song came to an end and the audience went wild. Beaming and red with pleasure Suzanne made her way back to the table, leading Jo by the hand. Everyone hugged and congratulated them. Stewart took advantage of the moment and planted a huge kiss on Suzanne's cheek, making her turn even more crimson.

"Brilliant! Brilliant!" Eve said, still clapping. "You sounded like professionals!"

"Lady Vicar! A touch of the Whoopi Goldberg's I do believe!" Natalie said, hugging Jo and then Suzanne. "Right little Sister Act, the two of you!"

"Oh what a shame Deano's not here to see how well you sing!" Geri said nastily. "Where is he, by the way?"

"I have no idea," Jo said, in spite of the fact that he'd phoned her to say he was going to have an early night. They'd talked for half an hour with Deano emphasising that the only reason he wasn't coming down was because he was tired and had a headache. He'd told her he couldn't wait to see her again the following morning. Jo found him as easy to talk to as he was on the eye. But she'd glanced at her travel alarm clock and said she had to go or she wouldn't have time for a shower before dinner. But she wasn't going to get into any kind of conversation with Geri about Deano, who'd told her what had happened after she'd gone to bed the previous evening. At least, his version of what had happened. He'd seemed a bit put out when Jo asked him why he hadn't just gone to bed and left Geri to her own devices.

Geri was angry with Jo for her abrupt answer; but she was even angrier with herself for making such a catty remark in front of everyone else. She didn't want them all thinking she was a bitch and she was still unsure as to what she had actually said or done the previous evening and who might have seen her.

Determined not to let Geri's remarks spoil anything everyone settled back in their seats as Charlene from North Carolina went into *Macarthur Park.*

"Oh my God!" Michael groaned to Eve. "Save me from this!"

"I take it you don't like this song, Michael?"

"It's about forty verses long! It's music to slit your wrists by!"

Eve laughed at him.

"I know what you mean. And it's usually sung by someone who hasn't got much of a clue," she said, as Charlene went for her third change of key.

"See what I mean?" Michael said. "I've got to hand it to you, Eve; I couldn't do your job. You know, it looks great, and I think we all thought at first that you had the life of Riley, but it's harder than it looks, isn't it? I mean, listening to this time and time again for a start!" he joked.

"When it's all going right it's the best job in the world, but when it goes wrong it goes wrong with knobs on," Eve agreed.

"You must meet some awful people; there must be times when you just want to tell people to fuck off, surely?"

"Perhaps. But what good would that do? My job is to diffuse trouble, not make the situation worse."

"Have you ever lost it with anyone, though?" Michael persisted.

"Once or twice," Eve grinned, remembering a few incidents where she had indeed lost it. She took a sip of her Diet Coke.

"I bet you've seen some things, enough to write a book," Michael said and Eve nodded in agreement. "But what I think is so great is that I thought going on a singles' holiday had a bit of a stigma attached to it. You know what I mean? I thought that coming on a singles' holiday was a bit like admitting that I had no friends. I was a bit worried what they'd all be like. I mean, I know we've got a couple of strange ones but on the whole everyone's great."

Eve knew exactly what he meant. It was exasperating, sometimes, to see other people's attitudes to singles groups. Yet more and more people were booking them; more and more people were choosing to go away with a singles' group because of the freedom it gave them.

"D'you eva get any journalists? You know, pretendin' to be jus' someone normal in the group but then writin' orrible fings?" asked Dave, who'd caught the tail end of Michael's comments.

"I've never had a journalist infiltrate the group, at least not as far as I know!" Eve laughed, "But I've had two come along to write articles. One was a really lovely man, who wrote a smashing article that really showed the group and the holiday in a positive light, but the woman was awful; a real queen bee, she was."

"Bet you ad to be on your best be'avya!"

"To be honest, and if you'll excuse my language, she pissed me right off, big time! She'd got the whole trip for free in exchange for writing an article about the holiday. It was a West Coast USA trip; Las Vegas, San Francisco, Los Angeles. We only had three days in Las Vegas and she spent the first two days going off on trips to research other articles she was writing and trying to get a free helicopter ride over the Gran Canyon. She was annoyed with me because I couldn't get a freebee for her. I couldn't even get one for myself! She went out of her way to stir up trouble in the group; she knew just what to say to press a button, know what I mean? Like, telling people they could get the trips a bit cheaper if they went and queued up instead of getting the tickets through me because I was earning commission; encouraging complaints about everything; trying to get the group to say nasty things about each other, that sort of thing."

"She sounds like a right cow."

"She was. In the end when the article came out, all she'd done was rubbish the holiday and take the mickey out of the people on it. She practically said they were all desperate to find a partner and were a bunch of losers!"

"What a bitch! Oh, thank God for that!" Michael said, as Charlene finally closed the gates on *Macarthur Park* and Shivonne announced Jason singing *Sweet Caroline*. Once again the Travel Together group got to its feet to welcome one of its own and Jason didn't disappoint. Throwing himself into the song he had the whole audience standing up holding hands and swinging them in the air at the chorus.

Geri watched with interest. She and Trevor hadn't gone up to do their number yet, but she knew she wanted to sing a song with Jason; he was fantastic. She thought she'd suggest it to him when he came back to join them. One way or another she was going to be the centre of attention in this group; she was going to make people take notice of her. Deano included. Even if he wasn't there.

***

Frances squatted on the edge of a floral armchair and looked around the very ornate, slightly ostentatious living room of the little wooden house, stuffed full with furniture, pictures, ornaments and knick-knacks, unsure of how she'd got there. She'd stopped asking herself what she was doing a couple of hours ago. The evening had been interesting and now that she was loosening up she was beginning to enjoy herself. They'd had a couple more drinks at Macy's Bar, during which time Frances had discovered very little about Neville, other than he wasn't Antiguan.

"Dy-a-me-kkan," he'd said, stretching it out into four syllables. "You know it?"

"No, I've never been to Jamaica. I've never been to the Caribbean before this trip."

"It's a beautiful country; far more beautiful than Antigua. It's the most beautiful country in the Caribbean with the most friendly people. Not like here!" he added with venom. Frances refrained from asking why he was in Antigua if he disliked it so much. He wasn't married, apparently, but he did have two children with an Antiguan woman that he didn't live with.

"Do you see your children?" Frances asked, curious as to his domestic set-up.

"Every day. I take care of them," he said proudly as if taking care of your kids wasn't something fathers were supposed to do. Then Neville had suggested going back to the hotel with her.

"You can't come into the hotel!" she said, panicking, knowing that she'd be mortified if anyone saw her and besides, security was strict at the Mango Tree Resort. She couldn't imagine the security guard on the gate letting her waltz back in with Neville on her arm.

"We'll go to mine, then," Neville had said, signalling for the bill, which somehow she had ended up paying. She vaguely remembered something about him not having any change. They had left the bar and got into his car or *'vay-hi-cal'* as he called it, a black Toyota that looked as if it had quite a few miles on the clock. It had roared them along the coast road and then inland over a big hill with a wonderful view of St John's, a mass of lights, and then through some narrow streets with corrugated iron fences and stray dogs, screeching to a halt outside a humble wooden house painted a lurid shade of green.

"Where are we?" Frances asked, feeling slightly nauseous from the effects of the spliff, the exhaust fumes and the speed Neville had driven at.

"Just outside St John's," he'd replied.

Frances was startled out of her trance by the opening of the door as Neville came back into the room. He had taken off his shirt to reveal his handsome body, the muscles defined like a Michelangelo statue. He was barefoot.

"You need the bathroom?" he asked.

Frances nodded and he indicated the door he'd just come through. Frances kicked her shoes off and went into the tiniest bathroom she'd ever seen. There was a toilet and small shower cubicle with no curtain. She shrugged; it served its purpose after all. She quickly had a wee and splashed water from the shower between her legs.

Shit! No towel!

214

She grabbed some toilet paper and dried herself, flushing the paper down the loo. Then she stood unsure of what to do. Should she take off her dress and walk back into the room half undressed the way he had? Or should she leave it on for the moment? She decided to leave it on. Coughing nervously she opened the bathroom door and stepped back into the living room to find that Neville had pulled the sofa down into a bed and he was lying across it stark naked, his braids held up in a hairnet, his hands caressing his groin. Frances looked away but found her eyes drawn back to Neville again.

Jesus!

She'd only ever seen two erect penises before; her ex-husband's and a boyfriend called Alan's that she'd had sex with on just two forgettable occasions. Both were lolly sticks compared to what was before her. She stood looking at him, afraid to move. Realising she was there, Neville stopped his stroking and turned to her.

"Come here, baby," he said, pulling her to him and lifting her dress over her head in one fell swoop. He leaned forward and started to kiss her; Frances could feel him pressing up against her. Well, it was hard not to! Very hard, in fact! He flicked the back of her bra and it came off as he pulled her down onto the bed alongside him. This was the bit that Frances had been dreading. No man had seen her naked since her operation. Neville ran his eyes over her body and then his hands followed. When he reached her left breast he gently touched the deep dent and the puckered scar tissue and then leaned forward and placed a tender kiss on the spot where his fingers had been.

"Looks like you've had a rough time," he said, stroking her hair. "Let's try to make it up to you. Tonight I'm gonna make you feel like a whole woman again."

And that's just what he did.

***

So much for an early night!

The karaoke had been a huge success with the Travel Together group taking all the accolades. Even Trevor and Geri had made a good stab at *Something Stupid*, but when Jason had got together with Jo and Suzanne to sing *Valerie* followed by *We Are the Champions* it had brought the house down. Shivonne had spent ten minutes consulting the public before deciding that all three deserved the Best Singer Award, and so each had been given a large bottle of Cavalier rum. Eve had surprised herself by actually having a good time and she knew that at least this had been a way of taking her mind off Melv. If she'd gone to her room she'd have only gone over the events of thirty years ago and the previous evening a hundred times. Gradually, the group started to break up as the day's excursion and the excitement of the karaoke and the great evening they'd spent together began to catch up with them.

"I can't believe I've got to get up early again tomorrow," Natalie grumbled good naturedly. "I'm supposed to be on holiday and I'm getting up earlier than if I was at home!"

"We don't have to be ready until twenty-five past eight," Michael said, "You talk as if it was five o'clock. Oops! Steady!" He put his arm out to support her as she stood up and wobbled to one side.

"That's those bloody rum punches," she giggled. "I'm not drunk, but I lost count after the eighth one!"

"And that was before lunch on the boat!" Michael said. "Ouch!" He clutched his arm where Natalie had swung her bag in mock offence and hit him with it.

The two of them walked off together towards their rooms. Eve followed them with her gaze.

"They're just good friends!" Grace leaned over and said to her. "At least, that's what they keep on telling us!"

"I'm sure they are," Eve said, "but they do make a nice couple!"

"Do you get many couples forming? Serious couples I mean? Not just a holiday shag."

"I've been to one wedding of two former group members, and there are three or four other couples who got together and are still together as far as I know."

"I suppose it'll happen when you put men and women together!" Grace said, philosophically. "Can't say there's anyone who's taken my fancy, though, I have to admit. The men are nice, but mates rather than romance material."

"What's your type then?" Eve asked her.

"I don't know if I've got a type. I'm more, see someone and know I fancy them or I don't. Do you know what I mean?"

"I know exactly what you mean," Eve said, nodding.

"After all, if I look at all my exes none of them really look alike, but they all had something, some quality, that I went for. Oh! Listen to me! *All my exes!* Anyone would think there'd been hundreds of them."

"And there have only been a few?" Eve asked. She usually didn't ask personal questions, but they were both relaxed, talking together like friends and Eve thought there was an air of mystery surrounding Grace. She'd heard that she was a high ranking police officer.

"There are just three of any significance. One I met at university. We were both studying English Literature but it sort of fizzled out when we got into the real world. I went into teaching and he went into the Civil Service."

"Oh! You were a teacher!"

"I was, but not for very long. I hated being at the local bog-standard comprehensive. What a dump! People say grammar schools were selective but they gave bright working class kids, like me, the chance to get a really good education. The place I worked was the pits. Everyone brought down to the level of the lowest common denominator; kids who wanted to learn unable to, distracted by those who thought the only reason to be in school was to muck around; teachers unable to discipline kids, it was a nightmare. Anyway, after three years I left and joined the police and I soon met a fireman, Rob, and we were together for eight years." She paused to take a sip of her drink before continuing. "And then I started seeing my guv, who was a detective chief inspector when I was a lowly detective sergeant and Rob found out and finished it."

"And what happened with you and your guv?"

"We had an affair for over fifteen years; until I woke up one day and realised I wanted out. He'd decided to take early retirement and set up a security firm. His kids were off-hand, they knew about us and liked me, and he'd started talking about us finally moving in together. That made me sit up and realise I actually didn't want that. He was coming up for retirement, I wanted promotion; it seemed like it was the natural end to it. He wasn't happy and it turned a bit nasty for a while but he eventually accepted it. We broke up, he set up his business and I became DCS. And that's it in a nutshell; Grace's love life!"

"Well, thank you for sharing that!" Eve said and both women laughed.

"Excuse me, ladies, but I'm turning in. Goodnight." Jason went, leaving Eve with Grace and Geri. She couldn't help notice Geri's eyes following him, unsure of whether to go after him or not. Eve hoped she wouldn't; Geri was the kind of woman who'd always measure her success by whether or not she had a man on her arm or in her bed. She was man-mad and Eve knew that was often a sign of low self-esteem. Geri watched Jason disappear and then turned her attention back to her drink and her two companions.

"You must meet loads of men in your job, Eve," she said.

"Yes I do," she said making both women laugh at her tone which made it very clear that they were men she didn't want to get involved with.

"But have you never had a fling with someone in your group?" Geri persisted.

"No, never. I don't see the men as potential partners. I mean, that's not to say that I don't sometimes look at someone and think how nice he is or how fit, but all the dancing and chatting I do is done from way behind the professional line that always stands between me and the group."

"It must be lonely for you sometimes," Grace said. "You're with the group but not of the group, as it were."

That's it exactly. And anyway, I've got in trouble before for dancing with men in the group," she laughed.

"Got in trouble?" Grace asked in disbelief. "How?"

"Oh you know, you try to get the group up on the dance floor so you get one of the men to dance with you and then a woman in the group who fancies him will either warn you off or write in about you when they get back."

"You're kidding!"

"I'm not. I think that's one of the most disappointing aspects of the job, really, when someone gives you a hug or a handshake at Heathrow and thanks you for the fabulous holiday they've had and is then absolutely vile and nasty about you on their questionnaire or on the company's website."

"How hypocritical! But that says far more about them than it does about you!" Grace said, indignant on Eve's behalf.

"Of course it does, but it ruins your faith in human nature sometimes."

"And do you ever get men making a pass at you?" Geri asked.

"Sometimes, but I've learned how to deal with it. It all comes with practice and experience," Eve laughed.

"But it must be hard when you're supposed to be nice to people, to have to give someone the elbow," Geri said.

"There's being nice and there's accepting sexual harassment and they're not the same thing," Grace said. "I've come across it time and again in my job. You know, blokes who think that if you smile and say 'good morning' you're really up for a quick shag in the back of the patrol car. Although, I also have to say that women can be very silly sometimes, too. I mean, if you are prepared to have a quick shag on the back seat of the patrol car, you can't blame your fellow officers for treating you with distain. Whether you're male or female," she added.

Geri looked a bit awkward. She yawned theatrically and stood up.

"I'm off to bed. See you all at breakfast!"

"Goodnight, Geri!" Eve and Grace chorused as she walked away.

"I think I'm going to turn in, too," Eve said.

218

"And me. Thanks for a great day, Eve," Grace said, collecting her bag and stacking the empty glasses into a pile. "I'll take these over to the bar to help the lovely Elvis out."

"Good night, Grace."

Her heels clacking on the tiles, Eve went back to her room with a warm, happy and contented feeling.

That was always a bad sign.

***

Geri swiped the security key in the slot, closed the door behind her and pulled the safety chain across. She was bursting to go to the loo so she had a wee and then cleaned her make-up from her face, thinking all the time about the various conversations that had gone on during the day. She was still smarting from Deano's comments on the boat.

He really fancies himself! Bastard!

She wiped the face cream off with a tissue enjoying thinking nasty thoughts about Deano, who'd started off the holiday by encouraging her all he could and then had very publically turned away from her for the pious Jo. She just didn't understand what she'd done wrong. She hoped she wasn't one of those needy women that Eve and Grace had been talking about. It was alright for them to go on about not running after men and not needing to have one all the time, but they were strong and they hadn't been through all that she'd been through.

And what's needy about wanting a man to want you every now and again?

She threw the dirty tissue in the bin and cleaned her teeth. She picked up her knickers from the floor and walking into the bedroom started pulling her dress over her head when she froze in fear.

A huge, black cockroach was on the curtains; stark and ugly against the pale floral pattern.

Oh shit!

As much as it terrified her, she couldn't take her eyes off it and, what's more, she knew she couldn't afford to because with one leap it would either land on her or disappear and then she knew she'd never get to sleep if it was loose in the room. Eve's words at the information meeting came into her head.

Ring security!

But to do that, she had to get to the phone, which was on the bedside table on the far side of the bed, next to the curtains where the bloody giant cockroach was poised ready for take-off. Moving very slowly she edged her way towards the bed, holding her dress in front of her as a barrier between them. She gradually slid her left knee onto the bed and then drew her right one to join it, while never taking her eyes from the curtains. She was breathing fast and she could feel her heart thumping and her pulse racing. Her mouth was dry and she licked her lips as she crawled very slowly forward across the bed towards the phone and salvation.

Just as she reached out with her left hand, slowly, controlled, and inch at a time to grab the phone she had a flashback. Blinking myopically, she leaned towards the curtain and then collapsed back on the bed laughing hysterically. When she had been getting undressed after the boat trip, she'd seen that the curtains were gaping open and she'd held them closed with her long black hair slide. And that's what it was! Not a cockroach but a hair slide.

I've been frightened of a bloody hair slide!

Geri laughed and laughed until she almost cried. And she felt better than she had in a long time.

***

DAY SIX

As the sunlight struck her face through the curtain-less windows Frances was aware that someone was moving around in the room. For a moment she didn't know where she was and then a pair of bloodshot eyes hovering above a huge grin appeared in front of her.

"Rise and shine! Time to go, baby!" Neville said.

Frances shot out of bed, looking round for a clock before she realised she was wearing her watch. It was showing six thirty. She blinked rapidly, trying to remember what day it was and what she had to do.

Eight twenty-five! Jeep safari!

It was then that she realised Neville was already dressed in his pristine Arawak uniform. He stood at the table putting things into a backpack-style bag, smiling at her kindly as he did so.

"You need to shower?"

"No! No! I'll do that back at the hotel."

Frances felt shy getting out of bed, naked and looking for her clothes, which she found folded neatly over the back of one of the dining chairs. Neville must have done that; her memories of the previous night didn't include folding up her clothes. She got dressed quickly as Neville waited patiently for her, giving her bottom a friendly whack as she bent over to put her feet into her knickers. As soon as she was ready he picked up his bag.

"I can't take you back to Mango Tree, 'cos I'm a little low on gas," he explained. "But I can take you to the bus stop."

Frances wasn't sure how she felt about that. Probably it was the lesser of two evils as she'd have died of embarrassment getting out of Neville's car in full view of the security guards on the front gate, not to mention any members of the hotel staff who might be arriving for work or Travel Together holidaymakers who had chosen this morning to go for a jog.

Neville's car spluttered twice and then roared into action, weaving its way along the narrow streets and out onto the main road again. He pulled up at a wooden bus shelter where two men in chef's trousers and a stunningly beautiful young woman immaculately dressed in a maroon skirt and jacket were already waiting. Neville leaned over and planted a kiss on her lips.

"You get the number twenty-two. You can take the twenty but that only takes you to Jolly Harbour, then you've got to walk about a mile and a half. Twenty-two takes you all the way."

"Okay," Frances said, opening the car door.

"You enjoy yourself?" Neville asked her, grinning. She nodded.

"You said you're in room two twenty-one?" She nodded again. "I'll give you a call when I finish work," he said planting another kiss on her lips before she slid off the seat and joined the people at the bus shelter. Frances felt very conspicuous standing there in what were so obviously the previous night's clothes.

"Good day!" the young woman said.

"Good morning," Frances replied. And the two men nodded their greeting to her.

The bus appeared after just a minute or two. It looked quite full to Frances and she was sure there was no room for her, but suddenly the front passenger door of the minibus opened and a man jumped out, signalling to Frances to jump in. She did so and then he squeezed back in sandwiching her between himself and the driver. Frances hoped he wasn't going to try to strike up a conversation with her. Her luck was in; he smiled but kept quiet, obviously not wanting to talk any more than she did. Frances leaned her head back against the seat and closed her eyes. Scenes from the previous night kept playing themselves behind her eyes and she couldn't help but grin at them. She'd never had sex with a man in a hairnet before. She'd always thought that smoking marijuana slowed you down. That wasn't the case with Neville. The sudden joyful, moist surge between her legs that the memories evoked almost lifted her from the seat and made her squirm.

Get a grip!

 After all this time, after all those years, at almost fifty-one, Frances had become multi-orgasmic.

***

Eve was ready and waiting in reception at quarter past eight. She knew she'd have to wait around, but she also knew she had to be there before the group. That said Trevor, Jo and Grace were already sitting, prepared and waiting when she came into the reception hall.

"Morning, everyone!" she said. "You all well?"

"Fine thanks," Grace answered for all three.

"I'm a little loose in the bowels this morning," Trevor said.

Thank you for sharing that with us!

"Trevor!" Jo and Grace both said, looking at him with distain.

"Well, I just thought Eve should know. I mean, do you think I'll be okay for the trip," he asked Eve.

"Only you know how badly your stomach is upset," Eve said, trying to put it as diplomatically as possible. "Have you taken anything for it?"

"Yes. I took some Imodium. Are there toilets on the way round?"

"Yes, at everywhere you stop there'll be a toilet. The first one will be about forty-five minutes after you leave here."

"I think I'll be alright. If I find I'm not I can always get a taxi back home early, can't I?" he said.

Eve looked out and wondered if they'd all be coming back early. Although the day had been sunny initially, it had clouded over and there was that heavy stickiness that meant rain was on the way. There could be no doubt that a storm was coming.

Donna and Dawn came rushing up to Eve, clutching dollars as they came, both dressed in Birkenstock's, navy cut-offs and blue t-shirts; Donna's light blue and Dawn's baby blue.

"We've got our money," Dawn said thrusting it into Eve's hand, quickly followed by Donna doing the same.

"Thanks," Eve said, counting the money. "I've put you both on the group ticket." She looked around the group and counted nine heads. "Frances and Deano missing, I think."

"Deano was at breakfast, but I didn't see Frances," Donna said.

"Here's Deano," Natalie said. "What happened to you?" she asked as he came limping into view and sat down heavily on one of the sofas.

"I walked right into a big planter; one of those concrete ones."

"What? With the palm trees in them?"

"Yes."

"You mean you nevva saw a great big eff-off palm tree?" Dave asked in wonderment.

"It didn't have a palm tree in it. It's got a smaller plant of some kind. I didn't see it because I had my sunglasses on."

"Well, why didn't you take em off? It ain't sunny is it?"

Deano looked uncomfortable. He sat rubbing his shin, which had a graze and a bruise forming.

"I'll get someone from reception to bring the first aid kit," Eve said, walking away.

"No don't! Don't fuss! I've got some antiseptic ointment in my bag I can put on it. I'm fine."

Geri, who after another uncomfortable night had combed her braids out that morning, couldn't help grinning to herself. She watched as he applied the ointment to his shin. Deano seemed to be quite accident prone. Yesterday he had the brush with the rock, today with the planter. At that moment Frances came hurrying up to join them. She was beaming as she greeted everyone. Eve, catching a whiff of marijuana, looked at her intently, remembering how she had been all dressed up the previous evening. Eve knew Frances must have had a date with one of the Arawak boys. She was glad for her, but hoped that Frances wouldn't be swept away by it all and do anything silly; Eve had seen it all before.

"Aren't Suzanne and Stewart coming?" Donna asked Dave.

"Nah. Suzanne didn't wanna do two days on the trot an so Stew said e'd stay wiv er."

"Ooh! I see! We've got a romance in the group, have we?" Donna asked.

"I fink we've got more'n one. But Stew's right luvved up."

Geri couldn't understand it. Of all the people on the holiday it was Suzanne, fat Suzanne, who'd got off with someone. Not that she fancied Stewart! But even so... She felt insulted somehow, that he'd gone for Suzanne and not for her. She was probably a year or two older than Suzanne, but she was at least four stone lighter. She gave a sigh. This holiday wasn't turning out how she'd expected. She'd tried to sing a song with Jason last night, but by the time he'd sung two with Suzanne and Jo they'd run out of time. She'd hung around the bar for a bit to see if she could get him in conversation, but Grace and Eve had been sitting with them until everything came to an end. And when he'd stood up to go she felt she couldn't follow because Eve was watching. She looked at Natalie and Michael who were chatting quietly together. She was sure something was going on there, too. And even that hateful Murray seemed to be getting off with Deborah. Geri sighed again. Was everyone getting it but her? She felt alone and rejected and she'd never done rejection very well.

At that moment the open-sided jeep pulled up in the car park opposite reception and an Antiguan man of about thirty, smartly dressed in a safari suit, jumped out.

"This is us!" Eve announced and everyone picked up their bags and followed her outside to where the jeep driver was opening the rear door and unfolding the step. There were two rows of seats in the jeep, going lengthways facing inwards towards each other

"Good morning! Good morning!" the driver called out to them before spotting Eve who went over to give him the ticket.

"Eve! Good to see you!" he said hugging her as he recognised her. "Who you got for me today?"

"They're a great group of people when they're sober so just don't let them have too much rum punch," Eve warned him, teasing them.

"You mean we should stop when everyone's had a bottle each?"

"That's it!" She turned to the group. "You're really lucky today because you've got Larry, who's just about the best guide on the whole of Antigua."

"You're too kind. I'm blushing," Larry said, offering his hand to Natalie and helping her up into the jeep. "Good morning, Miss Gorgeous! Move right along, that's it."

Natalie took the seat furthest in; laughing, the rest of the group followed her. Deano pushed himself to the front and sat between Jo and Natalie.

Don't bother, Deano!

Geri watched his haste and almost laughed out loud. She'd taken on board what Eve had said the previous evening about their being eleven of them and ten seats in the back of the jeep. She waited until it was her turn.

"Can I sit in the front, please? I sometimes get a bit car sick."

"You sure can! Just jump in and put your belt on. There's some paperwork on the seat but just put it on the dashboard. I'll be grateful for your company."

"You won't be saying that at the end of the day," Deano said in a stage whisper as Geri got in the front. Then he saw that Eve had heard and was glaring at him, so he concentrated on doing up his seat belt.

"Okay! Is everybody okay? Everybody got their seat belt fastened? Great!"

Larry fastened the rear door and walked round to the driver's door, turning to Eve before he got inside.

"Nice seeing you again, Eve. I'll take care of them for you. You enjoy your day."

"Thanks! Have a lovely time, everyone! Don't forget, dinner in Pizza Pizzazz tonight!" Eve called out as Larry started up the engine and the jeep swept out of the car park and down the driveway.

*****

Murray was a happy as a pig in shit. As happy as a flasher on a railway embankment. Today, he would have Deborah all to himself. Almost everyone had gone out on the trip and those that hadn't never came to the Spa Pool anyway, so he was assured of her uninterrupted company for a good seven or eight hours. In preparation, he'd got down early and had claimed two sun loungers and an umbrella away from the bar on the quieter side of the pool, where they could converse with a degree of privacy. He'd gone and had breakfast as the others were going off on their trip and now, at eight fifty, he was back at the loungers waiting for Deborah to appear. He looked up at the sky and gave a sigh. It was clouding over and what looked like big rain clouds were forming behind the hills to the east of the resort. But Murray didn't care if it rained. Today he felt different. Today he felt as if he were a new man. He realised that taking off his shirt and facing up to the embarrassment of the tattoo had been liberating; like a butterfly escaping from its chrysalis, so the real Murray had been able to emerge from the cocoon he'd spun around himself over the last few years. And to celebrate the mental and physical freedom exposing his torso had brought, he'd put on his new Speedos. He sat down and looked at his body, completely exposed apart from a small, yellow triangle.

Not bad! I pass for a much younger man if I hold my stomach in!

He got out his book and started reading, but the heady anticipation of the day and the promise it would bring wouldn't allow him to concentrate. He found himself reading the same passage several times, until he put the book down and closed his eyes acting out behind their lids his fantasies for the day.

***

On the dining-room terrace, Eve finished her breakfast as Suzanne and Stewart appeared just a few minutes apart. Suzanne was already perspiring; although it was overcast the heat was intense.

"That's because there's a storm brewing," Eve said. "Look! Even the sea looks different today," she added pointing. Suzanne and Stewart followed her finger and could see that the sea, which had been like a mill pond since they'd arrived, was now alive with white swirls almost as far as the eye could see and had turned from cobalt to grey.

"Does that mean we can't swim?" Stewart asked.

"It'll depend on whether there's an orange or red flag on the beach. My guess would be that it'll be fine for a while this morning, but it'll probably be red flag by this afternoon."

"Perhaps we could go out for a bus ride," Stewart said, hopefully. "Is there anywhere you'd suggest, Eve?"

"Well, there's St John's, of course. From there you could take another bus over to the east coast or down to English Harbour to go round Nelson's Dockyard."

"I'm not sure I want to go anywhere where I've got to take two buses," Suzanne said. "I'd quite like to go into St John's. But what if the storm starts?"

"The storm isn't forecast to hit until tomorrow," Eve said. "You'd be fine going into St John's today, although you might be a bit hot walking around."

226

"Let's go to the beach first and see how we feel at lunchtime," Suzanne said. "At the moment all I want to do is lie down in the shade or sit in the water."

Eve was just about to excuse herself as Huw arrived for breakfast.

"Christ! I feel rough. I must have had much more than I'd thought yesterday. I don't know how they've gone off on a trip today!"

Eve smiled. She couldn't make her mind up about Huw. One minute he was arrogance personified and the next he seemed like a nice, normal bloke. It was the same with Murray. For the first three days he'd been Mr Obnoxious yet since Deborah had been showing a bit of interest in him he'd turned into Mr Nice Guy. Telling the story of the tattoo had really got a laugh yesterday, yet Eve thought that it must have taken courage for him to do that. Still, at least now that it was out in the open he'd be able to take his shirt off for the rest of the holiday, and hopefully for the rest of his life. Perhaps he'd discovered that when you showed a bit of humility, people laughed with you and not at you.

"Just drink plenty of water this morning and have an orange juice with a little bit of salt in it and you'll be fine," she told Huw.

"Salt? I've never heard of that one. Still, I'll give it a go. Anything to stop the hammering in my head. You seen Jason this morning?" he asked.

All three shook their heads.

"Perhaps he's hung over as well," Suzanne said. "He had a few drinks to celebrate our karaoke success."

"You did ever so well, didn't you? You'd never've got me up there, singing!"

"But you're Welsh," Suzanne said. "I thought all Welshmen were good singers."

"I might be Welsh but I'm the exception that proves the rule, see?"

Eve excused herself. She picked up her coffee cup and walked over to the bar to do her morning surgery until half past ten. Although most of the group were out, she still had to be there just in case the others wanted her. She'd brought her book down with her as she didn't think she'd have much to do this morning. As she sat down she felt her blouse sticking to her back. She looked up at the sky which, although mostly overcast, still had large blue patches shining through. Her mobile phone rang. Looking at the number she saw the caller was Sunny.

"Hey, girl! What's up?" Sunny greeted her.

"I'm well, thanks."

"Good day out yesterday?"

"Fantastic! Everyone loved it and we had a great time."

"Well, I hope they enjoy the jeep today because the storm has now been graded as a force four tropical storm, and the Met Office has said that there's every possibility it could be a fully blown hurricane by the time it hits us, which will be around early afternoon tomorrow. So you need to tell your people not to go off property."

"Okay. And I'll make sure I've got the Mango Tree's hurricane procedure to give them tonight when I see them."

"You'll probably find that they put a copy in everyone's room, but it won't do any harm to actually give them each a copy in their hand. Ask Mr McGrass, he'll make sure you get them. What do you think of him? Have you met him, yet?"

"Oh, yes, I've met him." Eve said.

"Isn't he great?" Sunny insisted, enthusiastically.

"Oh, yes, he's very nice. Well, thanks for giving me the heads up on the weather. It was a good job we did the boat trip yesterday."

"I told you so! You enjoy your day now, and if you want anything you know where I am."

Eve hung up and was just taking a sip of her coffee when the phone rang again. This time the caller was showing as the Mango Tree Resort.

"Eve speaking."

"Hi, Eve, good day. It's Carlo here. I'm sorry to trouble you, but I guess you've heard the bad weather report? You know there's a big storm coming?"

"Yes, I just heard about it."

"Well, we're going to have to evacuate everyone from the first floor, or rather the ground floor, as you call it. And that includes you!"

"You think it's going to get that bad?"

"Well, there might be some flooding, you know, under the doors and so on; it's so difficult to keep the water out. So, if you can call by and see us at the front desk we'll give you another key and the maids will help you move your things. Okay?"

"That's fine, Carlo. Thank you."

Eve sighed. So much for having some time to herself today! Still, it took half an hour to change rooms, and given the alternative was to find herself and her possessions floating round the room tomorrow she had nothing to complain about. *Rather,* she chided herself, *you should feel thankful that they're moving you in advance, you ungrateful cow!*

***

Deborah was holding Murray's dick and staring into his eyes. Slowly and deliberately, she leaned forward and placed it between her breasts, which seemed much larger now that they swung pendulously before him, free of any restraining bra or bikini top. As her breasts worked his dick up and down between them she leaned forward and stuck her tongue in his mouth, pushing in down into his throat, while making sexy, sighing groans that were driving him wild. At the same time she managed to whisper his name in a deep, sultry voice.

"Murray! Murray! You're snoring!"

His eyes shot open with a start. Deborah was now lying on the sun lounger next to him, grinning. Aware of the effect of his dream and the brevity of his Speedos he quickly turned over onto his front.

"I must have nodded off."

"You were dead to the world when I came along. I've been here about half an hour and your snoring's become increasingly louder. But when you started groaning I had to nudge you; people were beginning to look because you were disturbing them."

"You're joking. I don't snore. And I certainly wasnae groaning!"

"Murray! I've heard quieter intercity expresses!"

Bugger!

Now she knew he snored it might put her off. His mouth was dry and he could do with a drink but he still couldn't get up for the moment without drawing more attention to himself. He couldn't believe she'd been lying next to him for half an hour. It was a good job he'd only snored and not talked in his sleep!

"It's so hot! It must be the hottest day since we've been here. There's no air, is there?" Deborah said. "I bet they're hot on their jeep trip."

"Yes, but they'll be getting the breeze if they're driving around with the sides off. Has Frances gone?"

"Yes."

"What happened with you two? You seemed tae be getting on really well for the first couple of days, yet I canna help but notice you've barely spoken a word tae each other for a while now."

Deborah sighed. She had no wish to go into details of her private life and her domestic set up with Murray. Deep down, in her heart of hearts, she knew that what Frances said was right. But that didn't make Deborah a bad person and it didn't make her feel better or worse about Maurice. Two nights ago, after her fall out with Frances, she'd sent him a text

I need some time 2 enjoy this holiday without ur constant

calls. Switching fone off til I get back 2 London.

Call me then n we can discuss our future. Xxx

And then she'd turned her phone off and hadn't turned it on again. She'd spent a lot of time, years and years in fact, on Maurice. Now for a few days it was Deborah's time. She looked at Murray and smiled. Under the brash, Scottish exterior, could there be a sensitive soul? He certainly seemed to have mellowed in the last twenty-four hours. Last night the two of them had sat on the sea wall with their toes in the sand, looking at the water and chatting. He told her about his kids and it was obvious that losing them had broken his heart. She'd given him a hug; the panacea for all-know ills, the touch of another human being; the knowledge that someone knows, understands and empathises with your situation. And to her amazement she'd felt him sob. He'd clung to her for a few moments until he'd been able to control himself. Then he'd walked her back to her room.

"I'm sorry about that, you know... getting all soppy and pathetic on you," he'd said as she'd taken her key from her bag. "But thanks for understanding."

He leaned forward and planted a kiss on her cheek. She'd hesitated. It would have been so easy to have pulled him inside and sought relief for both of them, but it would probably have made things difficult this morning and she wanted to enjoy her day by the pool with him. She'd already fallen out with Frances; she didn't want to alienate Murray as well. She'd discovered that she really liked the man's company and attention. She'd actually seen Frances coming into the hotel at half past seven that morning, as she came out of the gym after her short, early-morning session. She was curious and keen to know where Frances had been and, most importantly, with whom. She realised that Murray was waiting for an answer to his question.

"Oh, we had just a difference of opinion on something trivial. I'm going to go out of my way to make the peace with her tonight. Drink?" she asked him.

"I'll have a Wadiddly," he said as they both laughed at his using Dave's malapropism.

Deborah stood up and stretched languorously, her arms above her head lifting her breasts almost out of her bikini top, before turning to signal to the waiter. Murray groaned. Just as he thought it was almost safe to turn over onto his back again!

***

Suzanne and Stewart lay side by side and hand in hand on the beach, each deep in thought, both deliriously happy. Suzanne was beside herself. By winning the karaoke the previous evening, albeit with the other two, she'd become a celebrity within the resort. On her way from breakfast and then down to the beach several people had stopped her to congratulate her on her performance and Steve from the Entertainments Team had rushed over and kissed her hand at breakfast as he made his way around the terrace trying to drum up two teams for beach cricket. She was bursting with pride at her success; bursting with pride, too, that Stewart had chosen to be with her. After they'd all won the karaoke prize she and Stewart had gone and sat in the gardens, where, he'd told her that he really, really, really liked her to the extent that he wanted to see her once they got back to England.

"But we've only known each other for a couple of days. Everyone will say it's just a holiday fling."

"I don't care what other people say. Only I know how I feel, Suzanne, and I know that this is more than that. I just love being in your company. Spending time with you on the catamaran today, you know, swimming together and just being together, enjoying ourselves. It was one of the best days of my life. Honest."

This was new territory for Suzanne. For years she'd dedicated her life to Mum and the shop. She'd never looked for a boyfriend and one had never turned up. She'd almost come to accept that in modern day UK where being young and being thin were the ways in which a woman's worth was measured, someone of her age and of her size, was often condemned to a sterile, single, solitary old age. And now, here he was, the man of her dreams; kind, considerate, sartorially somewhat extravagant, and completely indifferent to the few extra pounds she might be carrying. Well, extra stones, perhaps. And, there, in the gardens, surrounded by an explosion of tropical colours and perfumes, she'd admitted that she'd felt the same way.

"But I live in Norfolk and you live in Oldham," she'd said. "That's miles away."

"Is it eck? It's do-able. You could come up and spend a weekend, come to a gig."

"But, that's difficult. We open the shop every day."

"You'll find someone to stand in for you. Or I could come down and see you! I could even help out behind the counter, or do the hard graft, you know, lifting boxes and stacking shelves."

Suzanne wasn't sure how Mum would react to Stewart. But then, in a fit of bravado and abandon she realised that she didn't really care what Mum thought. It had taken her so long to find him, but here he was! This was her life, not Mum's. And from now on Stewart was going to be a huge part of it.

"I'd like that," she'd said, and her honesty and sincerity had touched his heart. He kissed her gently on the lips and before they knew it they'd completely enveloped each other and snogged away for a long, long time.

Now, lying on the beach, Stewart marvelled about Suzanne. He was completely captivated by her naivety and innocence; her honest, unpretentious attitude to life; her beautiful smile and her lovely soft, curly hair. He couldn't wait to lose himself in her huge bosom and feel her generous thighs open up to receive him and wrap themselves around his body. He just hoped his own ample belly wouldn't get in the way.

***

By lunchtime Eve was settled into her new room, 228. It was a suite, which was rather nice; spacious and with little touches of luxury missing from the room she was usually given. Carlo had handed her a copy of the resort's hurricane procedure when she'd given back the key to her previous room and assured her that everyone would have one delivered to their rooms by early afternoon. In spite of the air conditioning unit being turned down to 16C, Eve felt hot and sticky. Looking out to the gardens and the row of Royal palms beyond, she could see how still everything was; not one single tree was moving. And beyond them, far on the horizon, floating ominously, it looked like the first storm clouds were gathering. She was just thinking about having a dip in the pool to cool off when the mobile rang. It was a number she didn't recognise.

"Hallo. Eve speaking."

"Eve, it's Larry. You need to go to Mount St John's. One of your people's had an accident."

"What? Who?"

"Robert Dean. We were at Devil's Bridge. I told them to be careful because the Atlantic's pounding today and the rocks were wet. I told them to take care, but he seemed to trip and he fell into the water. I got him out but not before he hit his head and his leg is broken, I think. It looks nasty. The paramedics came and they're taking him now."

Struggling to take it all in, Eve was shocked at what Larry was saying.

"You dived in after him?"

"Of course I did! He went in fully clothed and head-first; I had to get him out." He said it matter-of-factly, not looking for praise; just a man who did what the circumstances dictated him to do. No waiting for health and safety checks.

"What about the others?"

"They're all fine just a little shaken and concerned for their friend, obviously. But Andy, my co-worker, was here with another group and he had some spare pants I've borrowed and I always carry a spare shirt so I'm going to carry on with the tour."

"Are you sure?"

"I think it'll be best for them; take their minds off what's gone on."

"I don't mean for them, I mean for you! Are you okay, Larry?"

"I'm fine, Eve. I also need to carry on. Thanks for your concern. But they need you to go to the hospital with his insurance details. You know how it works here."

"I'm out the door! Thanks, Larry. Thanks a million. Tell the others I'll see them as usual tonight," and with that Eve hung up. She grabbed her paperwork envelope and took out the page showing the clients' details; passport number, date and place of issue and insurer's name, the policy number and emergency contact telephone number. She could phone the insurance company once she knew exactly what medical treatment Deano was going to need, but she needed to let Travel Together know about the situation. She looked at her watch. It was one o'clock, which meant it was six pm in UK. There was probably nobody in the office now. She dialled the Travel Together emergency mobile number. It went to voicemail.

Why the fuck do we have an emergency number if it's switched off?

Growling with frustration, Eve left a short sharp message asking whoever was on emergency duty to call her back on the mobile number that Sunny had provided her with because she was dealing with a nasty accident. She picked up her bag, grabbing a bottle of water and stuffing it inside as she left the room. Experience told her she was in for a long wait.

Eve heard a distant rumble of thunder as she got out of the taxi and paid the fare; the storm was moving nearer. She tucked the receipt into her purse just as an ambulance was pulling into the emergency bay at Mount St John's Medical Centre. She ran across and sure enough, as the doors opened Deano was revealed, strapped onto the stretcher, conscious and grimacing in pain.

"Deano! I'm here!"

In spite of the East End and Essex Orange suntan that she'd secretly chuckled about, she could clearly see that he was in shock; pale and shaking.

"Stand back, please, miss, we have to take him inside," one of the paramedics said. Eve stood back to let them do their job.

"I'll come in as soon as they let me!" she called to Deano in the hope of reassuring him. "Don't worry about anything; we'll take care of it all!"

233

He looked awful; there was something so different about him, and it wasn't just the pain in his eyes. It was the colour of his eyes. No longer turquoise, they were a sort of non-descript shade of hazel.

***

In spite of Deano's accident, the trip had been a roaring success. Obviously upset by what had happened to him, everyone's first thought had been to abandon the rest of the day, but once the ambulance had gone, whizzing Deano away in a fanfare of claxons and flashing lights, it somehow felt wrong to just go back to the hotel.

"Look! I'm not being funny, right? But what good will it do now if we all just go back to the hotel? What will we do? Just sit around," Natalie had said. "It might sound a bit callous but we can't undo what's just happened to Deano."

"You're right," Grace said. "The whole point of coming out today was to see the island and we're only halfway round."

There was a moment's silence while everyone thought about this. Nobody wanted to appear hard or uncaring, but they all knew that what Natalie and Grace said made sense. Larry, who had been visibly shaken when he'd seen Deano plough headlong into the sea and who had wasted no time or even given any thought to his own safety but had dived straight in after him, joined in the conversation.

"It's your trip, your day," Larry said. "Now, you may think it's already been ruined, but we can salvage it, you know. Your buddy's in real good hands. Our new hospital is state of the art and they're gonna take real good care of him. Eve's gone to meet up with him there. I suggest we have a rum punch to steady our nerves and put us back in the right mood and I promise you guys, I'll do my best to make the rest of the day the best I possibly can. We still have the English Harbour and Nelson's Dockyard visit and guided tour and that's probably the best part."

They all looked at each other and started nodding. Donna gave Larry a great big hug.

"You're a lovely man. A hero. Without you he'd have drowned today," she said.

"That's true," Grace said. "You acted very quickly. Thank you."

"Well, I did what I had to do, you know, but I'm just sorry he went in. He seemed to stumble against that rock. Did anyone see it?"

"Yes, he was just in front of me," Trevor said. "He tripped over that large stone," he pointed at it, "Well, he walked right into it, actually and toppled forward unable to stop himself."

"Do you need us to sign any witness statements?" Michael asked him. "Because I know I'd be willing to confirm what Trevor's just said; that's exactly what happened. He didn't seem to see the stone, he just walked straight into it and it tripped him."

"It was them bloody glasses!" Dave said. "If e adn't ad em on, e'd of seen where he was goin'."

"Well, he's lost them now," Natalie said. "Isn't vanity a terrible thing?"

Everyone looked at her, puzzled.

"Oh come on! Was I the only one to notice?"

She faced a wall of blank looks.

"His eyes aren't turquoise; they're just a normal sort of non-descript colour. He must have lost his cosmetically enhancing contact lenses yesterday and that's why he didn't come down to dinner last night and why he kept his sunglasses on today!"

They all looked at each other in amazement. Geri couldn't help herself, she started to giggle. In spite of themselves, one by one, the others joined in, fuelled by the nerves and upset of what they'd witnessed they all started laughing until they almost cried.

***

It was five o'clock before Eve could see Deano again. By that time he'd been x-rayed and Dr Rodriguez, the consultant orthopaedic surgeon had called her in to bring her up to date with his findings.

"He has a break to his left leg below the knee, across the tibia, but he also has a compound fracture at the top of the femur and that one's going to be the difficult one to set. Both injuries must have occurred as he hit rocks just below the water surface. We can operate here, but it will be a considerable time before he is allowed to go home. Or, we can try to make him comfortable enough for him to be taken back to the UK for treatment. However, that will also take time, because we need to ascertain there is no head injury, because if there is he can't fly."

"And how long will that take?" Eve asked.

"At least twenty-four hours, possibly forty-eight. We have to run tests and keep him under observation until we are certain. And if there is no injury to the head we will have to wait for the insurance company to send out a nurse companion to accompany him back on the flight. So that is the situation. Quite a difficult one."

"Thank you, doctor. Have you spoken to him? What does he want to do?"

"He seems unsure." Dr Rodriguez took a large white handkerchief from a pocket in his white coat and wiped his face. "It is a lot for him to take in and quite frankly he is still in shock. It's probably best if you talk to him and then the insurers and his family in England and then a decision can be made. For the moment, he is comfortable and under light sedation. I've given him the strongest possible painkiller I can. Would you like to see him?"

Eve nodded. She followed Dr Rodriguez out of his office and down a corridor that sparkled with cleanliness and smelt sharply of disinfectant, into a side ward which housed several beds, each with the curtains pulled closed around them. Dr Rodriguez stopped at the second one on the left and pulled the curtain back, motioning Eve to step inside. She did so and Dr Rodriguez followed leaving the curtain open.

"Robert. Your tour rep is here," he said, looking at him closely with highly-practised eyes. He turned to Eve. "I'll leave you with him. Just five minutes so that you don't tire him." And then he walked out pulling the curtain closed behind him. Eve took two steps nearer to the bed.

"Deano," she said, in a stage whisper.

He opened his eyes and looked at her, taking a moment to focus and recognise her.

"What a mess," he said.

"How are you feeling?" Eve knew it was a stupid question, but it seemed like the obvious one to ask.

"I've been better."

"The doctor said he explained to you that you've got a leg that's broken in two places and one of the breaks is a bit nasty." She paused, waiting for confirmation that he'd understood her. Deano nodded. His eyes, his boring, light-hazelish eyes, filled with tears.

"It was because I had my sunglasses on. It was cloudy... overcast and dark and they made it even darker. I couldn't see where I was going and I tripped over this fucking rock."

"Why didn't you take your sunglasses off?" She couldn't help herself. Although she was sure she already knew the answer, she just had to ask. Deano gulped.

"Because I'd lost one of my coloured contact lenses when we were on the catamaran yesterday. I never thought of bringing a spare pair with me. I couldn't face everyone, you know, after they'd all made comments about what a gorgeous colour my eyes were. I felt a right twat."

"Is that why you didn't come to dinner last night?"

He nodded.

"But surely, you weren't going to spend the rest of the holiday with your shades on, were you?"

"I was going to say I'd got conjunctivitis," he mumbled.

In spite of everything, Eve felt quite sorry for him, as he lay in bed, a picture of misery, the thought of everyone seeing him without the lenses seemed to be causing him more pain that his actual injuries.

"I'm really sorry, but I've got to ask you a couple of questions. I've got your insurance details, but Travel Together will have to contact your next of kin to obviously let them know what's happened to you and then they'll have to discuss the best way of dealing with this with your insurers... I mean... whether it's better for you to be treated here or at home."

Deano nodded despondently, a tear running down his face onto his chin. Eve reached inside her bag and took out some tissues and patted the tear dry and put the tissue into his hand. She then pulled out her pen and notebook.

"So, who's your next of kin and what's their phone number?"

"Mrs Rachael Dean. 07009 098765."

Eve hurriedly scribbled down the name and number, repeating it out loud as she did so.

"Is that your mum, Deano?" she asked him.

"No." He closed his eyes tightly and then slowly opened them to stare at Eve. "It's my wife. She doesn't know I'm here. She thinks I'm at a trade fair in Spain."

***

The group had gathered at the bar at seven o'clock, as per usual. Those who had been on the trip had brought the others up to date with what had happened to Deano and how Larry had dived in and saved him.

"But why did he have his sunglasses on if it wasn't sunny?" Deborah asked.

All those who had been on the trip looked at each other; none of them wanting to be the one who brought up the subject of the contact lenses.

"That's the million dollar question," Jo said. On reflection she'd been ashamed of herself for laughing at his misfortune and although she knew it was human nature, didn't want there to be more laughter about a man who'd become their friend over the last few days and who was now seriously hurt. A man who she knew may very well have become more than just her friend if things had taken a difference course. "Let's just hope his injuries are not as serious as they first appeared."

Further questions to the group were avoided by the arrival of Eve; looking unusually flustered and still wearing the clothes she'd had on at breakfast time.

"Hi, everyone! Sorry to keep you waiting, but I've just this minute stepped out of the taxi from seeing Deano at the hospital."

"How is he?" they all asked at once, like the Chorus in a Greek Tragedy.

"Not good, I'm afraid. He's got a break and a multiple fracture to the same leg and at the moment it's all in the hands of the insurance company, who now take over and liaise with the hospital and Deano and his family to decide what the best course to take is."

"Do you want a drink, Eve? You look as if you could do with one," Michael said. Eve nodded, thoughtfully.

"I'd actually like a rum punch," she said, and a cheer went up around the group, in spite of the seriousness of the moment.

"You prob'ly deserve it. We all fink you've got a great job, but it's fings like this you av ter deal wiv that must make it ard. Like Larry. Wot a star e was!" Dave said. "If e adn't of fought so quickly, Deano would of bin killed."

"So I understand. I'm going to ring him in a while to thank him properly."

"And all because he wasna looking where he was going, so I believe," Murray said.

Eve had made up her mind not to mention the sunglasses or lost contact lens, and certainly not to mention the wife. Karma had, in its own inevitable way, stepped in to take care of Deano's transgressions. He wasn't the first man to be guilty of vanity and he was paying a heavy price. She was deeply angry that a married man had tried to use her holiday and her group as a way of having a week's extra-marital sex, but that was between him and his conscience and for him to sort out with his wife. It was really nobody else's business.

"Well, that's what an accident is, isn't it? Someone loses concentration for a split second and their life changes forever," Eve said.

"Can he have visitors?" Suzanne asked

"Well, not at the moment. He's quite heavily sedated."

"Perhaps before we leave," Jo said. Who knows? Their friendship might have lead to something and it might not, but now all she could feel was compassion for a friend who was suffering. "We could go in and say goodbye, because I take it he won't be coming back with us."

"No chance of that," Eve said. "Even if they decide to take him back home for treatment it's going to take until the middle of next week to sort that all out."

"Poor man!" Frances said. The group went very quiet as each became lost in their thoughts, grateful that it hadn't happened to them.

"Anyway, I've got a couple of things to tell you. First of all, the big storm that's been getting closer is probably going to hit early afternoon tomorrow, so please don't go off-property. It'll be very, very windy and there'll be heavy rainfall. We'll have to amuse ourselves reading or playing cards or doing a quiz or something. Everyone clear about that?"

"Is it a hurricane?" Suzanne asked.

"It's a tropical storm at the moment; Tropical Storm Charlotte. But these things are notoriously erratic and it could become a fully blown hurricane, and if it does then the resort will go into emergency procedures which we'll have to follow to the letter. The other thing is that when the storm hits the power may go off, Sunny may not be able to visit, all sorts of things may happen, so I'm going to ask you to give me your check-in forms back by tomorrow morning instead of Friday, please, so that I can process them. Okay?" She looked round the group brightly as everyone nodded their head. "So, apart from the accident, did you all have a good day?" Eve asked trying to lighten the mood.

***

Dinner in Pizza Pizzazz was a huge success. Everyone enjoyed the food and Eve thought that tonight there seemed to be a greater feeling of togetherness, of camaraderie, among this group of people, who had been brought closer by a disaster befalling one of their number. She noticed that Frances and Deborah seemed to be friends again.

Deborah, having decided she didn't want to waste any more time by not talking to Frances, had deliberately sat next to her at dinner and immediately started up a conversation by asking her about the trip. Frances, who was never one to bear a grudge, well, not unless it was against her ex-husband and his mistress, and who was basking in the feel-good sensation that rampant, uninhibited sex with Neville had brought on, was soon engaged in animated conversation with her again.

"You look really nice again tonight," Deborah said, as they were finishing their rum and raisin ice creams. "That lime green is such a beautiful colour on you and it makes you look really brown."

About to say 'oh, but it's old' Frances, bit her lip and accepted the compliment. She'd taken time getting ready tonight; had put a special effort into looking good. She had just been getting into the shower when Neville had called her.

"What's up, baby?" he said and she felt herself go moist as the sound of his deep, caramel voice evoked memories of what they'd done together less than twenty-four hours ago. "You coming again tonight?"

"Several times I hope," she said, amazed at her own daring.

Neville chuckled at the other end of the phone. They'd made arrangements for Frances to take a taxi to the standpipe after Gray's Farm Police Station at nine thirty where Neville would be waiting for her.

"I'm still a little low on gas for my vehicle, or I'd come and get you," he'd explained, by way of apology.

Frances didn't mind; she didn't really want anyone to see her with Neville. She wasn't ashamed of this fling, this love affair, in the slightest. But she didn't want to be the subject of any gossip. She knew that middle-aged men could go out with women who were thirty years their junior and nobody would bat an eyelid. But when it was the other way round, the woman was the subject of so much scorn. Several years ago, before the cancer, she'd mentioned to Darren that she'd quite fancied going on safari to Kenya. He'd laughed out loud.

"Just so long as you don't come back with a Masai Warrior!" he'd warned.

If you could see me now, my son!

"Have you got a hot date?" Murray asked from across the table. She looked at him, aware that he might have made the peace with Deborah, but the argument she'd had with him still rankled. She was also suddenly aware that there'd been a lull in the conversation and almost everyone was looking at her, waiting for her reply.

"Why wouldn't she have?" Natalie piped up from further down the table. "She looks like a million dollars!" Frances looked gratefully at Natalie and smiled her thanks. Encouraged by Natalie's support she answered up for herself.

"Yes, I have, as a matter of fact."

"What, you?" Huw asked his mouth dropping open, in spite of it being full of tiramisu.

There was a sharp intake of breath from all the women around the table, except Geri, who couldn't understand either how Frances, who must be older than she was and hadn't really taken care of herself, could have a date. Even one or two of the men were taken back by Huw's lack of tact.

"Why not me? Why wouldn't I have a date?" Frances asked Huw, looking him straight in the eye. He dropped his gaze, but she wasn't going to let him off the hook so easily. "Why are you so surprised that I should have a date?"

240

Huw struggled to regain his composure. He didn't like the way she'd answered him back in front of everyone. Who the fuck did she think she was? He looked up and caught Trevor's eye. That was it! She must have a date with him; two of the older ones going out together.

"Oh, no offence, I just didn't know that you and Trevor had got together," he said.

Trevor choked on his mango cheese cake, flattered yet stunned and surprised by Huw's mistake.

"We haven't got together. Why do you think I'm going out with Trevor tonight?" Frances insisted.

"Well, you know, I mean... well... he's your age group, isn't he?"

Everyone sat back in their seats, watching and starting to enjoy the spectacle. You could have heard a pin drop.

"Oh, I must be at least twenty years older than Frances," Trevor said, ever the gentleman.

"So, a woman of a certain age must only go out with her own age group, must she? And by *her own age group* you mean only men who are older than her?" Frances wouldn't let go. Huw shrugged, resorting to aggression as being the only way he knew how to deal with the derision he was beginning to feel coming his way from all sides of the table.

"I don't really give a fuck who you're going out with. I couldn't care less. I just never had you down for one of those women who go after the locals. It is some local, I take it?"

Frances held his gaze.

"It might be."

"One of those who get off with a different old dear every week, is it? One of them beach bums who pick up geriatric foreigners who are gagging for it in the hope they'll bung them a few quid. I mean, no offence, but no man's going to shag an old woman if he can get a young bird, see!" He sat back, pleased with himself, looking round the table at the men, expecting to see nods of agreement, finding only blank stares as they all, even those that might secretly agree with him, kept well and truly quiet. Even Murray held his tongue and showed no emotion, aware that to do so might mean he'd never ever get any further with Deborah.

Frances leaned forward, trapping him in the headlight of her stare, never taking her eyes from his face for one single moment.

"Let me tell you something, Huw. There are those men, who are the equivalent of the trainee jockey; lacking experience and fearful they'll be found wanting. They will only go for the young fillies, some only ponies, because they know that as they haven't really got a clue either, a short fast ride that brings a moment's excitement will be all that's expected. Then there are the confident, experienced riders; those who know that wherever they take their horse, both of them will enjoy every single second of the ride. They'll enjoy the initial contact, the preparation, and understand that once he gains her confidence the two of them will have the time of their life. And that jockey relishes and appreciates an older horse, because he knows that as he wins her trust, she'll go wherever he may lead her, and that she may have a few tricks or touches of her own to bring to their encounter and make it even more memorable. So together they set off; walk, trot, canter and then gallop, over fences, across rivers, up mountains and down through valleys, going hell for leather, riding as one. He gets such pleasure and satisfaction from seeing his older mare reaching heights that the filly can only dream of and she takes him with her every single time. And as the two of them cross the finishing line together, sweating, hearts pounding, triumphant and victorious winners, they know their souls have soared together, sharing something so very special."

She paused for him to take in what she'd said and never taking her eyes from him she lifted her glass and sipped some more wine. Nobody moved a muscle; they all sat in absolute silence, watching, waiting to see what would happen next. Huw looked surly but gave an unconscious gulp. But Frances hadn't quite finished with him.

"So perhaps one day you'll become a man confident enough in his own skin and sexual performance to realise why a younger man might choose to go out with a geriatric foreigner."

"Woo hoo! Way to go, Frances!" Natalie said, clapping her hands, and all the women, except Geri, joined in with the spontaneous applause. Grace and Deborah both leaned over and high-fived Frances.

Huw stood up, humiliation turning his face blood red, spite and venom showing in his voice.

"I don't have to fucking listen to this!"

"No you don't," Frances agreed, also standing up. "But don't leave on my account, because it's time I was off." She unhooked her bag from the back of her chair and stepped round it and then pushed it back under the table. "Tonight I'm riding in the Grand National and we're under starter's orders."

And with that she sashayed out of the restaurant.

Blimey where had that all come from?

There was a few seconds' silence. Huw sat down again, downed the remains of his beer and then muttered something vile.

"Please don't use that language," Eve said, hearing what he'd said. "It's unacceptable and unnecessary."

"What you trying to tell me what I can and can't say? It's a free fucking country and I'll say what I like. Who the fuck do you think you are?"

242

"Don't take your anger out on me, please, Huw. I'm just telling you that I find that word very offensive and I'd prefer you not to use it in my hearing, especially about a member of the group."

"Well, she is! That's just what she is!"

"Is what?" Suzanne turned to ask Stewart. He whispered in her ear and she looked shocked. "No she isn't!" she called out to Huw.

"Huw, your attack on Frances was in front of everyone and totally unprovoked. She'd done nothing to deserve that. You can't blame her for answering you back. You brought it on yourself," Grace said.

"If you dish it out you've got to be able to take it," Donna added, surprising herself at how wound up Huw had made her feel.

"And you can just fuck off as well!"

"Don't you think that's enough?" Michael said. "You're out of order talking to Eve and Donna like that. I think you need to calm down a bit, mate."

"I'm not your mate."

"Huw, leave it," Jason said, putting a restraining hand on his arm.

Huw stood up again shaking off Jason's touch and looked round the table for support. But he found none as the only person who seemed unaware of the hole he was digging himself into, was Huw himself.

"And the rest of you can fuck of too!" And with that he strode out.

Everyone looked around at everyone else and gradually smiles broke out on their faces, in turn quickly turning into hoots of laughter and comments.

"Well, Frances really told im!" Dave said.

"He's a man who's got a big chip on both shoulders and probably a very small penis," Natalie observed. "I bet he's one of those men who drive around in a convertible with the top down in all weathers, you know the ones; their car's a penis extension."

"I drive a convertible," Michael said, straight-faced for a few seconds until the look of horror at having put her foot in it on Natalie's face caused him to laugh out loud and shake his head in contradiction.

"Or those that drive Pajeros!" Trevor said.

"What's wrong with a Pajero?" Stewart asked. "I use one to shift all my deejay stuff. They're great motors."

Trevor looked abashed. He went red at finding all eyes on himself for the second time in as many minutes, wishing he'd kept his mouth shut. But everyone was looking at him waiting for his answer. He coughed.

"Well, I think I told some of you that I go to Spanish lessons, didn't I?"

A few heads nodded.

"Well, when we had our Christmas party, some of the group were a bit naughty... you know... the sangria was flowing... and they asked Mari Angeles our teacher to tell them some swear words in Spanish. And Pajero is the Spanish for wanker."

The gale of laughter that followed this could have been heard in St John's as Stewart sat open-mouthed at what he'd heard.

"Right! I'm straight down the showroom when I get back home and trading it in!"

Alone, sitting on the seawall, anger and bile seeping from every pore in his body, Huw heard them all laughing and was certain it was about him.

***

Given that the weather was going to change and that they might be confined to barracks for the next day or so, some of the group decided to go out for a drink after dinner.

"How exciting! Going under the wire!" Grace said.

"I don't know if I can be arsed," Natalie said, yawning. "I'm tired after yesterday, last night and today."

"Oh come on Natalie! Just for one drink!" Suzanne said.

"Alright then! God! I'm so easily led" she laughed.

In the end everyone had decided to call a taxi to take them down to Jolly Harbour where they had the choice of two or three places where they could sit and have a drink. Jason had thought about finding Huw but when all said and done, although the two of them had become drinking buddies, that's really all it was. Huw was a real bigot. He wasn't someone that Jason would have had much to do with in the outside world. In fact, he reminded him of a PE teacher in his own school that he always avoided like the plague. If they hadn't both been teachers and more of less of the same age and sports enthusiasts, he doubted he'd ever have really got into conversation with him. And although there were a few people he didn't have much in common with on this trip, nobody was really gross or nasty and he'd been getting on fine with all of them. He liked Natalie and Jo and Michael; Dave was a right laugh and even Dawn and Donna had grown on him now that they'd settled down a bit. And Stewart might look a bit weird, as if he was going to a fancy dress some of the time, but they'd had a couple of great conversations about music because he certainly knew his stuff. Even Trevor was a nice enough bloke; he reminded him of his Uncle Geoff. He didn't want to end up being ostracised because Huw was an idiot and didn't know when to shut up. It wasn't the first time he'd caused a scene. He'd behaved like a little boy at Shirley Heights when the two American girls had started dancing with two local guys. No. He'd let Huw go off on his own. Tonight he was being one of the group.

***

Although she was dead tired, Eve went with them to Jolly Harbour. They were a nice group and she also felt the need to enjoy herself a bit tonight after the shocks she'd had to face during the day. As she was asking Paloma on the front desk to call a taxi big enough to take sixteen people to Jolly Harbour, or two smaller ones if that's all that were available, she'd caught a glimpse of lime green getting into a taxi, which headed down the driveway. She smiled to herself as she relived Frances, monologue in her mind's eye. She'd certainly put Huw in his place. Just as she'd started to think he was an alright guy! She smiled at the thought of Frances with a young, local man. From what she'd had to say, she'd obviously enjoyed herself and the evidence was she was going back for more. Eve just hoped she was being careful. She gave a mental shrug. She wasn't Frances' keeper. She was a woman of fifty; old enough to take care of herself.

They clambered out of their taxi and poured into the Sports Bar after the short ride from the Mango Tree Resort to Jolly Harbour and the taxi driver gave Eve his card so that she could phone him when they were ready to leave and he'd come back for them. The bar was quite lively; a local band was playing and a dozen or so people were on the dance floor, while others sat at tables, eating or drinking. Five men sat in a line on the bar stools watching a game of basketball on the large screen that hung above the bar. The group pushed their way through and congregated at the far end in a space next to the edge of the veranda. Drink orders were taken and delivered and everyone was talking and animated. Jo squeezed her way past Dawn, Jason and Geri to get to Eve. She leaned in and spoke to her so that nobody else could hear.

"How is Deano? Really?" she asked.

"Pretty much as I said. I mean, he's obviously in shock and he's sedated so that he can deal with the pain."

"Will you go in and see him tomorrow?"

"Probably. It'll depend on the weather but I was planning on going during the morning sometime."

"Do you think he'll be treated here?"

"I honestly don't know; all that's out of my hands now really. I'll go and see him whenever I can before we leave, but the decision about what happens to him will be taken by Deano himself and his insurers."

"Would you let him know I'm asking after him, please, Eve?"

"Of course I will!" Eve felt awkward and a bit sorry for Jo, who'd obviously been getting close to Deano in the last couple of days.

What the hell did he think he was playing at?

Jo was a truly lovely woman, who'd already had a lot of heartache in her life. She didn't need a married man messing around with her. Eve felt like telling her she'd had a lucky escape but knew she couldn't. Instead she patted Jo's arm.

"I'll tell him you send your love," she said.

At that moment a table of local people who had been eating together on the veranda stood up and started to make their way through the Travel Together group, nodding and smiling as they came, to a background of *"excuse me"* and *"oops, sorry"*. Eve went to take a step back to let an elegant woman in a pale lemon trouser suit pass when she heard a voice that stopped her in her tracks.

"You're all out having a good time I see?" Melv said to the group as he came through, his hand guiding the elbow of the woman. Recognising him, the group members returned his greeting. He was inches away from Eve and the woman had stopped right in front of her, turning to see who her husband was talking to. Melv switched his gaze to Eve.

"Good night, Eve. I heard one of your people suffered an accident today," he said, his manner totally composed and professional. "How is he?"

"He's in a bad way; two breaks to his left leg, one of them compound," Eve said, surprised at how calm her voice sounded when her heart was banging away louder than the drummer in the band.

"I'm really sorry to hear that. If there's anything that we can do please don't hesitate to let me know, will you?"

"Thank you," she muttered.

"And you're aware of the storm coming? You know we'll inform you if it turns into hurricane force."

"Oh yes, I've moved rooms, in case of flooding. I'm in two twenty-eight now."

Shit! Why did I say that? Could I be a little more obvious!

Melv didn't react. The wife smiled at Eve and Eve smiled back, but if either woman expected Melv to introduce them she was in for a disappointment. He took his wife by the elbow again and smiling around at the group he said goodnight to all of them and they left. Eve, who suddenly found she'd been holding her breath, gave a huge sigh. So, that was Mary.

The fragrant Mary McGrass.

She was younger than Eve had expected, but then again she often found it hard to put an age to people in the Caribbean, their skins were usually so good. She was average height, shapely without being overweight, and had beautiful makeup and hair. And walking behind them was a gorgeous younger version of Mary in jeans and a slash-neck t-shirt that just had to be Juliette. Eve breathed deeply again and blinked twice. The band was playing a salsa number. She put her glass down on the bar.

"Come on! Everyone on the dance floor! Let's party!" she said, leading the way forward.

***

An hour later and Eve was all danced out and ready to leave. Fortunately, so was everyone else. Eve went out onto the boardwalk to tell Natalie and Michael, who had gone off to sit quietly together when the others had hit the dance floor that they were leaving. The two of them were sitting close together in deep, earnest conversation.

"Sorry to interrupt, but we're all ready to leave," she said.

Michael jumped at the sound of her voice and sat back in his chair. Natalie smiled at Eve and said, "We're just coming." Eve was sure that Natalie and Michael had got together and that everyone had noticed, so she didn't really understand why they both seemed so guilty. Perhaps they didn't want everyone gossiping about them; a group could be malicious sometimes. Yet, they made no secret of sitting alone together. She mentally tossed the problem aside; it was nothing to do with her.

When the taxi turned up everyone piled in, some of them were giggling and some yawning loudly.

"I'm even too tired for a Wadiddly for the road," Dave said as they pulled up at the Mango Tree Resort. "I won't need no rockin' tonigh'!"

There was a chorus of agreement and then of goodnights as everyone went off to their rooms. Just Trevor took up Geri's suggestion of a nightcap. But they were too late; the bar had already closed for the night.

Stewart and Suzanne, sweat running down their bodies in rivulets, sticking their clothes to themselves and each other, embarked upon a serious snogging session in the corridor. Both of them wanted to invite the other one to take it further, but neither wanted to be the first one to make a move.

Natalie gave Michael a long hug before they parted on the second floor, then stood back and looked into his kind, gentle, handsome face.

"Good luck." she said, giving him another shorter hug before turning to go off to her room. He watched her disappear round the bend in the corridor, gave a deep sigh and walked the other way toward his own room.

Deborah quietly slipped into two forty-four, closing the door behind her and leaning against it. She'd managed to give Murray the slip by diving into the ladies' washroom in the reception area while his back was turned talking to Dave and then waiting until he'd gone before sneaking along the corridor at lightning speed. He was growing on her, but she was too tired to take it any further that night and she didn't want to be in a position to fight him off either.

Alone in her room, still oblivious to the truth about him, Jo got onto her knees to ask her God to do his best to heal Deano's broken body and to give him the strength to deal with whatever the next few weeks might bring.

And from her room Eve looked out at the night sky which was still, heavy and dark, the moon and stars hidden behind thick clouds.

Christ! What a day!

The painful memory of seeing Melv with his wife and daughter pierced her heart just like the forks of lightning she could see in the distance stabbing at the sea. She turned from the window, letting the pink and green floral curtains fall closed behind her. She slipped under the sheet and the events of the day fought each other to take over her mind. She replayed Larry's phone call, her visit to the hospital, Deano's confession, Frances's delightful put down of Huw, Huw's tantrum and then every second of the scene in the Sports Bar with Melv again. She squeezed her eyes tightly shut to get rid of the image and kicked the sheet off. Even with the air conditioning as cold as she could get it, the heat, which had become increasingly intense as the day had worn on, now hung over Antigua like a huge, heavy, woollen blanket. The storm was only hours away.

***

DAY SEVEN

Eve rang the hospital as soon as she was awake to enquire about Deano.

"He's as comfortable as can be expected," she was told by the nurse who'd answered her call.

"Please can you tell him that Eve will be in to see him later this morning?"

"Of course, my dear. You have a good day, now."

Eve made plans to go at ten thirty, after she'd finished her *morning surgery* as she liked to call it. That way she could see him and be back at the resort before the storm hit. She switched on the TV set in the room which was tuned to ABS, where *Good Morning Antigua and Barbuda* was giving the latest weather information; that Tropical Storm Charlotte had veered slightly east during the night and would not hit Antigua full on.

"However, the Meteorological Office and the Leeward Islands Hurricane Protection Service warn that wind speeds will still be extremely high and rainfall heavy and people are advised to take all protective and preventative measures possible to lessen the effects of Tropical Storm Charlotte. Members of the public should seek refuge inside from midday," the presenter was saying.

Eve quickly showered and made her way to the dining room. She needed to make sure that everyone knew the situation. She was going to suggest that they gathered in each other's rooms during the worst of the storm. That way everyone had company, and everyone could be easily contacted if anything changed or the situation worsened. She'd got some sets of playing cards from the resort shop at the beginning of the week when Sunny had first told her about the storm and Steve from the Entertainments Team had given her a Trivial Pursuits and a Monopoly set so that the group could entertain itself.

"We can always watch films," Donna said, when Eve was telling the group this at breakfast. "There's that channel, two I think it is, that shows great films continuously."

"The trouble is, the power might go off. In fact, it will go off. The resort has its own generator, but be prepared to use the candles in your rooms and for heaven's sake, please be careful! We don't want any fires!"

"The rain'd put it aht!" Dave joked.

"I've got a Travel Scrabble," Ursula said. Eve had been pleased to see that she had come along to have breakfast with the group that morning.

"You know how to have a good time!" Stewart ribbed her and she'd giggled girlishly.

"Has anyone seen Huw or Frances?" Eve asked.

Everyone shook their heads.

"Does anyone know where they might be?"

"Well, not together, that's for sure!" Natalie said, laughing.

"Not unless she's givin' im a ridin' lesson!" Dave added making them all laugh.

Jason suddenly realised that most eyes were on him and he coughed nervously.

"He... er... he was talking yesterday about going on a bike ride."

"A bike ride!" Eve heard herself splutter. "Didn't he listen to a word I said?"

"He thought that he'd just go off this morning and be back by about half two or three."

"But the storm's speeded up! It's hitting before that! I've just said everyone should be inside by midday!" Eve shouted, her frustration making her take it out on the wrong person. "Sorry, Jason. Why am I shouting at you? I know it's nothing to do with you. Anyway, nobody's going to rent him a bike today."

Jason gulped.

"He picked one up yesterday afternoon and took it for four days. He'd planned to leave about seven this morning and cycle to English Harbour. He wanted to go round Nelson's Dockyard."

"He must be mad!"

"He's arrogant," Grace said. "He's never been here, never experienced a tropical storm, but he knows better that you, Eve!"

"Serve him right if he gets washed away," Natalie said.

"No! We don't want anything to happen to him! We've had enough with Deano's accident," Eve said. "Just think of my paperwork," she added to lighten the tone. Everyone laughed with her.

"And where's Frances? Not back from her hot date yet." Stewart said.

"She might be having a lie-in," Eve said.

"She migh' be aving sumfink!" Dave said to more laughter.

Eve joined in but she hoped that if she wasn't in her room Frances would get herself back to the resort soon. She looked at her watch to see it was nine fifteen. She decided to change her plans.

"I'm going to see Deano now I think. That way I should be back by eleven. Lunch is going to be served in Pizza Pizzazz as it's the only restaurant that's not open to the elements. They can't seat everyone at once so there are three sittings. As I understand it, our group has been allocated two o'clock for lunch."

"That's a bit late." Deborah said. "Do we have to go at two? Can't some of us go earlier?"

"No, we can't. It's going to be a logistics nightmare for the hotel today and possibly tomorrow, so we're going to have to co-operate and have lunch a little earlier or a little later than we may have preferred," Eve said, bristling at Deborah's selfishness. What was it with some single people that they'd become so wrapped up in themselves, they turned into petulant children the moment their plans were challenged? Deborah pouted, unimpressed.

"And does that mean we'll have to eat at a certain time tonight, then?"

"I don't know yet. Quite possibly, yes."

"What? In Pizza Pizzazz again? We ate there last night."

God! Give me a break!

Most of the group looked at each other, eyebrows raised.

"With respect, some of you haven't got a clue!" Michael said. "I was in a tropical storm once in St Vincent. I've never seen *nuttin'* like it. It'll be raining so hard you probably won't be able to leave your rooms let alone get to Pizza Pizzazz!"

"We can't do anything about the weather, can we?" Suzanne said. "That's an Act of God!"

Several people looked involuntarily towards Jo.

"Don't drag us into it!" she joked.

"Well, worst case scenario, we'll eat in Pizza Pizzazz again tonight!" Eve said, unable to avoid the sarcastic tone in her voice. "But we'll have a better picture later on. I'll keep you all informed as soon as I know anything. I'll see if I can find Huw and Frances. If you see them before I do please bring them up to date."

"Give Deano our love," Natalie said as everyone chorused agreement.

"I will!"

251

***

Frances slowly felt herself waking up from a deep, dreamless sleep. The atmosphere in the room was sultry and hot and in spite of the fan that was blowing on them from the low table next to the bed her naked body was covered in a film of sweat. She was aware of Neville, already hard and prodding against the cheeks of her backside, while his right hand smoothly caressed her belly and thighs, working itself nearer and nearer to her pubic triangle, slowly parting her lips and massaging her clitoris with his fingers.

"Nice, wet, juicy pussy," he said, which made her even wetter than she already was.

He flipped her over and started to kiss her breasts. She marvelled to herself at how at ease and happy she felt in his company; her scarred breast caused her no discomfort, because he hadn't been repulsed by it as she had once feared some men might. He kissed her nipples, sucking them and rolling his tongue around them. Then he worked his kisses down her belly until his tongue slid right inside her producing her first orgasm of the morning.

***

Melv McGrass had been in his office since six o'clock preparing for the emergency meeting with his Heads of Departments that he had called for seven fifteen. At the meeting they had discussed the emergency procedures and they had drawn up a plan to keep their guests and staff safe and protect the property as best they could from any damage. For the tenth time that morning he checked that the a/c unit in his office was actually working and he sipped his fifth coffee of the day. Caffeine never bothered him in any adverse way and besides, he was going to need to stay awake for a long, long time. Checking his inbox he saw an email from Clayton Richards, the Watersports Manager, confirming that all the Hobie cats, surfboards, pedalos, kayaks and mattresses had been securely warehoused and the sun loungers throughout the property had also been stacked and chained. Another email from Osbert Joseph told him that a lunch roster for Pizza Pizzazz had been prepared and distributed among the guests explaining the situation and thanking them for their co-operation and the restaurant staff had all been briefed and were now preparing Pizza Pizzazz for lunch. He was just about to open a further email from Wesley Campbell, the Head Chef when his phone rang.

"I'm sorry to bother you, Mr McGrass," his secretary said, "but there's a guest who's asking to see you."

Mentally groaning at the interruption on what was probably his busiest, most problematic day of the year so far, Melv knew, nonetheless, that good manners dictated he give the guest a few moments. At least he hoped it was going to be a few moments.

"Send him through, Lucinda," he said, hanging up the phone then standing up to greet the guest, who turned out to be the young black man in Eve's group.

"Come in! Come in! Good morning," Melv said, extending his hand to Michael, who shook it tentatively. "Take a seat." He indicated the leather chair on the opposite side of his desk. "Well, it's certainly hot today!" Melv said, making polite conversation, waiting to hear the reason for the visit. Michael nodded and looked right at him.

"And I think it's about to get a little hotter, Mr McGrass."

Melv held his gaze, surprised and a little wrong-footed by Michael's tone. Michael licked his lips, nervously, his actions belying the belligerent aggression in his voice. He wiped the palms of his hands against his trousers and leaned forward in his seat.

"You see. I have reason to believe that you are my father."

***

Stewart stood outside the pharmacy in the village, sweat running like a river down his back and chest and took a deep breath. Quickly, before his nerve failed him he pushed the door open and stepped into the cool interior to see he was the only customer. Unsure as to whether this was a good thing or not, he started looking around to see if he could see what he wanted out on the shelves.

"Good day. Can I help you with something?"

A female voice, which seemed to come from nowhere made him jump out of his skin. He looked over to the counter and saw that it belonged to an elegant, middle-aged woman, wearing a smart navy-blue blouse and skirt, her hair braided neatly and tidily up high on her head and stylish gold earrings swinging from her lobes, matching the chain around her neck. Stewart swallowed nervously.

"Just looking, thank you!" he called across to her, wondering why he suddenly felt like a teen asking for beer in an off-licence while knowing he was legally too young to buy it. He made his way along the two aisles, eyes flashing from side to side taking everything in. Toothpaste, mouthwash, toothbrushes, denture fixative, talc, baby lotion, baby shampoo, baby food on the right and indigestion tablets, vitamins, shaving cream, shaving balm, razors, shower gel, tampons and sanitary towels on the left. He quickly averted his gaze from them as if he'd been caught looking at a dirty magazine. He was at the end of the aisle and face to face with the main counter and the woman behind it. Now he was close he could see her name badge. *MISS BAPTISTE.* She looked at him quizzically and smiled. Then she turned slightly to her right and pointed over her shoulder to two shelves which carried a large and varied supply of condoms.

"Is that what you're looking for?" she asked sweetly.

Stewart gulped and nodded.

"Do you want Rough Rider, Pleasure King or Ecstasy?"

"Er... I don't know. What's the difference?" Then he kicked himself for asking.

"Rough Rider are ribbed, Pleasure King are very, very thin and Ecstasy comes in three flavours, strawberry, banana and chocolate."

He couldn't believe he was having this conversation with such a lovely genteel lady.

"Er... are they all the same size?"

Miss Baptiste nodded, giving a little wry smile as she did so.

"All the same size. They're universal size. They adapt to fit all types of men."

"I'll have Rough Rider, please," Stewart said, with an air of confidence he wasn't feeling.

"Small, medium or large?"

"I thought you said they were all the same size. Universal."

"I'm asking what size pack you want. Three, ten, or twenty?"

Stewart thought about it. He was unsure; Suzanne hadn't agreed to anything at all yet so twenty might be a bit presumptuous. Then again they still had four full days to go and if things did take off...

"Ten please," he said with another sudden surge of confidence.

Miss Baptiste put the box of condoms into a plain brown bag and took Stewart's money.

"You enjoy your day now!" she said to him, smiling.

"And you, yours," Stewart said as he scuttled out the door to smack against the wall of sheer heat waiting for him outside.

***

Neither Huw nor Frances had been in their rooms. Although she was aware that the storm might take out the telephone system, Eve had left both of them a voicemail message telling them about lunch and asking them to touch base with her so that she knew they'd got the message and were accounted for. Then she called a taxi and headed off to Mount St John's to visit Deano.

He was more alert this morning but also more agitated. A local representative of his insurers had visited him earlier and told him that he was going to be taken back to UK for treatment, but that it would be the following Wednesday before he could go as that was the first available flight with room enough to accommodate him on a stretcher plus the nurse-companion and his wife, who was going to arrive on Saturday. Rizwana, Travel Together's Customer Liaison Manager had phoned Eve when she was on her way to the hospital telling her she'd informed Mrs Dean of the situation and she'd decided to come out. Deano told Eve that he hadn't spoken to his wife.

"I'm hoping that when she actually sees me, sees the state I'm in, she'll go easier on me. I don't want to talk to her on the phone; I don't want a bollocking. By the time she gets here she might have calmed down."

Ever the coward, Deano! Ever the coward!

"Everyone sends their love, Jo especially."

Deano had the grace to blush.

"She wants to come in and see you, but she can't until the storm blows over. Saturday might be a good time."

"No! No, tell her not to come! Please!"

Eve was quite enjoying seeing him squirm.

"Thank them all, but tell them I don't want them to see me like this."

Eve had left as quickly as she could. She felt great sympathy for Deano's injuries; it had been a nasty accident, even if it had been brought on by his own vanity. But seeing just what a spineless coward he really was just made her angry. He'd been prepared to use a lovely woman like Jo; probably crow about it to his mates in the pub when he got back home about how he'd pulled a female vicar, with not a thought for her feelings or dignity in the slightest. And even in the unlikely event that he had fallen for Jo, it still made her really mad that he was married yet had come on a Travel Together holiday just to try and pull a woman.

Sunny had left a voicemail message while her mobile had been switched off during the hospital visit, to say that she'd picked up the Check-In forms. And as her taxi was coming through the main gate of the Mango Tree Resort at a quarter to eleven, Eve's mobile rang again. Lifting it to her ear she looked out of the window and saw the trees were all unnaturally still. There wasn't a breath of air to be found anywhere.

"Eve speaking," she said, seeing that the caller ID showed the resort and expecting it to be Huw or Frances.

"Eve."

Her stomach flipped and her heart stood still at the sound of his voice.

Why, dear God? Why?

"Are you back from the hospital? Are you on property?"

"I'm just coming up the drive."

"Can you come to my office, immediately, please?"

Eve felt suspicion rising; was this some sort of ploy to get her alone? Or was she flattering herself?

"What's this about?"

"You'll see once you're here." And with that he hung up.

Slowly and deliberately, breathing hard as she went, Eve climbed the staircase to the right of the front desk which lead to the Administration Department where Melv's office was, while trickles of perspiration made their way down her back and legs. She stopped to take a wet wipe from her bag and pass it over her face, which she was certain was red, puffy and sweaty, annoyed with herself for caring how she looked in front of Melv, yet knowing she wanted to look her best. She knocked on the door, heard Melv call out "Come!" and went inside. She was taken by surprise to see Michael sitting there with an expression on his face that she couldn't decipher. She looked from one to the other, her smile disappearing as she became aware that the atmosphere inside this room was as heavy and expectant as that outside.

"Take a seat, Eve." Eve sat on the other empty leather chair.

"Can I get you something to drink?"

"A Diet Coke would be nice," Eve said and Melv stood up and went to a fridge in the corner and pulled out a can, which he opened and then gave to Eve with a glass containing a couple of ice cubes. She noticed that Michael was nursing a beer and there was a glass of what looked like rum on Melv's desk. Melv took his seat again behind the desk and looked at Eve for a moment before he spoke.

"Eve, Michael has something to say, that I think may interest you."

He turned to look at Michael, whose confidence seemed to have ebbed away again. Michael sipped his beer and then placed the can on the edge of Melv's desk.

"Eve. I came here this morning to tell Melv that I think... well, that is... I know that he's my father."

Eve thought she was going to faint. Luckily she'd put the glass of coke on the small coffee table to the right of the chair or she knew for certain she'd have dropped it. She looked at both men, drinking in their features, seeing the likeness that was now abundantly clear, in spite of Michael's lighter skin and slightly finer features.

256

O Spyros mou!

"Now, I've already told Michael that I can't possibly be his father, because, well, no woman, other than my wife, that is, has ever told me she was carrying my child," Melv said, without blinking.

There was a pause. *A pregnant pause,* Eve thought, afraid she would giggle from nerves. She couldn't trust herself to speak. Unable to bear the silence Michael jumped in.

"This is crazy! What has all this got to do with Eve? Why did you have to drag her in and tell her my... or rather our business? I know that you're my dad. I told you I found my original birth certificate. My father was a Bajan national; Melvyn Alexander McGrass. That's you! And my mother was a Greek woman..."

"...called Paraskevi Stefanou," Eve finished the sentence for him.

"How do you know that?" Michael's eyes popped out of their sockets.

Eve looked at this handsome, good, decent young man. Her baby.

"Because I'm your mother, Michael," she said.

"No you're not! You can't be! You're not Greek!"

"Eve, do you want to fill us both in?" Melv asked the pressure of the day suddenly forgotten. "Because I think that both of us are a little confused and you've got some explaining to do."

She nodded, turned to face Michael, took a deep breath and began her story.

***

"I was born in Lefkimmi on the island of Corfu on 28th February 1962 the third child and first daughter of Lefteris and Maria Stefanou, who ran a small taverna offering bed and breakfast to those first, early tourists to the island, mostly Italians who came across on the ferry. I was christened Paraskevi, which soon became shortened to Evi by my two older brothers, Spyros and Lefteris. After me came another girl, Maria, and then a younger brother, Iannis, which meant my parents had five children under eight. My childhood was a happy one even though from the age of eight or nine I worked hard as I was expected to help out with the family business. I knew no better, I knew nothing else and so it was second nature to me to make beds, wait tables and wash dishes throughout the summer months as I turned from child to teenager, while my brothers danced the nights away on the terrace of our taverna, entertaining tourists.

By the time I was seventeen it was the late 1970s and my father decided to send me to England to improve my English. I was the brightest of my siblings as far as studying was concerned and my father had plans for building a hotel on a large piece of land his family had passed down to him on the coast. He hoped that by going to England I would not only speak perfect English, but also make the right contacts within the tourism industry to further his plans. So, in September 1979 I set off for England where an agency had set up a job for me as an au pair with the Morris family in Windsor and where I was to attend intensive English classes three nights a week.

I fell in love with Windsor at first sight and was really lucky in getting a place with the Morrises. Their two-year-old twins Melissa and Naomi were a gorgeous handful; a round pair of cherubs, all dimpled elbows and knees, and it was impossible not to love and adore them. Janet, Mrs Morris, was a kind woman to work for and she made a point of taking me round to her friends' houses to introduce me to their au pairs, Conchi from Zaragoza, Astrid from Malmo and Maria from Florence, who quickly became my friends. On our nights off we used to meet up and go to Blazes, a disco club just outside Windsor where we'd dance the night away, enjoying ourselves as only the young and the problem-free can.

And it was in Blazes one Saturday evening in November 1979 that I met Melv McGrath from Barbados, who was in his final year of a Business Studies degree. For me it was love at first sight. I had never met anyone like him and soon we became inseparable; every spare moment was spent in each other's company. I didn't abandon my friends, though. Often we would all go out together, to Blazes or the cinema, or to sit in a pub and chat and put the world to rights. But sometimes, I would sneak back to Melv's digs and into his bed, where he took me gently over the threshold from girl to woman. Lying next to each other in the dark, we'd whisper our plans for the future. Neither of us had any uncertainty whatsoever that ours was a storybook love affair; nobody had ever loved like us before and nobody would again. Melv was returning to Barbados in May as soon as his degree finished and I was going to complete my year with the Morris family in September and then follow him. We'd marry as soon as I got to Barbados and start up our own hotel; we were heading for the stars. I'd made up my mind I wouldn't be going back to Greece, at least not for the time being. My father would never understand my actions; he would regard them as treachery. I'd wait until my parents had grown used to the idea of me being married to a Bajan, and until I had produced a couple of grandchildren for them and then we'd all go to visit. In the meantime, my brothers would have to pull themselves up by the bootstraps to help my father fulfil his plans and dreams. There were four other children who would have to do their share now

258

because Evi's life was going in a completely different direction from the one her father had mapped out for her.

I was so in love and my rose-tinted glasses were wrap-arounds that wouldn't let anything through that might thwart my plans.

Melv flew back to Barbados during the last week of May 1980. Heartbroken, I cried so much I thought I'd never stop. He promised to write and he was true to his word; I got a letter from him almost daily. They were beautiful letters in which he told me in detail of his life, how his parents were waiting to meet me having eagerly found where Corfu was in their Atlas. He told me how he'd already got a job on a post-graduate programme in a large hotel and that he'd been looking at land to buy for us to build our own house.

I was so caught up in all this that it took me a few weeks to realise that the weight I appeared to be gaining wasn't just from comfort eating because Melv had gone. I sat up in bed with a start one morning as it hit me that I hadn't had a period since 20th March. It was now 18th June. I'd never felt more alone or more afraid.

I met up with Conchi and Astrid in the park that afternoon. Maria was no longer part of our circle, having set up home with the father of the family she'd been living with. We'd last seen her in April when she'd told us she was leaving Windsor. She had a black eye, which Leonora, the lady of the house had given her when she'd realised what had been going on. Maria and Andrew were now living in a flat in Kingston-upon-Thames.

I burst into tears as soon as I saw Conchi and Astrid walking across the park towards me. Conchi wrapped me in her arms as we sat on the grass and Astrid, ever the practical Swede, said that she didn't really think there was a problem. Perhaps there wasn't in Sweden, but I knew I could never go back to Corfu with any child born out of matrimony, yet alone a black one. While Conchi rocked and soothed me, Astrid pelted down to the chemist's to get a pregnancy testing kit for me.

"There's no point in you being so upset when you might not even be pregnant!" she'd said.

But I knew I was. And the test confirmed it the following morning. I sat on my bed with the results in my hand and decided to do some practical thinking.

My contract with the Morris family ran until September, by which time I'd be six months pregnant. That meant that I could carry on working for them and they might not even notice my pregnancy. If I saved my money from now on, I could probably keep myself until the baby was born.

But then what would I do?

Sitting on the bed, faced with the stark reality of my situation, I realised I didn't know what to do. I threw myself down, sobbing. I was crying so hard that I didn't hear Janet gently push the door open and come into my room to bring me that day's missive from Melv, which the postman had just delivered. When she saw me crying she was genuinely upset for me. Thinking it was because I was missing Melv, she lifted me up and hugged me, making *sshhhh –ing* noises, until she suddenly realised what I was clutching.

I have never ever had so much love and support from anyone in my life as I did from Janet and Pete Morris during 1980. They let me carry on working for them as long as I could, and in the final weeks of my pregnancy fussed and looked after me as if I was a special princess who needed to be pampered. At dinner, after the twins had gone to sleep, we would discuss endlessly the possibilities for me and for my baby. They couldn't understand why I wouldn't tell Melv; why I wouldn't give him the opportunity to take responsibility for his child. I knew that Melv had loved me when he was in England; I knew that he probably still loved me now and was expecting me to go to Barbados, although his letters had dropped down to just one a week, the last one telling me that his father had died unexpectedly and that he now had to take care of his Mother. And because of that something deep inside me caused me to fear telling him. Making plans to marry me was one thing; feeling obliged to marry me because there was a child involved was something else, especially when he suddenly found himself with other responsibilities. Perhaps by now he was beginning to see me as some sort of holiday fling. I'd seen my own brothers swear undying love to gorgeous, young, yet naive, girls from all over Europe, swiftly forgetting them as soon as they'd left and another one had arrived. Being back in his own country, among his own people, surrounded by beautiful, Bajan girls, Melv might be asking himself what he'd ever seen in me. Pete said I wasn't being fair to Melv, that I should at least give him the benefit of the doubt and not make his decisions for him. But I knew that I couldn't ever tell Melv what had happened; I feared his rejection too much. Our love affair was over.

I also knew that I couldn't take my baby to Corfu, either. Janet said that she thought I was judging my parents harshly.

"Mum's always come round," she said.

"Not mine!" I replied.

If I'd got pregnant by a fellow Corfiot it would have been scandalous enough. My parents would have had to arrange a very quick wedding and given a huge dowry to the groom's family in order to enable them to overcome the *shame* of taking on such a wanton girl as their daughter-in-law, even though, the pregnancy was a good sign because it would mean that I was fertile and likely to produce lots of children for the family business, whatever that may be. But to return home, from England, without having completely mastered English and pregnant to boot, by a black man who'd left me and was five thousand miles away, was totally unthinkable. The black population of Lefkimmi in 1980 was precisely zero. The child would have been treated in a way that he didn't ever deserve, was completely unacceptable and which I knew I could never allow.

One afternoon Janet arranged for a kindly, middle-aged woman, with greying hair escaping from a bun and a gentle smile to come and visit me; Ruth Welbelove. By the time she left two hours later, we had agreed that my baby would be put up for adoption. She reassured me that he would go to a good, home; to parents who would love and cherish him and who wanted him one hundred percent. I so wanted that to be true.

On 24th December 1980 after a long, hard labour, worse than anything I could ever have imagined, feeling that God was giving me extra pain because I was such an awful person who was going to give her baby away, my beautiful little boy was born at 5.15pm, weighing seven pounds and ten ounces. I called him Spiridion – Spyros for short – after the patron saint of Corfu, who, I hoped and prayed would look after him and protect him for all his life.

Everyone had told me not to look at him because I would make it much harder for myself, but nothing could have stopped me. The young midwife understood and, having checked him over, wrapped him in a clean sheet and placed him in my arms. I had never felt such overwhelming love in my life for anything or anybody. It was a love I would have given my life for; a mother's love. He looked at me with huge dark eyes; wide awake not closed or screwed up like some newborns. I kissed him, told him I loved him more than anything else in the world, made him a promise that I would never ever forget him and begged him to forgive me. The midwife gently eased him from my arms and took him; he became the best Christmas present ever for someone else and I screamed and screamed until they gave me an injection that knocked me out until the following morning, when, although it was Christmas Day, the Morrises came and took me home. I stayed in bed for a week, face turned to the wall, refusing food, words and comfort. I was in my own private hell, where my heart wasn't just broken in two; it had been ripped out of my body at the moment when my child had been wrenched from my arms.

Eventually Janet and Peter said that if I didn't eat something they would have me taken into hospital. I realised that I was placing an unfair burden on them. They had shown me nothing but kindness and had gone out of their way to help and support me and I was repaying them by adding to their worries. I was giving them more work than the twins. So a week after I'd given away the best gift that life could ever have given me, I got up out of bed, showered, dressed, had a bowl of soup and made the conscious decision to get on with my life. I knew that I would never, ever forgive myself, or forget my little boy. I just had to hope and trust that the family that had taken him would give him the happy life he deserved.

And after a few weeks I decided I would go back to Corfu at Easter. Janet was happy for me to stay with them and continue to take care of the twins until then. I don't know why I made that decision really, probably because I was young, still only just nineteen, and I had faced such a major trauma away from my family. And after all, when your belly hurts you always run to Mum, don't you? So I went back to Corfu, to the newly extended Stefanou Taverna in Lefkimmi, the proud English-speaking daughter, with my head held high.

But I couldn't settle back into the old life. Even my father's plans for a big hotel, which I would help to run, left me cold and couldn't make up for a life I felt I was missing elsewhere. I'd left my small island; I'd experienced life in the outside world. Okay! I'd messed up, but that didn't mean I couldn't have a second chance. I'd been used to coming and going as I pleased, of making my own decisions and doing what I wanted. The claustrophobic atmosphere of life in the taverna, where my father and brothers watched my every movement was unbearable. Every night they would toy and flirt and dance with the tourists while my mother, Maria and I waited tables, cooked and cleaned. By now Spyros was engaged to a girl from Benitses, Alexia, whose family owned lands on the east coast south of Aeolos, which would be her dowry. Both her father and mine had plans to expand their empires and build a further hotel there. Alexia was a beautiful girl, both inside and out, who now also helped out working with us in our taverna. Once we'd finished our work in the kitchen, we would serve drinks and sit and watch the men. Although my mother and Alexia were present, my father and Spyros still danced and flirted and talked to these foreign women, often, I'm sure, taking things much further. I felt my mother's humiliation. And I felt trapped. I saw myself in her place in twenty years' time; watching while my husband danced and chatted with other women while I was suppose to sit humbly by and accept it. And I knew that there was no way I would allow myself to do that. And besides, I knew that nobody else's love would ever measure up to the wonderful true love I'd had with Melv. No other man would ever feel the same as him, touch me, love me or treat me the same way he had. I would often find myself lost in a daydream about him, wondering if I dare run away to Barbados and try to find him. I'd even fantasize about him suddenly turning up at the taverna one morning to pick me up in his arms and whisk me away before my father and brothers could do anything about it. Maria knew there was something wrong with me and often questioned me about my life in Windsor, but I stuck to stories of the Morrises and my au-pair girlfriends. The hunky Bajan I'd loved and the beautiful child I'd given away remained secrets locked deep in my heart.

 My opportunity to escape the unbearable claustrophobia came in the form of Brian Mitchell.

Brian was an English guy, the rep for a small British tour operator that brought guests to our taverna. I felt myself drawn to Brian, not because he was handsome or because I fancied him in any way, but because he was a link to the outside world; a link to England, to Windsor, to the wonderful freedom I'd know for a short time before I'd blown everything and thrown it all away. And he was a part of that secret outside world where my child was living and, as I prayed with all my heart, thriving. We would often sit and chat, always chaperoned by Maria or Alexia or one of my brothers. Heaven forbid that I, a nineteen-year-old Corfiot girl, should be alone with a man! But as the summer wore on, I could see that Brian liked me and I knew that he was going to be my ticket to get away from Corfu again.

As the summer slowly came to an end Brian asked my father for my hand in marriage. My father, thinking as a businessman, agreed and so we became officially engaged. Brian had to leave Corfu in mid-November because he had put in a bid to buy out the tour operator he worked for. And he was already building an apartment block in Kavos that he wanted to contract out to his company, thus securing a local livelihood for us when he returned in March.

We had a huge Corfiot wedding the following October. On my wedding day nobody could have guessed as I stood in the church in Lefkimmi and smiled and made my vows to one man that the face of another was all I could see.

I tried my best to be a good wife to Brian. He was a decent, steady man and there were even some times when I found myself at ease with him and loving him, but it was always the love of a sister I felt and not that of a wife or even less, a lover. Brian, through no fault of his own, just didn't excite me.

We began to travel often to London and with the ability to wrap him around my little finger I soon persuaded Brian to let me run the office in London taking care of the bookings for a while. We soon settled in a nice little terraced house in Epping, where I'd take the Central Line every day to our offices near Tottenham Court Road. But Brian's plans were always to spend as much time as possible in Corfu; whereas the longer I stayed away the less I ever wanted to return. I bided my time and waited until the night before he was going over to Corfu on one of his many business trips. We had been married for two years by this time. I'd prepared his favourite dinner, braised beef, and as we ate I told him that I wanted a divorce.

He didn't take it well. He was shocked and disbelieving. He said we'd talk about it when he came back from Corfu the following month, but by that time I'd moved out. I found myself a job in a travel agent's in Chelmsford and rented a small flat and never looked back. I worked hard and within three years had become the manageress and at the World Travel Market I was introduced to Bill Wickes, the owner of Travel Together. We just clicked from the first moment and he phoned me the following morning to offer me a job as Operations Manager. Within weeks we had become lovers and moved in together. I worked my socks off to make Travel Together a success and when Bill and I both realised a few years ago that our relationship was coming to an end; he paid me a generous lump sum and continued to employ me, at my own request, as a tour manager.

And the job has taken me all over the globe; I've been to the glaciers of Patagonia, the deserts of North Africa, the tropical rain forests of Indonesia, the mountains of Western Canada and visited the most exciting cities in the world, seen its most breath-taking monuments and bathed on its most beautiful beaches. And all the time, without realising it, I was being led on a winding, meandering path towards Antigua, where I would finally be reunited with my son and his father, the two great loves of my life."

**

Eve's head fell forward, her chin resting on her chest, exhausted. Her blouse was soaking wet from the tears she hadn't even realised she'd shed. The silence in the room was as tangible as the heavy pre-storm stillness outside. Suddenly the phone on Melv's desk let out a shrill ring making the three of them jump. Melv snatched it up.

"I told you to hold all calls," he snapped. He paused, listening. "I don't care! Tell them to give me ten, fifteen minutes."

Michael moved in his seat, his own face as wet as his mother's.

"Well, I didn't see that coming. I wasn't expecting that. I came looking to confront my father, to ask him why he abandoned me and I've found out that he didn't even know about me because my mother didn't tell him. Oh, but by the way, she's here, too! And she's my caring, kind-hearted, loveable tour manager!"

Eve shuddered at all the hurt and pain in her son's voice.

Please don't hate me! Please don't hate me! Please don't hate me!

She looked at Michael and then at Melv, the shock and disbelief they both felt etched on their faces, their identical faces; one darker, one lighter; one older, one younger, but undeniably the same face; the same genetic pool; the same DNA. Melv coughed to clear his throat and then he looked at both of them.

"I think we all need a little time to take in the events of this morning," he said. "Perhaps we could meet up later after we've had time to come to grips with what we've just learned and with the situation that we are in?"

"Oh, that's right! Let's adjourn and reconvene at a more convenient moment, shall we? With a bit of luck, I might go away and then you won't have to face up to me at all!" Michael spat out as he leapt to his feet.

Melv looked at him with compassion, in spite of the obvious distress he was feeling.

"Michael," he said, standing to face his son across the desk, "it is not my intention to brush you off, or treat you discourteously or disrespectfully. We have all been taken by surprise to say the least. None of us has had the morning we were expecting. You were obviously geared up to confront me with my abandonment of you and you've then had to face not only my complete ignorance of your existence but also finding out that your mother is, in fact, a woman that by the strangest of coincidences is here with us, too. I have been shocked and surprised, pleasantly surprised, to discover that I have a son whose existence my former girl-friend chose to keep from me. And Eve has had perhaps the greatest shock of all; she's finally come face to face with the child she gave up and she's had to finally tell the man who fathered him and who she cast aside the full story of what happened. I'm not sure which of us has had the biggest shock and this certainly isn't a game of point scoring. We have a big storm coming and I have things to do, procedures to implement to keep this property and everyone on it safe. I have to do my job. And we all need time to take in what's happened."

"Michael, I understand you must be feeling angry...." Eve said.

"Angry? Angry? You have no fucking idea how I'm feeling!"

Michael choked back a sob, turned on his heel and marched from the room slamming the door almost off its hinges. Eve and Melv looked at each other for what could have only been ten seconds, but to Eve they felt like an eternity. Melv shook his head.

"I can't believe you wouldn't have told me something like that. Why did your being pregnant make any difference to us? Why did it stop you from coming to join me in Barbados?"

Eve didn't answer, she just lowered her head, which, she just realised, was throbbing. She raised her fingers to her temples and massaged them.

"Not now, Melv, please! It doesn't even make much sense to me anymore, but it was a lifetime ago and things were different then." She looked at her watch and saw it was time to meet the group. "I have to go," she said as Melv came round from behind the desk. He opened his arms and she suddenly found herself wrapped inside them, sobbing her heart out, her tears soaking his shirt as his own dripped slowly onto her hair.

***

Frances realised she felt thirsty. She opened her eyes and looked at her watch. It was 12:45.

Christ! We've been in bed for fourteen hours!

Fourteen hours and five orgasms. Five full, throbbing, body-wracking, all-consuming orgasms. Three last night and two this morning. And each time Neville had matched her, orgasm for orgasm, his obvious pleasure and enjoyment reaching a climax that gave him a wild, exciting look that almost made her come again.

I'm having the time of my life!

She slowly turned over, causing Neville's hand to fall between her thighs as she did so. She giggled to herself, tempted to shift down on the bed a little more until his fingers were touching her pussy again.

Pussy!

She chuckled to herself again. She'd never used that term, yet now it seemed the natural thing to say. Resisting the temptation of yet another orgasm she slid from the bed and opened the little fridge on the other side of the room. She reached in and took out an unopened bottle of water, which she gulped from thirstily. She knew she had to get back to the hotel. It was irresponsible to stay here when the storm hit; Eve and the others might be worried about her.

"Come back to bed, baby," Neville said, looking at her across the room, his braids, splayed out across the pillow, his muscular arms open and inviting and his dick already on the rise. Who could resist him? Frances climbed back onto the bed and into his arms, pushing her belly against his and loving the effect it was having on him. He started to nuzzle and kiss her neck.

"I have to let Eve know I'm okay," she said, "I'll just ring her."

She reached into her bag and switched on her mobile as Neville continued to kiss her neck and her nipples. She'd put Eve's mobile number into her phone on the first day, in case of emergencies. She hit the number and after a couple of seconds heard the phone ring. Neville, meanwhile, had started kissing her belly and had slid his fingers into her, slowly rubbing and squeezing. She could feel herself responding just as Eve answered.

"Eve? It's me. Frances," she squeaked, aware that another orgasm wasn't too far away.

"Frances! Thank God! Are you okay? Where are you?"

"I'm with my friend at the moment. I thought I'd better let you know I'm safe."

"Thanks for that. You know the storm's on its way, don't you? It'll be hitting us very soon."

It certainly will!

Frances was now squirming as every cell in her body began to pulsate in response to Neville's fingers and lips.

"I'll probably ride it out here. The storm I mean. The storm." She couldn't concentrate on what she was saying.

"Well, keep in touch, Frances. Let me know you're okay, won't you? I've got your number now so I can call you, too."

"Yes, Bye!" Frances hung up as the first wave of orgasm drew a deep moan from her throat.

At the other end, Eve, who had heard it, grinned, in spite of her own upset and misery.

"You go, girl!" she said, as she put her mobile back in her bag.

***

"Oh my God!"

Natalie's mouth and eyes couldn't have opened any wider as she tried to take in what Michael had just told her. She blinked and then smiled.

"But that's lovely! I mean it's one of those life-is-stranger-than-fiction moments, but it's like a fairy story."

"Oh give me a break! Some fucking fairy story! I confided in you, Nat, because I thought you understood my feelings and where I'm coming from. Don't turn it all into *They all lived happily ever after*!"

"What's wrong with you, Michael? For a minute, just stop wallowing in your own self-pity."

"I'm not!" Michael half turned his back on her as the two of them propped on a rock at the far end of the beach; the same place Natalie had run to when she'd seen the wedding.

"You are! Look at your body language! You're behaving like a spoilt child."

Michael continued to ignore her and look out to sea. He was upset and disappointed with her; he thought she'd been on his side. Natalie decided to try a different approach.

"Did you, or did you not, have a happy childhood?" she asked him, her dark eyes blazing at him like two lamps searching into his soul.

"I've told you I did. My mum and dad are two of the most decent, kind, honest, loving people you could ever wish to meet."

"So although you were adopted, you never felt you missed out or were treated differently?"

"No. They couldn't have treated me better if I'd been their own flesh and blood. My childhood was idyllic. I was one of the family, a huge extended family. My aunts, uncles, cousins, all accepted me, in fact, it was a shock when they sat me down when I was twelve and explained that I wasn't their natural child. People always used to say how much I looked like my dad. They took me on holidays back to St Vincent to meet the family there, and I'd felt so much a part of it all. And once I was eighteen they even encouraged me to find my birth parents. They've loved and supported me all of my life."

"So, you never felt, different, or as if you didn't fit in?"

"Not at all! But as time's gone on, I've become more and more curious. Even more so when I discovered that my dad was Bajan and my mum Greek. I mean what a combination!"

"Yes, you'd never know Eve was Greek, would you? I mean, her English is perfect. But then, if she's lived in England for so long it's bound to be." She paused for a moment; this mention of Eve hadn't sent him off on one and that was a good sign.

"So, if your childhood was great and you were loved and cherished, why are you so angry with your birth parents? It's not as if you were left in a bus station like poor Dave was, is it? You didn't grow up in a series of children's homes, did you?"

"No, I didn't! But she didn't know that, did she? I could have ended up anywhere as far as she knew!"

"Oh, Michael, stop it! Stop throwing your rattle out the pram! It must have been a shock for her to find herself pregnant; she's already told you that. She's also already told you about

268

her circumstances. She was alone in London, miles away from home. And home was Hicksville, Greece more than thirty years ago. She couldn't have taken you back there. And all credit to her, she could have had an abortion and you'd never have existed, but she didn't do that either. That would have been the easiest way out."

"But she could have told Melv! He wanted to marry her; he'd have been overjoyed to be a father. He told me he would!"

"He says that now, but would he have done? You know, my parents had a terrible marriage. They stayed together for me and my sister and in the end four people ended up being very unhappy. What makes you think that if Eve had followed Melv to Barbados that it would have all turned out wonderful or that your life would have been so much better than the life you had growing up in High Wycombe and Durham?"

Michael said nothing. He sat in a petulant silence, scuffing the sand with his foot. But Natalie wasn't going to let him off the hook so easily.

"Your adoptive parents, what were they called?

"Alice and Bertram."

"Alice and Bertram did their very best for you because they loved and wanted you. They made sure you were happy; they made sure you had a carefree childhood and a university education. They were in a position to do so. Eve had wanted the best for you, too, but she couldn't give it to you, so she handed you over to someone who could. How lucky are you, Michael Brown? You've got two lots of parents who love you and wanted the best for you. You're being too hard on Eve. She was only nineteen years old. Do you remember how it felt to be nineteen? I mean, I know at nineteen I thought I knew it all, and in spite of being confident on stage and in front of the camera, inside I was shy and insecure and found it hard enough to choose what to wear to go out clubbing. I don't know what I would have done in her position. She was miles from home. She knew her parents would go spare. Melv's letters were dropping off. And I know he says he'd have been delighted to know he was going to be a father, but would he? I mean, he's hardly likely to say now that he wouldn't have accepted responsibility for you, is he? He might have run a mile and wanted nothing to do with you. He was thousands of miles away, after all and that would have been easy enough to do."

Michael shifted uncomfortably and reluctantly nodded his agreement with what Natalie was saying.

"And he's got the biggest cop out of all; Eve didn't tell him, so he can wash his hands of all responsibility and say that he's the good guy and he would have looked after you. I know that sounds harsh. He's had the shock of his life today and I'm not taking away from that. But just make sure you don't crucify Eve between the two of you. She was afraid Melv would reject you both thirty years ago. Don't make the mistake of rejecting her now."

Deciding she'd said enough. Natalie sighed and shut up. Michael sat quietly for a couple of moments and then he let out a deep sigh.

"You're right, Nat. I've behaved like a petulant child."

His voice became choked and Natalie could see from the way that his chin quivered that tears weren't far away.

"It's all been such a shock. I don't even really know what reaction I was expecting to get from Melv. I think I was expecting him to take me into his arms and call me 'son' and tell me how he'd spent his life searching for me. When I saw he never had a clue I'd ever been born, it wrong-footed me. And then finding out that my mother was actually here and that I'd know her for a week already....." He started to sob and Natalie wrapped her arms around him and held him tightly. Her heart ached as she felt his pain; huge sobs of agony shook his body for several minutes until he finally became still and quiet. He pulled away from her, averting his gaze and wiping the back of his hand over his face.

"I'm sorry."

"Why are you apologising to me?"

"Because... because... for being a wuss, I suppose. I've just met my parents. You're right, I should be happy." He shrugged his shoulders. "Perhaps finding out I was adopted all those years ago affected me deep down. I thought I'd handled it well, but perhaps the feeling of... abandonment... perhaps I buried that and it's all come out today."

Natalie took his hands in hers and made him turn and look at her.

"Okay, you've recognised your hurt and your feelings of being abandoned, even though you were loved and well-cared for. Now how are you going to deal with what you've found out today? Are you going to be glad and accept both your birth parents and forge a grown up relationship with them? Or are you going to be hurt and bitter for the rest of your life?"

***

Eve looked around Pizza Pizzazz nervously.

"We're over here!" she heard and turning saw Stewart standing up and waving at her.

Making her way over to their long table she logged that Huw wasn't there and neither were Michael or Natalie. Eve sighed; she felt as if she was working on autopilot. Her mind was racing and her stomach lurching. She just wished this bloody storm would break; perhaps some of the rest of the tension would disappear with it when it did.

"Sorry I'm late. Hope you've left me something," she attempted a feeble joke.

"Well, there wasn't much to start with, what with our having to come to the last sitting," Deborah grumbled.

"Oh give it a rest!" Grace said. "The lunch has been perfectly substantial; there was a big salad table and a choice of two meats and fish and burger and pizza. That's enough choice for anyone."

"And you've spent the holiday eating less than a sparrow and turning your nose up at the rest of us tucking in," Stewart added. He'd been particularly incensed at breakfast that morning when Deborah had watched Suzanne walk away from the table and then expressed her surprise to Murray and Geri, in a stage whisper, that Stewart would have found someone who was *'the size of a house'* attractive. Geri had sniggered her agreement, but just as Murray was about to say something he looked up and saw the murderous look on Stewart's face.

"She's not a house; she's a beautiful, majestic mansion. She's big, warm and welcoming, and she's all-woman" he'd said remembering what the mango seller had said about her. "She's not one of these skinny, cold, bitter bitches who spend their lives pushing a lettuce leaf round their plates, but knocking back the wine and slagging everyone off. Suzanne's loving and kind and I don't just find her attractive, I've fallen in love with her!"

That had shut them up!

Eve went over to the buffet. Eating was the last thing she felt like doing, but she knew she should. She helped herself to some barbecued chicken and some fries and went back to the table.

"Anyone heard from or seen Huw?" she asked.

"No, we ain't," Dave said.

"Nor Frances," Deborah said.

"I've heard from Frances," Eve said. "She's fine. She's aware of the pending storm and she's somewhere safe." She kept her eyes on her plate, refusing to meet any of the inquisitive looks that were rebounding round the table.

"But Nat and Michael haven't been seen for ages," Trevor said.

"It's not like them to miss lunch, either!" Stewart put in.

Eve continued to eat without looking up.

"I'm sure they haven't gone far," she said, hoping in her heart that they hadn't. She pushed the rest of the food on her plate to one side and put down her knife and fork and looked out the window. Nothing moved.

"I'm going to get a coffee and sit in the bar until the storm starts," Eve said. "It's so hot in here. Do you want to join me?"

Everyone said they would and they stood up en masse and made their way to the bar where they pulled chairs round and all sat together. All the bottles and glasses had been stored away and a sign read: *DUE TO THE IMPENDING STORM ALL DRINKS ARE BEING SERVED IN THE CONFERENCE ROOM*

"We're circlin' the wagons," Dave said, chuckling.

"It's stifling," Jason said. "There's not a breath of air."

"The lull before the storm, indeed," Trevor agreed.

"Look!" Eve raised her finger and pointed to the palm trees. Very slowly they were starting to move; a gentle sway, barely perceptible.

"Is that a good sign?" Dave asked her.

"It means the storm's here," she said, taking out her note pad and pen. "I think we should decide who's going where."

"Me an' Stew was talkin' abaht playin' some music in my room. Bring a few Wadiddlys an av a bit of a party. You're all welcome," Dave said.

Most of the group decided they'd go along, except Dawn and Donna, who wanted to go to Donna's room and do their nails, and Ursula who wanted a siesta. Geri looked at Jason and said she was going to her room. He said nothing. He'd thought he was going to get stuck with her the previous evening when she'd followed him around a bit. But she obviously hadn't given up.

Eve said she was going to be in her new room and gave them its number, saying if she didn't see them before she'd see them at seven in Pizza Pizzazz. She reminded everyone to take care. As they all stood up to go their different ways, they could feel the wind, which was now making the palm trees wave wildly.

"Who'd have thought it would get up this quickly?" Trevor asked nobody in particular. "Five minutes ago it was as still as a grave."

"Let's go and get our drinks and go to Dave's room, then, shall we?" Jo suggested.

"Here comes the rain!" Eve said as the first splashes from the huge, heavy raindrops hit the tables and chairs and ground around them. Within seconds the rain was pouring down. There were squeals and shouts from the group as they tried to outrun the rain and reach cover before they were soaked. Eve didn't move. She had an overwhelming desire to stand and be whipped by the wind and lashed by the rain. She turned from the bar and walked along the path to the beach. The sea was unrecognisable from the deep turquoise mirror of the previous days;

272

big grey waves were climbing high and smashing down. Eve stood looking at it with the rain hammering against her face and her whole body, enjoying the therapeutic, cleansing power of the water and praying that it would wash away all the guilt of the last thirty years and leave her with some peace of mind at last.

***

Huw had started to deeply regret hiring the fucking bike hours ago. He hadn't realised how hilly the road along the south west coast was, and although he considered himself to be fit, cycling up and down steep inclines in the stifling heat and intense humidity, while trying to avoid potholes, kamikaze bus drivers, plus the occasional mongoose that scurried across the road in front of him had taken its toll. If he didn't find somewhere to stop soon he was going to keel over; he'd finished his bottle of water ten minutes into the ride. He hoped the next village had a bar as well as the obligatory six churches. He'd passed quite a few places that looked like bars, but they were all closed. Of course, Huw didn't appreciate that other people took storm warnings seriously and the bar owners had all gone home to take care of their properties and their families.

Suddenly, as if from nowhere, he felt a strong wind start up and the next thing he thought he could hear a child's voice.

"Daddy! There's a white man and a bicycle in the yard."

Opening his eyes he could see he was lying on a lawn next to a very large cactus with the bike on top of him. And then it started raining.

"Karena, go inside! Go inside!" he heard a man's voice say. And then the same voice again, much closer to him. "You alright, buddy? What happened to you?"

Huw sat up realising that the only thing that hurt was his pride.

"The wind blew me off my bike, I think," he said.

"Let's get inside, the rain's coming," the man said, lifting the bike from across his legs and helping him to his feet. "We'll put this in the car port," he said wheeling the bike into a space under the canopy between a black Nissan Micra and the house. "You come inside with me," he said, striding ahead of Huw, "You can wait with us until the storm passes."

The man slipped off his shoes just inside the door and Huw thought he'd better do the same, pushing his trainers off by rubbing one toe against the other heel. He followed the man into a large open plan living room where three children suddenly switched their attention from the large TV to their visitor. The man pushed the children along the sofa to make room for Huw.

"Please, take a seat," he said. "I'm Bronson. Bronson James."

"Huw Jones," Huw said, taking Bronson's proffered hand.

***

Soaked to the skin, Eve was turning the key to get into her room as the phone started ringing. She rushed and grabbed it, letting the rain in and trailing puddles of water right across the room.

"Eve speaking!"

"Hi, Eve. It's Natalie."

Eve gulped and tried to stop hyperventilating. Natalie must know the whole story by now. Eve had realised that what everyone had mistakenly believed to be a budding romance between Michael and Natalie had only been him confiding in her.

"I just wanted you to know that Michael and I are okay. We didn't want you to worry about us. Sorry we missed lunch."

"Oh that's okay. I mean, I'm sorry you missed it, too. I'm not sure if they'll be serving afternoon tea, what with the storm and everything. We're all meeting up at seven in Pizza Pizzazz."

You are gabbling! Shut up!

"Oh, we'll last until dinner. We were just wondering where the others are."

"Most of them have gone to Dave's room for drinks and music."

"Okay. Thanks. I'll probably pop along and join them, if I can brave the rain."

There was a short silence.

"Natalie."

"Yes?"

There was another short silence.

"Is he alright?"

"Yes, he is I think the two of you probably need to have a long chat."

"Yes you're right. We do."

"Can I say something to you, Eve?" Natalie asked.

"Yes," Eve said, bracing herself for the lashing from Natalie's often barbed tongue.

"I think you did the only thing possible when Michael was born. It was a brave decision. You must have been terrified being on your own and so far from home. I mean, it's not really any of my business," she said, as if she were fearful of Eve's reaction. "But I think you did the

274

right thing and I've told him so. I think it's well cool you being his mum," she added with a little giggle.

"Thank you." Eve's throat constricted and her eyes welled up for the umpteenth time that day.

"And I'm not going to tell anyone. If you and Michael want to make it public knowledge, that's up to the two of you. But nobody's going to hear it from me. Okay?"

"Okay. Thanks."

"See you later."

Eve put the phone down and heaved a sigh. She peeled off her soaking wet clothes and had a quick shower and wrapped herself in a sarong. She was just hanging up the towel on the rack when a huge crash of thunder made her jump out of her skin. Seconds later the power went off. The resort had its own generator that kicked in after a moment and just as it did Eve heard a knocking on her door. She opened it to find Michael standing there. He was soaking wet and holding out a bedraggled bunch of mixed tropical flowers he'd obviously just picked from the gardens. He looked at Eve apprehensively and then smiled. He held the flowers towards her.

"I think I've behaved like a bit of a prat," he said.

***

Huw had never heard rain like it. The noise of it bouncing against the galvanised roof was deafening, so loud that he had to strain to hear what was being said to him. Bronson had served him some water and now a large, ice cold glass of mango juice, which was going down a treat. He didn't think he'd ever been as thirsty in his life as he had that morning. He was annoyed with himself for getting like that; he was a PE teacher, for God's sake! He knew about hydration and the effects of heat on the body. He also knew that he was his own worst enemy. He'd behaved like a stubborn twelve-year-old going off on a bike like that when it was so hot and there was a storm on the way. He suddenly realised that Eve would probably be worried about him. After all, although she'd spoilt his fun a couple of times and ran the trip a bit like a sergeant-major in his opinion, she was only doing her job, he supposed. He'd always had a problem with bossy women. He liked a woman who knew her place and showed a man some respect. Even so, he thought he should let her know he was okay.

"I don't suppose I could make a phone call, could I?" he asked Bronson, raising his voice to be heard over the rain.

"Yeh mon, no problem," Bronson said, lifting the receiver, only to find it was dead. "It's cut off because of the storm," he said. "Let me try my cell phone."

Bronson disappeared into one of the bedrooms that led off a short hallway on the right hand side of the living room. He came back looking at it in the palm of his hand and shaking his head.

"No signal. That'll be because of the storm. We'll just have to wait until it passes."

"How long is that likely to be?"

"Not for a good few hours yet. Probably all night."

"All night?" Huw was shocked.

"This is a Caribbean storm. Not like those little showers you have in the UK. This is proper rain, man! What's up? You need to let people know where you are?"

"Yes." Huw found his voice sounded small and scared.

"Don't worry. There's nothing you can do now about it. You're welcome here with us. How about a beer to help pass the time?"

**

In Mount St John's Medical Centre, Deano rested back against the pillows listening to the rain. He had never felt so alone in his life. The agonising pains in his leg had now calmed to dull aches that he was getting used to. He felt really sorry for himself. How could he have got into this situation? All because he'd opened his eyes under water and lost one of his turquoise contact lenses. Why hadn't he brought a spare pair with him? Why had he been so bloody vain to wear them in the first place? He thought about the time he'd spent in Antigua before his accident. He'd had a great holiday up until then. He'd made friends; he genuinely liked most of the group. He thought about them all; Dave his Wadiddly-drinking buddy; Michael who shared his sense of humour; Stewart who they'd teased about the condoms and Suzanne, the lovely woman Stewart was falling for. Deano thought about Suzanne. Until this holiday he wouldn't have looked twice at someone like her. He'd have just dismissed her as a fat woman that his mates would have only chatted up for a bet. But getting to know her through Stewart's eyes he'd realised what a great person she was. And Natalie. And Grace. And Trevor. Even the Dolly Sisters. And, of course, Jo. Gorgeous, curvy, loving, smart, kind... she was all those things. Yes, of course, at first it had been a bit of a novelty when he'd found out that the woman he was chasing was a vicar. But that had soon become unimportant as he'd got to know her better. But now here he was, stuck in hospital in a sorry state and they hadn't even had a shag! That was all because of that stupid Geri. If she hadn't followed them on Tuesday night, who knows what might have happened. He could murder her. But it wasn't just about getting Jo into bed. He'd surprised himself at the depth of his feelings for her. He hadn't fallen for a woman so quickly since, well, since he'd met Rachel.

Just as he thought of her name a loud thunderclap brought him back to the present moment and he looked at the window pane where water poured down. The storm was well and truly here now. And then, on Saturday there'd be another one when Rachel arrived. He closed his eyes tightly. He felt sick when he thought about how he was going to have to try to explain this away to her. Throughout their marriage he'd been unfaithful; there'd been a couple of women he'd met through work or in pubs and he was sure she'd never really suspected anything. Once or twice when it looked like she might have unwittingly caught him out he'd always been ready with an excuse, an answer and an explanation for everything. He was Deano – Jack the Lad! But now, there was no getting away from this; he was in deep shit. He felt his eyes stinging behind the lids. A huge sob of self-pity escaped from his lips and a tear slid from under his right eyelid and down his cheek. It had all gone so fucking wrong.

***

A flash of lightening lit up Geri's room, waking her from her siesta. She looked at her watch and saw it was five o'clock. She sighed with disappointment. Jason hadn't come to her room. She wondered if he'd been knocking and she hadn't heard him, but even she thought that unlikely.

What am I doing wrong?

She'd been certain he'd follow her this afternoon. As soon as she'd got to her room she showered and put on a sarong and stretched out on the bed waiting for the arrival she was certain was going to happen, but didn't. She thought about the others; Deborah and Murray had obviously got together and so had Suzanne and Stewart. Natalie and Michael were always in a corner whispering or going for a walk together. Even trying to stop Jo muscling in on Deano hadn't worked. He was seriously out of action now. She just couldn't understand it; she was younger than Deborah, several sizes thinner than Suzanne, yet the men seemed to find her completely unattractive, or at least, not attractive enough to spend time with. She was lonely; she wanted male company and she wanted sex. She thought about Frances. The rumour around the group was that she'd got off with a local, one of the boys from the catamaran. She certainly seemed to be having a good time; nobody had seen her since yesterday.

Perhaps that's what I should do.

She thought about the local men available. It would have to be someone in the hotel; a member of staff. Elvis was nice. She thought about the way he looked at her and smiled every time he served her a drink. Perhaps he'd been giving her the come-on and she hadn't realised. Perhaps he'd wanted to take her out or take her to bed. The more she thought about it the more she convinced herself that she was right. Elvis wanted her and she hadn't realised!

She decided to get showered and changed and to seek him out. Her holiday was just about to change for the better! Sod the blokes in the T2G group. She was going for the local experience!

***

"What's New Pussycat!" Suzanne shouted.

Jason shook his head and continued to crawl around on the floor of Dave's room. The others were sitting on the bed, which had been pushed up against the far wall, or on the chairs that had been brought from their various rooms, each holding a beer or a rum punch, watching Jason's actions.

"Dog! Reservoir Dogs!" Dave shouted.

Jason shook his head and then raised his hands, cupping them around it.

"Headache? You've got a headache?" Stewart suggested.

Jason shook his head again, looked frustrated.

"Come on! Try!" he said.

"You mustn't talk!" Suzanne admonished him.

Suitably chastised, Jason continued to crawl around the room on his hands and knees, now opening his mouth widely and waving his arm, with the fingers splayed like claws in front of his face.

"Tiger!" Grace shouted.

Jason shook his head.

"Lion, then?" she added.

Jason nodded vigorously.

"The one-eyed lion!" Dave shouted.

"How can it be? He's already said it's three words," Deborah said.

"Ain't *one-eyed* one word?" Dave asked.

Natalie roared out laughing.

"Dave you're priceless!" she said.

"The Lion King!" shouted Suzanne.

"Hoo-bloody-ray! At last!" said Jason, getting up off his knees and dusting his shorts. "I deserve another Wadiddly after that," he said, grabbing one of the large plastic water bottles that Dave and Stewart had got Elvis to fill with beer and rum punch to bring to the room. Although it was only four o'clock the room was quite dark and a row of emergency candles

278

supplied by the hotel in each room were lined up on the dressing table, giving the room an eerie light.

"We should have a séance," Dave suddenly said.

"No we shouldn't," Jo said quietly but firmly.

"Don't you fink people should dabble?" Dave asked her.

"No, I don't. I've seen people seriously disturbed by doing silly things like the Ouija Board."

"I was only kiddin'" he said, to try to appease her.

"I'm sure you were," she said. "Come on, Suzanne, your turn. You got Lion King right."

"Oh, I don't want to play anymore," said Suzanne, "it's too hot without the air conditioning or the fans working properly. Let's have a rest and listen to some more music!"

Everyone nodded in agreement. The hotel's generator didn't have the full power of the mains supply and it was hot in the room. They'd opened the patio doors about three inches; any more meant that the wind blew out the candles and the rain started coming in. Dave got up to put a new set of batteries in his i-pod docking station and CD player.

"And let's have a break from *Loofah!*" Natalie said. "I mean, I like him," she added quickly when she saw the murderous look that Dave had given her, "but let's listen to something else."

"Some Abba, or something we can sing along to," said Suzanne, swigging on her fourth rum punch of the afternoon and beginning to feel in party mood in spite of the heat.

"Anyone know any good jokes?" Jason asked.

Everyone thought about it for a moment and shook their heads.

"I'm not good at remembering jokes," Trevor said. "And I must admit, I don't always find modern jokes very funny."

"I think you've got a point there," Jo said. "Most modern humour goes right over my head."

"I dinnae think you can beat Billy Connelly," Murray said.

"He's alright," Suzanne said, "but I don't always get so-called comedy. I don't see how just being a man swearing profusely in a regional accent or an ugly woman makes you funny."

Everyone burst out laughing at that, most of them nodding in agreement. Jo looked at Suzanne and blew her a kiss.

"Suzanne you crack me up!" she said. "You always hit the nail right on the head."

"I know!" Natalie suddenly shouted. "Let's play *Confessions*!"

"That sounds ominous," Stewart said, looking doubtful.

"No, it's not. Look, in the first round you just say, or confess, rather, what is absolutely non-negotiable in a partner. For example, for me it's cleanliness. I could never go out with a bloke who didn't use deodorant or cologne. I like a clean man. See? Grace? You go next."

"A non-smoker. That is absolutely non-negotiable. I can't stand the smell of cigarettes on someone's clothes or breath."

"But what if he was the real man of your dreams? Wouldn't you overlook that?" Stewart asked. "I'm sure you would!"

"I wouldn't!" Grace snapped back.

"Okay! That's Grace then. What about you, Deborah?" Natalie asked.

Deborah drained her glass and stood up.

"I'll pass on that and leave you to it. I'm going to run the gauntlet of the rain and go back to my room for a while for a short nap and a shower," she said.

"I'll join you," Murray said, also standing up. Deborah turned to look at him.

"You won't!" she said as the others laughed and whooped. Murray went scarlet.

"I didnae mean I'd join you for the nap and shower; I meant I'd join you in running the gauntlet. I'm going tae my own room for a nap and shower," he explained, spluttering as they both climbed over legs and around chairs to get out of the room. As they opened the door the rain lashed against them. The floor of the open corridor was under at least an inch and a half of water and Deborah's flip flops slid on the tiles.

"Steady!" Murray said, grabbing her arm just in time to stop her landing on her bottom.

"Whoops! Oh, thanks!" she said, standing upright and taking a hold of his arm. "I'll hold onto you in case I slip again."

Bracing themselves and huddled against each other they made their way along the corridor. By the time they reached Deborah's room they were both soaked to the skin and struggling to stay upright. Masterfully, Murray took the swipe card from her, held it slowly and firmly and opened it first time. Deborah dashed in, pulling an astonished Murray behind her. She slammed the door and pushed him against it, the drops from their bodies making puddles on the floor.

Christ!

He couldn't believe his luck. Their faces inches apart, Deborah stared at him and slowly licked her lips. He could already feel himself getting hard.

"Murray, let's get it on!" she said, starting to kiss him.

As he peeled off her wet blouse and unhooked her bra he finally saw the pert, cherry-topped breasts that had teased him all week up close and in glorious Technicolor.

I've died and gone to Heaven!

***

"Want a top-up?" Jo asked Grace and Natalie as she slid off the bed. The game of *Confessions* had turned into *Snog, Shag or Stab,* with Dave insisting he'd rather stab himself than have to snog or shag Nancy Dell' Olio but it had then gradually petered out as the rum punches and beers took their toll.

But in spite of the amount of alcohol they'd already consumed Natalie looked at Jo and the two of them then both said in unison "Has a rag doll got cloth tits?" and then burst out laughing. Natalie held out her plastic cup, which Jo took, as Grace turned towards her.

"So what happened to you and Michael earlier? And where is he now?"

"Oh, we'd just gone for a short walk when the rain started, so we sheltered down by the water sports centre until it became clear it wasn't going to let up, so we made a dash for it. I went back to my room to get dried off and I suppose he's done the same."

Grace looked at her sharply. Years and years of interrogating suspects had given her a good sense of intuition for when someone was lying to her. She was certain there was more to it than Natalie was saying; the two of them had been acting a little strangely for a couple of days. Jo and Suzanne had said they thought they were having a little holiday romance and didn't want the rest of the group to know, but Grace knew that couldn't be the case. If they were having a secret fling they'd never be seen together. Yet she was sure that something was definitely going on. And Natalie and Michael would tell them in their own good time, if they wanted them to know.

***

It had got very dark; just one candle burned in Eve's room throwing long shadows up the walls as she and Michael sat across from each other, she on the bed and he on the chair. Three hours had passed in a whirl of storytelling and catching up. Eve had questioned him intensely about the Browns – Alice and Bertram – and his upbringing and felt herself overwhelmed with gratitude towards this couple who had made such an excellent job of bringing up her son and caring for him. They had raised a thoroughly decent young man.

"Do you think they'd agree to meet me?" she'd asked him.

"I don't see why not. They've supported me every step of the way in my search for Melv. And for you. But searching for you was hard; you seemed to have just disappeared off the face of the earth. And the Greek Consulate couldn't help. Now I know why. You'd become Eve Mitchell with a British passport."

"I just want to give them a hug and say thank you for doing such a great job with you. You're a son any mother would be proud of. I can't believe my luck at being your mum and at finding you." Then it was Michael's turn to get choked again.

Michael had finally realised what it must have been like for Eve to find herself pregnant and alone just months after her nineteenth birthday. He'd also accepted Eve's reasons for not looking for him; first of all, she thought he might never have been told he'd been adopted and she could have stirred up a real hornet's nest; secondly if he had been told, he might want nothing to do with her and she couldn't have taken his rejection, and thirdly, she couldn't have borne it if his life had been unhappy or if he'd ended up on the streets. He soon started talking animatedly, wanting to know everything about his Greek family and Corfu. Eve explained that she'd seen very little of them over the years; for a long time after she'd left Brian and stayed on in England she'd barely seen them at all. Her father and brothers had been angry that she'd gone away in the first place and even more so when she'd chosen not to go back after her divorce. She used to secretly ring her mother every week at a time when she knew that she'd be alone so that they could talk and catch up and for the last five or six years she'd actually gone back to Corfu at least once a year to see everyone and now her relationship with her father, who was in his seventies, and her brothers was more cordial than it had been in a long time.

"Perhaps at some point in the future you could visit with me," she suggested, "although you need to give me a chance to explain it all to them first; to warm the waters."

"I've never been to Corfu. I nearly went a few years ago on a lads' holiday to Kavos, but it fell through. It's funny, now I know you're Greek I can see it," he said, laughing. "You've got that European look about you."

"Have I? I've never denied my roots; it just became easier to become Eve over the years, especially working all the time with Brits. And I know my English is good, that I've got no trace of a Greek accent. In fact, when I speak Greek I struggle sometimes. You know, I forget the Greek word for something or I form a sentence with English grammar structures. You wouldn't ever believe it was my mother tongue!" she laughed.

"When I first saw my birth mother's name; your name and realised you were Greek, I asked a Greek Cypriot friend to teach me some Greek. The first thing I learned was *I manamou.*"

"*My mother*," Eve said, tears springing into her eyes again. God! Would she never stop crying?

Michael looked at his watch.

"It's half past six, Eve," he said. He didn't think he'd ever be able to call her anything else; certainly not *'Mum'*, that always had been and always would be Alice, his adoptive mum.

"Good God!" Eve said jumping up. "We're supposed to be meeting in Pizza Pizzazz at seven." She peered through the curtains. It was dark outside, but the rain was still lashing down and the wind was rocking the palm trees back and forth.

"I'll go and have a wash and see you there. Don't let's say anything to the others yet. I mean, Nat knows, but she won't say anything."

"I'll go along with whatever you think. I have no problem acknowledging you as my son, but I do have to work with these people."

"I know, but I still need some time to get my head around it. And really it's nobody else's business, is it? Bloody hell!" Michael had opened Eve's door to find water running down the open-plan corridor. He slipped his feet out of his deck shoes and paddled off along the corridor.

***

At dinner there was a great sense of camaraderie among the guests, who revelled in the idea of all pulling together to face adversity.

"Was it like this at Dunkirk?" Dave asked Trevor.

"I don't know!" he replied laughing. "I was only months old when the war ended, you cheeky bugger!"

"Oohhhh! Trevor swore!" Natalie said, teasing him.

"I think the staff have done a marvellous job getting us fed tonight," Grace said. "It can't be easy cooking when you can hardly see and it's so hot. How can they bear it in the kitchen?"

Everyone nodded their agreement. Even Deborah, who seemed in a very good mood tonight.

"Any more news from Frances?" she asked Eve, who shook her head.

"No. But I'm sure she's fine. It's Huw I'm worried about. Nobody's heard anything from him, I suppose?" she asked, looking around the table.

"He's a right tosser if you ask me," Jason said. "Just taking off like that. He could be anywhere."

"I'm going to see if I can get in touch with the police as soon as we've finished eating. I suppose if he'd had an accident we'd know about it, but as Jason says, he could be anywhere and anything could have happened to him."

"How much longer do you think this storm's going to go on for?" Donna asked.

"It could be a couple more hours," Eve replied, "I don't think the worst has passed yet."

"Yes," Michael agreed. "It's been raining for a long time but the real eye of the storm isn't over us yet. There are usually great flashes of lightening and huge claps of thunder, that we haven't really had, have we? Just the odd one or two so far."

"The hotel staff are going to play music in the small conference room and once they've cleared away the final sitting of dinner in here they're going to set up a limited bar facility so that people can gather here if they want to," Eve informed them all.

"I think I might have an early night," Suzanne said. "All that rum punch this afternoon has made me sleepy."

Dave noticed Stewart looked crestfallen. He nudged him in the ribs.

"Cheer up, mate! That was a come-on if I ever erd one!"

"Do you think so?"

"Course it was, you dozy sod."

Leaving the group to their own devices for a while, Eve paddled her way to the front desk where Carlo was dealing with the guests with his usual aplomb. A grey-haired man in a Manchester United shirt and jogging bottoms stood before him.

"Will the bar open as normal tonight?" he asked Carlo.

Carlo looked from the man to the rain that was falling in sheets and being blown into the reception area by the gale-force wind; to the buckets and towels that covered much of the floor of the reception area and to the sandbags that were pushed up against the office doors on the far side to stop the water going underneath them.

"As normal, sir? As normal?" he asked incredulously.

The man looked at him and nodded his head.

"We'd like to be able to get a drink. After all, we've paid for all-inclusive."

"There are bar facilities and some music in the small conference room, which is to the north of the main corridors and there will be further bar facilities in Pizza Pizzazz once dinner is over."

"Oh! We've got to walk all the way over there? In the rain?" the man asked, disbelieving.

Carlo's eyes flashed and his mouth drew into a sneer. Everything he had ever learned about customer service just blew away with the wind.

"Sir, the main bar is under three feet of water. The evening bar staff can't get in because their homes and the roads here are flooded. The staff members who are working in the make-do bars tonight have been here all day. They don't know if their homes or families are safe or not, because we are surrounded by water and they can't get out and the storm has taken out the telephone lines. Yet in spite of that they are still working to enable you to enjoy the all-inclusive holiday that, as you so rightly point out, you have paid for."

The man tutted and turned to walk away, deliberately catching Eve's eye as he did so.

"It's not good enough, is it?" he said. "You'd think they'd be a bit more organised than this, wouldn't you? After all, they reckon it rains heavily here every summer."

"Yes, you'd have thought they'd have found a way of diverting hurricanes away from all-inclusive resorts by now, so that holidaymakers who choose to come here at the cheapest time of year would get exactly what they paid for, wouldn't you?" Eve spat at him. He didn't realise she was attacking him at first and smiled and nodded in agreement at what she said. He was soon left in no doubt as she continued. "You stupid man! Listen to yourself! Everyone's knocking themselves out here for you. What more do you want? You should be ashamed of yourself!"

Taken aback by Eve's response, he shuffled off. She glared at his disappearing back and then turned to look at Carlo and the two of them burst out laughing.

"What an idiot!" Eve said.

"Well, you certainly told him, girl!" Carlo said and high-fived her.

Eve just started to explain about Huw's disappearance to Carlo when the door to the back office opened and Melv came out.

"Perhaps Mr McGrass can give you better advice than me on this one," Carlo said.

Eve and Melv both looked at each other uncomfortably for a moment, but Eve knew that they had to put all the personal stuff aside now. She needed Melv's help and she wasn't too proud to ask for it.

"Do you have any idea where he might have gone on the bicycle?" Melv asked her once she'd finished telling him how Huw had gone off.

"Not really. One of the guys in the group that he's been friendly with said that he wanted to see Nelson's Dockyard. But he's been gone since really early this morning. He must have had breakfast at seven and then set off. Nobody's seen him all day."

"Our Head of Security has a radio link to the local police station. I'll see if we can put out a message to them. But if he'd had an accident we'd probably have heard."

"But he might be lying somewhere hurt, where nobody can see him."

"Then there's nothing we can do about that. Nobody's out tonight; no cars, nobody. The whole island is under water; trees are down and roads are blocked. If he is lying hurt somewhere nobody's going to come across him until the storm abates and that will probably be in the early hours of the morning."

Eve sighed. She knew Melv was right. She was so mad at Huw that she almost hoped something had happened to him to teach him a lesson. Then she quickly corrected the thought. One group member in hospital with serious injuries was enough for any trip! She looked at Melv and saw the tension and problems of the day etched on his face.

"How is everything?" she asked.

"Not good. The whole surrounding area is under water, which means that we're cut off from the rest of the island at the moment. The forecast is that it's going to get worse in the next couple of hours when the storm proper hits, so it'll be tomorrow morning before we can really assess the damage and sort everything out."

"Well, if I can do anything... you know it goes without saying."

"Thanks. We've sorted out accommodation for the staff; fortunately it's low season and we've got enough rooms empty to accommodate them, three and four to a room. My concern is that the water's going to rise a lot more yet. It's not draining away because it's raining too hard and the drains can't cope." He sighed and ran his hand over his head. "People throw their garbage carelessly without realising that they're blocking the drains. Others don't cut their hedges back and that causes blocking, too. We can just hope it's not going to be so bad that we get completely flooded. We've now got sandbags down all along the whole ground floor corridor to protect the rooms there. It's a nightmare!"

They smiled at each other in spite of the seriousness of the topic of conversation.

"I was just going along to Pizza Pizzazz for a drink. Would you care to join me?"

"Yes! Yes, I would," Eve said, hoping she hadn't sounded too eager.

"I'll just radio the message through to security about your missing man and then we'll have ourselves a rum punch. It's going to be a long night."

***

The missing man was, meanwhile, having the time of his life at home with the Jameses. He'd discovered that Bronson had once played cricket at a fairly high level, having attended two selection trials for the West Indies. And his son, Paul, was a rising cricket star. The youngest daughter, Karena, the one who had found him in the garden, was a gymnast and the older daughter, Alanna, was a tennis player who'd won the Junior Antigua and Barbuda Championships the previous year. They'd talked cricket and sport for hours; the children being chuffed to discover their surprise guest was a PE teacher. He, in turn, had enjoyed himself when they'd played a made-up sports quiz to entertain themselves for an hour or so. He and Paul had taken on Bronson and his two daughters and had narrowly beaten them.

"That wasn't fair!" Alanna said at the end, "All the questions about rugby and English sports. How we supposed to know that?"

"Don't be a bad sport!" her father admonished her, laughing.

Huw couldn't help noticing the great relationship Bronson had with his kids. They cracked jokes and fooled around yet they were respectful to him and very well-behaved. He wondered about Mrs James.

"Do you live with the children on your own?" he asked, feeling that their new-found friendship allowed him to do so without feeling he was prying.

"Their mother's in St Kitt's. She went to visit her sister, to take care of her for a couple of weeks after she had surgery. She's an unmarried lady with no children, the sister, so Annalee, that's my wife, looks out for her the best she can, even though we're on different islands. She's due back next week. I expect she'll be concerned about us as she can't contact us now the phone's down and the cell phone's not working. She'll be praying to the Lord that we're safe."

Huw couldn't help wondering if Eve or anyone else in the group would be praying to the Lord that he was safe. Somehow he doubted it, yet he knew he had nobody to blame but himself.

***

The thunderbolt that hit the dome roof of Pizza Pizzazz sounded like a meteor crashing. Fortunately, there were only about thirty people in there at the time, including the T2G group, who had stayed on after dinner. Eve had been sitting at the bar making small talk with Melv about everything and nothing; both of them carefully avoiding the events of the day. There was no sign of Michael. He'd excused himself after dinner and gone to his room. He was mentally and emotionally exhausted. His three-hour conversation with Eve had been an emotional rollercoaster, but he'd soaked up all the information she'd given out about Greece and her family, like a man in the desert quenching his thirst at an oasis. And he still had to go through the same with Melv, to find out about his Bajan roots. The others, except for Deborah, Murray and Ursula were all sitting at a table chatting. Geri was draped on a stool further along the bar from Melv and Eve, trying to engage Elvis in conversation, oblivious to the fact that the man was just about on his knees having done fourteen hours at work so far.

The whole place was pitched into darkness, people started screaming and rain poured in through the hole the thunderbolt had left and the wind threatened to rip off the rest of the roof.

Melv and Elvis both started shouting orders and trying to calm everyone down.

"Ladies and gentlemen, stay calm! Please stay calm!" Melv shouted as weak emergency lights clicked on. "We're going to get members of staff to escort you back along the path and through the corridors until you get safely to your rooms. We cannot serve any more drinks here now. Please do as we ask and return to your rooms!"

Elvis and two other waiters appeared with large torches and started to pull on Wellingtons and rain jackets.

"Elvis, you stand at the start of the path and shine the torch so people can see. Gareth! You take the people in rooms on the south side and Carlton can take the north." He turned back to the guests. "Please listen, everyone! Those of you in rooms on the north side, that's rooms one to thirty on each floor please follow Carlton now! You may need to take your shoes off. Please be careful the path is slippery." He waited until people started to shuffle out following Carlton to where Elvis stood holding the torch up high to illuminate the path. That almost wasn't necessary as the lightening was now flashing every couple of seconds. Once nobody else was moving behind Carlton Melv spoke to those remaining.

"Those in rooms thirty-one through eighty please follow Gareth."

Eve watched everyone leave but stayed where she was. Melv was hastily trying to secure the bar and she dashed round behind him, helping however she could. Three members of staff came into the restaurant having heard the thunderbolt and in spite of the tiredness they were feeling stacked tables and chairs and helped secure whatever else they could. Eve's arms ached, but she couldn't let up now; she was needed. She put glasses into crates and crates into cupboards while the rain poured down on her head and the wind blew everything out of her hands.

This is only a tropical storm. What must a hurricane be like?

Gareth and Carlton returned from escort duty and immediately started to help.

"Where's Elvis?" Melv asked. They shook their heads. They hadn't seen Elvis on the path when they'd fought their way back to the restaurant.

Melv radioed security at the two gates on the perimeter fence who reported *"Property secure"* as did the head of security, who was in his office in the Admin Block, although he added, "well, as secure as it's gonna be in these conditions, Melv."

"I know what you mean," Melv said, shaking his head. He turned to his staff and thanked them.

"Guys, you know I'm more than appreciative of what you've all done tonight and all through, today. Go and get some rest now; tomorrow's going to be another long day. "

"Good night, Mr McGrass, good night, Eve," they all said as they walked to the door, each one bracing himself for the wind and rain outside.

"I'm going over to my office. You want to join me?" Melv asked Eve. We can dry off a bit and I'll see if there's any news about Huw." Eve nodded in agreement. She took off her shoes and put on the waterproof coat that Melv offered her and then giggled at the sight of the two of them.

"Very attractive!" she said.

"What every well-dressed Antiguan is wearing this summer!" Melv joked as he took her arm tightly and the two of them tried to walk as steadily as they could along the corridor and back to Melv's office.

***

By midnight the storm was directly overhead. The lightening was so frequent that you could have read a book by it; it was like a florescent light. Jo got out of bed to look out of her window at the sea and was surprised to find she was paddling.

I'm on the first floor! The water can't be that deep!

She reached for the light switch, but then realised the power was off completely. Probably just as well as she was up to her ankles in water. Another flash of lightening showed that the water had come in through the slats in the door and underneath it. She paddled round the bed and pulled the curtain back to a wild sight. The whole scene was completely unrecognisable from the idyllic, travel poster they'd all fallen in love with. The lightening was now a permanent feature displaying nature's power in all its force. The trees, including the huge, majestic royal palms, were bent double and bushes were almost horizontal on the ground. The sea looked like it was having a party; a rave. Waves shot up in the air, then fell tumbling down; mini tsunamis raced each other along the beach. Jo looked on in awe.

"How great Thou art! How great Thou art!" she found herself whispering involuntarily.

*** ***

In a small, wooden house not far from Gray's Farm Police Station, Frances writhed on the bed, sexy, sensuous and sultry and slowly opened her eyes to drink in the sight of Neville, who was rising above her, the lightening illuminating his black skin, shimmering with perspiration and his braids, dancing around his head to a seductive rhythm of their own and she was mesmerised. She'd now lost count of the orgasms and the number of times they'd made love. After each session they would hold each other, share a joint, sleep for a while, then wake up, have a drink and start all over again. Conversation had become less and less. Frances thought it strange they had nothing much to say to each other. They just screwed each other's brains out. It was as if he was a machine and it never occurred to Frances to refuse him; she was making up for the last twenty years! She'd always considered herself somewhat reserved where lovemaking was concerned. Martin had accused her of being frigid when they'd broken up; it was one of the excuses he tried to explain his affair, to put the blame on her. But now she knew she wasn't frigid. She'd just had to wait for the right man to come along with the key to unlock the door and free the sensual woman who'd been imprisoned inside her for such a long time.

Earlier Neville had produced some chicken from the small fridge next to the sink and a pot of sauce and they'd eaten it with some bread. Fortunately his stove was gas so they'd been able to heat the sauce which they poured over the cold chicken. It was too hot to have the gas on for any length of time and the wind was rattling through chinks in the wooden slats that the house was made of and Frances was afraid it might catch fire,

As he thrust into her again and again, his hair flying back and forth his face a wild, handsome mask of pleasure, Frances wished she could savour the sheer thrill of the moment for ever. He was young, he was different, and he was exciting. As he came to his climax the thunder crashed and roared outside, the lightening lit up the room and the sound of the rain and the wind came together giving Frances the most electrifying night of her life, Neville collapsed next to her, nuzzling her neck and holding her tight as her clitoris throbbed and sheer exhilaration seared through her body.

I know I'm alive! For the first time ever, I know I'm one hundred per cent alive!

***

In room 320, Suzanne couldn't sleep, which wasn't surprising given the heat and the noise that nature was causing outside. She jumped out of her skin as another thunderclap echoed through the night sky. She felt alone and scared, like a small child. She was kicking herself for not asking Stewart to stay with her. But she'd thought he was going to offer, so she waited and waited and then they were all accompanied back to their rooms and she'd lost sight of him. She'd definitely made up her mind that she wanted to take things further with Stewart, but now it looked like the holiday was passing and they weren't getting past the kissing stage. And today they hadn't even done that! Well, she had nobody to blame but herself. Stewart had made it obvious that he liked her from the start. She'd been the one to hold back because she hadn't wanted him to think she was that kind of a girl. Whatever *that kind of a girl was*! It couldn't be her; after all she was thirty-eight years old and had never had full sex. But she didn't want him to think that because she'd never had sex that she was desperate, either. She thought she'd talk it over with Grace and Jo and Natalie in the morning. They would know what she should do. Or perhaps she should just talk to Stewart. Another clap of thunder startled her so much she felt tearful. And then she was aware of a faint tapping on the door. She jumped out of bed, knocking her knee on the bedside cabinet as she did so. The lightening illuminated a long candle on the dressing table just at that moment and she picked it up as a weapon and crept towards the door, slowly realising as she did that her feet were wet.

"Who is it?" she said in a stage whisper.

"It's me. Stewart. I'm just checking to see you're alright."

Suzanne dropped the candle, her fingers fumbled to unchain the door and then she opened it wide. Rain, wind and Stewart all came tumbling into the room.

"Oh, Stewart!" Suzanne said, throwing herself into his arms and nearly knocking him over.

"Oops! Steady on!" he said, nervously. "You okay?

"I am now," she said, pulling him towards the bed.

An hour later Stewart considered himself to be the luckiest man alive. He snuggled up behind Suzanne, her large, dimpled, warm backside fitting nicely against his belly like two very sweaty pieces of a jigsaw; his hand across her breasts gently caressing her left nipple and listening to her snoring very quietly. The world could come to an end tonight and it wouldn't matter. He'd finally found complete happiness. Tonight he'd come home to this wonderful woman; he was where he belonged. And the condoms had fitted perfectly. He'd had no worries in that department.

***

In the village of Liberta Huw slept like a baby. The rum that Bronson had plied him with as they'd exchanged more and more stories of their own sporting prowess had had its effect. He was oblivious to the storm outside and the fact that the Royal Antigua and Barbuda Police Force had a missing person's alert out for him. He was dreaming that he was scoring the winning try for Wales against England at Cardiff Arms Park and the noise of the thunder was, in his dreams, the roar of approval from the home crowd.

***

In room 274 Geri sobbed into her pillow. Her lip was swollen where her tooth had gone through it and fear at what was about to happen paralysed her. She'd stopped struggling when she realised it seemed to turn him on, that he seemed to like it.

"Please! Please, don't!" she whimpered, hating herself for begging.

"What? You don't want it?" his voice said, close in her ear, dripping with sarcasm. "You've wanted it all week. I've been watching you. Tonight you couldn't have made it more clear. You've been gagging for it. And now you've got it. So just relax and enjoy it!" Her back arched, tensely, anticipating the pain. He roughly pushed her head back down sending her face into the pillow and for a moment she panicked as she couldn't breathe.

"Relax. Don't fight it. You'll actually enjoy it, you'll see," he said as Geri's scream was drowned by the next clap of thunder.

***

Deano couldn't get comfortable. Sleep was impossible, partly due to the storm and partly due to his own discomfort. Not his physical discomfort – he barely registered the pain now – but the mental anguish that the thought of Rachel's visit brought him. He squirmed in bed at the thought of it. Her plane was due to land at one o'clock on Saturday lunch time. That was less than thirty-six hours away. Perhaps it would be delayed by the storm. Perhaps it would go down in the storm.

Stop it! What are you thinking?

A nurse popped her head in the door and saw he was awake.

"Can I get you some water?" she asked him, smiling. He noticed she had a beautiful face; huge almond eyes and high cheekbones with luscious, full red lips. He started to imagine what it might feel like to have those lips on his body, kissing his chest, his stomach and then slowly, deliberately closing around...

"Mr Dean? Can I do something for you?" she repeated, rousing him from his fantasy.

"Can you lie down next to me on the bed?" he said.

"Pardon me?"

"Yes, water would be great, thank you."

***

As Murray came for the second time that day he thought it must be his birthday. He hadn't had sex twice in one day since... since... well, for a very long time. He preened as Deborah came just a second or two after him. He'd proved to a classy woman like her what he was worth.

He'd made her happy again tonight, just like she'd said he had during their earlier session. Then, the first time, it had been a little rushed, but tonight they'd been able to take their time and it had been magic.

Glorious!

He rolled over onto his side and looked at her. Yes, she might be a bit older than he'd have liked but she still had a good body; she'd obviously taken care of herself. Seeing her eyes on him he pulled his stomach in. He didn't exactly have a six-pack, but it wasn't a barrel either. Her damp, black hair fanned out over the pillow and a strand stuck to her cheek. He peeled it away and she smiled as he did so.

"I'll err... just go to the bathroom," he said, pointing vaguely in the area of his crotch where a condom hung like a week-old balloon from his rapidly shrinking erection. He leapt up as athletically as he could manage and promptly skidded on the wet floor.

"Bloody hell! You could kill yourself on that," he grumbled as he disappeared into the dark depths of the bathroom. "I can't see," he complained. Deborah raised her eyebrows.

"That's because the power's off!"

Then she smiled to herself. As she heard him fumbling around she turned onto her back and put her hand between her legs. It hadn't been the best sex in the world but it hadn't been the worst. This afternoon she'd come easily because she'd been dying for sex by the time they got to her room. The build up to the storm had created a sexual tension and urgency in her that she'd had to meet. And she'd surprised herself by actually discovering she wanted sex with Murray. He'd grown on her over the last few days and she enjoyed his company. And once she'd got round the problem with his breath – she'd told him he needed to drinks loads and loads of water to avoid dehydration, which, consequently had diluted his stomach acid and got rid of the rancid smell his breath sometimes carried – she'd found him quite attractive. And she was curious to have sex with someone who wasn't Maurice. And God only knew if she'd ever have sex with him again, given his present condition. Tonight she had wanted to take things slower, but Murray's slow and tender was just a bit faster than Jenson Button in an F1 race. Murray had been in a hurry. So, this time she'd done what millions of women have done since Eve bit the apple; she faked it. God knew, she'd faked it enough with Maurice over the years to avoid hurting his fragile ego. She'd had an orgasm thanks to the *pulsate* mode on the hand-held shower head hundreds of times after letting Maurice think he'd taken her over the finishing line. Tonight she'd known Murray was nearly there and wouldn't last long enough so she'd pretended. Now with him safely in the bathroom she started to finish herself off.

***

In room 356 Michael went over the events of the day for the umpteenth time. Hugging himself, he felt like a kid on Christmas morning. He'd decided that life was a funny thing, and he had come to realise that he was lucky, so lucky to have Eve as his birth mother. He'd liked her from the off and after their talk that afternoon he saw she was a good, decent woman who had done the only thing she could and then paid the price for the next thirty years, only for him to come along and behave like a right idiot. Nat had been right.

Thinking about Natalie brought another smile to his lips. Thank God she was on this holiday; she'd proved herself a real mate. He found himself hoping they'd stay in touch once they got home. Okay, he was in Durham and she was in Hertfordshire, but there were motorways and trains. And several times a month he travelled down to London. He'd made up his mind that on his next trip he'd go to Windsor and try and find Blazes. He also wanted the address of where his father had lived, just to see where he'd really started life. He was going to ask Natalie to go with him.

And tomorrow, or once things got back to normal at the resort, whenever that was, he'd talk to his father and ask him about Barbados. He liked both his birth parents as people and really hoped they could all enjoy a good relationship from now on. He was just sorry that the phone lines were down because his mum and dad must be anxiously waiting to hear from him how the meeting with his birth father had gone. He had so much to tell them now; they wouldn't believe it.

He turned towards the wall with a huge grin on his face and went through every moment he'd spent with Eve all over again, oblivious to the storm raging outside.

***

And in the General Manager's office, Michael's birth parents found a solace in each other. The radio had brought no news of Huw, but Melv was reassured again by his staff that the resort was as secure as it possibly could be until daylight. So they allowed themselves the luxury of sharing a few drinks, memories, stories and finally a passion that was totally natural and whose depth and intensity matched the storm raging outside. And one they both thought had well and truly died.

***

DAY EIGHT

The crackle of Melv's radio woke them both up instantly as they lay cocooned together, wrapped in each other's arms on the large leather sofa in the corner of his office. They looked at each other sleepily surprised to discover where they were and who they were with. Disentangling himself from her, Melv stood up and answered his radio, while Eve stretched and went to look out of the window. It was 5.15am and it was just light. The rain had stopped and the wind had slowed right down but the little she could see, just a small section of the gardens, was completely submerged. Large palm branches was strewn everywhere. Melv held a crackly conversation with Spencer, the Head of Security, who was bringing him up to date on the situation; the surrounding area was still under water, although no more rain was forecast so it was just a case of waiting for the water to subside and then staff and supplies could get in and out and operation clean up could begin. Spencer said that the department managers who'd actually managed to get home last night had agreed to try to get in as soon as it was safe to do so. He was expecting some of them by boat shortly.

Eve turned towards Melv as he finished his conversation. He'd gone into work mode and seemed almost unaware of her presence. He pushed his feet down into Wellington boots and started for the door, before suddenly turning sharply to face her. He stepped back towards her and planted a kiss on her forehead.

"Go and get some proper rest," he said, "at least for a couple of hours."

"No, I want to come with you. I want to help," she said, feeling irked by his apparent casual indifference to her. "There must be something I can do."

"Okay. I'll take you through to the kitchens, perhaps you can help with breakfasts."

They walked apart from each other as they went along the corridor of the Admin Block and down the stairs into the reception area. It was clear that the water was already subsiding and there was an absolute silence and calm everywhere. If anyone was surprised to see the two of them together so early in the morning, they showed no signs of it. Eve strode alongside Melv, her mind going round and round, glad to have something to do to take it away from all the events of the previous twenty-four hours, which had culminated in something that up until a week ago she had never imagined happening in a million years.

***

Slowly, Mango Tree Resort came awake to face the damage done and to wonder and discuss the strength of the storm. Large signs were put up around the reception area advising everyone that breakfast would be served from 8am in the main restaurant and offering apologies and asking for understanding and co-operation. A further notice informed everyone that there would be a temporary bar set up on the restaurant terrace until the main bar could be cleaned, repaired and restocked. It was hoped that would happen by that evening. Eve had taken a look at the bar, which was still submerged under two feet of water and felt that the notice was somewhat optimistic.

She had kept busy since reporting to the kitchen at five thirty. Edward, the Assistant Chef who was leading the operation decided to make scrambled egg and bacon, although Eve personally thought they should just offer cereals, toast, fruit and yoghurt. Surely people would understand in the circumstances?

Would they ever!!

In spite of knowing the situation, that staff couldn't get in and seeing how Eve and six members of staff from various hotel departments were trying hard to stock the breakfast buffet and keep the food coming, people were still just eating and walking away, leaving their used plates and cups on the tables apparently unaware there were no waiters. Consequently, others couldn't sit down as the tables were dirty. The final straw for Eve was when she came out of the kitchen with a tray of Danish pastries to face an irate Geordie, scruffy Peter from Newcastle who'd murdered *Chasing Cars* at the karaoke, asking if he was going to have to wait much longer for beans.

"Beans?" Eve asked incredulously. "Beans?" she said again, raising her voice this time and throwing the tray of pastries onto the table in disgust with a loud clatter that made people turn around. Grabbing a chair, she stood on it and started shouting.

"Can I have your attention, please? Excuse me, everyone! Please listen up! Now some of you appear not to have noticed but we had a bit of as storm last night. Consequently the surrounding villages are flooded and we are cut off at the moment. Cut off means that nobody can get in or out. The staff that are still here, have been here for thirty hours and have worked tirelessly and ceaselessly during that time. The rest of the staff can't get in and even if they could they would have to leave their children, because schools are closed, and their homes, which as I've already said, are flooded. So" and at this point she stared right at Peter, "if the worst thing that happens to you today is that you don't have any beans to go with your egg and bacon, consider yourself blessed! And, can I please ask you to at least clear up after yourselves? Please stack your dirty plates and cups on the service table and put the cutlery in the bucket next to it. Thank you!"

As she stepped off the chair there was a rush of shamefaced people, grabbing dirty cutlery and dishes and asking how they could help. Much to her joy she saw Trevor, Dawn, Donna, Natalie, Grace, Dave, Jo and Michael form a chain gang passing dirty plates into the kitchen and bringing clean ones out. She beamed at them.

"Morning, Boss!" Dave called out. "We fought we betta get stuck in or you'd give us a righ' bollockin'" he added, laughing.

"Thanks, guys," she said, smiling at them all, yet feeling curiously shy when her eyes met Michael's.

If you only knew what your father and I got up to last night!

***

Huw was wading around the edge of Bronson's property with him, checking on everything and assessing the damage. A large palm tree had lost several branches and there were mangos and coconuts on the ground, which was itself under several inches of water. Huw's hired bike was lying on its side by the side door of the house where the winds had blown it. Looking up at the roof, Bronson tutted.

"We got a little problem up there, I can see. I'll have to fix that later. I got some supplies in. I always do that before hurricane season starts, you never know what you're gonna need."

Huw couldn't help admiring the well-kept pale-lemon house with its orange window frames.

"Do you do all your own repairs?"

"Yes, I enjoy a bit of DIY, as I believe you call it in England. Sorry, Britain."

They'd had a long conversation the previous evening about the nations that make up the United Kingdom of Great Britain and Northern Ireland and about Welsh nationalism. Huw never really considered himself to be a Nationalist; he couldn't speak Welsh and had a certain degree of contempt for those that did, seeing them as bumpkins and pedants. Yet last night he'd become a convincing debater, arguing eloquently and forcefully the case for separatism. He'd quite surprised himself.

"I suppose I'd better be getting back through the rain forest to the Mango Tree," he said, inwardly shuddering at the thought of the ride back.

"No way! That road'll be flooded and cut off. You'll have to take the All Saints' Road back to St John's and then the coast road along. But that way may be blocked, too. Things got a little wild last night and it always takes us a few days to get back to normal."

"A few days! I'm leaving on Monday."

"Wait a while and see if the bus comes by. If the bus is running you can put the bike on the bus and take a ride back to the hotel."

Huw smiled to himself. That sounded like a better idea. Bronson told the children to fix some breakfast while he and Huw looked round for further damage. The fence on the south east side was down; that was where the wind hit worst.

"How often do you get hurricanes like that one, then?" Huw asked.

"That wasn't a hurricane, oh no!" Bronson shook his head vigorously. "Last night we were lucky the wind didn't come."

"But it was howling. Look at the state of the place!" Huw argued.

"That wasn't wind, Huw. That was a gentle breeze compared to what a hurricane would bring. What we had last night was a tropical storm. A hurricane is much worse. Much, much worse."

Huw shook his head in disbelief. He looked at Bronson, who never stopped smiling as he assessed the repairs he had to do to his property and the cleaning up of the gallery and kitchen area where the water had got in, in spite of the sandbags and he felt humbled. At home the whole country came to a standstill when it snowed for a couple of hours, or when the wrong leaves got onto the railway lines. And everyone grumbled and complained.

"How do you put up with it? Doesn't it get you down?" he asked.

"I guess it's the price we pay for living in paradise," Bronson said, laughing out loud.

An hour later Karena, who was on bus-watch, announced that she'd just seen one go by.

"Good! That means that in a short while he'll be coming back and you can take this bus through All Saint's Village and into St John's. Then depending on the roads you can cycle back to Mango Tree Resort or take the Bolans bus."

Huw was glad he'd be able to get back to the resort, although he was expecting a dressing down from that bossy cow Eve. Still, he'd show them. He'd tell them what a fabulous time he'd had with his new friends in Liberta Village.

He and Bronson swapped e-mail addresses and promised to keep in touch.

"I can't thank you enough for all you did for me last night and this morning," he said, shaking Bronson's hand.

"It was my pleasure! We weren't gonna leave you lying in the yard!" Bronson joked and to Huw's surprise he found himself and Bronson locked in a warm, brotherly embrace. Stepping back, Huw held out his arms and one by one the three children came into them and gave him a huge, warm, goodbye-hug.

"Your children are a credit to you," he said, feeling suddenly emotional. He looked at the three of them, well-behaved, polite, interesting and intelligent and thought of all the ill-mannered wasters he taught in the glum, grey comprehensive back in Hereford. Perhaps he could organise a transfer?

So, it was with a touch of sadness that he clambered onto the bus with his bike. The driver wasn't very happy about taking him.

"You taking up three seats with the bicycle, man," he said. "Careful you don't mash up me upholstery."

"Well, I'll pay for three tickets, then," Huw said, bringing a smile to the driver's face. He endured an uncomfortable ride on the back seat with the bike balanced precariously across him, the pedals digging into his nether regions. The devastation from the storm was evident everywhere. He saw houses with their galvanised roofs lifting off; others with water butts turned on their sides or with doors and windows smashed open or missing altogether. Cars were strewn by the roadside, where their owners had abandoned them, or where the wind had tossed them.

Several times the bus slowed right down as the driver manoeuvred over craters that had opened up in the road or gullies that had appeared during the storm, where water flowed along, but finally, with great relief, they pulled into the Bus Station in St John's and Huw got out.

He asked the driver where he could get the bus to Bolans or the Mango Tree Resort.

"No buses running that way," the driver said. "The whole area from Jennings south is under water."

Great! Now what?

***

Geri shuffled from the bed to the bathroom. She desperately hoped the shower was working now. She balked at the sight of herself in the full length mirror on the outside of the bathroom door.

That can't be me! I look about ninety!

Her top lip was swollen and dry blood caked her cheek. Her eyes were so swollen from crying that each was like a little slit in the middle of a red, puffy lump of raw meat. Her body ached from being hunched up on the bed; she didn't think she'd ever be able to stand up straight again. Visions of the previous night flooded into her brain, in spite of her attempts to block them.

Stop it! Don't think about it! Don't let him think he's won! Get under the water!

With relief she saw the water spur from the showerhead. She stood under it and grabbed the soap, lathering it all over her body, scrubbing, rubbing, trying her best to get rid of any trace there might be left of him on any part of her. The water ran over her head, down her face, over her shoulders and her torso, down her back, between her buttocks, between her thighs and down her legs, where it sloshed around her feet before disappearing down the drain. And all the time she stood there, she cried and sobbed; with relief, with pain and with disgust at herself.

"You've been gagging for it all week."

His words went round and round in her head, making her cry out loud in anguish.

"I haven't been gagging for it! I haven't! I haven't! No! No! No!"

Slowly, after a long, long time, she turned the water off and wrapped herself in one of the bath towels on the rack, for a moment taking solace at the soft downy feeling, the nearest thing she'd had to a hug in a long time. She went back into the room, and suddenly ripped the sheets from the bed and threw them on the floor. She'd rather sleep on a beach towel than get back into those dirty, filthy, disgusting sheets that smelt of him and what he'd done to her. She climbed onto the bed and pushed herself right up into the corner between the pillows and the wall, tucking her legs up underneath her, her head, turbaned in a hand towel, resting, exhausted against the headboard. And she started crying again.

This wasn't how it was supposed to be! My lovely holiday; ruined, wrecked.

Just like her life was, she thought. And all because of one, stupid mistake.

***

"Is there any damage to the house?" Frances asked Neville as he wandered naked back into the room from the bathroom, scratching his chest.

"Not that I can see. We're lucky. The houses are close together here, so we're protected," he said.

He looked into a small bag that was on the table. *'Me weed bag'* he'd called it yesterday. Was it yesterday? Frances was losing track of time.

"I'm gonna need to go and get some supplies," he said. "You got any money?"

"Supplies?" Frances queried, thinking he meant food. "Don't get anything for me. I've got to go back to the Mango Tree at some point today."

His expression turned serious.

"You spend two days with me, eat me food, smoke me weed and you just gonna go off?" he asked, sucking his teeth to show his disgust.

"No! No! Of course not! I mean, I've got to go back to the hotel, but, of course, I'll chuck in some money for supplies," she said, smiling to try to lighten the atmosphere.

She got off the bed and walked across the room to where her bag was sitting on a large, ornate dresser that was squeezed in between two upholstered chairs. She opened her purse.

"How much do you need?"

"Give me a coupla hundred," he said, pulling on his shorts over his bare backside and slipping a vest over his head.

She peeled off two one hundred notes and gave them to him.

"Could you get me something to drink, please?" she asked. "Juice, soft drink, anything."

He nodded.

"There's a bucked I filled in the bathroom so you can put water on your skin" he said, smiling again. "West Indian style," he added, grinning again.

Frances went through to the bathroom and had a stand up wash, thinking as she did so that she hadn't had one since she was a little girl. She laughed out loud as she realised there were a lot of things she hadn't done for a long time that she'd done repeatedly in the last forty-eight hours. She could smell the marijuana, thick and cloying in her hair. It would take more than a stand up wash to get rid of the smell of that, she knew.

What would Darren say?

She remembered a conversation they'd had when he was about fourteen and she was trying to put the fear of God into him about drugs. Good job she didn't have to have that conversation now, the hypocrisy would show in her face, although she realised that a few puffs on Neville's joints didn't make her a junkie. She patted herself dry with the small towel that was on the rail and walked back into the room like John Wayne getting off his horse after riding the range all day. Her pussy felt sore. She giggled to herself again at the word. She'd always call it that from now on she decided. She also realised that she quite liked this walking around naked. Martin would have thought she'd taken leave of her senses if she'd taken her clothes off in the house while they were married, yet here, with Neville, it just seemed so natural. Reaching into her bag, she turned on her mobile phone to see if there was a signal. She waited a couple of moments and then LIME appeared on her phone and three bars. She dialled Eve's number. She had to let her know she was still safe and that she would be back sometime later.

***

Huw pushed his bike along the coast road. He'd been able to cycle for a mile or so, but then he'd come across a section where the road had almost disappeared under stones and earth that had been washed down from the surrounding hillsides. The storm may have passed and the humidity lessened but it was still bloody hot. He stopped to brush the sweat from his face and to take a swig from the bottle of water Bronson had insisted on giving him. He'd also insisted Huw put on sun block and with the sun penetrating the thin veneer of cloud he was grateful he had. He could hear a vehicle coming up behind him and he stopped, trying to keep as far to the right as he could, facing on-coming traffic, to let it pass, but the vehicle came to a halt next to him. He turned to see it was a Police 4x4, with two officers inside. The one in the passenger seat looked out at him.

"Mr Jones? Huw Jones?" he asked.

Huw nodded.

"We've been looking for you, sir!"

***

By lunch time Operation Clean Up was well under way. The water had receded faster than expectations which meant some staff could get in and the maintenance department was power-hosing the public areas to clean them up. It would, of course, be several days before the rooms on the ground floor would be ready for guests again, but they weren't needed at the moment, much to Melv's delight. To add to his delight, Michael had sought him out and told him he wanted to help.

"But you're a guest here, Michael," he'd said, "We don't expect the guests to get themselves dirty now the staff are here. Breakfast was different," he said as they both thought of Eve's outburst.

"Yes, well, Eve certainly didn't mince her words, did she?" Michael said as they both laughed at the memory.

"She certainly didn't! Listen! I'll have some time this afternoon, after lunch, things should have quietened down a bit by then. Why don't you call by my office and we'll have a chat and a catch up? Meanwhile, thanks for the offer of help, I really do appreciate it, but we're fine."

Michael went to find the others, who were all sitting in their beachwear on the restaurant terrace drinking.

"I'll get ya one, mate!" Dave called out as Michael approached the table. "I'm jus' gettin' anuvva rand in fr'us."

"With any luck the beach'll be open again after lunch," Natalie told him. "They've got what look like little tractors down there at the moment, going up and down and cleaning it up."

"I must say, they've done a great job," Dawn said. "I mean, I was saying to Donna, wasn't I, Donna? If this'd been England it'd be days before everything was back in working order, wouldn't it? If it was England it might be weeks even and people wouldn't all muck in like they do here in Antigua."

"Well, if my aunt had balls she'd be my uncle!" Trevor said and they all burst out laughing just as Eve came up to join them.

"No sign of Huw?" Grace asked her.

"No," she said, shaking her head. "And I haven't seen Geri all morning, either. Have any of you seen her?"

"The last time I saw her was last night when we were in Pizza Pizzazz, before the thunderbolt hit," Suzanne said. "She was sitting at the bar talking to Elvis."

The others all nodded in agreement. Nobody had seen her since then.

"And Murray and Deborah were here til about ten minutes ago and then they went off. Together." Stewart said raising his eyebrows.

"Err, pot, kettle, black?" Natalie said, roaring with laughter as Stewart and Suzanne both went bright red.

"Any news from Frances?" Grace asked.

"Yes, she left me a voicemail about half an hour ago. She's fine and will probably be back sometime this afternoon."

The group members exchanged looks with each other, which Eve saw.

"And no comments, you lot, when she does come back!" she warned as they all laughed.

"We were just saying what a good job the hotel's done getting things back to normal," Dawn said to Eve. "I said, if it was England it would take weeks, wouldn't it?"

"They are on the ball," Eve agreed, "Oh, lovely! Thanks" she added, taking the Diet Coke that Dave was offering her from among the tray of Wadiddlys.

"I can't believe some people!" he fumed. "You've got a temporary bar, right? The two young gels servin' be'ind it are obviously not bar staff. I mean they're all dressed up like they work in the offices or somefink. An' there's stupid bastards askin' fer cocktails and then complainin' when they don't know ow t' make 'em. I arsk yer!"

At that moment, Carlo appeared on the terrace. He looked around and then spotting Eve made his way across to the group.

"Sorry to interrupt," he said, "but is Mr Owen here?"

"Yes! That's me!" Trevor said, looking at him in surprise.

"Could you come to the front desk, please, sir? Someone is going to call you back in five minutes time."

"Me?" Trevor asked in amazement.

"If you're Mr Owen, sir, yes."

303

Trevor jumped up.

"My mother!" he said. "Something must have happened to her!" as he rushed off behind Carlo, back to the front desk to wait for his call.

"His mother? She must be about a hundred!" Jason said.

"Don't be nasty!" Natalie said. "Trevor's only in his early sixties. She could be late seventies. That's no age now!"

Jason pulled a face and supped his beer. Michael and Eve caught each other's eye and exchanged beaming smiles. That kept on happening. Eve was surprised nobody had noticed.

"You all going back to the beach as soon as it opens?" Eve asked.

"As soon as it opens we'll be on it!" Stewart said. "I don't know about the rest of you but I'm dying for a swim." Murmured agreement echoed around the group. Eve's mobile phone rang.

"Eve? It's Carlo! Can you come to the front desk, please?"

"Now?" she asked.

"This minute, please," he said, hanging up.

"I'm wanted at the front desk," Eve said, standing up. "It must be Trevor. He's had bad news," she said, hurrying off to the front desk.

But when she got there, it wasn't Trevor, who was nowhere to be seen. A sheepish-looking Huw was standing with the hired bike between two police officers. The Police 4x4 was parked on the reception forecourt.

"Good day, Eve," Officer Ross said. Eve had met the tall, upright, extremely efficient yet pleasant man on two previous trips to Antigua; the first when one of her group, a man who knew everything and consequently couldn't be told anything, had ignored her words of caution about buying tickets from unknown people on the beach and had claimed he'd given 'a young local man' $90 US for a boat trip that never existed and the second when two men in the group had started fighting each other over a woman in the taxi on the way back from Shirley Heights.

"Good morning, Officer Ross," she replied, looking first at him and then at Huw.

"We've found your missing person," he said. "And we've told him he should never have been out in a storm like that. Yet alone on a bi-cycle."

"I'm glad you're back safely," Eve said as evenly as she could manage to Huw, who couldn't meet her eye.

"Well, you are safe this time," Officer Ross said, "but in future, you take notice of what this young lady tells you. She's almost one of us. She knows how dangerous a storm here can be. You heed her words now," he added, tipping his cap at Eve as the two men returned to their 4x4.

"Yes, Officer Ross!" Huw said in a childish, sing-song voice, but not until the two officers were out of earshot. Eve rounded on him.

"I wouldn't have expected any other reaction from you!" she said sharply, raising her voice. "You should be thanking those two men, not taking the piss. I really don't care where you were or what you did. You're a stupid, irresponsible man!"

"Don't you call me stupid and irresponsible! I'm going to write to Travel Together about you as soon as I get home."

"Please do! Meanwhile, just try to cause as little upset as possible in the time we have left. You've had a real attitude since you got here. You've been rude to other members of the group, you've been rude to me and you've sulked and behaved like a petulant child. But going off, on a bike, when you knew, you'd been told and warned that a tropical storm was on the way was irresponsible, selfish and reckless. Just stay out of my way!" She turned on her heel and marched off, leaving Huw the subject of curious stares from the dozen or so people who had witnessed the exchange standing alone, red-faced and defiant clutching onto the bike.

***

Eve was just finishing her lunch when Jo and Grace approached her. She smiled up at them as she put her knife and fork together on the plate.

"Was it Trevor's mother?" Grace asked. "Had something happened to her?"

"What, when I went to reception? No, it was Huw. He'd had a ride in a police car."

"What happened to him?" asked Jo, wide-eyed.

"I've no idea," Eve confessed. "To be honest, I'm just glad he's safe, but he's behaved like an idiot and I told him so."

"Good for you!" Grace said. "He's done nothing but sulk and insult people since we got here. Look at his little outburst with Frances the other night! That was completely unprovoked and uncalled for. He's obviously got a problem with women."

"Yes, well, that's as may be, but he's got no right to carry on the way he does. But to answer your question, I don't know what happened to Trevor. I haven't seen him since he went off to take the phone call. He certainly wasn't in reception. Hasn't anyone seen him?"

"No. Not since he went to take the phone call. I knocked on his door to see if he was coming to lunch but there was no reply. That was about half an hour ago," Jo said.

"I'll see if I can find him. I hope everything's okay."

"We don't want to pry," Jo said, "after all, he's quite a private person, but we just want to know he's alright."

"Of course you do! And I'm sure he'll appreciate that."

Eve stood up, collected her bag from the back of the chair and walked towards the front desk to try Trevor's room again.

Please, God, can I just have a couple of hours without something happening?

***

Murray and Deborah couldn't keep their hands off each other. The idea of sneaking away from the group and having sex again at lunchtime appealed to both of them and this time gave a slight edge to their love making. They were just working up to the climax of their second session of the afternoon when Deborah's mobile rang.

Shit!

She'd turned it on earlier just out of curiosity to see if there was a signal or not, as most people were going on about the phones being down. She'd obviously forgotten to turn it off again. Murray stopped mid-thrust.

"Do you want tae get it?"

Deborah hesitated. She was certain it could only be one person; Maurice. But then again it could be her sister. It could be anyone. Her mind was working overtime. If she didn't answer it she wouldn't be able to concentrate on Murray for the rest of the afternoon because she'd be wondering who it could have been, until she checked the phone. But if she answered it and it was Maurice, she couldn't talk to him in front of Murray. But she could see it was him and switch the phone off! Pushing Murray off she lunged across the room to grab the phone. Too late! They'd rung off. *Missed call* was showing on the screen. She pressed the button and saw it was *Caller Unknown*.

Bugger!

Now she was none the wiser. It could have been anyone. She tossed the phone back on the dressing table and climbed back onto the bed and sat astride Murray who was doing his best to keep his erection.

"Bad timing!" he said.

"No it wasn't; it gave you the chance to play with yourself," she joked.

"I'd rather you played with me," he said, guiding her hand onto him. She started to work him up and down and he was soon a bit harder. Not ramrod straight but at least hard enough to enter her. And just as he did *I Will Always Love You* rang out from the mobile, advising Deborah that she had a voicemail message.

"Leave it!" Murray said, coming over all masterful. There was no way he was going to lose his erection for the second time. He thrust himself up into Deborah whose thoughts were now once again with the bloody mobile. The only way forward was to let Murray come and then she could listen to the message while he was in the bathroom. She'd do without an orgasm this time.

Within two minutes Murray was *Oh God*-ing and it was all over. Deborah collapsed onto him as if she'd just had the ride of her life.

"Was it good fer you? Did you come?" he asked, still getting his breath back.

What is it with fucking men? Why do they always ask that? Bloody fragile egos!

She nodded and smiled. Well, she had enjoyed herself and come in the earlier session. She climbed off him and lay down, waiting for him to go to the bathroom. Instead, he took her hand and squeezed it, holding it in both his. Okay! She'd play along for a few minutes. But after five minutes he still showed no signs of moving.

Are you deliberately trying to wind me up?

"I just need to go to the bathroom," she said, in the hope that when she came back – quickly – he'd then go in.

"Just wait for a moment. I want to tell you something."

Please don't let it be you've got herpes or crabs!

"You've made me a really happy man these last few days and I'd like tae carry on seeing you when we get back home. I mean, I know it's early days but I havnae felt like this about anyone fer a long time." He turned his head and looked into her eyes, pleading; scared she was going to say no. Deborah swallowed. She was sort of enjoying this fling, but she wasn't sure she wanted to take it home with her.

"Let's just take it slowly, shall we? I mean, I know we've slept together but we've only known each other a week, haven't we?"

"But we could, you know, date properly in London. Go out fer a meal or tae see a film, we wouldn't have tae be always jumping intae bed. Well, not unless you'd want tae, of course," he added hastily, anxious not to turn down any possible future opportunity of taking Deborah to bed. She smiled.

"Yes, a film and a meal sounds nice," she said. "Thank you. Now, please excuse me before I disgrace myself," she said, sliding off the bed and going into the bathroom where she waited for thirty seconds, flushed the loo, rinsed her hands picked up the phone and pressed the *Play Messages* function, shocked to hear that she had twelve un-played messages. That meant she'd have to listen to the other eleven to hear the last one. She couldn't do that now as Murray would start knocking on the door to check she was still alive if she took that long.

Sod it!

Whoever, whatever it was would have to wait.

***

Eve hadn't been able to locate Trevor. She left a voicemail for him on the room phone hoping it hadn't been bad news and saying she'd see him later. Nobody had seen Geri, either. She wasn't answering her phone, so Eve left another message. She was getting tired of grown-ups behaving like children; tired of all the attention seekers that Travel Together groups seemed to attract. Geri! Huw! Deano! She'd had enough of the lot of them. She was exhausted. The events of the last few days were whirling round in her head. It had all been too much. She wanted time with her son.

My son!

How wonderful did that sound? She offered up a prayer of thanks to a Greek Orthodox God, and to Saint Spiridion, neither of whom had ever quite disappeared from her life. It was a prayer of deep gratitude that came from the bottom of her heart. She knew that Michael was spending time with Melv that afternoon and she felt a sudden surge of illogical jealousy. After all, they were father and son and she'd spent a couple of hours with him yesterday afternoon. But it hadn't been enough; she wanted to spend days at a time with him, talking, laughing, and sharing stories and secrets, until they had made up for thirty lost years.

As for her feelings and thoughts about Melv, she didn't even want to go there. For the moment she told herself that they had been two people who comforted and found shelter in each other during the storm. There had been nothing else to it. That's what she kept telling herself as she leaned back against the pillows and finally, as everything caught up with her, fell into a deep, deep sleep.

***

Down on the beach it was business as usual. Dave had been the first in the queue for sun loungers and now he was in the usual spot with Natalie, Grace, Jo, Jason, Stewart, Suzanne and the Dolly Sisters, as he still insisted on calling Donna and Dawn.

"Where's Michael?" he asked Natalie.

"Don't know," she said. "I haven't seen him for ages."

"And still no sign of Trevor," Suzanne said. "I do hope he's alright. You don't think something's happened to him, do you?" she asked anxiously.

"What could have happened to him?" Stewart said, in an attempt to reassure her.

"Well, anything could have," she said.

"Let's have a swim!" he said, pulling her up in an attempt to change the subject. "I'm hot."

"Me, too!" said Donna, jumping up to join them.

"And me!" said Dawn.

"And me!" said Dave.

"And me!" said Natalie.

"Party poopers!" Grace shouted after them. "Can't you see they wanted to be on their own?"

"Oh well, we might as well all go" Jason said starting to jog across the beach after them. Grace followed him before turning to Jo.

"You coming?"

"No. I'll stay here and watch the stuff," she said, grateful for the peace and quiet, in spite of being hot. She closed her eyes and gave thanks that the constant flow of beach vendors had been stemmed today, probably because of the storm. Although some of them sold nice bits and pieces of jewellery and most of them were good entertainment value, like Palinda who regaled them with tales of her son Elvroy who had dreams of making it big in show business, she wanted to be alone with her thoughts; her thoughts about Deano. She felt uncomfortable that he was languishing in the hospital while they were all enjoying themselves. Her inborn compassion told her she should do something. She would have felt like that even if he'd been a stranger, let alone someone she really liked. The truth was, she wanted to see him. Not just to minister to him; but because she was honest enough with herself to realise that she really did have feelings for him and she hoped against hope that one day, in the future, when he was back home and all mended, that they could perhaps meet up and see what the possibilities were.

Providing he feels the same, of course!

She winced at the thought. Of that she had no certainty; perhaps Deano, in spite of his protestations of really liking her, had only seen her as a holiday fling. Perhaps. But if she never saw him again, then how would she ever know? Eve had said he didn't want visitors as he was in pain. But she'd made up her mind. She was going to see him tomorrow afternoon, while the others were off on their helicopter ride!

***

Michael and Melv had been talking for over an hour and in spite of seeing the tiredness and strain of the last twenty-four hours on his father's face, Michael just couldn't bring himself to leave. He'd heard all about his late grandparents and the army of aunts and uncles and cousins back in Barbados; surprised to discover that Melv was one of eight children. He couldn't believe just how large his extended family was.

"We will, of course, go to Barbados together one day," Melv said. "And I mean that as a promise. I will introduce you to everyone; you'll meet them all." He swallowed and looked away. "But just give me a while to break the news nearer to home, will you? Please?"

He was aware of Michael's intense stare. He lifted his head and looked his newly-found son in the eye.

"Don't start thinking that I don't want you, or don't want to acknowledge you or anything like that! It's just... well... it's complicated."

Michael continued to say nothing. Melv knew that he had no intention of making things any easier for him and he didn't blame him, really.

"In the eyes of the world, Mary and I are a happy, loving couple with two wonderful kids. The reality is somewhat different. We've both known for a very long time that our marriage was empty and wasn't working for either of us. For a while both of us found company elsewhere, and one night three years ago Mary had just told me she was leaving me for someone else, when the police called to say they had our daughter who'd been involved in a joy-riding accident and was drunk and showed signs of using other substances. We'd been so wrapped up in our own selves that we'd turned a blind eye to Juliette running round with a wild crowd, doing things that she's now ashamed of. But that night was a wake-up call for us and we decided to put our differences behind us and pull together to save her. Our daughter's wellbeing was more important to us than anything else, so we worked hard at being parents and providing a loving family circle and home again, and fortunately it all came together. Juliette's now just finished high school and she's doing really well. Mary and I both know that once Juliette is older, twenty-one, twenty-two, once she has a career or a husband or family of her own, then we'll both go our separate ways again. But she's already warned me that she wants at least half of all we have, and although, as I've said we've both had partners outside our marriage, I don't want to do anything that might upset the apple cart."

He paused and looked at Michael who slowly nodded; taking in and understanding what Melv was saying.

"I will need to pick my moment to introduce you very carefully; especially when she discovers who your mother is and that she's a regular visitor to Antigua. She'll never believe we haven't been having an affair the whole while," he added ruefully. "And she'll do all she can to use that against me when we finally divorce. Now that makes me sound like a real coward, doesn't it?"

"I understand your position. And while I don't want you to sweep me under the carpet and act like I never existed, my intention was never to totally disrupt your life, either," Michael said. "I can see what the situation is."

Melv sighed heavily.

"Thank you," he said. "I know that both Radley and Juliette will be excited at the news they have an older brother and will want to meet you. We just have to take it a step at a time."

Michael beamed.

"You know, it's like I told Eve, that my parents will always be my parents. They've done too much for me, sacrificed too much for me for me to turn my back on that. But I'm so glad that my birth parents are you two. I mean, I can see how you had a fatal attraction all those years ago."

"Eve's a remarkable woman and as we say in these parts, she's still hot!" Melv said hoping that Michael wouldn't detect something was going on with him and Eve. Michael laughed again and then he really saw just how tired and exhausted his father was looking.

"I'm going to go and leave you in peace now. You must be shattered after the storm and all the problems and extra work that brought you. Without me turning up!" he added.

Both men stood up and hugged each other in a warm, natural embrace. Just as the door flew open and Mary walked in. She looked at her husband and the handsome young man who stood with their arms around each other and smirked.

"What? So now you're an anti-man?" she asked.

Melv put his head back and burst out laughing at his wife's comment.

"Mary, this is one of our guests, Michael Brown. Michael, my wife Mary," he said as Michael shook hands with the elegant woman in the brown and white floral sundress.

"I was just thanking Melv and his staff for the great job they did during the storm," Michael said, surprised at how easily the lie slipped off his tongue. "And for how they've got everything back to normal so quickly."

"Yes, it was some storm, wasn't it?" Mary said, shaking her head and smiling. She turned to her husband. "I was just wondering if you needed a ride home."

"Yes, I think things are under control here. I'll come home and see what the damage is there."

"It's minimal. Just a few branches gone from the coconut palm at the far end of the yard and one piece of fencing loose," Mary said.

"Well, that's something!"

"I'll be getting along, then, I won't hold you up any longer," Michael said, eager to make his escape. There was something he was unsure of about Mary; her smile didn't reach her eyes. "Thanks again, Melv. It was nice to meet you, Mary."

Mary smiled her mouth-only smile again and he left the office. He stood outside the door and sighed.

What more had I expected?

When he'd set out to face his father he'd told his parents that he had no intention of ruining anyone's life yet he had known deep down inside that he really hoped he would make his father suffer and be sorry for abandoning him. Now he knew the whole story he knew there was no way he'd want to upset Melv or cause his family any distress. Yet he felt a sense of disappointment that he couldn't be introduced to his half-brother and half-sister for the time being. Still, he gave himself a metaphorical shake, and thought about a trip to Barbados with his father to meet the dozens of family members he'd never ever dreamed existed. And suddenly he felt happy. Dozens of aunts and uncles and cousins in Barbados and dozens more in Corfu! And he still had Eve, his mother, right here with him, even if he did have to share her with the rest of the group. He decided to go back to his room and phone her with the news of how the meeting with Melv had gone.

***

Geri looked at her face in the mirror. She was starving; she'd eaten nothing all day. She shrugged as she looked at herself. Her fat lip was still obvious, in spite of the witch hazel she'd put on it. She wondered if she could disguise it with make-up. Possibly, but probably not. She didn't want to face the others for dinner. She didn't want to face them ever again. She just wanted to go home. She picked up the phone and rang the front desk to ask for room service.

"We have no room service available at the present time, due to the reduced conditions we are working under brought about by last night's storm," she was informed.

So there was nothing for it; if she wanted to eat she would have to face them. Then it occurred to her that Eve might help. She dialled Eve's room. She was sure the voicemail service was just about to engage when she heard Eve lift the receiver.

"Hallo. Eve speaking," she said groggily.

"Eve, it's me. Geri."

"Hi, Geri! Are you okay?" Eve asked after a moment.

"Yes. I took a tumble in the rain last night and it shook me up a bit, so I decided to spend the day in bed getting over it. I must have been in the shower when you rang earlier. Thanks for ringing."

She's being nice!

"You're welcome, Geri. We were all concerned because we hadn't seen you," Eve said, sincerely hoping Geri hadn't interrupted her sleep just to thank her for the phone call. "Can I do anything for you?"

"Well, I don't fancy coming to dinner tonight, so I wondered if I could have my dinner served in my room. I rang the front desk and they said it wasn't possible."

"They've been under such pressure because of the storm they're not offering room service at the moment, but I'll bring a tray to your room if you want."

Geri was wrong-footed. She thought Eve would say she'd send a waiter with the tray not that she would bring it herself. If she did, she'd see her fat lip. Still, perhaps she could tell Eve that she'd done that when she fell over in the rain.

"That's kind of you. Anything will do. Whatever's on the menu," Geri said.

"Well, we're meeting in the bar as per usual, and going into dinner about half past seven, so I'll bring it to you then. Okay?"

"That's fine. Thank you."

"Is there anything you don't like?"

"I eat most things," Geri said, thinking at that moment that she'd eat whatever was put in front of her, she was so hungry.

"Righto! I'll bring whatever I can."

"Thanks again," Geri said, and hung up.

She sighed in relief. Only an hour to go and she'd have food! And Eve had obviously believed her story. She was so glad she wouldn't have to go into the bar tonight.

***

Finally, Murray had gone back to his own room to shower and change ready for dinner. As soon as he'd closed the door behind him, Deborah had leapt off the bed and grabbed the phone and started listening to all her voicemail messages. Every single one was from Maurice, at first

313

from his mobile phone and then, when he'd seen she wasn't replying, he'd withheld his number. His tone had gone through several changes as the messages progressed.

BEEP!   **Deborah, it's me. Your phone appears to be off, or perhaps you're in a part of the hotel that has no signal. Please call me back within the next hour, while I'm alone.**

BEEP!   **Deborah, I called you about forty minutes ago, but you haven't called me back yet. Please ring me if you get this within the next twenty minutes.**

BEEP!   **Deborah, I don't know what's going on but I've left you two messages. Your phone is going straight to voicemail. Perhaps it's a poor signal where you are. Anyway, I'm going to bed now so don't ring me back tonight. Call me first thing in the morning, your time.**

BEEP!   **Deborah, what are you playing at? It's not a poor signal, is it? I've just read your text message. Why is your phone switched off? Have you met someone? Is that it? Call me!**

BEEP!   **Darling, it's me again. Sorry if I sounded a bit upset a couple of minutes ago, but I'm worried about you. It's not like you not to answer, is it? Especially when I know how much you've been looking forward to my calls. Please let me know you're safe and well. Love you lots.**

BEEP!   **Deborah, what the hell is going on? It must be dinner time in Antigua, which has been a good time to call you up to now. Or have you gone out to dinner somewhere with someone?**

BEEP!   Deborah, I don't know if you're trying to prove a point, but this has gone too far. If you're enjoying yourself I won't be cross. I want you to have a good time. But I don't like being ignored. I'm alone all day today so you can ring me back at any time.

BEEP!   Deborah stop playing games! You must have been awake at least an hour now; it's eight o'clock in Antigua. We've missed so many opportunities to talk over the last two days will all this silliness. You're behaving like a child! Just call me.

BEEP!   This is your last chance. If you don't call me back by six o'clock tonight, that's one o'clock lunch time in Antigua then that's it! You'll never hear from me again! Don't say I didn't warn you!

BEEP!   Deborah, it's six o'clock and you haven't called. Don't ring now as Sadie will be home any minute. Call me tomorrow.

BEEP!   Deborah, I never want to hear from you again. It's over and I mean it. I've made a promise to Sadie tonight that I will never have any contact with you again, and she's standing here with me now. I won't take your calls. So don't phone me, don't contact me, EVER AGAIN!

Well! She was taken aback to say the least. And she was surprised at her own reaction to the messages. She thought back to her conversation, well, argument, really, with Frances and she realised that everything Frances had said was right. It was as if she was listening to Maurice for the first time. She could hear all the manipulation and control in his voice, the change of mood, and the change of tactic, to try to get her to call, to try to interrupt her holiday. That's what it was! She'd thought he cared about her, that he was calling because he loved her. But now she could see that he was calling to disrupt her holiday, to make sure that if she was enjoying

315

herself a little too much, he was still there, still present and he could pull her away from her new friends. And to pretend in front of Sadie that *SHE'D* been the one phoning him! Well, he'd gone too far this time. She was going to call his bluff; she wanted nothing more to do with him.

What a bastard!

But then she corrected herself. She had *allowed* him to be a bastard. She had *allowed* him to control and take over her life for the last thirty years! She had been his own little Barbie Doll. She'd dressed the way he'd told her to, worn her hair the way he'd told her to, and eaten what he'd told her to. In fact, she'd only ever done whatever he'd told her to since she'd known him, She'd been taken out of the box and put on show whenever Maurice was around and then put back in the box again for nobody else to see. Frances and Samantha had both been right.

But what on earth does that say about me? I've wasted my life on a married man.

Thank God for Murray! Boy, oh boy, was she going to give them both a treat tonight. Her *Edinburgh Rock* she'd called him as she'd given it a few licks, his delight and growling ecstasy so great he didn't even tell her she'd got the wrong city. Well, Eddie Rock was in for a night to remember! She wondered for a second if it was wrong to just use Murray in this way. But she shrugged. After a lifetime of putting a man first, she was now going to look after number one. And besides, Murray wasn't complaining.

***

Jason and Huw met up in the bar. In spite of privately thinking that Huw was a prat for what he'd done, Jason wasn't prepared to ostracise him the way some of the group had. After all, up until the night before last when he'd launched his attack on Frances they'd got on fairly well. At least he was a drinking buddy.

"So, where did you end up, then?" Jason asked him.

"Right down in the south of the island. I'd got as far as English Harbour and saw all round Nelson's Dockyard," Huw lied, "and then I met this lovely family who suggested I had lunch with them and wait out the storm."

"What? Local people?"

"Yes. The guy had played professional cricket and his daughter's an up and coming tennis pro. Beautiful girl. She's invited me back down over the weekend," he said, omitting to tell Jason that she was only in her early teens.

Jason laughed, impressed and slapped Huw on the back. Huw grinned. There was no need to tell Jason the whole truth; let them all think he'd fared better than he had.

"So, what's been happening here while I've been away?"

"Well, apart from the storm, not much really. Stewart's finally got into Suzanne's knickers..."

"Now there's a thought!" Huw interrupted, managing to swig his beer and sneer at the same time.

"And Murray's been locked away with Deborah."

"Fucking hell! How did he manage that? I mean, she's getting on a bit, but she's a good-looking woman. I like Orientals, do you?"

Jason nodded his agreement.

"Oh yessss!" he said. "Where's she from? Do we know?"

"I think someone said her dad's English but her mum's from the Philippines. Now they know how to please a man, they do, the Philippine women."

They both thought about that for a moment, silently nodding in agreement, although neither of them had ever even dated a Philippine woman yet alone had one pleasuring them.

"And Frances hasn't been seen since she left dinner the night before last."

"I bet she won't get a slapped wrist from Mein Fuehrer when she gets back like I did!" Huw said in his best hard-done-by-little-boy voice.

"She's phoned Eve a couple of times, apparently, to say she was alright. Perhaps that's what you should have done."

"Oh, bollocks to that! I'm a grown up, I can go where I like and do what I like without having to phone in and ask permission!"

They saw Dawn and Donna arrive further down the bar and then how Elvis immediately engaged them in banter.

"Nothing happened to either of them then?" Huw asked.

"Not that I know of. Mind you, they don't shut up long enough for a shagging, do they? You'd have to do them with your fingers in your ears."

"Or shove your cock in their mouths. And even then I wouldn't guarantee it!" They both laughed out loud, just as Eve, Stewart, Suzanne and Michael joined Dawn and Donna.

Eve had been cheered up by Michael's phone call. It had taken her by surprise and filled her with delight.

"I just wanted you to know that I spent some time with Melv this afternoon and he's filled me in on Barbados and that side of the family. Bloody hell! I've gone from only child with three known cousins, to one of fourteen Greek cousins and twenty-two West Indians," he laughed.

"It must all be a bit overwhelming," Eve said.

"It is. It's a lot to take in, but I have to say I'm really pleased. It's cool. It's cool. And I thought I'd phone you because, well... it's a bit difficult us talking... in front of the others, I mean. Isn't it?"

"Yes, it is. Still, I'm here whenever you want and I'm hoping we can see each other when we get home." She hadn't meant to say that; it had slipped out. Now she held her breath.

"Too right! I'm not letting you slip out of my life again, Paraskevi Stefanou!"

Now, at the bar, in front of the others, they smiled at each other as they listened to the conversations going on around them and both gave an inward sigh of contentment.

Jo, Grace, Natalie and Dave joined them, and then, to everyone's delight, Ursula put in an appearance.

"What's the latest on Deano?" Jo asked Eve.

"Oh, bloody hell!" Eve put her hand to her head. "I was going to ring this afternoon." She didn't want to have to explain why she'd been so tired, let them assume it was because the storm had kept her awake. "Officially, he's not mine anymore," she said, making inverted commas around *mine* as she spoke. "Someone from the Consulate Office will have gone to see him and the insurer's rep will take care of him, but I'd like to see him and check he's doing alright and knows we haven't forgotten him."

"Perhaps we could all go in on Sunday and say goodbye," Natalie suggested.

"Yeh! That's a good idea!" Dave said. "I'd like t'keep in touch wiv 'im. 'E's a good bloke."

"Well, I'd have to run that by the hospital staff," Eve said, knowing that Rachel would doubtless be at the hospital on Sunday and neither she nor Deano would appreciate a herd of singles turning up. "I'll see what they say," she added, already having made up her mind to say they wouldn't agree to it.

"Trevor!" Natalie screeched his name and ran and put her arms around him as he appeared in the bar; looking good in his Bermuda shorts, lime green polo shirt and smart sandals. "You're a sight for sore eyes! We thought something had happened to you."

Trevor smiled and blushed as Natalie pulled him down the bar to where the others were standing, watching him and welcoming him with warm smiles.

"You alrigh', mate?" Dave said. "Wan' a Wadiddly?"

"Yes, I'm fine, thank you, and a beer would be wonderful, thanks, Dave."

"Elvis! One more Wadiddly, please!" Dave shouted his order down the bar.

Eve smiled at Trevor, without saying anything. It was obvious that he was fine and she was sure he'd tell them what had happened in his own time. Elvis slid the beer down the bar and Dave caught it and shoved it into Trevor's hand.

"There yer go! Cheers!" he said.

"Cheers!" Trevor said, sipping the beer.

"So, what happened to you then? Has your mum died?" Suzanne asked as everyone except Stewart groaned at her lack of sensitivity. Stewart saw it as her naive innocence.

"No, Mum's fine. It was... well... the phone call was from my daughter."

"You don't have to tell us, Trevor, not if it's personal," Jo said, glaring at Suzanne.

"No. I don't mind you all knowing; it's good news really. You see, I've been somewhat estranged from her for a while now. Well, since she came out, in fact." He said the words *came out* as if he were trying out a phrase in a foreign language. "I'm what you might call a traditional kind of man, I suppose, and it's been hard for me to accept her chosen lifestyle. I mean, I like her partner, Sonia, I think she's a nice woman. And she doesn't sort of go in for the dungarees and very short hair and neither does Rose. Not... er... not that it would matter if they did, of course. Anyway, things were always awkward between us. She and Sonia came to stay with me and I felt uncomfortable having them share a bed so I'd put Rose in her old bedroom and Sonia in the guest room. Well, Rose was annoyed. She said if it had been my son and his wife visiting I'd have put them in together, and of course she was right. And she said she'd also noticed that I seemed to have a problem introducing them to people. So they left and Rose said that I'd always be welcome at their house because I was her father, but that she'd never visit me again. Three months later she sent me the photos of her civil partnership ceremony with Sonia. She said that she hadn't felt she could invite me because of my obvious feelings of animosity towards her and Rose and their lifestyle. But yesterday she'd been on the internet and seen that the storm had hit Antigua and she knew from my son that I was here. She said she'd been trying to reach me for hours. She rang Travel Together and was told we were all safe, but she'd wanted to hear my voice; to know that I really was safe and sound. Isn't that nice?" he looked around the group, beaming, waiting for their approval.

"Oh, that's lovely!" Natalie said, and Jo leaned over and gave him a hug.

"But what happened to you then? You weren't on the phone all that time, were you?" Suzanne asked.

"No. Once I'd spoken to her I realised what a stupid old fuddy duddy I've become. How I was risking losing my daughter for ever because of my own narrow, bigoted views. So I went off on my own for a long, long walk during which I gave myself a proper telling-off. And I sat on the sand and watched the sea coming and going and just felt at peace with myself for the first time in a number of years!"

"Wow! A real spiritual experience!" Natalie said.

"Sort of," Trevor replied, smiling round at everyone secretly pleased that they'd missed him.

"So, are we all here? We're starving!" Donna said.

"Are Murray and Deborah joining us?" Eve asked.

Nobody knew.

"Geri's not here, either," Stewart said.

"No. She's not coming to dinner. She's having it in her room. She had a fall and doesn't want to come out," she added by means of an explanation.

"Oh, more attention seeking I suppose!" Grace said, as they all made their way towards their tables while Eve went to get a tray to take Geri's meal to her just as Deborah and Murray scuttled up to the tables together, with Frances close behind.

"Frances!" everyone chorused.

"Alright! Don't make a fuss! I'm back in the fold," she said, taking a seat between Trevor and Dave, hoping she'd managed to wash the smell of marijuana out of her hair and from her skin. It seemed to cling to everything. When he'd realised she meant it when she said she had to get back to the hotel, Neville had walked her back to the main road and flagged down a car belonging to someone he knew.

"You give him forty EC and he'll take you to Mango Tree, okay?" he'd said. "I'll call you tomorrow. I'm not sure if I'm working yet or not. When you leaving?"

"Monday," she told him, somewhat miffed as this was the third time she'd told him. He'd seemed surprised when she said she was going, but Frances needed a break from hot-sex for a short while at least. She was a flesh and blood woman, true, but flesh and blood women couldn't exist on joints and bits of cold chicken. She needed a square meal. She wanted a hot shower. And she wanted a change of clothes, or rather; she wanted to put clothes on. Being completely naked for two whole days was beginning to lose its appeal. She needed a few hours' break and then the orgasm-fest could begin again. She felt a little ripple in her pussy as she thought about it and giggled to herself.

320

She wondered how Martin had spent the last two days.

"You coming, mate?" Jason asked Huw as he got off the bar stool at seeing the others move towards the dining room.

"Yes, I'll come. Just don't let any of them start, that's all, or they'll get a right mouthful from me," he warned.

As it was, he was disappointed. Nobody paid him the slightest attention.

***

Eve had almost dropped the tray in surprise when she saw Geri. Her puffy eyes showed she'd obviously been crying and her top lip looked as if it was swollen, too, with a faint bruise showing through.

"So, what happened to you?" Eve asked, placing the tray on the dressing table.

"Oh, I slipped on the wet path when we were all being led back to our rooms. I must have gone over on my ankle, or something."

"But your face! How did you cut your lip? It is cut, isn't it?"

"I don't really know. I think I must have put my teeth through it as I fell."

Both women looked at each other knowing that that was highly unlikely. Eve decided not to pursue it. Whatever trouble Geri had got herself into she was probably better not knowing unless Geri wanted her help.

"Well, enjoy your dinner. Hopefully you'll feel better by breakfast time and we'll see you then."

"Yes, hopefully you will. Thank you for bringing my tray," she said as she showed Eve out. She closed the door and leaned against it. She could do with a drink, she should have asked Eve to bring her one. She thought about going quickly to the bar, but decided against it. Elvis might be there and she didn't want to see him. She crossed the room and sat on the bed, the thoughts of the previous evening racing through her mind again, going round and round like washing on a never-ending cycle. She clenched her whole body as she re-lived every moment of what had happened, and within minutes she collapsed across the bed, sobbing again.

***

Eve's surprise at seeing Geri was soon replaced by a deep feeling of disappointment. Michael had mentioned that Melv had gone home. She kept telling herself that having sex with him had been a mistake and he obviously felt the same because he'd made no attempt to contact her and she hadn't seen him since mid-morning. And now he'd gone off and even though her sensible side told her that he had to be absolutely shattered after the storm, she was pissed off with him.

He could have phoned me today. He could have come and looked for me.

Then she was angry for herself for being so needy. Why couldn't she just walk away the way he had? For days she hadn't wanted anything to do with him so why was it a big deal that he didn't want her now? Why was she playing games? Irritated and angry with herself, she shook her head and concentrated on dinner.

"What we all doing tonight?" Natalie asked.

"Why? What do you fancy doing?" Michael asked her.

"I'm open to suggestion!"

"Why don't we play pool?" Jason suggested. "Anyone up for it?"

Most of the group nodded their agreement.

"We could have the women against the men," Trevor said.

"Nah! We'd beat em too easy!" Dave said.

"You might be sorry you said that, Dave," Jo said. "Some of us might be really good."

"Yeah! An' pigs migh' fly!" he said, laughing.

"Well, who's playing?" Jason asked, "Hands up!"

Trevor, Michael, Huw, Dave and Stewart all put their hands up.

"You not playing?" he asked Murray.

"I'm not sure," he said, obviously waiting to see what Deborah was doing.

"Okay, well that's six men. How many of the girls want to play?"

Natalie, Grace, Jo, Donna, Dawn, Suzanne and Deborah put their hands up.

"So, seven of you. Well, that's okay then. We'll play six of us against seven of you."

"I'll play, too!" Murray said, seeing that Deborah was playing.

"Why don't we get a tournament going?" Eve suggested.

"Good idea!" Jason said. "We can play in pairs, a man and a woman in each team. Unless you want to play, too, Frances?"

"No thanks. I'm a bit tired. I'm going to have a couple of drinks and listen to the band and then I'm going to bed."

"Right! Come on, then!" Eve said, anxious to be doing something to take her mind off Melv; scared she might be tempted to phone or text him. "Let's go and grab a table before someone else does!"

***

Across the island in Crosbies, Melv was dead to the world. Eve could have spent the whole night ringing and texting, he'd never have heard her. Having slept for two hours in the previous forty-eight, he was now in a deep, impenetrable sleep, where he was dreaming of Michael and Eve waving to him from on board a motor boat that was pulling away from a beach and leaving him behind.

***

And in Mount St John's Medical Centre Deano couldn't sleep. By tomorrow afternoon Rachel would be here. And that didn't bear thinking about.

***

DAY NINE

"I'm so excited!"

Suzanne clapped her hands together as she sat at breakfast. She looked out at the scene before her and couldn't believe the difference from this time yesterday. The sun was shining; the sea was calm; the resort was all cleaned up and back to normal. And today, she was going on a helicopter ride for the first time in her life.

"I can't wait for three o'clock."

"You have to be ready at two fifteen, don't forget," Eve said.

"Oh, yes, I know! But the actual take off is at three, isn't it?"

"Yes it is! And it's a lovely day for flying. You'll have such a great time!"

"Are you okay, Eve?" Suzanne asked her, looking at the large sunglasses Eve was wearing and noticing her general air of tiredness. "You look a bit tired, not like your usual self."

"I'm fine. Just didn't sleep very well and I think I might have a touch of hay fever this morning," she said. "And I think the excitement of the pool competition kept me awake," she added quickly, eager to change the subject.

"Oh yes! Fancy me and Stewart coming second!"

"You did really well," Eve said, genuinely pleased at the outcome. "At one point I thought you were going to beat Dave and Jo."

"I got your love letter," Stewart said to Eve as he joined them; referring to the departure information she'd sent everyone. He kissed Suzanne on the top of the head as he did so. "Are you absolutely sure we've got to leave on Monday? Nothing you can do to give us a couple of extra days?"

"I'm afraid not! You'll just have to make the most of the time left."

"Oh I intend to!" he said.

Eve excused herself and stood up, taking her coffee cup and her bag with her and headed over to the terrace to do her usual morning stint; her *surgery*, although she doubted anyone would have any problems or things they wanted to discuss today. Everyone would be making the most of the beautiful weather again, although some had said they'd join her on a trip into St John's as it was going to be the only chance they had now of going. She saw the T2G tables slowly fill up as the other group members came down to breakfast. Geri hadn't appeared yet, but Eve was sure she was fit and well enough to come down to breakfast and wouldn't need her to take it up to her room. She slowly sipped her coffee and observed the group from a distance. If she were a betting woman she'd put money on their subject of conversation and who it was that would be raising the objections.

And she was right.

"I don't see why we have to tip, do you?" Huw was asking the table in general.

"No I don't," Murray agreed with him. "The holiday's expensive enough without having twenty-five pounds added tae it."

Natalie, Grace and Michael all exchanged a look.

"Yes, that's what I object to, being told how much you have to give," Huw said, through a mouthful of bacon sandwich. "It should be left up to us entirely to see if we want to give or not."

"Can you read?" Natalie asked him.

He looked up at her with a surly expression on his face, while still chewing.

"Of course I can fucking read. What you asking me that for?"

"Well, if you can *fucking read*, you'll have seen that in Eve's letter it says that twenty-five pounds is only the *suggested* amount. So that means you can put in however much you like."

"Twenty-five pounds is only just over two pounds a day," Suzanne said. "That's nothing, is it? I mean, when we go to Majorca we tip every time we have a round of drinks or something to eat, and that must come to much more than that."

"And a lot of people work here," Stewart said, "It has to go a long way."

"Well, I'm not tipping on principle," Huw said.

"What principle's that, then?" Grace asked.

"Well, on the principle that I don't believe in tipping."

"What? You don't think there's one boy or girl in this hotel worth two pounds a day?" she asked, raising her voice, astounded at his attitude.

"I don't think the service has been all that good. We've had to ask them to fill up the wine at dinner..."

325

"Oh shut up! That's not an excuse for not giving them a tip, just because you had to ask to have your glass filled up once or twice. Perhaps you shouldn't have drunk it so bloody quickly! It's not the staff's fault if you knock it back so fast they can't keep up with you," Natalie spat at him, her disgust evident for all to see.

"And how can you say the service hasn't been good? The staff have been brilliant!" Grace said.

"Look how hard everyone worked during and after the storm to look after us!" Natalie continued, feeling like she could punch Huw.

"That's their job!" Huw retorted. "I work hard and nobody tips me!"

"Oh shut up! You're a bloody teacher! The service industry relies on tipping. People like these get low wages."

"Well, then, the hotel should pay them more. If we keep on tipping it'll only encourage them not to put wages up."

"But if wages go up, the prices of the holidays will go up! Can't you see that?" Natalie was indignant. "And what are you talking about Murray?" she turned on him, even though he'd, wisely, kept quiet since he'd seen how the group had rounded on Huw. "You're a taxi driver. You practically demand a tip from your passengers!"

"I dinnae do that!" he said, going red-faced.

"But you expect people to tip you," Grace said. "So what's different about here?"

"I dinnae tell people how much to tip."

"Well then, put in however much you like, but put *something* in the envelope," Deborah said, giving him a stern look.

"And anyway, how do we know the staff get it?" Huw said, unwilling to let it drop.

"What are you suggesting?" Michael butted in, glaring at him, "That Eve keeps it?"

"No! I'm not suggesting anything. I'm not saying she keeps it. I'm just saying that once she hands it over it could go anywhere."

"God! You're such a nasty cynic!" Grace said. "The staff here are smashing and they've all bent over backwards for us as a group. I mean, look! We've had great service. Nobody else has had their tables reserved; they've all had to queue up every time for a table for breakfast or dinner. We just come and sit down. Nothing's too much trouble for them. We've had them running up and down fetching ice-creams, topping up the wine, bringing drinks from the bar..."

"Yeah! An' look when we was in my room durin' the storm! They give us them big bottles of drinks, the rum punches an' beers an' that. They didn't av to!" Dave said, joining in.

"Well they're getting fuck all from me!" Huw said, standing up and marching away from them.

"Tight arse!" Natalie called after him. "Uurrggghhh! I hate mean people! You know the other afternoon I said a man had to be clean, well I'd rather he was dirty than tight-fisted!"

Deborah turned to Murray and gave him a steely stare, before slowly wiping her mouth with her napkin.

"You might like to reconsider your take on tipping the staff," she said to him as he blushed again. "Because, like Natalie, I find meanness to be the worst of human traits."

"Oh, aye!" he said, standing up. "Excuse me, I'll go and get some sun loungers for us." And then he hurried away quickly as the rest of the group burst out laughing.

"You've got him under the thumb!" Michael said to her, grinning.

"He's all talk. You know, he'll bluff and bluster his way with something, but he's not malicious like Huw is."

"You're right there," Grace said, "there's just something about Huw that I can't stand!"

"Well, when I first met Murray I couldn't stand him, could I, Frances?" she said, drawing Frances into the conversation.

"No, you couldn't, well, neither of us could. He was so negative. Every time he opened his mouth it was to moan about something; everything about the resort, the holiday, and the people was wrong," Frances said.

"Yes, but he's mellowed a bit."

"Probably because you've given him a bit of TLC," Michael said, making Deborah laugh.

"But Huw's a different type. I'm sorry to say it but I think he's nasty," Deborah said.

"I couldn't agree more!" Grace said. "Look at all the trouble he's caused. He's wanted outsiders to join the group, he's sulked, he's gone off in the storm without saying where he was going and now he decides at the end of the holiday that he's a Communist!"

"Unfortunately, he's quite typical of a lot of male teachers, isn't he Donna?" Dawn called across from the adjoining table. "Some of them are more childish than the kids! Ohh! Sorry, Jason, I didn't mean you!" she added quickly.

"No worries!" Jason said. "I'm sorry that I've got to agree with most of what you've all said. He's alright when you're on your own having a drink with him, but he's got a strange attitude. He won't be told about anything."

"You mean he's a man!" Natalie said, to much shouting and derision from the men.

At that moment Eve reappeared at the table, having had her coffee in peace.

"Oh, just the person!" Grace said. "I wanted to ask you how I go about getting an upgrade on the way back."

"You'll have to ask the staff who come to the resort to do the check-in. They'll know the passenger load and whether there are any places available in *Select*."

"I might upgrade, too," Deborah said. "It depends how much it costs. I had twin toddlers sitting behind me on the way over, whose parents thought the whole aircraft was being entertained by bloody Tilly and Lola's antics! If the wheels on the bus had gone round one more bloody time I'd have opened the rear door and jumped out!"

Grace screeched out laughing, while nodding her head in agreement.

"You're so right! The day someone starts up an adults-only airline they'll make a fortune."

"Isn't that Business Class?" asked Trevor.

"It used to be," Grace retorted, "but you can't even be certain that Business is a child-free zone nowadays."

"Well, as I say, ask the staff at check in. It usually costs about a hundred and ninety-nine pounds," Eve said. "Now, I'm doing a shortened surgery today, because I'm going into St John's with those who want to do a bit of shopping and have a look around. Who's coming?"

Natalie, Grace, Trevor, Suzanne, Stewart, Michael and Dave all said they would.

"Okay, meet me in reception at half past nine; that's in ten minutes time," Eve said, consulting her watch. "We need to be back in time to give those going on the helicopter ride time to have some lunch before they go off."

"You not going?" Deborah asked Frances.

"No. I've seen a bit of St John's and to be honest I don't want to trail round the shops. I'd rather stay here and get some more sun."

"Me too. Are you going by the Spa Pool?"

"Probably."

328

"Well, join us then. Please."

"Okay, but I don't want to be intruding," Frances said with a smile.

"You won't be! It'll be nice to have a catch up. I want to hear all about your new man," she said pausing for a moment. Then she added, "And I want to apologise for our fall out. I've had a series of texts from Maurice that you wouldn't believe!"

"I bet I would!" Frances said as they both laughed.

"You not coming into town, Jason?" Eve asked.

"Not me! I'm going to play water volleyball at eleven. I've already told Huw to put my name down."

"And we've already been in," Donna said. "We've done all our shopping, haven't we, Dawn?"

Dawn nodded in agreement.

Eve went back to her room to drop her bag and clean her teeth. She thought she'd let Ursula know they were going in case she wanted to join them.

"Oh yes please! I was going to go in by myself at some time today. Going in with the group will be more fun!" she said.

Then Eve thought about Geri, who still hadn't put in an appearance when Eve had left the dining-room. She dialled her room and Geri picked up.

"Morning! It's Eve here. I was just wondering if you wanted to join us, we're going into St John's for a couple of hours."

"What time are you leaving?"

"In five minutes."

"Well, that's not much notice, is it?"

Eve found herself mentally counting to ten. Geri was really pushing a button!

"No. Sorry, it isn't. But I was looking out for you at breakfast to tell you."

"Well, who's going?"

"Stewart, Suzanne, Dave, Michael, Natalie, Trevor, Grace and Ursula."

Geri hesitated for a moment.

"I'll come!" she said. "I'll be down as fast as I can!"

***

Saturday is the busiest day of the week in St John's. It's not only market day, but it's the day that Antiguans – freed from the restraints of Monday to Friday working – go out and shop. A full bus was pulling away as they got to the stop outside the resort, but within a minute an empty one had pulled up. Eve was asked for the sixth time in as many minutes how much the bus fare was as they clambered on board.

"Three dollars twenty-five if you're paying in EC, or give him two US and you'll get some change," she said, wondering why nobody ever listened.

The bus took off at lightning speed with the radio blaring out a local evangelical station. About a quarter of a mile along the road it screeched to a halt to let an immaculately-dressed woman in her mid-twenties with a three-year-old child and a young baby get on.

"Open the door f' she!" the driver called out to Dave, who was sitting by the door.

"Oh! Sorry!" Dave said, sliding the door open and finding the baby thrust into his arms, while the young mother agilely got on board and sat the other child on a seat between her and Michael.

"Good day!" she said to everyone and they all chorused "Good day!" back. She then turned to Dave to take her baby back. "Thank you," she said as she took him.

"You're welcome," Dave said, blushing.

"That suited you, Dave!" Stewart called out from the back seat, where he was sitting hand-in-hand with Suzanne. "There's still time for you to be a hands-on daddy!"

"Wha'eva!" Dave called back, laughing.

"Why didn't Jo want to come?" Natalie asked Grace, who was sitting next to her. "I thought she said she wanted to have a look round when we were talking about it the other day."

"I'm not sure. She just said this morning that she wanted to spend time on the beach as it's such a nice morning."

"Have you got anything special to buy?" Trevor asked Geri, feeling he should have some kind of conversation with her as they were sitting together.

"Not really. I just want to get out of the resort for a bit. I might get a couple of small souvenirs, you know, t-shirts or something like that. How about you?"

"I want to get something to take back to the office. We always do when one of us has been away. Something to share out, like boiled sweets or toffees."

Boiled sweets! I'm glad I don't work with you!

"I want to take some photos," Ursula said to Trevor from his other side.

"I thought as much," Trevor said, eyeing the huge black Canon with its long lens hanging from her neck. "That must weigh something, mustn't it?"

"Yes, it does drag my neck forward a bit," she said, "But it takes such wonderful photos I can't bring myself to trade it in for one of these smaller digital ones."

"You're not under cover for some down-market tabloid, are you?" Trevor asked her. She laughed and shook her head. Geri relaxed back into her seat. Nobody had questioned her fat lip, which could be passed off as a sun-blister or a mosquito bite, so she felt more comfortable. And behind her sunglasses, her eyes had almost entirely gone back to their normal size, shape and colour.

The bus, which was now full of the sounds of a church choir singing their hearts out, suddenly lurched to a halt and then started to reverse.

"Oi! Oi! We're going the wrong way!" Dave said.

"People coming down the road," the lady with the baby and the child said to him. And then they all realised that the driver had seen two young lads who were at least two hundred yards up a side road, yet he had known they wanted the bus. He reversed to the junction with the road and waited for them.

"Just like at home!" Natalie said. "NOT!"

The boys boarded, saying their "Good day" as they did so and the bus set off a high speed again. They whizzed through villages, along a winding road that went up and down hill, and in no time at all they pulled into the West Bus Station.

"This is where you get the bus back should we get separated and you not come back with me," Eve said as they all got off. "Now, I'm going to do a slow walk from here to Heritage Quay, pointing out things of interest on the way. I know someone wants an ATM and someone else wants a pharmacy..."

"That ain't you, is it Stew? You ain't run outta condoms already, 'ave ya?" Dave asked, interrupting. Stewart stuck two fingers up at him.

"And if there's anything else you want, please ask, and keep a tight hold on your belongings," Eve continued as they set off up Market Street. She walked them at a slow pace so they could take in their bearings and look around them. They soon came to the huge head and shoulders statue of VC Bird, the first Premier and Prime Minister of Antigua and Barbuda, which Eve pointed out to them.

"This is a statue of Vere Cornwall Bird, Antigua's first Prime Minister, you know, the guy the airport's named after," she said. "This statue was a gift from the people of Cuba. So if

331

you get lost, just look for the statue or ask someone and then you know the bus station is just a few yards past it."

Ursula went into a photo-taking frenzy, snapping from every angle. Eve waited for her to finish.

"We'll never be home in time for lunch if she's going to take twenty photos of everything," Geri grumbled.

"We'll give her a minute or two," Eve said, biting her tongue about the length of time Geri had kept the whole group waiting at Shirley Heights, only not to turn up at all. Dave, Natalie and Michael also took photos on their mobile phones and Suzanne delved into the large beach bag she was carrying and pulled out her camera, asking Grace to take a photo of her and Stewart in front of the monument. When they'd all finished they continued their walk up Market Street, looking at the wares on the stalls, mainly fruit, CDs and DVDs, the clothes being at the beginning before the bus station. When they reached the junction with Redcliffe Street they turned left and Eve found a spot of shade to talk to them again.

"If you want to see the museum or the cathedral continue up Market Street," she said. "The museum's a small building on your left and just beyond that right at the top of Market Street, if you turn right at the T-junction, you'll see the Cathedral. It's a magnificent building. You can't go inside at the moment as it's being restored but you might like to take some photos from the outside. And some of the headstones around it are particularly interesting."

She turned and led them down Redcliff Street until she came to the corner with Thames Street and stopped again. This time she pointed out the shops in Redcliffe Quay over on the left hand side, telling the group that the area had once been warehouses which had been restored externally and modernised internally and now housed boutiques, jewellers, craft shops, restaurants, a wine bar and an ice-cream parlour. They then made their way along Thames St, passed several nice clothes stores, as Eve showed them the Vendors' Mall, where they could buy their t-shirts and fridge magnets; the pharmacy and just beyond it in St Mary's Street, to the right, Hemingway's Restaurant, which was a great place to have a lime daiquiri and a lobster lunch.

"Shame we've got to be back for the helicopter!" Stewart said.

"We could always have early lunch," Suzanne suggested. "As long as we're ready for quarter past two."

"I'd quite fancy a lime daiquiri!" Grace said, "Although perhaps not for an hour or so!"

They stopped just inside Heritage Quay and reassuring the waiting taxi-drivers that they didn't want a tour of the island, Eve pointed out the ATM machine and the various high-class jewellers, duty-free shops, boutiques and art shops.

"Something for everyone!" she said. "So, I'm going to buy two things then I'm going to be sitting in the bar over there," she said, pointing at the B'Hive, "and I'll be there until quarter past twelve. It's half past ten now. If you're going to come back with me, then meet me there by twelve fifteen, if not I'll assume you're making your own way back. And those of you going on the helicopter ride don't forget you have to be ready for quarter past two."

With cries of "Thanks, Eve!" and "Where do you want to go first?" the group split up. Eve went to buy a copy of the Daily Observer and to get a carton of cigarettes from the Duty Free shop for her neighbour Ruth, who always watered her garden while she was away and generally kept an eye on things for her. Ruth was a chain-smoker and although Eve had never smoked herself, she accepted Ruth's right to. And at least by buying her cigarettes she was saving Ruth some money. Once she'd done that she took a seat on the B'Hive terrace , ordered a Diet Coke and settled down to read the paper in peace for, she hoped, at least half an hour!

**

"So how many orgasms did you have then?"

"To be honest, I lost count. Probably more than I've had in the rest of my life, though!"

Frances and Deborah were on adjacent sun loungers next to the Spa pool. Feeling left-out and unwanted, Murray had gone off to play pool volleyball for half an hour, leaving the two women to catch up on the other's events of the last few days. Deborah was open-mouthed and goggle-eyed at Frances' stories of her three day love-in with Neville.

"So which one was he?"

"The one that looked like that boxer. What's his name?"

"You're asking me? I haven't a clue. Is he the one with the braids?"

"Yes, that's him. The one I danced with."

"Bloody hell!" Deborah giggled at the thought of Frances having an affair with a young guy with a body to die for who was only just a bit older than her son. "And are you seeing him again? Before we leave?"

"Oh, yes! I just needed a bit of a rest. There's only so much action a pussy can take, after all."

Deborah screamed with laughter.

"Pussy!"

"I know. I can't stop saying it now. Still, it trips off the tongue easier than vagina. From now on, I'll never think of it as anything else. But to answer your question, I'm supposed to be seeing him again tonight. He's calling me when he finishes work."

"Well! Who would have thought it? I mean, no offence, but you came across as so straight-laced."

"Not straight-laced, just indignant. When all's said and done, I really do believe that an affair is nasty. It's betrayal. I'm not having another go at you! But I'd been deeply hurt by a woman who'd had an affair with my husband. Our lives together ended because of it and it upset me to listen to you slagging off Maurice's wife when she's the innocent party when all's said and done. Neville and I aren't hurting anyone; we're both free agents. And anyway, this is just a little holiday fling, you know, my mid-life crisis! It's the female equivalent of a man going to the gym, getting a toupee and buying a sports car."

Deborah paused to take in what Frances had said. She found herself nodding her head in agreement.

"You're right. And, do you know what? Maurice turned out to be a right bastard. When I decided to turn my phone off so that I could enjoy my holiday you should have heard the messages he sent me! He ended up by saying that his wife was with him and he was telling me for one last time to leave him alone!"

"What? He tried to pretend that you were ringing him?"

"Yes. Pathetic, isn't it?"

"And what about you and Murray, then?" Frances asked, as she replenished the suntan cream on her arms and across her chest. "Will you see each other when you get home or is it just a little holiday romance, too?"

"Oh, it's just a holiday romance! I mean, I quite like him. Obviously, I couldn't have got involved with someone I didn't like, but I don't see him as a boyfriend. He's been quite a laugh, really, someone to show me that there are more men than Maurice in the world, but I wouldn't want to go out with him."

"And how does he feel about that?"

"He's a bit keen for us to carry on seeing each other in London; you now, he keeps on dropping hints. But I've no intention of doing that."

"Why not?"

"I just haven't. I don't know why not. But I don't want to see him once we've left here. I'll just make sure I let him down gently. What happens in Antigua stays in Antigua!"

"Do you think you'll get back with Maurice, then?"

"No way! Not after the way he's treated me. And besides, he'll never be able to get away to see me ever again. No, I've got to put all my energy into finding a job. I have to find a way to earn a living and to pay the rent."

"What will you do?"

"Well, I've done a floristry course and aromatherapy. Perhaps I'll update my skills and look round for something. I'll survive! Do you want a drink?" she asked as she spied Murray making his way back towards them.

"Oh yes! It's not too early for a rum punch, is it?"

"Who cares if it is? Murray! Bring two rum punches with you, please!"

***

Geri was walking slowly back along Market Street, having been to see the Cathedral. Ursula had gone with her, but they'd split up as she wanted to wander around the shops whereas Ursula wanted to take some more photos of it from the other side. She turned into a side street heading back towards Heritage Quay, trying to walk in the shade as she'd forgotten to put on a sunhat or to rub in any suntan cream. She'd bought a t-shirt from a shop in Long Street, her only purchase so far, and now she stopped to look in a dress shop, where a couple of beautiful bright dresses had caught her eye. As she did, Natalie and Grace came out.

"Hello!" Natalie said. "Been buying?"

"Oh, just a t-shirt."

"They've got some beautiful dresses in there. Look!"

She opened up a pink and white striped plastic bag and pulled out a pale lime green sun dress and held it up for Geri to see.

"It's gorgeous!" Geri enthused. "Can I ask how much it was?"

"Twenty-five US. That's about eighteen pounds. Nothing, is it?"

"And I've got one in mauve," Grace said. "I know that's a bit Donna and Dawn, but we live at opposite sides of the country when we get home so there's not much chance of us both turning up at the same do wearing the same dress."

"I'm actually looking for something for my daughter," Geri said. "She's nearly seventeen and she's going to Turkey in a few weeks' time. A pretty sundress would be a nice present, wouldn't it?"

"Yes! We'll come back in with you," Natalie offered and the three of them went into the shop. Natalie and Grace showed Geri the racks of summer dresses all at twenty-five US dollars. In the end, Geri settled for a very light pink maxi dress with a shimmer to it for her daughter.

"That's what they're all calling *nude*. It's the latest colour. The Middletons wear it all the time. Very this year!" Natalie said as they left the shop and made their way back towards St Mary's Street and Heritage Quay. But when they got to Hemingway's Natalie and Grace stopped.

"We're meeting the others here for a lime daiquiri. You going to join us?" Grace asked her, smiling.

"Yes, I'd like to," Geri said, surprising herself. And the three of them went up the stairs to find a table to wait for Suzanne, Stewart, Trevor and Dave.

"Three lime daiquiris, please!" Grace said to the waitress, who'd showed them to a table overlooking the street.

"Coming right up!" she said and sashayed off to get them.

"So, have you just got the one daughter?" Natalie asked Geri as they waited for their drinks.

"Yes. One daughter and one son. He'll be fourteen in September. I've got him a t-shirt."

"And are they home alone while you're gadding about the Caribbean?"

"No, they've gone over to their dad's. It's only half an hour from me... us... so it's easy for them to get to school and college from there."

"So your divorce was all amicable then, was it?" Natalie asked.

Geri nodded her head. She felt obliged to answer but before she could she was relieved to see the others all arrive at the top of the stairs.

"Over here!" Natalie called to them, waving her arms around and nearly knocking the lime daiquiris off the tray that the waitress was carrying. "Oops! Sorry!" she said, laughing her head off.

The four newcomers sat down and showed the others what they'd bought, which was mainly fridge magnets (Trevor, Dave and Suzanne), a couple of local CDs (Stewart), a silver bracelet (Stewart for Suzanne), a jade and silver pendant (Trevor for his daughter) and some duty free (everyone).

"Wew, it mus' be serious. Buyin' er jewellery," Dave observed to Stewart.

"Stop embarrassing us! I can spend my money on Suzanne if I want to, can't I?"

"Course you can! I fink you make a lovely couple," he added, pretending to wipe his eyes on a napkin.

"Are we going to have lunch here, or are we going back?" Suzanne asked eager to change the subject away from her and Stewart.

"What's the time?" Natalie asked Trevor.

"Half past eleven," he said, looking at his watch.

"It's a bit early, isn't it?" Grace said. "Shall we just have a drink and go back to the Mango Tree for lunch?"

Everyone agreed with her and they settled back in their chairs to sip their drinks and watch the world go by in the street below them. And for the first time in the whole holiday Geri felt settled; quiet and at peace with herself, she was part of the group, with nothing to prove.

**

"This bleedin' drive gets longer every time I walk dahn it," Dave complained as the group plodded along in the heat towards the main hotel entrance.

"Yes, it does," Suzanne agreed with him as she huffed and puffed with sweat running down her face and most of her body. "I'm going to have a nice shower and change before my helicopter ride. Lunch first, though, I think."

"Proper lunch or snack?" Natalie asked them.

"Proper lunch!" was the reply from everyone and within ten minutes they were all sitting together eating and drinking. As they did Michael's mobile rang. He fished it out of his pocket and looked at the screen.

"Excuse me, everyone," he said, standing up and moving away from the table.

"Oi! Oi! He got anuvva bird, Nat?" Dave asked, knowing it would wind her up.

"Why are you asking me? I'm sure Michael's got lots of birds, as you so nicely refer to us."

Dave chuckled and bit into his pork chop. There was nothing he liked more than stirring, but he never did it maliciously. It was always just a bit of fun as far as he was concerned. Elvis appeared at the table with a tray of beers. He started to serve them when Geri jumped up without looking at him and quickly walked away towards the washrooms. Eve watched closely and she saw that Elvis had registered Geri's departure. Something had gone on the other night, she was sure of it, not just Geri's cut lip and tearful face but the way she'd just reacted. But with Elvis? He didn't seem the type to upset a woman. But what was the type? And then again, perhaps he hadn't. Perhaps Geri had been telling the truth after all and she'd simply fallen over. She was tempted to ask her, but then reprimanded herself. It was none of her business and besides, Geri was a grown woman and she seemed to have enjoyed herself this morning. She reminded herself again of the old Greek saying of her grandmother; *if you don't want a terrible stench don't stir up shit.* She couldn't argue with that!

Michael came back to the table with a huge grin on his face. Dave looked at him and also grinned.

"Mind your own business!" Natalie admonished him before he could open his mouth, though. Michael burst out laughing.

"It's alright, Nat. I'm going to tell everyone."

Eve went pale. The colour drained from her face like water from an upturned bottle. She didn't want everyone to know. How dare he tell everyone without consulting with her?

"Michael..." she started to protest.

"It's okay, Eve," he interrupted. "I want to tell them what's been going on; about my father."

Everyone's curiosity was aroused by this time and they'd all stopped eating. Geri had arrived back at the table and she slipped into her seat unnoticed as all eyes were on Michael. And Eve suddenly realised to her great relief that the way he'd emphasised the word *father* meant he was only going to tell the group half the story. He cleared his throat.

"Well, one of the reasons I came on this holiday, the main reason, actually, was because I found out a few years back that I had been adopted as a baby. My parents, the ones that I've always called Mum and Dad and the ones that brought me up, had adopted me when I was just a few days old. I love them to bits and I'll always love them because they loved me unconditionally and took good care of me and they're two amazing people who couldn't have done more. But, I had this curiosity to find out who my birth parents were and my adoptive parents discussed it with me and agreed that they'd give me their support in trying to track them down. Anyway, to cut a very long story short, I finally discovered that my father was from Barbados, but that he was now living in Antigua and working at this hotel. Coming here with Travel Together meant that I could come here as part of a group and suss him out at the same time." He paused to take a sip of his drink. Nine pairs of eyes bore into his face.

"So that's why you was questionin' me abaht not knowin' your parents an' being adopted!" Dave exclaimed, the penny dropping.

"Yes. You've dealt with it really well, Dave, and I admire you a lot for that, but for me it was different. I needed to know who my parents were. Anyway, the other day I finally worked

338

up the courage and confronted him and he was totally shocked. He didn't know I existed until that moment because my birth mum had never told him. But he's come round and we're getting on fine. And he's just phoned to ask me to go out fishing with him tomorrow. He wants us to spend the day together, to get to know each other a bit more before I leave."

Eve thought her heart was going to burst when she looked at the joy on Michael's face. His smile was huge and his eyes sparkled and she felt a great surge of happiness well up inside her that her son and his father were forming a relationship. She also felt a tug of jealousy pulling at her heart that she hadn't been included, but seeing Michael's elation she rejected her selfishness.

Everyone was smiling and laughing along with Michael, except Suzanne who had tears in her eyes.

"The only person I told was Natalie. So when you saw us talking together and going off together it had nothing to do with fancying her. I was just confiding in her."

"Oh, thanks, Michael!" Natalie laughed as Michael, quickly realising his mistake, hugged her to him.

"What an amazing story!" Grace said. "And are we allowed to know who he is?"

"It's Mr McGrass, the General Manager," Michael said. "I don't care that all of you know. I want you to know. But can I just ask that you don't say anything to him or to anyone else outside the group about it yet. He's got a family and he wants to introduce me slowly. I came here to meet him, not to rock the boat and cause trouble for him."

"What about your birth mother?" Geri asked. "Did your father tell you anything about her?"

"That she was a young Greek student he met while he was also studying in London; that they were very much in love and he'd hoped to spend his life with her."

"So what happened?"

"Nobody knows. He didn't know she was ever pregnant."

"Fancy not telling him!" Stewart said. "She should have done, shouldn't she?"

"Yes, she should of told im," Dave said. "A man as a righ' to know he's a father."

Eve felt herself colouring up. She squirmed in her chair and felt uncomfortable. Just in case she hadn't done it enough herself, now the group were going to start beating her up.

"It must have been a hugely difficult decision for her if she was young and alone and pregnant in a foreign country. It couldn't have been easy. And she must have done what she thought was the best for her baby. If she couldn't look after him then she made sure he went to someone who could. I think she was very brave." Natalie said passionately. Their eyes met and Eve blinked her thanks and a faint smile played round Natalie's lips. She'd kept Michael's secret for him so far and she wasn't going to break her word now.

"I've certainly no complaints, anyway, about my upbringing. Like I said, I couldn't have gone to a better couple."

"And tomorrow you're having a blokes' day with your dad. Woo hoo!" Natalie said to lighten the atmosphere.

"This calls for another round of drinks, I think!" Trevor said, signalling to a passing waitress. "We have to drink to Michael and his dad!"

A far-off rumbling sound made Eve look up and she saw a Virgin Atlantic 747 in the distance as it turned over Jolly Harbour ready to cross the island from west to east and land at VC Bird in less than a couple of minutes. She also remembered who was on board and a sudden realisation dawned on her.

"Has anyone seen Jo since we got back?" she asked her head snapping round the group.

Nobody had. Eve sighed. She knew where Jo was. She also knew there was nothing she could do about it. It wasn't her business to stop Jo getting hurt or Deano getting into any more trouble. She'd had a lot thrown at her during this trip and the secret of being a successful tour manager was knowing when you'd reached the point where you could no longer do anything and just letting go. She joined the others as they raised their refilled glasses.

"To Michael and his dad!"

***

Deano heard the door open slowly and footsteps walk falteringly towards his bed and then stop. He braced himself and opened his eyes to find himself looking into two beautiful green ones that were staring at him intently. Jo! He couldn't stop himself smiling and when she saw his reaction to her, she smiled, too and then leaned forward to give him a kiss on the cheek. He was overjoyed at seeing her, yet petrified at the same time.

"You look better than I feared you might," she said, pulling the plastic chair away from the wall and positioning it next to the bed. "I know you said you didn't want visitors but I couldn't leave without coming in to see you. I didn't want you to think that we'd all abandoned you, because we haven't. We all ask Eve about you constantly."

Deano smiled again and took her hand, his mind in turmoil with so many conflicting emotions. He'd dreaded her coming in, yet now he was so glad to see her. His hand tingled at her touch and he felt a real longing to hold her, nothing more, just to hold her in his arms forever. He'd

340

thought he'd feel foolish because of the whole contact lens episode, but he sensed it wasn't even an issue for her. She was more attractive than he'd remembered; shining, long, red hair; shapely figure; gorgeous smile and a loveliness that he couldn't qualify or define. They sat in contented silence for a few moments, just looking at each other, hands entwined, perfectly relaxed and at ease in each other's company, each feeling again that dangerous spark of attraction between them. Jo could feel her heart thumping away at the nearness of him. A warm glow began to burn inside her. She was sure he could see it. She coughed and tried to start a conversation with him.

"Are you in pain?"

"Some. It's become a dull ache, really, you know, sort of discomfort rather than pain, although the first day or so was pretty horrendous. I'm in charge of my own pain control now and I'm just keeping it at a minimum."

"Everyone sends their love. They've told me to get your e-mail address so that they can all keep in touch with you when we're home and they can follow your progress."

"Yes, that's great," he said, having no intention whatsoever of keeping in touch with any of them. It was all too embarrassing. He just wanted to scrub the last week out of his life and never hear the name Travel Together ever again. He'd been stupid, really stupid and although they were a great bunch of people, especially Dave and Michael and Grace and Natalie, there was no way he wanted to be reminded of what he'd done and what had happened to him in Antigua. And if they knew the truth about him they'd probably hate him anyway.

"And so would I," she added shyly. "Like to follow your progress."

He looked at her again and a feeling of shame crept over him. How had he ever thought it was a laugh to play with the feelings of such a good, kind, beautiful person like Jo? He'd have to give a false e-mail address. He couldn't possibly tell her the truth about how he'd come to get away from his wife for a week in the hope of having uncomplicated no-strings-attached sex. It wasn't that things weren't good with Rachel; he'd just wanted a change from the same old routine. His was the lament of the adulterous bastard: *I love my wife but I'm not in love with her.* He'd been unfaithful to her more times than he cared to remember in the ten years they'd been together but no woman had ever meant anything to him at all until he'd met Jo. And even then his ego had let Geri almost spoil it, although he knew that it was probably just as well that things hadn't gone any further with Jo, given the way it had now turned out. If they had had sex he'd be feeling even worse; probably very guilty.

"Terrible storm, wasn't it?" he said, changing the subject.

"You can say that again! The whole resort was under water and we were cut off for quite a while. I thought it rained in the West Country, but that really beat it. And the thunder and lightning!"

341

"Yes, it really was quite something, wasn't it?"

"Deano, you didn't say anything just now, when I said I'd like to keep in touch with you."

"I don't have to say something, do I? I've already said I'll give you my e-mail address. I'll keep in touch, don't worry!"

"Well, I'd like to know how you're doing, you know, how you're healing and coping with things again. You know. Perhaps see each other again."

There was a tangible pause. Jo looked at him and then slowly turned scarlet as she nodded her head and gave a nervous, tight little smile.

"Okay. I get it. This was never going to be anything more than a quick holiday fling."

"No! No! It was! I wanted it to be. I really did but we have to be realistic. I am going to be out of action for months. I don't even know if I'll ever walk properly again."

"And you think that would matter to me?"

"I just don't want to say that we'll see each other and then we don't. Let me see what the prognosis is once I get back home and perhaps a few months down the line, when I'm a bit more mobile and the future's a bit clearer we can see each other, then."

Jo didn't say anything. She just looked at him, but she slowly slid her hand out from inside his as the door opened and a nurse bustled in.

"I've come to take your blood pressure," she said walking round to the far side of the bed and sliding a cuff up Deano's left arm. Then she turned and smiled at Jo. "Oh, hello! He will be happy now that you're here. We weren't expecting you so early. You must have got through Immigration and Customs very quickly today. You're a happy man, nah? Now that your wife's here!" she said to Deano.

Deano looked at Jo, his eyes pleading her forgiveness. She sat still, like a statue for a moment before speaking.

"I'm not Deano's wife. I'm a minister of the church who was in the hotel and I've come to visit him to offer solace.

The nurse looked at her as she pumped up the blood pressure gauge, her eyes agog.

"You're a minister? Well, I'm amazed. You don't look like no minister I've ever seen," she chuckled.

Her eyes were agog again a moment later when she took the blood pressure reading.

"Hmm! It's very high today. I'll come back and take it again in a while. Probably all the excitement of your wife coming." she said, leaving the room.

"I'm not surprised it's high!" Jo said, standing up.

"Jo! Please! Let me explain!"

"Explain what? That you're married? That your wife's on her way here? If I were you I'd save your explanations for her!" She strode towards the door.

"Please don't go! Not like this! Jo, please, let me explain how I feel about you!"

Jo turned back into the room and took two steps towards the bed.

"You've got a minute."

"Look, I know what I did wasn't nice. I wanted a short holiday in the sun away from my wife. Just a break. Honest!"

"So, are you telling me that she knew you were here? In Antigua? On a singles' holiday?"

"No. No, she didn't. She thought I was at a trade fair. I travel a lot in my job, I told you that. We've been together ten years and things have got stale. I wanted a break, a change, some excitement and, yes, I admit it, I was looking for sex. But I wasn't banking on meeting you. I thought I'd just have a quick fling with some woman and that would be that. Then I met you and I thought you were gorgeous. I still think that. You must believe me! Look! I could have had a fling with Geri, couldn't I? She did her utmost to get me to go with her, but I wasn't interested in her because I wanted you. And then, just as we were getting close, this stupid accident happened."

Jo had to admit that at least that part was true. If he'd wanted just sex he could have gone with Geri. She began to feel herself weakening and that annoyed her.

"Please give me a chance! Give me a few months; wait for me. I want us to get to know each other. I want us to be together. But I have to get better first, to be up and walking and back on my feet. Then, when I am, I can leave her and you and I can really make a go of it."

Something in his demeanour made Jo snap. He talked about leaving his wife as if he were discarding an old sweater or a pair of shoes; something he'd once really liked but had no use for any longer. And Jo was expected to just sit and wait to be summoned once he was ready.

"Oh, can we? Your arrogance is unbelievable. Who do you think you are? When I arrived here today, I would have been prepared to try to forge a relationship with you. I thought I could travel up to see you, help you get better and be a part of your life. We could see how we really felt about each other and get to know each other as you recovered. That would really

343

have been a test. But you obviously have other plans. Your poor wife is going to nurse you back to health and then be dumped unceremoniously. Or will you stay with her but hope that I'll be willing to be the third side of the triangle? Well, let me tell you straight, Deano, I'm not getting involved with a married man, not you or anyone. It's a carrousel to nowhere that I'm just not getting on. So my advice to you would be, forget me!"

Jo turned to leave just as the door swung open again and a short, thin, blonde woman, not unlike Geri to look at, wearing an above-the-knee cream dress and high heeled shoes, carrying a smart holdall came into the room pulling a maroon suitcase behind her. She didn't look very happy and her expression turned even more sour when she looked at Jo and then across to her husband.

"You must be Mrs Dean?" Jo said, gathering her wits before Deano did. She leaned forward and held out her hand, which Rachel took automatically, wrong-footed by Jo's approach. "I'm the Reverend Joanne Walsh."

"Reverend?" Rachel's face was a picture.

"Yes, I'm staying at the hotel and I just came by to minister to your husband, but I can see that now you're here he's in very good hands." She delved into her handbag and pulled out some bookmarks that she always carried with her, each featuring a Bible quotation and turned back to Deano, whose face was an unfathomable mask.

"I hope you find some comfort in these words," she said, putting them on the bedside cabinet. "Goodbye, Mr Dean. You will be in my prayers and have my very best wishes for a speedy recovery."

And with that she was out the door, striding down the corridor as the first tears began to roll down her cheeks.

***

There was an excited buzz inside the helicopter as Suzanne and Stewart, who were facing forward, Michael and Trevor, who were facing backwards, and Grace, who was next to the pilot, did up their seat belts. They had all watched the safety information video when they'd checked in at the office in Jolly Harbour and so they adjusted their headsets accordingly.

"Can everyone hear me?" the pilot asked.

"Yes!" they chorused. Unfortunately, though, they had all forgotten to press the control button so the pilot couldn't hear them.

"Press the button to speak to me, guys," he said, patiently. This happened all the time.

"Oh, sorry!" they all chorused again and then burst out laughing.

"Okay. My name's John and I have the pleasure of being your pilot for today. So, hold tight, we're ready to rock and roll!"

None of them had ever been in a helicopter before, except Grace, and it was a strange feeling for them as they took off vertically, completely different from an aeroplane. John told them they'd be going along the coastline for a short distance and then they'd head west south west towards Montserrat.

"As you can see, we have the whole of Jolly Harbour and the Jolly Beach Resort below us now, with Sugar Ridge over on the port side, that's to say on our left."

"Will we see the Mango Tree Resort?" Suzanne asked and then had to ask it all over again because she'd forgotten to press the button.

"That's just ahead of us now. It'll be to our left as we swing out over the water. You'll get a great view of it going out and coming back."

Five pairs of eyes searched the resort below, squealing like children as they were able to identify landmarks within the resort.

"See if we can see any of the others!" Stewart said. "Yes! Look! That's Huw and Jason playing cricket on the beach!"

The five of them waved frantically, completely unaware that they couldn't be seen inside the helicopter, but everyone on the beach turned and looked up towards it and started to wave.

"They've seen us!" Suzanne shouted, not realising there was no need to shout and therefore deafening everyone.

And then they were over the Caribbean Sea. John pointed out Cades Reef, where they'd stopped for snorkelling on the catamaran trip and then he started to tell them about Montserrat and that terrible day in August 1997 when the Soufriere Hills Volcano erupted after two years of grumbled warnings.

"As you can see," he said, as they approached the island, "it was mainly the south of Montserrat that was affected. You can see as we fly closer the pathway of the pyroclastic flows and you'll notice the smell."

They all sniffed and realised they could smell sulphur. John pointed out where Plymouth, the capital, had been and talked about the destruction caused.

"Twenty-three people died, most of them in the old airport area," he said, "and the population took a huge drop from twelve thousand to just above five. I mean, most people were refugees; they'd lost their homes. You can see how the whole of the southern end of the island was wiped out. And every rooftop you can see sticking out from the lava signifies a family's life destroyed."

Everyone became subdued and quiet as they took in just what it had all meant to the people of Montserrat.

"It's just like Eve said, like a modern day Pompeii," Trevor whispered.

"I feel quite tearful, it's so poignant," Grace said.

"Well, let's see if we can cheer you up with some wildlife on the way back!" John said, in an attempt to lighten the mood. "Has everyone taken all the shots they want?"

Everyone had and so he swung the helicopter back towards Antigua. After a moment or two of flying over the sea he suddenly became excited.

"Look! Down there! Straight ahead of us! Dolphins!"

His five passengers all got their cameras at the ready as John came down a bit lower and suddenly they could see the two animals leaping through the waves as they flew over them.

"Oh, that's made my holiday!" Suzanne said. "I love dolphins!"

"You're lucky to see them today, we don't always see them," John said. "And they put on a little display especially for us. Did you see them dancing through the waves there? Beautiful!"

And two minutes later they saw a catamaran below them, which seemed to have stopped and they realised they were looking at a large Hawksbill Turtle, which could be seen clearly in the water beneath them.

"That makes up for the one I couldn't see on the catamaran!" Grace said gleefully, clicking away with her camera.

"And we're going back in over Mango Tree and along the west coast to Jolly Harbour," John said as they got their cameras ready for some final pictures of their resort from the air.

"That was the best afternoon of my whole holiday!" Trevor said as they got out of the helicopter.

"I agree!" Grace said, as she stepped down from the front of the cabin.

The other three nodded. It had been the second best for Stewart and Suzanne and Michael hoped his best afternoon was still to come.

**

"Can I join you?"

Natalie looked up from her book to see Geri standing nervously next to her.

"Course you can! Here! Put your stuff on that sun lounger. I was saving a couple for when the others get back off the helicopter trip, or for Jo, but I haven't seen her at all since breakfast."

"What was she doing today?" Geri asked as she sat down next to Natalie.

"No idea. She said she didn't want to come into St John's so I assumed she'd just be on the beach when we got back. But she wasn't and she didn't come into lunch. She's probably just having a quiet day to herself."

"It's funny her being a vicar, isn't it?" Geri said, spreading lotion on her neck and face.

"Not really. You've got to be something, haven't you? What do you do?"

"I work in an estate agent's. Very boring. You're a dance teacher aren't you?"

"I am. And I love it. I've really missed my classes while I've been here. Oh, not that I haven't enjoyed the holiday! It's been fantastic, even with the storm, Michael's search for his dad, Deano's accident and my little wobbly over the wedding." She laughed at herself. "It did me good, actually, to have other people who didn't really know me telling me what my friends and family had already told me a hundred times. And I really do feel now, that I'm over it all. No more guilt trip!"

"You don't regret calling off your wedding, then?"

Natalie paused for a minute and thought. She hadn't really liked Geri much and here she was deep in conversation with her and being asked all sorts of personal questions. She gave a mental shrug. This is what a singles' holiday was all about; talking openly and intimately to people you'd never met before and who you'd never see again. And sometimes talking to a stranger did you good.

"No. We weren't right for each other, really. That's why I couldn't do it. And as everyone keeps on telling me, it took a lot of courage to do that. The easy path would have been to go through with it. You know, it was a bit like poor Princess Diana, when her sister said she couldn't call the wedding off because her face was already on the tea towels."

She paused while they both laughed and she took a big swig from her bottle of water.

"And it would have been wrong to stay get back with him just because he got injured. Although that sounds really hard it's the truth. I'd been struggling with guilt since it happened. It really believed it was my fault he'd got shot and injured. His mother and sister sent me the most awful e-mails."

"Listen! Nobody's got the right to judge you. We all make decisions for whatever reason that sometimes have far-reaching consequences. But what's done is done. And anyone can see that you not marrying him had nothing whatsoever to do with him getting blown up."

"You sound like you've got a story, the way you said that," Natalie said.

"Not really!" Geri said quickly. "My life's boring. I work in an estate agent's, I have two kids, I probably drink too much and I can't get another man interested in me for love nor money," she laughed, bitterly.

"I think you try too hard. Sorry! I was out of order saying that. But, you know, that's the impression you give, the way you went off with some local at Shirley Heights and then you sort of threw yourself at Deano, even though you could see he liked Jo. Please don't take this wrong, but perhaps you should be a bit more laid back, not quite so eager. Don't try to be centre stage all the time." Natalie shut up, fearing she'd gone too far.

Geri gave a wry smile and nodded her head.

"That's me all over," she said as her eyes welled up with tears. "I've always had this need to be important, to be needed by people. But I always seem to alienate everyone and do everything wrong. People think I'm a gossip and a busybody."

"Oh, don't cry!" Natalie jumped up and knelt beside Geri putting her arm around her shoulder. "You'll get a nice guy one day, you'll see. Sorry. That was patronising, but you really will, Geri. Just take it easy and don't rush at the first man who smiles or talks to you."

Geri nodded and wiped her tears away with the back of her hand. Natalie perched on the sun longer alongside her.

"Getting traded in for a younger model didn't help, either," she confessed, unable to believe that she was telling Natalie this. "I'd had no idea he'd been seeing someone and suddenly it was all over. Sixteen years of marriage over in a flash!"

"No! What a bastard!" Natalie said, in solidarity with her new best friend.

"He's a pilot and he'd had this young stewardess on the go for a while before it all came to light," she said. "But there you are! What can you do? Other than hope that one day she'll trade him in for a younger version and then he'll know what it feels like."

"Although it doesn't usually happen that way round, does it?" Natalie said. "You know, you don't get many younger men interested in older women. In spite of what Frances said the other night! She made me die! Just cracked me up! Good for her if she's off with some young bloke. Just seeing the way she shut up that obnoxious Huw was priceless!" she giggled. Geri smiled, too, although inside she was annoyed with herself. She hadn't wanted anyone to know anything at all about her private life and she was still unaware she'd said anything to Deano the night she was drunk. And although she'd given Natalie a much edited version of her breakup and divorce, she still felt she'd said too much. She quickly changed the subject.

"You seeing anyone back home?"

"Not at the moment. The dancing school and the agency take up a huge chunk of my time and to be honest, after what happened with Andy I'm beginning to wonder if I'm a bit of a commitment-phobe. Maybe later on. This time next year. Who knows? How about you? Nobody at home?"

"No. I don't really go out much to meet anyone."

"Have you tried internet dating?" she asked her.

"More times than I care to remember! They're rarely what they say they are and the ones I've met up with were only interested in getting me into bed and once they had I never saw them again. It was just a series of one-night stands. Or two-night stands. There was even a three-night stand. Then he told me that his late wife had been in touch with him through a local medium and had told him I wasn't the woman for him!"

Natalie just couldn't help herself, she burst out laughing and to her relief she saw that Geri was laughing, too.

"Well, that's original!! Natalie said, through giggles. "I've never heard that one before."

But he didn't tell me when we met up that evening. He waited til we'd gone back to his place and done the business and then he told me!" Geri screeched with laughter.

"Well, at least you can laugh about it now. And, you know that's something perhaps you can take from this holiday; something you've learned. Sex and love and affection are not the same thing."

"Oh, I know that!" Geri said, nodding her head. "I had a stupid one-night stand with someone that turned ugly a couple of nights ago. I've learned my lesson."

"No! Who? Not one of the group?"

"No. Just someone. It won't happen again. I've made a decision to start valuing myself a bit more from now on. I've looked around at some of the women in the group and I've realised that you don't measure your worth by the man on your arm. I mean, look at Grace. She's a high ranking police officer and she's done it all herself. And even Eve. She hasn't got a man, has she?"

"I don't know. I don't know much about her, she sort of mucks in with us but keeps her private life private, doesn't she?"

"Well, I'm going to be more like that from now on," Geri nodded.

"Good on you! Fancy a dip?"

Natalie pulled her new friend Geri up by the hands and the two of them ran down the beach together and threw themselves into the cool, white foam.

***

Frances was ready for afternoon tea. She'd had a lovely day in the sun, chatting and laughing with Deborah, and occasionally Murray, drinking a couple of rum punches and having a couple of refreshing dips in the Spa pool. She stood up and stretched and started to pack her towel, book and suntan lotion into her bag.

"Are you coming to tea?" she asked Deborah.

"Ooh, yes! I hadn't realised it was that time already."

"Yes, indeed, it's Tiffin Time. I'm going to miss this next week. By this time I'm usually looking at my watch and counting down to five o'clock and thinking about what to have for dinner."

"Are you coming, Murray?" Deborah asked him, noting that he looked a bit dejected, lying back with his hands behind his head.

"Er, no. I'm going along tae play volley ball at five o'clock with some of the others. I said I would and I cannae not turn up."

"Okay! See you at pre-dinner drinks then!" Deborah said, wiggling her fingers at him and tottering off behind Frances in her high-heeled mules. Murray sighed deeply as he watched her backside disappear from view. On one level he was ecstatically happy. He'd had sex with the most desirable woman in the group. Well, probably the most desirable after Natalie, but she was too young for him. And, more importantly, he'd had sex more than once! But today Deborah seemed to be shutting him out of things. She'd spent most of the day giggling and whispering with Frances. When he'd asked what they were talking about she'd said it was just *'girls' stuff'* but he'd been put out by it. After all, it was bad manners to whisper when you were with other people. And all day he'd been hoping that Frances was going to go off again so that he'd have Deborah all to himself. They might even have gone back to his room or hers for a nice siesta together but Frances had stuck around. Even at lunch. They'd had a table for three in the restaurant until Dawn and Donna had joined them. And then to say the conversation had become banal was an understatement.

God help the kids of today with the likes of those two teaching them!

They'd bored him senseless with talk about their line dancing classes and the supposedly-funny story of last parents' evening, when Donna had taken Alfie Someone-or-other's mother to task about his late arrival every morning due to taking his younger brother to school only to find out that he was an only child.

Ha – bloody – ha!

Deborah had tried to include him a couple of times by cracking jokes. She'd said that all the men in the hotel must be asking themselves what aftershave he was wearing as he was sitting with four gorgeous women.

"Are they heck!" he'd said. "They've probably all come tae the conclusion that I'm stone deaf!"

The four of them had smiled, but it hadn't gone down too well. And now, Deborah had gone off to have tea with Frances, when he'd wanted her to have tea with him. Alone. He hadn't arranged to meet the others for volley ball, but he'd rather do that than have to have tea with the two of them carrying on and leaving him out. He saw Huw and Jason making their way along the beach towards the volleyball net and just behind them were Trevor and Dave. He sighed again and stood up and stretched. He might as well play with them. He wasn't using up his energy any other way at the moment.

***

Eve had spent the afternoon quietly sprawled on the padded sun lounger on her little terrace, reading her book. Although, if anyone had asked her what the story was about she couldn't have explained one word of it because her mind had been elsewhere. On Melv. Several times she'd picked up the phone in the room to check it was working. She'd lost count of the times she'd checked her mobile phone to see if she'd missed a call from him. And all the time she was angry with herself for doing that. She'd made it perfectly clear to Melv that she'd wanted nothing to do with him.

But what about the night of the storm?

Well, he'd obviously seen it for what it was; two people finding a solace in each other after a frustrating, difficult time. And she couldn't blame him because she'd behaved like some sort of neurotic idiot. She'd said she didn't want anything to do with him and then she'd had a night of wild passion with him. No wonder he was confused. She was confused! And she was also in turmoil at all the feelings that had come to the surface since their paths had crossed.

Stop it! Don't go over it all again!

She was driving herself nuts. She was getting on her own nerves. She had to be grateful that she'd found her son, that he didn't hate her and that he was going to get to know his father and hopefully her, too. That was a blessing, something she'd never thought would happen.

Be glad and thank God you've got Michael back in your life!

When the phone rang she nearly hit the ceiling. She jumped up from the sun lounger and rushed into the room, throwing herself across the bed to grab the receiver before the call went to voicemail.

"Eve speaking!" she said, breathless. There was a silence.

"Hello! Hello! This is Eve," she said again.

"It's Jo, Eve. Have you got five minutes, please?"

"Yes, of course," she said with a sinking heart. She knew what this was going to be all about. "Do you want to meet me in reception?"

"Actually, would you mind coming up to my room, please? It's three two one."

"I'll be five minutes," Eve said.

Jo looked calm and serene enough when she opened the door, which Eve was pleased to see. She went inside and sat on the end of the bed and Jo took the room's only chair.

"I won't beat about the bush, Eve," she said, "I know you must know about Deano being married." Eve sighed deeply and waited a moment before replying.

"Yes I do. He told me when I went in to see him after the accident. She, the wife, that is, thought he was at some auction or trade fair apparently. He asked me not to say anything to anyone and so I didn't."

"Well, I can understand that, I suppose."

"Look, Jo. Something like that puts me in an awkward position. What goes on between adults on these holidays is their business and not mine. Of course I feel really sorry for Deano when he had his accident, but when he told me he had a wife I was really mad. Men like him do our company's reputation no good whatsoever. Travel Together is a company for single travellers, and that includes those who might have a partner who can't travel with them because they're sick or don't like flying or for some other reason. No, we're not a dating agency but we're not a leg-over week away for predators who think we're 18-30s for grownups, either. We're supposed to provide a degree of protection for those who feel vulnerable travelling alone, not offer them up on a plate!"

"I understand. I know you have no control over who comes on these holidays. You can't get people to prove they're single or have good intentions. I'm not blaming you or the company in any way, Eve."

"Well, I'm glad you understand why I didn't say anything to anyone. And obviously that's why I said he didn't want any visitors. He was scared that his wife would find out it was

352

a singles holiday, I think, although she would have realised that the moment our office got in touch with her. How did you find out?"

"Well, I went to see him today. In spite of what you said, I wanted to see him, you know, to see how he was and because... well, because I wanted to see him! And then his wife walked in!"

"Oh, Jo!" Eve feeling a huge compassion for the beautiful young woman sitting opposite her leaned across and took her hand.

"I introduced myself as the Reverend Joanne Walsh, left some scripture quotations on the bedside table and made a quick exit!" Both women laughed at this, but Eve could see that Jo was teetering on the brink of tears.

"We were getting close before his accident and I really was hoping that he'd let me into his life when we got back home and that whatever the outcome might be, whether he'd walk again or be left with a limp or even confined to a wheelchair, we might have some sort of future together. Perhaps even be a couple."

She looked up at Eve's face, her green eyes brimming with un-spilled tears, reflecting the hurt and bewilderment she was feeling.

"I know! It's crazy, isn't it? I've met him for just a few days and he's turned out to be a selfish user, and yet I'm talking like some silly schoolgirl with a crush on a rock star."

"Sometimes holidays, especially to magical places like this, affect us deeply. They turn us all into silly schoolgirls for a while; they give us a thrill of excitement and everything we see and do is magnified to be larger than life and just wonderful. And that includes the people we meet. A holiday is a place where real life is suspended and where fantasies, romance and adventures take over."

Eve stopped abruptly, surprised by her own words. Jo was nodding at them.

"You're right," she looked at Eve and smiled. "Thanks for coming to see me. I know through my faith that when we're troubled we're always sent a message, you know, it can be something we hear on the radio or overhear in the queue at the bank or read on a billboard. And other times we're sent a messenger to personally deliver the special words that we're meant to hear. Some might call that messenger an angel. You've been my angel this afternoon."

"Well, I've been called a few things in my time!" Eve laughed.

"I mean it! You said exactly what I was meant to hear. It makes letting go of Deano so much easier. I'm not one to live by what might have been. I just felt such a fool when first the nurse thought I was his wife and then moments afterwards she actually walked in. I've just got to accept that he was playing with me and I let myself been sucked in."

353

Eve sighed. Over the years she'd seen so many people hurt and upset when a holiday romance had gone wrong. She'd like to personally wring Deano's neck; Jo was a lovely woman who hadn't deserved to be messed around like this.

"Still," Jo continued, "no harm done! I'm truly sorry he's had such a terrible accident and I really do wish him all the very best for a speedy recovery and that he finds a measure of peace in his personal life. He'll be in my prayers for a long time. But... I've still got forty-eight hours of holiday left and I mean to enjoy every single minute of every single one of them!"

"Good for you!" Eve said standing up. The two women looked at each other and then shared a hug.

"Thanks again," Jo said.

Walking back to her room Eve's own words echoed inside her head.

"Sometimes holidays, especially to magical places like this, affect us deeply. They turn us all into silly schoolgirls for a while; they give us a thrill of excitement and everything we see and do is magnified to be larger than life and just wonderful. And that includes the people we meet. A holiday is a place where real life is suspended and where fantasies, romance and adventures take over."

She nodded at her own wisdom as she went back into her room. She had to take her own advice.

***

The two topics of conversation all the way through pre-dinner drinks and dinner itself were *Michael Finding His Dad* and *The Helicopter Ride over Montserrat*. No adjective was considered too descriptive when the Montserrat Five were telling their tale and showing their photos.

"Oh I really wish I'd gone on it!" Natalie said as she flicked through the pictures on Grace's camera with Jo looking over her shoulder.

"Never mind! Something to come back for!" Jo said.

Only Huw and Murray were showing little interest in the photos or in Michael's news. Deborah nudged Frances and inclined her head slightly towards Murray who was sitting opposite them.

"I think he's still sulking!"

"Well, tomorrow I'll probably be missing for part of the day so he'll have you all to himself again!"

"What? You're going back to Neville-land tonight?"

"I am indeed. Pussy's nicely rested and raring to go again!"

They both screamed with laughter. Murray looked across at them and felt a real stab of jealousy. He was wishing that Frances had stayed with her local lover-boy and not come back and elbowed him out of Deborah's arms. But he was determined to get Deborah alone again tonight. And tomorrow night! The holiday was really racing by now and he knew he was going to be very sorry to see it end.

The band had struck up and from the very first number most of the group had decided to shake a leg.

"Oh, my God! Go Ursula!" Natalie suddenly shouted out as she went to join the others. "Look!" she told them, pointing at Ursula who was dancing her way across the floor in the arms of a very dapper little man with a shiny, bald head. She looked at them looking at her and gave a beaming smile, without missing a beat.

Eve was sitting watching them enjoying themselves when Michael pulled up a chair next to her.

"Not dancing?" she asked him.

"I will be in a minute. I just wanted to... well... check I suppose... that you're okay with me spending the day with Melv tomorrow."

"Me? Of course I am! Why wouldn't I be?"

"Well, I didn't want you to feel left out. I asked Melv if he'd invited you but he said you'd have loads of time to spend with me in England, whereas he'd only really got tomorrow left."

"Oh, Michael!" she gave him a hug and was so happy to feel him respond. She let go of him and sat back in her chair, studying his handsome face, looking for signs of herself in it and just getting a glimpse of her father in his expression. His sensitivity to her situation made her feel great. Her son was a kind, decent human being and she was extremely proud of him. "I'm so glad that we've all found each other and words can't express the love and gratitude I feel knowing that you want to forge a relationship with me as well as Melv."

"And I can't say I'm sorry enough for behaving like a twat. You are going to get so sick of me. I'll be making that journey down from Durham to Essex at every opportunity."

"Good! You go and spend time with your dad tomorrow and I really hope you both enjoy yourselves. What am I talking about? I know you will! And thanks for not telling the group the whole story."

"What? You really thought I'd tell them you're my mum? Not that I don't want to!" he added quickly. "I want to shout it from the rooftops, but I know you're in the middle of a job here with these people and it wouldn't be right."

"Thank you."

"So," he stood up and offered her his hand, "I'll keep our little secret but it's going to cost you a dance!"

Eve stood up, laughing, and still holding onto his hand the pair of them shuffled towards the dance floor in time to the music.

"I'm going to have my first ever dance with my mum!" Michael said, looking at her and grinning from ear to ear.

"The next one will be a *sirtaki* at your grandparents' taverna in Lefkimmi," she said, finding she was beaming, too, as they joined the others who were flinging themselves around to a reggae medley with Donna and Dawn performing one of their intricate-stepped line dances across the centre of the dance floor.

***

Frances stepped out of the taxi just beyond Gray's Hill Police Station and saw Neville standing waiting for her. He gave her a smacking kiss and then took her hand and they wandered over to a stall that had set up selling barbecued chicken that smelled delicious.

"I've already eaten," Frances said.

"I haven't and I'm hungry," Neville said, still holding tightly to her hand.

"Give me a chicken an fries," he said to the young woman who was turning a line of chicken breasts over on the barbecue grill with great dexterity.

There were three other people waiting for food and Frances felt as if the whole world was looking at them; this mismatched couple – one black one white – one old one young. Although Neville had told her he was thirty-two, she was sure he couldn't be more than about twenty-six. She in turn had told him she was forty-four. She gave a mental shrug.

So what? Who cares what they think? Not me!

The young woman was an expert and within a few minutes she'd served up the chicken and chips in a polystyrene container and handed it to Neville.

"Twelve dollars."

Neville felt his pocket and shook his head.

"Me nah brought me money," he said, looking at Frances.

Feeling somewhat flustered, although she didn't really know why, Frances delved into her bag and pulled out her purse, passing a fifty dollar note to the seller, who shoved it into her apron pocket and pulled out the change, which she gave to Neville, who pocketed it swiftly, then put his hand under her elbow to lead her away from the stall.

"I'll give it to you when we get by me," he said.

As soon as they were inside the house, Neville forgot about eating. He put his meal on the table and then turned swiftly to Frances, pulling down the top of her dress to expose her breasts and starting to kiss and suck them. She could already feel him growing huge against her belly and she felt herself responding instantly. Within seconds the two of them were sighing, squealing and soaked in sweat as tonight's endless sexathon started up.

***

As the band played their last song at the Mango Tree Resort Murray was all smiles. Deborah had danced a long slow dance with him, pressing up against him and singing quietly in his ear; showing all the signs of a promising night ahead. He gave a big grin as he returned to the table with drinks for both of them and mentally rubbed his hands together. He yawned theatrically as he looked towards the others who were having a group dance. They'd formed a circle and everyone was taking it in turns to strut their stuff in the centre of it. They were obviously all having a whale of a time. Only Huw hadn't joined in. He sat at the bar talking to two girls who had just arrived that afternoon. Deborah hadn't reacted to Murray's yawn, so he yawned again, louder and longer this time, leaning back in his chair and opening his mouth wide.

"Oh dear! I'm sorry. It must be nearly ma bed time," he said, hoping that Deborah would take the hint. She took a sip of her drink instead.

"It must be all that lying round the pool all day. It's made me tired."

"That's a shame," Deborah said looking at him and placing her right hand on his knee. "I was hoping you'd be up for a night of passion. But if you're tired, well, too bad. I'll have to look around for someone else," she added, standing up quickly and moving nimbly between the tables and chairs to join the others on the dance floor. Murray nearly spat out his beer in surprise.

I just cannae figure out that woman!

"Eve! What's open tonight? Where can we go?" Natalie asked as, music over, they came back to their seats, fanning their faces and wiping their brows. "It's Saturday night and we're leaving Monday. We just have to go out tonight!"

"The Sports Bar in Jolly Harbour," Eve suggested. "That'll have music until twelve. Or if you want to go into town you might like Coast. That has music until two."

"Yay! Who's up for going into St John's?" Natalie asked looking round the table.

Dave, Michael, Jo, Dawn, Donna, Trevor and Jason all decided they were.

"You not coming, Grace?" Natalie asked.

"No, thanks. I've really enjoyed myself tonight but I'm too tired to go out now. I'm old, don't forget!"

"Ow abaht the luv birds?" Dave asked Stewart and Suzanne.

"If you mean us, thanks but no thanks. I think I peaked this afternoon seeing Montserrat," Stewart said as Suzanne nodded in agreement.

"Geri? You'll come, won't you?" Natalie urged her. Geri hesitated. She wanted to go out with them, but she didn't trust what might happen if she did.

"Er... I'm not sure."

"Oh, come on!" Natalie said, surprised that after their earlier conversation Geri had appeared a bit jumpy and quiet this evening. "This time next week we'll all be watching the telly or in bed reading a book and wishing we were here."

"Okay! I'll come!" she said.

Murray held his breath as Natalie turned to Deborah. But before Natalie could ask her anything Deborah shook her head.

"Not me, thanks, Natalie. I've had a great evening, but I'm going to bed," she said and Murray's heart sank.

"And I'm off to bed, too! Thanks for a lovely time!" Ursula scuttled away from the table like one of the little mongooses that lived in the grounds. Everyone could see that her dancing partner was waiting for her at the other side of the terrace.

"Ah! Bless!" Natalie said smiling at them.

They went back to their rooms for money and a tidy up, leaving Grace, Murray, Deborah, Stewart and Suzanne at the table. Stewart and Suzanne soon excused themselves saying they were going for a stroll along the beach. And off they set, arm in arm, cocooned in a cloud of love.

"Aren't they sweet?" Grace said, watching them go. "I wonder if they'll end up together."

"Why not?" said Murray. "They seem tae have really hit if off here. And they dinnae live too far from each other, do they?"

"I'm not sure. But even if it comes to nothing, they've had a good holiday," Deborah said, smiling.

Grace finished her drink and picked up her bag and her shoes, which were heaped on the chair next to her.

"I can't face putting these sandals back on. They've given me blisters tonight, but it was lovely, somehow, dancing barefoot. I haven't done that in years."

"I know what you mean. There's something really liberating about having nothing on your feet, isn't there? It's a bit like taking your clothes off."

Grace laughed as she stood up.

"I don't want to do that," she said. "I wouldn't want to frighten anyone!"

"Tssk! You're in fantastic shape," Deborah said. "Good night. Sleep well!"

"Thanks, Deborah, you too. Good night, Murray."

And she meandered off, swinging her bag and shoes, her shiny bob bouncing in time with her steps, past Elvis, who took a break from collecting glasses to swing her round in an exaggerated ballroom hold then kiss her hand and release her, and along the path towards her room. Deborah looked at Murray over the rim of her glass.

"Alone at last," she teased him.

"I thought you said you were going tae bed."

"I am. With you."

Murray gulped as her hand reached out and grabbed the front of his shirt and pulled him towards her and she planted a long, lingering kiss on his lips. He gulped again as she pulled away.

"Shall we go?"

"Oh, aye!" Murray leapt out of his seat and started walking around the pool towards the rooms, assuming Deborah was following him.

"Er, no!" she called out to him.

He stopped abruptly and turned round with a bewildered look on his face.

"We're not going to bed. I've changed my mind. We're going to fulfil one of my fantasies," she said, smiling. She licked her lips and took his hand. She turned around and led him through the gardens towards the beach. She smiled to herself at her confidence. Frances's stories of what went on in Neville-land had made her hungry for her own adventures. As they reached the sand she kicked off her mules and Murray took off his sandals. They walked along the beach past the water sports centre and the Crazy Conch, until they came to a spot where the resort lights didn't reach. Just the silver glow of the almost full moon reflecting across the water provided their only illumination.

Deborah dropped her bag and shoes on the sand and pulled her dress over her head, revealing matching pink lace bra and panties. Murray's jaw dropped open. He couldn't quite believe his luck. He pulled off his shirt and then unbuckled his trousers and let them drop without taking his eyes off Deborah, who had flicked off her bra and was stepping out of her knickers.

Fucking hell!

In five seconds he stood naked beside her. She playfully slapped his erection.

"The water will soon get rid of that!" she laughed. "Come on! We're skinny dipping!"

"Woo hoo!" Murray shouted as he ran behind her into the waves.

***

Coast was heaving with people, noise and atmosphere. Eve was glad she'd brought them here. It was a place she loved and they were getting to see how some Antiguans enjoyed themselves on a Saturday night. There were other places she could have taken them; but Coast covered all ages and styles and offered a safe environment for everyone to enjoy. Two local men had made a beeline for Donna and Dawn as soon as they had arrived and after dancing to the band for a while they had gone inside to the *dark room* as Eve called it, where coupled danced closely together Caribbean style, like two spoons. Jason was sitting at a table on the opposite side from the bar deep in conversation with two men. Eve sat at the bar with her drink while the others were on the dance floor. Only Geri sat beside her. She seemed subdued.

"Not dancing?" Eve asked her.

"No. I prefer to sit and watch the others."

"But you're a good dancer. I've seen you on the dance floor at the hotel."

"Yes, but I'm happy to sit and watch now. You know, just drink in the atmosphere. It's a great place, isn't it?"

"Yes. I like it here. I mean, there are other places I could have taken you, but the music probably would have been a bit heavy for all of you. And, of course, apart from Natalie, we're not in our twenties anymore!" she laughed.

"Tell me about it!" Geri laughed, too and then seemed to freeze.

"Good night, ladies," a voice said as a man stood between them. Eve looked up to see Elvis, standing there, holding one of the pretty young girls that Huw had been talking to by the hand. "Nice to see you out enjoying yourselves."

"You, too, Elvis."

"Can I get you a drink?" he said smiling at both of them.

"I've just got this one," Eve said, "but thanks, anyway."

"How about you, honey?" he asked Geri and she shook her head and murmured, "No, thank you," without looking at him.

"Well, you have yourselves a good night, now," he said, smiling again before walking off towards the dance floor, his date teetering behind him in five inch heels.

"Have you got a problem with Elvis?" Eve couldn't resist asking Geri. "Only I can't help noticing that for the last day or so you've been uncomfortable around him."

Geri went scarlet and continued to stare at her drink. But Eve wanted to know just what had happened. So she waited. After a moment or two Geri sighed and looked up at her.

"I made a bit of a fool of myself with him on the night of the storm. I'd been sitting at the bar talking to him and we were getting on really well. He was definitely chatting me up. I mean, I'm not stupid, he really was! You know, asking me all sorts of personal questions, and so when we had to evacuate the restaurant I deliberately waited behind along the path in the hope of... well... I don't know what it was in the hope of, really. Of him coming back to my room, I suppose. But I'd completely misread the signs. When I appeared he just looked startled and he got angry and said I should have gone with the others; that I was putting myself in danger and putting him in danger. I sort of threw myself into his arms and we both fell over. He pulled me up and dragged me along the path, shining the torch until we reached the first rooms where the emergency lighting was on. Then he told me to stop behaving like an idiot and to go back to my room. And off he marched." She paused and looked at Eve. "You must think I'm so stupid. I don't know how I misread the situation so badly, I mean, he seemed really interested in me."

"Yes, but don't forget, being nice to people is part of his job. And, of course, you'd had a few drinks. I'm glad it was no more than that. I thought someone had roughed you up when I saw your lip and how upset you were."

Geri went scarlet and looked down again. For a moment Eve thought she was going to burst into tears.

Dammit! I can't even have a few drinks in a club at one o'clock in the morning without having to play Agony Aunt.

"I just felt really stupid, that's all," Geri said. "I've felt awkward seeing him again since then, although, he hasn't made any reference to it. I mean, he's been really nice, you know, just acted as if nothing happened."

I know exactly what you mean! I've got one who's acted like nothing happened, too!

"Well, I should just forget it. He obviously has. Women making passes at you is an occupational hazard when you're a waiter in the Caribbean. Especially a good-looking, charming one like Elvis. And he was mad at you because he knew how bad and dangerous the storm was and you didn't. Just forget it!"

Geri smiled and at that moment Trevor, who was on his way back from the loo, whisked up to them and grabbed Geri off the stool and onto the dance floor as the band ripped into another number that made the glasses on the tables and the bottles behind the bar rattle as if there was an earthquake. Eve took a long sip of her drink and looked towards the dance floor. A statuesque blonde was dirty dancing with a hunk and they were both waving at her at the same time: Georgina and Cranleigh. She smiled and waved back. She admired Georgina because she was a woman who knew how to enjoy herself and nothing got in her way or stopped her. Then she scolded herself.

Don't sink into self pity!

She had nothing to complain about at all. In fact, she was rejoicing because she'd found her son. Her eyes wandered across the dance floor to Michael, her gorgeous, grown-up son, who was having a ball dancing up close to Natalie.

"Thank you, God," she whispered as gratitude swept through her entire body.

"Can I get you a drink, Eve?" Jason asked, standing beside her.

"Thanks, Jason. A rum and diet would be nice. Haven't I seen your friends at the hotel?" she asked nodding towards the two men he'd been sitting with.

"Yes. They're from Trinidad," he said, raising his voice to make himself heard above the music that had gone up a notch. "Nice guys. They're here on business and staying at Mango Tree. They had a few hours off and joined in the water polo this morning, that's how I know them. A rum and diet coke and three beers please, mate," he said to the barman.

"I thought you'd have been on the dance floor," Eve said.

"No. I'm happy to chat. I mean, I like dancing, but we're talking cricket at the moment!"

"Well, as long as you're enjoying yourself," Eve said, taking her drink from him. "Thanks, Jason. Cheers!"

"Cheers, Eve!" he said and wandered back to the table.

***

"No means no, you wanker! Now let go of my arm before I scream my head off for security."

Huw let go of the girl's arm giving her a rough push at the same time. She stumbled backwards and sat down abruptly on the sand, mini skirt rising up over her waist exposing her tiny thong. Scrambling to her feet she swung her bag with as much force as she could muster and slapped him around the head with it. Now it was his turn to stumble.

"And just stay away from me!" she spat as a parting shot, before she marched back up the beach towards the lights of the gardens and safety.

Huw rubbed his temple, where he could feel that a buckle on the bag had cut his skin and felt very sorry for himself. He sat down on the sand and leaned back against a stack of sun loungers. He was in shadow; a large tamarind tree blocking the moonlight. He hadn't fancied her much anyway, he told himself, lacking conviction. He'd preferred her mate, but she'd gone off into town with Elvis. They'd asked them to go with them, but Huw hadn't wanted to go out and spend money on a girl, when she'd already had a few drinks and he'd been sure he could get what he wanted from her by just going for a walk. She'd surprised him. She'd been alright when they'd started kissing but as soon as he tried a bit harder she'd suddenly sobered up and turned nasty. He wriggled down in the sand, trying to get a bit more comfortable as he sank further into his pit of self-pity. He heard muted giggles and conversation and looked up to see Suzanne and Stewart, arms around each other, coming along the beach towards him. They'd obviously been up to something. Suzanne's hair was wet and Stewart was carrying his bright green and purple striped shirt over his arm. He watched them as they stopped to kiss, laughed out loud and then carried on up the beach towards the hotel, singing *Take a Chance on Me* as they went. Huw curled his lip at the sight of them, telling himself that he wouldn't do Suzanne if she was the only woman left on Earth. He didn't know how any bloke could be interested in a fat girl. But then again, he didn't know what woman could fancy a man like Stewart, who lived in some sort of colour-blind-anything-goes-and-the-louder-the-better world.

After a few minutes of further wallowing, he was just about to get up and go back to his room when he looked to his right and saw Deborah and Murray coming down the beach. They didn't see him deep in the shadows underneath the tree. They walked past him and stopped about twenty yards further on. He watched as, oblivious to his presence, they pulled their clothes off and turned and ran into the water, the dimples on their white arses wiggling and reflecting the moon's glow. He watched them splashing each other with their arms and legs; giggling and laughing as Deborah tried to escape from Murray who ducked her under, then pulled her up, smothering her face with kisses. He watched as they kissed more frantically and held onto each other tightly in the water. He watched as it became obvious that they were doing much more than that.

Fuck! Am I the only one not having a shag tonight?

He watched as Deborah flipped onto her back and folded her legs around Murray's waist, pulling him into her. Murray began thrusting and Deborah began groaning, the sound floating across the water towards him. And then he had an idea.

***

In the lush, warm water, Deborah and Murray were having the time of their lives. Alone with the whole Caribbean Sea for just the two of them, they each relaxed, let themselves go and enjoyed the best sex they'd ever had. Deborah knew what it must feel like to be a mermaid. Her hair floated out around her and the sea formed a warm, welcoming womb that totally embraced her. The gentle slapping sound of the waves on the shore added a backbeat to Murray's frantic rhythm. She concentrated hard and suddenly experienced an explosion as her body shuddered with the biggest orgasm of her life. She gave a scream that was almost primeval as her body lifted from the water and then splashed back down again as Murray collapsed, his legs buckling underneath him. He turned onto his back and they lay side by side, gently touching each other, both exhausted and spent.

"How was it?"

Why the fuck do you have to ask that every single time?

"Didn't I sound as if I was enjoying myself?"

"Oh, aye, you did! They mustae heard you in the village."

Deborah didn't answer. She didn't want to talk, she just wanted to live in the moment and remember it always: sex in the warm sea under a bright silver moon and her biggest ever orgasm. Just thinking about it made her feel horny all over again.

Pussy's happy!

She giggled to herself and thought of Frances, who she knew would be proud of her. Her magnificent moment was brought to an abrupt end by Murray splashing around as he struggled to put his feet on the ground.

"It's getting a bit cold, isn't it? Shall we get out?"

"You go. I want just a couple more minutes."

Murray waded out of the water and she smiled at the peace and quiet that covered and settled all around her as she stared up at the moon and a feeling of absolute contentment and serenity rippled through her body.

This is what happy feels like!

And she realised that she was smiling; that there was a huge grin on her face. She'd found peace, perfect peace. Which was then completely shattered by Murray's frantic shouting.

"Deborah! Deborah!"

Seething with annoyance she turned around to see him waving his arms at her from the water's edge.

"What?" she snapped at him.

"Our clothes have gone! Our clothes have gone!"

"Oh, don't be ridiculous!"

She waded out taking big angry strides, furious at him for spoiling her idyllic moment. But then she saw that they had indeed gone.

"But where have they gone?"

"Well, it's bloody obvious. Some bastard's taken them!"

"Who? Who's taken them? There's nobody here but us."

They both looked around puzzled, eyes searching. And then they were both blinded by the dazzle from two searchlights that were suddenly turned on them. Murray shoved his hands in front of his groin and Deborah raced back into the sea for cover as the lights came closer.

"Can we ask what you're doing, sir?" a voice called out from behind one of the spotlights.

"Well we're nae having our dinner," Murray said. "Can't you turn that bloody light off?" He raised his right hand to shield his eyes while keeping his left one in place at his crotch.

Two security guards, one tall, one shorter, approached him, turning off their very large torches as they did so.

"Are you aware that you are breaking the law, sir?" the shorter one asked Murray. "It's illegal to expose yourself in this country."

"I'm nae exposed!" Murray firmly placed both hands in front of him again.

"Well, you're not fully clothed, sir," the taller one observed.

"I'm on the beach."

"And it's illegal to be naked on the beach unless it's one of the designated nudist areas, sir."

"Look. We just wanted a wee skinny dip. It's dark and we dinnae think anyone could see us. They couldnae see us. We left our clothes here, on the beach. Right here," he said, indicating the spot where he was standing, "but when we came out of the water they'd gone!"

The two security guards looked at each other and then looked back at Murray.

"You're absolutely sure you left them here?" the shorter one asked.

"Aye! Right here!"

"And were you wearing jeans and a dark blue shirt?"

"Aye."

"And the lady was wearing a long red dress?"

"Aye. How do you know that?"

"Because we just found them on a stack of sun loungers next to the Crazy Conch as we started our patrol," the guard said.

"Maybe you've been the subject of a practical joke, sir," the tall one said. "If you like to wait here, I'll fetch them for you." And he set off back along the beach. The other guard smiled at Murray.

"We know you folks like to come here to have fun, but you should be careful going into the sea at night. There might be jelly fish, there might be something bigger. Or you just might get into trouble and there's nobody here to see or hear you," he said.

Murray nodded his head. He'd had such a great time and this had sort of put a damper on it. The tall guard came back carrying their clothes, shoes and Deborah's bag, which he handed to Murray.

"Here you are. Now get dressed, please, sir, and we would appreciate it if you didn't repeat tonight's behaviour again."

"Aye, your colleague's just told me that."

"We want you to have fun, but we want you to stay safe. Tell your lady she can come out of the sea now. Good night, sir,"

"Good night!"

Murray waited until the two guards were well on their way before he called Deborah out of the water. She came splashing out, laughing as she did so.

"What a hoot! Who on earth would have taken our clothes?"

"Well, the important thing is that we've got them back. I thought we were gonna have tae walk back tae our rooms stark naked." Murray placed the clothes on the ground and sorted through the pile for his underpants. As he bent forward to pick them up Deborah wrapped herself over him, wetting and chilling him, yet immediately exciting him.

"No! Not here, Deborah! We dinnae want those guards coming back and finding us at it again."

"Coward!" she whispered in his ear.

"Aye! I am! At least as far as doing it again here's concerned."

"Let's get dressed then and go back to my room. Perhaps we could do it on the balcony!" she suggested sweetly licking his ear as she spoke.

Murray shivered with excitement and anticipation. He couldn't get dressed quickly enough.

***

Eve dropped her bag on the bed and kicked off her shoes, looking at her watch as she did so. Ten to three. She smiled to herself as she thought back over the last couple of hours; getting a group of people who'd all had way too much to drink into a taxi and home wasn't easy and had resulted in three trips back into Coast to find those who'd managed to get lost between the doorway and the taxi, which was all of thirty yards. And then Natalie had somehow managed to miss her seat completely and ended up sprawled on the floor with her legs and arms in the air like a beetle that's flipped onto its back and can't right itself. Dawn and Donna had been in hoots of laughter at the dirty dancing they'd been doing.

"I couldn't believe it!" Donna was screeching. "I think he must have been a policeman. His truncheon kept on digging into my bum and I didn't even know what his name was!" Everyone roared.

"I didn't care what was going on round the back," Dawn retorted, "I just didn't want his hands anywhere near my purse!"

"*'Keep your hand over your threepenny bit'* my dad used to tell my sisters," Trevor joined in, provoking more screams of laughter from everyone.

Still, none of them had been nasty; they were all giggly, nice drunks, even if they were, in the case of Natalie and Dave, rather loud. She yawned and took her local cell phone out of her bag to set the alarm ready for getting up. She was surprised to see six missed calls, all between half eleven and twelve o'clock and all from Melv. There was also a voicemail message from him, which he'd left at midnight.

Hi, Eve. I've been looking for you around the resort but I can't find you and you're not answering the phone in your room. I wanted to see you. Erm... you possibly know I'm spending the day with Michael tomorrow. Anyway I'm going to be here for a while, if you get this message, say in the next hour, before one o'clock, then call me please.

Too late!

She'd been waiting all day and all evening and he hadn't called. But he *had* called! And with all the noise in the bar she hadn't heard the phone ring. She leaned back against the headboard and tried to think clearly.

What do I really want?

She lay there quietly for a moment and thought that she didn't even know what she really wanted. She was so good at giving advice to other people – Ms Agony Aunt – yet she didn't even know what to tell herself. Yes, she still found him attractive and yes, their for-old-times-sake night together had been good. More than good; it had been great. But, Eve realised that having great sex with your ex didn't mean you were in love with him again. It just meant that both egos had been pandered to and a ghost laid to rest.

Or had it?

If Melv had got her on the phone tonight, would she have had sex with him again?

Probably! Correction! Definitely!

But that didn't mean they were in love, or even starting up their relationship again. They were two people who'd found excitement and briefly revisited a beautiful period of their youth through finding each other again. They now had something that tied them together forever and that was their son, Michael. But they weren't a couple now and Eve felt that they never would be. She turned over and bashed the pillow and then fitted her head in the hollow she'd made, curling her knees up to her chest. Melv was married. He had a family and she had no plans to elbow in on that at all. But, perhaps, when Travel Together sent her back to Antigua, as they would, because she planned to request it, then it would be nice to think that she and Melv could perhaps spend some time together and perhaps even make each other happy for a while. She smiled to herself at the thought that Melv would be in Antigua waiting for her whenever she came back and then fully dressed and make-up still on, she fell into a deep, dreamless sleep.

***

DAY TEN

This is what I missed! This is what his first day at school would have been like...

Eve felt a lump rise in her throat as she watched Michael, who showed no signs of being hung over, finish his breakfast, then lift his rucksack onto his back, give her a cheery wave and then stride off down to the jetty where his father had arranged to pick him up for their day out. Even from the bar where she sat doing her morning *surgery* she could see, looking through a mother's eyes, his eagerness yet his apprehension at what might unfold during the day ahead. She grinned and waved back, trying not to look as if she was fussing, or taking too much interest in him. She couldn't wait until they were back home; then she and Michael could start their relationship properly. She'd watched the others wishing him luck. Natalie and Jo had given him a big hug and Dave, Stewart and Jason had all shaken his hand as he'd left them behind and strode off through the bar and gardens towards the beach. Her thoughts were interrupted by the ringing of her phone.

"Hi! Eve! At last! I was trying to reach you for the longest while."

"No, Melv, you tried to reach me for half an hour last night!"

She heard him chuckled down the phone and the sound of it gave her a warm feeling.

"Sorry. I forgot how pedantic you can be. I tried to reach you for an hour last night, Eve."

"Well, if you'd tried to reach me a bit earlier, like any time during the previous day and a half, you'd have got me," she couldn't help retorting, although she immediately regretted it. She didn't want him to think she cared that much. "Anyway, now you've got me. So what can I do for you, Melv?"

"I was just checking that you knew that Michael is coming out on the boat with me today."

"Yes, I knew. He told me last night."

"And you're okay with that?"

"Why wouldn't I be?"

"No reason! I just wanted to check you knew, that's all. I mean, you'll have him all to yourself from tomorrow and I just wanted to spend some time with him, to get to know him a bit more... for him to get to know me... you know how it is."

"Melv I really haven't got a problem with any of it. I'm honestly glad, from the bottom of my heart that you're spending the day together. Really and truly."

"Great!"

There was an awkward pause. Eve looked around the bar and restaurant, watching Natalie, Dave, Trevor, Stewart, Suzanne and Grace heading off towards the beach, making the most of their last full day in the sun.

"You're going to have a great day for it, too. Not a cloud in the sky!" she said and then mentally kicked herself for talking about the weather. Melv wasn't one of her clients that she had to make polite conversation with. She didn't have to speak to him at all if she didn't want to. But she did want to! She heard a cough down the line as Melv nervously cleared his throat.

"Eve, I was wondering, could we meet up later? Perhaps you could come down to the boat when we get back?"

"Oh that would be nice! The three of us having a drink together," she said, being deliberately obtuse.

"I meant the two of us. I'd like us to spend some time together later."

"It's difficult. It's our last night and we're all having dinner together. I've got a special table arranged for eight o'clock."

"Well, meet me at half five. Please, Eve! Come down to the jetty at five-thirty. I'll be waiting there. I want to see you."

Shit!

She'd made up her mind last night that she was going to treat him as a fuck-buddy for her trips to Antigua. And now here she was, stomach churning, heart flipping, pulse racing, at the thought of being alone with him for an hour or so.

"What do you think? Eve? Are you still there?"

"I'm still here." She took a deep breath. "Okay. I'll come to the jetty at five-thirty."

"Great! Thanks. I look forward to that. Oh, here comes Michael."

"Well, have a great day the two of you. And take care of him on the high seas," she joked to try to lighten herself up as much as the atmosphere between them.

"I will."

And he was gone.

She slipped her phone back into her bag and looked up to see Dawn and Donna making their way towards her, in matching romper suits, Donna's yellow and Dawn's apple green, both waving envelopes.

"We thought we'd give you the tip money now," Donna said.

"Then it's done with and we haven't got to think about it anymore," Dawn finished the sentence for her.

"Oh, thank you," Eve said, taking the envelopes and putting them inside her folder and ticking their names on her *Staff Gratuities* list.

"We've give the suggested amount and we're gonna leave the chambermaid a little something, too," Dawn said.

"We know they ask us not to tip individually but she's a nice woman. And we're gonna leave her our toiletries as well," Donna declared.

"I'm sure she'll really appreciate that. Are you off to the beach?"

"Yes. We're gonna have a real full day of serious sunbathing so we can go home as tanned as possible. The others have gone on and Dave said he'd save two beds for us."

"You coming down to join us?" Dawn asked.

"I might later on. Just a few last minute bits and pieces to do, you know, paperwork. And I really ought to go in and see Deano to say goodbye."

"Well, give him our best!" Dawn said as the two of them flip-flopped their way down to the beach to join the others.

Eve thought that they were nice enough women, just a bit strange. But then she shrugged and laughed to herself.

Who wasn't?

She sipped her coffee and watched Deborah and Murray finish their cosy breakfast *a deux* and walk off together, with Murray's arms hovering around Deborah's shoulder. She gave her head a slight shake; she'd never have put those two together at the beginning of the holiday! Then she saw Geri arrive for breakfast and join Jo, who was alone at the table. She hadn't seen Frances this morning, but she giggled to herself as she imagined rampant sex with a man twenty years her junior was probably what she'd had for breakfast.

Good on you, Frances!

***

Frances was, actually, tucked up in bed in her room at the resort. She'd arrived back at quarter past seven in a taxi that had dropped Neville off at work and then brought her down the west coast to the Mango Tree Resort. When she'd gone to pay the fare, she was surprised to see only $10 US in her purse. She was sure she'd put a $100 US note in there last night. She always liked to have money on her. After all, you never knew when an emergency might present itself. She excused herself to the taxi driver, who looked at her suspiciously when she said she had to go to her room for more money.

"I'm in room two twenty-one. Honestly. You can check at the front desk," she said, although she'd really rather he didn't. She didn't want to let everyone see she was just rolling home.

"It's alright. I'll wait for you right here," the taxi driver said.

Frances rushed back to her room and opened her safe. She grabbed a fifty dollar bill from the wad of US dollars, pinging the elastic band as she did so, and rushed back down to the front gate of the resort where the taxi driver was patiently waiting.

"That's fine! Keep the change!" she trilled at him, thrusting the fifty dollar bill into his hand.

"Thank you, lady," he said, surprised at the size of the tip, putting the taxi into gear and speeding off before she could change her mind.

Frances looked at her watch and saw it was almost seven thirty. She felt peckish but she didn't want to see the others and she certainly didn't want them to see her in last night's clothes with the whiff of weed wafting around her. She made her way towards the breakfast buffet, where she helped herself to two Danish pastries and a cup of tea, which she took back to her room, with her head down to avoid seeing anyone. She stripped off her clothes and stood under the shower for a few minutes then wrapped herself in a thick fluffy towel and lay back against the headboard, sipping her tea and eating her pastries, thinking about the money. It was easily done, she supposed. It was the second time she'd made a mistake. The first night she'd gone out with Neville she'd thought she'd taken three fifty dollar notes but it turned out they were five dollar bills. The lighting in the room was what could be called *atmospheric*, which was really another word for dim. And last night she must have grabbed a ten dollar note, thinking it was a hundred. She'd changed the fifty dollar note she'd already had in her purse when she'd taken the taxi to Neville's and then the change had gone on his supper. She shrugged.

Be more careful next time!

And of course, she'd been in such an eager rush to get back to Neville that she hadn't really been concentrating on what she was doing. She stretched out on the bed. She felt tired and so did pussy, which felt swollen and *oh God!* wet again! She only had to think about Neville and what they did together and she became so aroused she thought she could have an orgasm there and then. *Think Yourself to Orgasm.* It sounded like the title of an article in *She* or *Cosmopolitan.* She giggled as she thought about starting a blog aimed at older women. What could she call is? *Bring Your Pussy Back to Life. Pussy Pulsates. Orgasmathon. Licking the Lollipop.* She giggled again at the two words - *pussy* and *lollipop* as if she was a ten-year-old in a sex lesson. Then she felt a wave of sleep coming over her. She relaxed and let it embrace her. Licking the lollipop was tiring business.

***

Geri took a sip of her coffee and put the mug back on the table.

"Jo," she said, turning to look at her, "I've been hoping to see you on your own before we left. I just wanted to apologise to you for my behaviour... you know... around you and Deano. I behaved like an idiot and I'm sorry that I spoilt the time that you two could have had together."

Jo gazed back at Geri and saw the signs of hurt and bitterness etched on her face, alongside the damage that drink was also doing. In spite of her tan, Geri's skin looked sallow; her nose and cheeks had the beginnings of a drinker's spider veins and there were dark shadows under her eyes too deep to be removed by simply having a good night's sleep. She noticed, too, that Geri's hand trembled slightly as she picked up her coffee mug again and held it in front of her, both hands wrapped around it, clutching it like an amulet.

"There's really no need to apologise, Geri. We all do silly things and I'm sure that Deano played his part in it," Jo said. As angry as she had been with Deano, she didn't think it right that she should tell anyone else what had really happened between them or that he was married and his wife was actually in Antigua with him now.

"He did!" Geri agreed; glad to be able to share the blame. "He did encourage me. You know, from the first moment I saw him at Gatwick he was giving me the come-on, chatting me up, looking at me. If he'd hadn't I wouldn't have kept on hanging around him, would I?"

"I would hope not," Jo said.

"No, I wouldn't! Honest! I just... you know... he... well, he made out like he fancied me."

"Well, don't lose any sleep over it," Jo said. "I'm sure that if he hadn't had his accident we wouldn't have got very far together, and I've come to realise over the last few days that a quick holiday fling isn't really what I'm looking for."

"You mean, you want to get married again?"

"Possibly. Possibly not. But what I do want is a good, honest, kind, decent man to share my life with again."

"Huh! Some hopes!" Geri said.

"I managed to find one before and I think I can find one again. There are good men in the world, not all of them are bastards, you know."

She sipped her tea, looking at Geri over the rim.

"I suppose from your reaction that you had a bad marriage, did you?"

"Yes. I was married to a pilot who left me for a bloody trolley dolly."

"Oh dear! I'm sorry."

"Twenty years of my life I'd given him, sixteen as his wife, and then it was all gone in an instant. Twenty years of building a home, giving him two lovely kids was tossed aside when some young whore fluttered her false eyelashes at him."

"That's a bit harsh, Geri. After all he chose to have an affair with her, she didn't make him, did she?"

"I know. But it makes me angry. All because of her I went from living in a beautiful five-bedroom detached house with half an acre of garden, to a pokey flat. From being able to spend freely on whatever I liked to having to watch every penny. And from travelling the world in Business Class and staying in five-star hotels to having to come away on a singles' holiday because I've got nobody else to travel with."

"We're not so bad, are we?" Jo asked, looking her straight in the eye.

"Oh, no! I didn't mean that. I didn't mean any offence to anyone on the holiday. I think everyone's great and I must admit a lot of them are the sort of people I wouldn't have imagined would have to come on a holiday like this."

"Perhaps they didn't *have to* come on a holiday like this. Perhaps they wanted to; they *chose* to. Stop thinking of the group as a bunch of losers. And yourself. Because you're not. You're a woman who chose to come on a singles' holiday to meet new people and make new friends and because she didn't want to travel alone."

"It sounds better when you say it."

"But it's true whoever says it."

"I wish I had your confidence and your... your... serenity. That's what it is! You have an air of serenity about you. I suppose it's down to you being religious, is it?"

"My faith is the foundation of my life and I am blessed to know and love Jesus Christ. And because of that I believe that everyone would find peace and serenity if they also followed Him."

She saw a cloud pass over Geri's face and she smiled and gently touched her forearm.

"It's okay, Geri, I'm not going to preach to you or try to convert you. I'm merely telling you why I've found serenity after the turmoil and bitterness that had been my life."

"Do you think I should start going to church then?"

"Not unless you want to. But I do think you'd benefit from counselling. Perhaps you could do some work on self-worth and self-esteem. You can be happy, very happy without being *wife-of*."

"But I feel like I can't compete with bloody Lucy. That's the trolley dolly. I mean, my kids love her, too. Sometimes when they come and see me I think I'll scream if I hear her name one more time!"

"So, they live with their dad, do they? That must be hard for you."

"Oh, they spend weekends with their dad. They're with me the rest of the time, of course they are!" Geri said quickly. *'Too quickly'*, Jo thought. "We struggle along but we're happy. But she can buy them things that I can't and I feel like she's completely taken over."

"I'm sure that's not true. We've all only got one mum and I'm sure your children know that. The best thing you can do is be a great role model. Show them that you're a woman who's living a happy, successful, independent life."

"But I get lonely. Don't you?"

"Sometimes, yes I do. But as I said to you, I've decided that I do want another relationship and I'm sure that sooner or later that's what I'm going to have."

"I wish I had your optimism," Geri sighed. She sat back in her chair, the story of her divorce and present circumstances vivid in her mind. She'd told it so many times now, she almost believed it herself.

Anxious for the conversation not to go round and round in circles, Jo took the last bit of her slice of toast and folded her napkin onto the table.

"Well, I'm off to join the others at the beach, but I just want to talk to Eve for a moment first. Are you going down?"

"Oh yes!" Geri said, brightening. "There's no way I'm missing our last day of sunshine."

"I'll see you there, then," Jo said, gathering her beach bag and making her way over to the terrace where Eve was sitting, waiting to greet her with her usual warm, friendly smile.

"How do you do it, Eve?" Jo asked her. "You're always smiling."

"You should see me on a bad day!" Eve said and they both laughed.

"Well, I'd have thought you'd have had enough bad days this week, but you're still smiling!"

"It goes with the territory. There must be days when you don't feel like standing in the pulpit or listening to the woes of one of your parishioners, but I'm sure that you put on a smile."

"You're right! But I can always walk away after a while whereas you're stuck with people twenty-four seven. Anyway, I was just wondering how Deano is. Oh, I know what I said and it was the truth. But we were all talking about him at breakfast and wondering how he is and whether or not you'll be seeing him before we leave."

"To be honest, I'm going to ring him. I have no wish to sit by his bed with his wife on the other side. And besides, it's not really anything to do with me anymore, but I did want to just say goodbye and wish him luck. As I'm sure you did, too."

"Yes. Even though I don't want to see him again I wish him well."

"Well, I'll tell him when I ring. Everyone's said they wish to be remembered. They've all accepted the fact that he said he didn't want any visitors so that's made things easier."

"We're down on the beach in the usual spot if you want to come and sit with us," Jo offered. "But I won't be offended if you don't come along."

"Thanks, but I have got quite a lot to do today," Eve said. Although she knew that she would spend most of it wondering what was going on at sea with her son and his father.

***

Her son and his father were having a wonderful time together. They'd cast off from the jetty at the Mango Tree Resort and headed north.

"I know you went south when you did your catamaran trip," Melv said, "so it'll be nice for us to go north today. Maybe up to Bird Island or Green Island, although I don't want to get too far into the Atlantic as it's still a little worked up after the storm. Or we could go out to Paradise Reef and do a little fishing."

"I'm not bothered where we go. It's just great being out at sea, but I would like to do some fishing."

Melv stood behind the wheel of the speed boat and Michael sat to his right, his legs dangling over the side, watching the coastline as Melv pointed things out to him. They followed the shoreline around Hermitage and Five Islands Harbour, up past Hawksbill Beach and Deep Bay.

"Want a beer?" Melv asked, pointing at the large cool box. "Help yourself."

Michael grabbed them both a beer and sat back again to enjoy the ride as they turned into St John's Harbour. He could see the twin domed spires of the cathedral slightly to the left with the yellow and dark orange stripes of Mount St John's Medical Centre looking down on the City from its hilltop location to the right. Seeing the hospital, Michael thought about Deano who was inside and wished him well. Melv expertly steered the boat alongside a huge cruise ship that had docked and whose passengers were spilling out along the board-walk. Michael saw the *Welcome to Antigua* sign on the terracotta rooftops of Redcliffe Quay as Melv spun the wheel and they turned back towards the open sea. Michael realised that the *Arawak Arrow* was alongside them, full with passengers from the cruise ship who were going on a *Sail and Snorkel* day. He waved at Amos who was at the helm and who recognised him and sounded the klaxon in salute and then waved back.

Melv opened the throttle and the boat sped forward turning north at the mouth of the harbour past Fort St James, Dickinson Bay and then heading northwest towards Paradise Reef. Once there, Melv tied the boat to one of several buoys bobbing on the surface of the water.

"Here!" he threw a snorkel and mask at Michael. "So you can get a good look at what we're gonna catch."

He adjusted Michael's mask and the two of them put on their fins and got into the water. Immediately they were surrounded by hundreds of fish; the water was teeming with them, and Michael was surprised at how close they came to him, encouraged by the small pieces of bread that Melv had dropped into the water ahead of them. He'd enjoyed the snorkelling at Cades Reef, but this was something else. This time he was snorkelling with his dad.

Back on the boat they let the sun dry their skin as they helped themselves to another beer each to take away the taste of the salt from their mouths and Melv set up the fishing line.

"You saw how many fish there are, so usually we take home quite a good catch from here," he said. "If we're lucky, you'll have enough for your whole group to eat at the Crazy Conch tonight."

"How did you know we're eating there?" Michael asked.

"I spoke to Eve this morning."

Michael grinned.

"What you smiling at?"

"I'm not naive enough to think that you and my mother will ever get together," he said, pausing to take a sip of his beer and sitting on the deck next to Melv who was lowering the line into the water, "but I just love it that you talk to each other."

"Of course we do! I've already told you that my marriage isn't good; it's only a matter of time before Mary and I go our separate ways. We would have done a few years back if it hadn't been for the problems with Juliette. If I was single now, who knows? But I already know that Eve has a life in England and I'm not that presumptuous to think that we'd get together again."

"Although you'd like to?"

"Mmm... yes and no. The romantic young student in me would love it, but the mature man knows that it's not likely to happen. We're both different people now from the two young lovers who were responsible for bringing you into the world."

He finished hooking bait on the line and dropped it into the water, dipped his hands in the sea to wash them and then went over to his bag and opened it up, bringing out a large brown envelope which he took to the seats under the canopy, motioning Michael to sit next to him.

"I've brought some photos along that I thought you might want to take a look at," he said, taking them out.

Michael felt a shiver of excitement go down his spine as he started to look through them with his father.

"These are some of me just before I went to study in England," he said, laughing. "I was probably about sixteen, seventeen."

"You're the dude with the hair?" Michael asked, incredulous at the sight of his father with a huge afro. Melv nodded. "Who are all the others?"

"They were my friends. Alan, Jaden, Wilson, Marty. We were all inseparable up until then. Went to the same school, hung out at the same places. You know how it is."

He showed Michael several pictures of the group of friends, drinking together, at the beach, fooling around.

"And this beautiful woman is your grandma," he said, putting a photo of an elegant, older woman wearing 'church' clothes. "That was taken about five years before she died so she's about seventy-two there. She died three years ago."

"She really was beautiful," Michael said, staring at her intently, brushing his finger over her face, trying but not seeing a family resemblance to himself at all.

"This is the guy I think you look like; my father."

Michael looked at the black and white photo of a man in shirtsleeves, wearing rimless glasses and holding a small baby in his arms, with two slightly older children standing next to him.

"The baby's me and the other two are my sister Deandra and my brother Broderick. We're in the yard of the house we all grew up in, in Barbados. Can you see the likeness between you and him?"

Michael nodded. He could see his own face in his grandfather's; lighter in colour, eyes a bit wider, but it was him.

"What was his name?"

"Reggie. And my mother was called Miriam."

"What did he do? What happened to him?"

He was a farmer to begin with, or rather his father was. But life on the farm was hard and his parents made sure he had an education, so when he left school he got a job as a clerk in a shipping company. Over the years he worked his way up and by the time that photo was taken he was the office manager. He worked long hours. He was usually gone before us in the mornings and he was rarely home before seven in the evening. His sight was poor because of the hours he spent bent over the books, laboriously recording all the vessels that left and arrived and where they were going and what they were carrying."

"How did he die?"

"He had cancer. He died a relatively young man; he was in his late forties. The year after I came back from England. That was another reason why I couldn't chase after your mother. I was needed at home. I had to find work and support my mother."

"Have you got any photos of the two of you together?"

"Of me with Eve? No. I carried a photo of her in my wallet for a long, long time. But then I married Mary and... well... when you're married you stop carrying pictures of other lovers!"

"I want you to tell me everything about the family there is to know and everything about you. Everything."

"I've told you most things already. But let's get ourselves some lunch first. I can't recall things on an empty stomach," Melv joked.

The two men got out the picnic and Michael settled back down under the canopy anxious not to miss any tiny detail about one half of his family tree.

***

Natalie drank half her bottle of water in two great big gulps. Like the others, she was feeling headachy and dehydrated from the previous night's drinking.

"I think it's time for another paracetamol," she said, diving into her beach bag. "Anyone else want one?"

"Yeah, I'll 'ave one, please," Dave said, holding his hand out for Natalie to place the tablet in.

"I can't believe how much water I've drunk," Natalie said. "We must have been really wasted last night. I can't remember much about it."

"Well, I remember you falling backwards into the taxi and you couldn't get up," Trevor said.

"Good job we was all drunk 'n' nobody took a photo of yer kicking yer legs in the air an' showin' yer knickers!" Dave said, placing the paracetamol in his mouth and swallowing it down with the remains of his warm beer.

"I'm so sad. I can't believe we're on our last day." Suzanne gave a deep sigh as she looked along the beach and out over the sea.

"Look at it this way; we've still got twenty-four hours left," Stewart said. "This time tomorrow we'll only be vacating our rooms. We've got the rest of today and tonight. And don't forget, we've got a special meal tonight, haven't we? And there's tomorrow morning as well."

"I know. But it's still sad."

"Think not with sadness that it is no more but with gladness that it was," Jo said to her. "Think about the great time you've had... that we've all had... and be glad!"

"Yes, don't you start me off, Suzanne!" Natalie warned her. "I'm a real softie. I know I'll be grizzling when we leave tomorrow and I have to say goodbye to you all, but don't start me off today!"

"I nevva 'ad you dahn fer a softie," Dave said to Natalie.

"It's not soft to be sad!" Suzanne corrected him. "Just sensitive."

"Yes, Dave! I'm sensitive!" Natalie said throwing an ice cube at him.

"I can't believe where the time's gone, though," Grace said. "It's flown by."

"Yes, but on the other hand, it seems like I've been away a long time. You know, since we were in Gatwick. And it seems ages since I last took a dance class. I'm looking forward to going back and seeing the kids again."

"Don't you break up for the summer holidays?" Geri asked.

"Just these two weeks. I can't really afford to close for six weeks, and anyway, I do a summer school during the day and loads of them come to it. Their parents are glad to have them doing something and not just hanging around the house."

"Well, let's hope all that hacking scandal's over by the time we get back," Trevor said. "I got to the stage where I'd have put my head in the oven if I'd heard the word *hacking* or *Murdoch* one more time!"

"Tell me abaht it! It got like a bleedin' witch unt in the end if you ask me," Dave said. "Yeah, it was terrible, but there's more pressin' fings appenin'."

"I think you're right," Stewart said. "It's all politics. None of them are whiter than white."

"What's your opinion abaht the Met an' all that scandaw, Detective Chief Superintendant?" Dave asked Grace.

"I think they handled it badly and shot themselves in the foot. The powers that be in the Met made a balls-up. What annoys me is that it then gives the whole of the police force, countrywide, a bad name."

"And it'll only be a few weeks and then the *X-Factor* and *Strictly* start again!" said Suzanne, clapping her hands.

"You won't be watchin' that, will ya?" Dave asked her. "You'll be spendin' the weekends wiv Stew in Oldham."

Suzanne and Stewart both blushed as the others all laughed at Dave's comment.

"She can still watch them in Oldham!" Natalie said, jumping to their defence.

"Course I can! And anyway, Stewart's probably coming to spend the weekends with me because I have to work in the shop."

"Yes, and besides, coming to me's a bit like *Meet the Fockers*," Stewart said, making them all laugh again. "What with my mum and my sister's kids it's a nightmare."

"What abaht yer gigs? You givin' em up?"

"No! We're gonna work something out, you'll see. Nothing's coming between us!" Stewart said leaning over and kissing Suzanne.

"Yeuk! Get a room, you two!" Natalie said, making Suzanne giggle.

"I love *Strictly*," said Geri. "I love the outfits and I love to see how the celebrities improve as the weeks go by."

"That's because you like dancing," Trevor said. "Did you do dance as part of your PE training?"

"Not really, just the odd bit of country dancing. I suppose I've always like exercise and dancing's part of that."

"Oh, are you a PE teacher? I thought you were an estate agent," Natalie said, noticing that Geri had turned pink.

"I used to teach PE. I gave it up when I had the children and now, well, I'd have to do some courses to update my skills and it just doesn't seem worth it. So I'm happy to carry on where I am," she said, praying someone would change the subject quickly. Grace answered her prayers.

"I was thinking about getting an upgrade on the flight going back," she said, stretching back on her sun lounger. "I've got a two hour wait at Gatwick for my flight to Manchester and it would be nice to think I could have a bit of comfort and get some sleep on the flight from here."

"How much did Eve say it is?" Trevor asked.

"About two hundred pounds, I think. I'd willing pay that, though, for some peace."

"Mind you, there's no guarantee you won't get children next to you even if you do upgrade," Jo said. "My sister and her husband treated themselves to an upgrade when they went to New York two years ago and they had a baby in front of them who cried for five of the six and a half hours the flight lasted!"

"And you do get some right chavs upgrading, too!" Stewart added. "I saw a woman going up the stairs to the top deck when we were boarding in Gatwick and she looked a right state."

"I don't mind her looking a state as long as she's quiet!" Grace said, laughing.

"Well, that's just it! She had about four kids with her and they looked like trouble, if you know what I mean."

"I wonder if she's the one I noticed when we were checking in," Natalie said. "She was wearing really nice sandals yet her toenails were yellow and her heels looked like lumps of Parmesan cheese."

Everyone roared with laughter at Natalie's description of the woman.

"Well, I'll ask to pay for an upgrade, but only if I can sit next to someone whose feet are nicely pedicured!"

"Will we all sit together, do you think?" Trevor asked. "Some of us were together on the way out, weren't we?"

"Well I hope so! I want to sit with Stewart!" Suzanne said, sounding like a five-year-old girl. "It might not be full, so we'll be able to choose our seats."

"If the airline people are bringing our boarding cards it sounds like the seat numbers will already have been allocated," Stewart said, taking her hand. "But don't worry, we'll ask Eve. She'll know what to do so that we can sit together." And he planted another kiss on Suzanne's lips.

"Put 'er dahn, Stew!" Dave said.

Dawn and Donna came strolling up the beach from their aquarobics session in the pool.

"Anyone want a drink?" Donna asked. "Shall we go and get everyone a rum punch?"

"Yeah, go on then!" Natalie said, laughing at herself and looking defiantly at the surprised faces of the others. "Well, why not? In two days time I'll be pining for all this and dying for a rum punch!"

"Natalie's right and besides, it would be rude to turn down the offer of a drink from two such charming waitresses," Trevor said, surprising himself at his response.

"Blimey! Have you all met my friend Trevor, the charmer and ladies' man?" Stewart said and they all laughed.

"Beer fer me, please," Dave said.

After carefully counting how many rum punches and how many beers they were fetching Donna and Dawn went up the beach to the bar to get the drinks in.

"I'm going back in the water, I'm boiling. Anyone coming in for a dip?" Grace asked standing up.

They all were. They made their way across the warm sand and into the cool, refreshing water, all flipping onto their backs, relaxing and floating, except for Suzanne and Stewart who bobbed about clinging to each other. After a moment of calm they were thrown about by the wash from two jet skis as Huw and Jason raced by them, a little too close for comfort.

"Tossers!" Dave shouted at them, pushing the water from his eyes as he surfaced.

"They want to be careful," Trevor said. "We don't want any more accidents!"

***

Eve put the phone down from talking to Deano, who'd sounded glum and depressed. But at least he was alone as his wife had just gone out for a cigarette and a cup of coffee so he could talk freely.

"Well, everyone sends their love and best wishes," Eve said in an attempt to cheer him up. "They wanted to come in and see you today, but I said that you still didn't want any visitors."

"Thanks. You heard about Jo coming in, did you? Did she tell you?"

"Yes she did."

"She couldn't have come at a worse moment; my wife walked in on us."

"It must have been quite a shock for her."

"No! Jo told her she's a vicar and that she was, you know, visiting the sick."

"I meant Jo. It was a shock for her. Finding out that you're married."

There was an awkward pause and then Deano gave a groan.

"I never wanted her to find out like that!" he said.

You never wanted her to find out at all!

"I wanted to tell her quietly, in my own time."

Eve didn't say anything, not trusting herself to refrain from giving him the bollocking he deserved.

"Has she said anything to you, Eve?"

"What about?"

"About the two of us. About wanting to see me again or keeping in touch with me?"

"No. She hasn't said anything about that; she just told me what had happened yesterday."

"Would you do me a favour and give her my mobile number or my e-mail address, Eve? Please?"

"No, sorry, Deano, I won't. I'm not your messenger. Especially after everything that's gone on. If she wants to contact you again she'll find you but don't drag me into it and don't ask me to do things like that for you."

"But I need to explain!"

384

"Then find another way of doing it. But if you really want my advice, leave her alone."

"Eve, please!"

"I hope that everything turns out for you; that your journey back home is comfortable and that your leg heals well and that you'll soon be up and around."

"But, Eve... Okay. I understand where you're coming from." There was another short pause. "Thanks anyway... for all your help and everything. I mean, before the accident as well."

"That's okay. You take care of yourself."

She ended the call and sighed to herself at the foolishness of some people. She thought about Deano and about his vanity.

Turquoise contact lenses!

She gave a little giggle. It all seemed so absurd. A married man comes away for what he hopes will be a leg-over week and then has a serious accident because he's lost one of his turquoise contact lenses and can't let people see his eyes are really hazel so he keeps his sun glasses on! She started to laugh at the absurdity of it. At times like this she believed in karma. Deano had paid dearly for his conceit.

***

Deborah and Murray had spent the whole morning together at the Spa Bar. They'd giggled repeatedly about the previous evening and the *Mystery of the Missing Clothes* and Murray had just loved the way it had turned Deborah on. They'd had a night of loving that he could only have dreamed about. Deborah had certainly got an appetite for sex, but then he supposed that was because she was finally with a real man. He stretched his arms above his head and looked at Deborah who was fast asleep beside him, knocked out by her night of action. He felt very self-satisfied. He also felt thirsty. He stood up to get a beer just as Deborah stirred.

"I'm going for a drink. Will I get you one?"

"A beer, please"

Murray made his way over to the bar with a huge grin on his face. However, it soon disappeared when he turned round to see that in the three minutes it had taken him to get the drinks Frances had appeared and was sitting on his sun lounger deep in conversation with Deborah. He stomped back over to them, handed Deborah her drink and then stood in front of Frances, waiting for her to take the hint that she was on his lounger, but she seemed oblivious to him and much to his dismay, so did Deborah.

"So, are you going back for one last session tonight?" Deborah asked, chuckling.

"What do you think? Of course I am! I'll be facing an indeterminate sex-famine when I get back home, so I may as well enjoy the feast while I can!"

They both roared with laughter and Murray felt decidedly out of it. He hoped Deborah wasn't giving Frances all the details of their encounter. But then he supposed it was different for Frances; hers was just a holiday fling. Having endless sex with a younger man must be somewhat of a novelty he supposed. But it just couldn't compare to what he had with Deborah.

"Well, we had a shag in the sea last night and while we were in there someone whipped our clothes," Deborah said.

"No! How did that happen?" Frances's eyes opened like saucers as she looked from Deborah to Murray with a huge grin on her face. Murray felt himself go scarlet.

"I'm just off tae the gents," he said, excusing himself as he walked off feeling suddenly very peeved. Bloody Frances was going to spoil his day, now. He just knew it. She'd probably tag along for lunch and play gooseberry all the afternoon. He'd been hoping that Deborah would be in the mood for a siesta, but there wasn't much chance of that now.

Fuck you, Frances!

***

At five o'clock Melv guided the boat gently back alongside the jetty. Michael jumped off and tethered the rope, securing it with the knot that Melv had shown him earlier in the day.

"Well done, first mate!" Melv said, high fiving him. He lifted the cool box that held their catch and passed it to Michael and the two men made their way along the jetty towards the Crazy Conch to ask Vaughan, the chef to prepare some of the fish for the Travel Together group who were eating there that night.

"Yeh mon! No problem. I'll put the wahoo on the grill for you," Vaughan said, lovingly running his hands over it in admiration. "It's a big one! More than enough for all of you."

Michael grinned, pleased with himself. Melv had taken his photo holding the wahoo, which was heavy. They'd also caught several snappers, two king fish, a mahi-mahi and a marlin. Melv was going to take it all home with him and clean it.

"Some of it the family will eat tonight or tomorrow and the rest will go in the freezer."

"I've had such a great day. Thank you."

"It's meant more to me than you can ever imagine," Melv said and Michael saw the tears in his eyes.

"Why don't you come and have dinner with us tonight? After all, you caught the wahoo really. I wouldn't have had a clue without you!"

"I'll take a rain check with you on that, Michael. I'm not sure if Eve would be okay with it. She's very protective of her group."

"She'll love it! Please! Come and eat with us. It's our last night."

Just at that moment Natalie, Grace, Jo, Dave, Geri and Trevor, who were walking the length of the beach along the water's edge saw them and came over.

"Hi! Hi! How was your day?" Natalie asked, although the beam on both men's faces already gave her their answer.

"Fantastic! And you should see how much we caught! The chef's preparing the wahoo for us for dinner tonight in the Crazy Conch. It's huge!"

"Woo hoo!" she gave her classic response.

"No, wahoo!"

They all laughed.

"Come down to the boat and take a look at the rest of the catch," Melv said leading them across the sand towards the jetty.

"Wow!"

They were all amazed at the size and number of the fish.

"What's that yellow and blue one?" Natalie asked.

"That's a mahi-mahi."

"Oh, didn't we have that for dinner the other night?"

"Probably. It's a nice, meaty while fish. Slightly sweet."

"An is the woo'oo bigger'n that then?" Dave asked.

"Oh, yes! It's huge," Michael said. "There'll be enough for however many want to try it tonight."

"Are you joining us?" Grace turned to Melv. "It would be nice if you did."

"I just invited him but he's not sure about Eve."

"Eve?"

"I just think she might have plans for you all as it's the last night," Melv jumped in, fearful that Michael might say something they'd all regret.

"She won't mind!" Natalie said. "She's well cool. And it'll be nice for you to eat together." She nodded at Melv and Michael and then froze as she realised what she'd said and that Melv might not know that Michael had told the group about their relationship. "I mean, as you both caught the fish, that is."

"Yes, and then you can tell your fisherman's stories together!" Jo said.

"Okay! It's a date! I'll see you all later," Melv said.

The group turned to walk back up the beach as Michael turned to his father.

"Thanks again," he said as they stood looking at each other and then the two men embraced, neither one wanting to be the one that pulled away first.

***

Eve had changed three times. Part of her problem was that most of her clothes were in the *dirty* side of her suitcase. On a trip she'd always put clothes that were dirty into the lid of her case where they could be zipped away from anything that she was taking home clean. Unfortunately, as this was the last day, there wasn't much left. She finally settled for a maxi dress that was fairly casual, but nice enough for her to keep on for dinner if she didn't have time to change. She did her makeup carefully, just concentrating on her eyes and with a quick layer of lip gloss over her lips. She piled her hair up on top of her head and held it firm with a comb. She eyed herself from all angles in the mirror.

Not bad!

As she made her way through the grounds down towards the jetty she saw Jason, Dave and Stewart juggling loads of drinks as they headed towards the beach.

"We're avin a group sunset watch!" Dave announced. "We're all dahn there. Ev'ryone. Even Ursula. We're gonna watch our last sunset all togevva. It was Nat's idea. You comin'?"

"I've just got something to do now," Eve said, feeling a bit guilty that she wasn't going to be part of this. But then again, the group didn't need or even want her to be there with them continually. They could have a bit of privacy from her. And besides she was anxious to hear from Melv how the day had gone. "You all enjoy yourselves and I'll see you a bit later."

"Okay!"

Eve veered to the left and kicked off her sandals making it easier to cross the sand towards the jetty where she could see Melv and his speedboat waiting for her. He took her hand and helped her step onboard. There was a moment's awkward silence and then they both spoke at once.

388

"How did the day go?"

"Have you seen Michael?"

They both laughed nervously and Melv insisted she go first.

"I was asking how your day went. Did you both enjoy yourselves?"

"I had a wonderful day. A beautiful day that I'll treasure forever. Michael's a great guy and I was able to tell him all about my family, you know, fill him in a bit more on their background and show him some pictures, so he gets some idea about the family tree. And we had a very successful day's fishing. I hope he enjoyed himself. I know I did."

"That's good. I'm pleased for you both."

"So, shall we go for a ride, somewhere?"

"Be a shame not to as we have a boat here."

"Where would you like to go?"

"You're the captain!"

Melv looked at Eve and smiled as he turned the key and started the engine. He loosened the ropes and pulled them on board and within two minutes they were heading out to sea.

***

After saying their *goodbyes* to Eve the three men walked down to the beach where the whole group had gathered together to watch their final sunset in Antigua. Sharing sun loungers or sitting on the sand they all relaxed and sipped their drinks, looking towards the sun that still had a way to go before it set.

"I just want to bottle this up and take it back to Merseyside with me," Grace said, "I just know it's going to be pissing down when we get back."

"Yeah, but we can still show off our tans," Donna said. "We're walking round in shorts whatever the weather, aren't we, Dawn?"

Feeling the effects of an afternoon of drinking rum punches, Dawn, who was sitting on the sand at the foot of Donna's lounger simply nodded in agreement.

"Yeah, I'm gonna wear all light colours, you know, white an' cream an' lemon an' that. Colours what show up yer tan," Dave said.

"I can't wait to see you in lemon!" Stewart said.

389

"Sorry, mate. I can't ear what you're sayin' over that shirt," Dave shot back, referring to Stewart's red and green palm tree shirt. Everyone laughed.

"That's no funnier now than the first time you said it!" Stewart retorted. "The trouble with you is you don't know quality when you see it! This is one of Palinda's best. Twenty US."

"You was robbed," Dave said, chuckling.

They watched Melv's boat cross the bay in front of them and head north along the west coast.

"You reckon there's something going on with Eve and the manager?" Jason asked looking at Michael.

"What makes you think that?" Michael asked him.

"Well, they're going off for a ride together to watch the sunset by the looks of it."

"Well, we're all sitting here together watching the sunset but we're not having a bang gang, are we?" Natalie said, the rum making her trip over her tongue.

Everyone laughed at her mistake, but she didn't care. She didn't want anyone to upset Michael; that was why she'd jumped in.

"Bang gang, gang bang, who cares?" she said, laughing and raising her glass high in the air. "Cheers everyone! Here's to our last night together!"

They all chinked glasses with each other. Even Huw, who seemed to have got over his strop joined in. He was sprawled on a lounger with his feet to one side with Jason balancing on the other.

"You enjoyed yourself, Ursula?" Grace turned to her right and asked her.

"Very much so. I felt so stressed out when I got here, but I feel so much better now; like I've really had a good rest."

"Seein yer boyfriend later?" Dave asked. Ursula sat very still for a moment and then gave a little grin.

"He's asked me to accompany him to a bar in the village after dinner. A place called Macy's"

"We wen' there the uvva night. Righ' fit barmaid."

"She's not going to be looking at the barmaid, is she?" Natalie said. "Especially if she's got a hot date!"

"You have a great night, Ursula!" Grace said to her.

"But don't let im av is evil way wiv yer!" Dave added. "Unless is long-term intentions towards yer are honourable."

"Why not?" Ursula asked, surprising them all. "You should always sample before you buy." The whole group fell about laughing. Even Huw had a smile on his face.

"You little hussy!" Natalie teased her. "You certainly have unwound on this holiday; all your stress has just disappeared!"

"Don't talk tae me about stress!" Murray said. "Just the thought of getting back intae my cab and intae the London traffic again is enough tae depress me. Cyclists! Pedestrians! Buses! Cars!"

"You forgot horse drawn vehicles," Deborah said, teasing him.

"I'd hate to drive for a living," Natalie said. "I don't know how you do it, Murray. I love what I do. I think that waking up and thinking '*oh fuck! I've got to go to work today!*' must be the worst thing in the world."

"Don't you find teaching stressful?" Trevor asked her.

"No! I love it. I love seeing my kids learning a new dance and going to auditions and getting jobs on the stage and on TV. I love it when we put on a big production. I just love everything about it!"

"That's because you're not in a fucking state school like the rest of us," Jason said. "If you were trying to teach dance or drama at the Municipal Dump Comprehensive, you'd feel different, wouldn't she?" he looked at Huw and then Geri, who looked away from him.

"Too right!" Huw agreed.

"Yes, teaching is stressful, but I'm always ready to go back to start a new term or a new year," Dawn said.

"What about you, Geri," Jason said. "Do you look forward to going back?"

"I'm no longer a teacher. I'm an estate agent," Geri said, looking out to sea.

"What did you used to teach?" Huw asked.

"Does anyone want another drink?" Geri asked, standing up and ignoring his question.

"I'll come wiv ya," Dave said, standing up. "Ya can't carry it all on yer own."

The two of them made their way back towards the bar, Geri striding along in a silent fury. Dave shuffled along trying to keep up with her until, out of breath he stopped and pulled her arm to bring her to a standstill and then swung her round to face him.

"Look! I know I ain't exactly bin yer favourite person on this olidee an' that we nevva got off to a very good start wiv me joke abaht Old Spice, but I fought we was friends nah."

"We are friends."

"So why ya dashin' along like ya don't want no-one to see us togevva? I offered ter elp ya wiv the drinks 'cos I knew ya couldn't manage. I'm tryin' ter elp ya."

"Oh, Dave, it's not you!" Geri said. "I'm just... just a bit upset with someone else in the group, that's all. It's not you. I'm glad you've come along to help me; I appreciate it, I really do."

"Oo's upset ya then? "What's it all abaht?"

"Oh, no-one."

"But you just said someone, oo's not me's upset ya."

"It's nothing. Honest. I made a bit of a fool of myself as usual. I really just want to forget it all. It's nothing to do with you. I'm not upset with you at all. In fact, I do hope we're friends. I'd like to think so."

"Course we are! As long as I ain't done nuffink to upset ya I'm appy!"

Geri squeezed his arm and he gave a beaming smile as they turned along the path towards the bar. Geri felt happy as they got the drinks, pleased that she'd cleared the air with Dave who she had really come to like. She looked at him closely, eyes hidden by her large sunglasses, and thought he wasn't bad looking. She'd never been attracted to bald men, but there was something... something... well, *nice,* about Dave. And now he had a deep tan his blue eyes really stood out and shone. Dave persuaded Elvis to give them two trays to carry the drinks on.

"We'll bring em righ' back," he said.

"Hey, no problem," Elvis said, smiling at both of them, glad that Geri was smiling back at him. "I'll send one of the boys to collect them in a while. You folks enjoy the sunset!"

Clutching their drinks and looking towards the west, a feel-good atmosphere of camaraderie was settling over the group when Jo had an idea.

"Group photo!" she announced jumping up and waving her camera. "All chush up together."

"But you won't be in it!" Frances said. She waited a moment expecting Deborah to offer to take the picture as she didn't want to be in it, but Deborah stayed where she was, happy to be part of the group photo. "Look! Ask him to do it!" she said, pointing at Lester, the waiter Elvis had sent down to collect the trays and the pile of empty glasses on them. "Excuse me! Can you take a photo of us, please?"

"Sure, ma'am," he said, taking the camera from Jo, who then went and positioned herself back on the sun lounger between Trevor's legs.

"Wait! Can you take one for me, too, please?" Ursula said, jumping up and starting a chain reaction which ended in poor Lester being draped in twelve cameras, half of which had switched themselves off before he could use them and needed their owner to get up and switch them on again.

Finally, Lester had taken the photo twelve times and each camera was back with its owner, when Suzanne let out a yell.

"The sunset! We've nearly missed it!"

They all looked round quickly, just in time to see the lower edge of the sun, now a dark tangerine orb, touch the sea. A silence settled over them. Stewart put his arms around Suzanne. Deborah found herself reaching for Murray's hand. Natalie put her head on Michael's knee, Dawn leaned back against Donna's legs and Jo felt Trevor reach for her hand and she gently squeezed it. Each one of them sat with his or her own thoughts as, through a mellow haze of rum, they watched the glorious sun set over the Caribbean Sea for the very last time.

***

Anchored among the large rocks known as Five Islands, Eve and Melv also watched the sunset. The dark tangerine orb had turned to a blood-orange red as it prepared to disappear completely, leaving streaks of pink through the few fluffy clouds that were suspended across the whole sky. They sat side by side, sipping champagne, legs swinging over the side, in companionable silence until Melv gave an embarrassed cough.

"Erm, I hope you don't mind, but when Michael and I got back we met some of the others and they saw what we'd caught and they invited me to join you all for dinner tonight. The chef in the Crazy Conch is going to prepare the wahoo for us all. It was a biggie." He looked at her shyly, afraid of her reaction.

"Why would I mind? As long as everyone's happy that's all I care about. And it's nice for you and Michael to eat what you caught together." She paused for a moment. "You do know that he told the group you're his dad?"

"Yes. I wasn't too happy about that, I mean, I don't want Mary finding out from anyone else but me, but he's assured me that they're all sworn to secrecy."

"Yes they are, and besides, we're leaving tomorrow so there's little chance of her getting to hear about it from anyone. I take it you are going to tell her?"

"Of course I am! Now that I've found him I'm not going to hide Michael away like I'm ashamed of him. Next time he comes I want him to meet his half brother and sister, but I just need to explain to the kids, well, and to Mary, why I haven't ever mentioned him before."

"That it's down to me, right?" she said, suddenly prickling.

"Well, yes. It is down to you, Eve. Whichever way you look at it, it's down to you. I couldn't tell them about a son I didn't know existed and the reason I didn't know he existed is because you didn't tell me about him."

"But I..."

"I know your reasons! Let's not go over this again, we've already discussed it to death. You had your reasons and I'm not blaming you or judging you. But the reason I didn't know about Michael was because I wasn't told; we can't get away from that. But, hell, let's not fight now! This is our last chance to spend some time together and I thought you'd like this little spot."

Chastised and knowing what he said made sense, Eve looked at her surroundings and smiled.

"I don't like this little spot; I love it! It's beautiful. And the sunset's a gorgeous one tonight."

Melv lifted the champagne bottle from the ice bucket and refilled her glass and then opened up a tray of snacks he'd picked up from the hotel kitchen and offered it to her, then placed it on the bench seat behind them.

"Whenever I see a beautiful sunset I always think of Corfu. It doesn't matter where I am in the world, wherever I've seen the sun go down it always reminds me of watching it from the beaches at home or from my father's fishing boat. It's the only thing that's ever made me homesick for Corfu, the sunsets."

"And now you can take Michael to see them."

"Yes, I hope so. But we've hardly spoken to each other really. You know, it's all so difficult with the group and well... it's not the ideal situation to get to know your son in."

"But now you have time. You can make plans when you get back home to meet up and to get to know each other properly. When's your next trip?"

"I haven't actually got anything for three weeks until I go to China, so it gives us time. But it has to come from him, doesn't it? Oh, he's said he wants us to spend time together and for us to have a proper relationship, but what if he has second thoughts? What if his mother..." she stumbled over the word, "his adoptive mother, what if she steps in and says she doesn't want him to see me? What if he decides when he's back home and all the emotion and excitement's died down that he just can't forgive me for giving him away and for not telling you about him? What then?" A tear welled up in the corner of her eye and slowly started making its way down her left cheek.

"Whoa! Slow down, Eve! You're getting ahead of yourself with all this *what if*. Don't cry!" He put his arm round her shoulder and drew her to him. She leaned against his chest, her tears flowing faster as all the pent up frustration of the roller-coaster ride that had been the last nine days caught up with her. "You've had a tough time, Baby. The storm; the guy with the accident; finding out about Michael..."

"Seeing you again!" she interrupted him.

"Yes. Seeing me again, too. And even when everything's going right your job is sometimes stressful. I must admit I don't know how you do it. You're in such close proximity with them all the time. Doesn't it drive you crazy?"

Eve lifted her head and grabbed a paper napkin from the tray of snacks to dry her eyes. She nodded at what Melv had just said.

"Yes, it does get me down at times," she sniffed. "I mean, this group's been nice, really, but some of them are so needy and they never stop whinging about things. You know," she shrugged, "sometimes it's like taking a school trip. You have these people who want to impress you with what an important job they do and how well-travelled they are yet they continually whine about the tiniest things. Like at breakfast this morning. Grace is a really nice woman, right, and I really like her, yet she was complaining because for the second day running there was no pineapple. I mean, didn't she realise that people wouldn't be out picking pineapples in a tropical storm? Or even take into account that the fruit and vegetable markets haven't been open since the storm passed? I told her that the heavy rainfall had ruined the pineapple crop and she looked at me as if I was mad and said, "But we've got watermelons". I mean; what have watermelons got to do with not having pineapple? And I know it sounds petty, but when you're listening to it day after day from twenty people... well, sometimes it gets to you."

Pushing her fringe back from her eyes, Melv reached for the bottle of champagne from the ice bucket and laughed at her frustration while refilling her glass.

"Perhaps she doesn't realise that pineapples grow in the ground. Most people think they grow on trees."

"Well, perhaps, but it's the subtle whinging that gets me down, you know, the ones that have something negative to say the whole bloody time. Still, on the whole they've been a nice group of people and it's home-time tomorrow!"

"And, will we see each other again soon?"

"I don't know; will we?"

"I'd like to think so." Melv took hold of her hand. "I'd like to think that we're going to keep in touch and that you'll come back to Antigua soon. Or that we'll meet up when I'm in London for the World Travel Market."

"What have you got in mind? Us meeting up for a quick fuck every so often?" she asked, staring at him and taking delight in watching him flinch at her words. He sipped his drink, dropped her hand and looked away from her, out towards the horizon where the crimson sun was now just a small segment sitting on top of the sea. He gave a deep sigh before he answered her.

"Look, what happened the night of the storm was unexpected and it was great. You know... the two of us together again, it felt good and it felt right. But, as you know, I'm married..."

"Well being married didn't stop you taking me to your bed, did it?" she interrupted him feeling her anger rising. "What was I? Just someone you wanted for old time's sake? Just an easy lay?"

She stood up intending to cross to the other side of the boat to sit away from him but he grabbed her wrist and spun her round, putting his left arm around her back and drawing her towards him.

"Will you just shut up for a minute and let me finish what I was going to say?"

Their faces inches apart, two sets of deep brown eyes looking into each other, she nodded her head.

"Mary and me, well... we're not exactly what you would call happily married."

"Oh spare me the *My-wife-doesn't- understand-me* speech!"

"Eve! For God's sake shut up, woman, and let me talk!"

He glared at her and she lowered her gaze, concentrating on sipping her drink.

"We both found out after five or six years of marriage that we had little in common. Mary is a hard woman. Don't get me wrong, I'm not criticising her for that; she's made her way in banking, which hasn't been easy, you know. She's a woman in a man's world. But her career always came before me as a result of me also selfishly putting my career before her. We've both had to spend time away from each other and the family and it's easy to drift apart and in a way we both competed against each other to see who could be more successful. My pride said it had to be me, but Mary fought against that. Who earned more money; who had most responsibility, all shit stuff that's really not important. You know, point scoring... childish immature behaviour. We even both took lovers and made no secret of it. But the one thing we have in common is our great love for our children. Several years ago my daughter went off the rails and we both realised then that we had to work hard together to get her back on track and that meant being responsible parents and making a safe, stable environment for her. Mary turned down the chance to be happy with someone else and to become the bank's first female senior manager. And in return, I made sure that she and both our kids had my full support. And that meant giving them time and attention."

Melv leaned across and poured the last drops of champagne into his glass, swallowing them in one gulp.

"But in spite of this united front, tough love and the blessing of Juliette finally getting herself sorted out, we both knew that we had stayed together for the children and that sooner or later, once they were both out in the world doing their own thing, Mary and I would also do our own thing and go our separate ways. Michael coming into my life won't affect that and he won't be the reason for any breakup. But I want to handle it my way."

He turned and took her hands in his again, pulling her close to him and looking straight into her eyes.

"But when the time comes, I'd like to know that you and I have at least the possibility of a future together."

"So I have to sit and wait for you to tie up your family ends and then when Mary's gone on her merry way you bring me in off the subs' bench? Is that it?"

"For Christ's sake, woman! Why won't you meet me half way on this? Huh? All I'm asking is for us to keep in touch, to see each other in London or here whenever we can. I'm asking for us to get to know each other all over again, to start from scratch. And who knows? We may discover we do indeed have a future together once I'm free."

Eve smiled at his suggestion, because it was almost exactly what she'd decided she wanted the previous evening. She *did* want to see him again. She *did* want to have a relationship with him and she mentally ticked herself off for playing games. He was being brutally honest with her and he deserved honesty in return.

"What? What are you thinking? What are you smiling at?" he asked looking into her face and brushing her hair back so he could see into her eyes.

"I'm smiling because I'm happy. I'm smiling because I had already decided that I wanted to get to know you all over again. And I'm smiling because I know we're just about to make love to each other."

Eve reached down and pulled her dress over her head. Melv pulled her to him and gave her a long, deep kiss, before they both shared a special love-making session up on the deck of the gently-bobbing boat while twilight, then darkness fell all around them.

***

Dinner was a riotous affair. Knowing that it was their last night had brought out the naughty child in many of the group and there was an element of hysteria about the event; even Trevor having enjoyed several glasses of wine had opened up, telling jokes and bawdy tales. And those who hadn't seemed to have much in common appeared to realise that they would soon be saying goodbye to their new best friends and so wanted so have as good a time as possible with them on their last night together. The wahoo was declared the best fish they had ever eaten and Michael and Melv were congratulated on their fishing skills and then Vaughan the chef was called for to be thanked, congratulated and the recipe begged. Glasses were chinked time and time again as toasts were proposed and agreement bellowed. And as if to make their last evening extra-special for them a band was playing at the Crazy Conch and some of the diners had gathered on the make-do dance floor in front of the band. As they finished their main courses Dave stood up and jingled his spoon against his glass, asking for silence.

"I wanna say on be'alf of the ol group that Eve's bin the best tour manager we could've wished for. We've ad such a good olidee, fanks to you, Eve. An this is a small token of our appreciation." He handed Eve a very large envelope and planted a huge sloppy kiss on her cheek as the group broke into a round of wild applause and cheers. Peeking inside, Eve saw a beautiful landscape painting of the beach by the local artist Heather Doram and a smaller envelope that obviously contained money. She flushed as she smiled, looking around the table.

"It's been my pleasure," she said. "I'm glad you've enjoyed yourselves. As first-timers I know it's not easy and we've had the storm and Deano's accident but I do hope you've enjoyed the Travel Together experience and that I'll meet some of you again," she said. There were nods of agreement all round the table.

Then Michael grabbed Eve's hand, pulling her onto the dance floor. He took her in ballroom hold and the two of them bobbed in time as the band played *Hot Hot Hot*.

"It's been difficult to get you on your own but I wanted you to know that I think you're cool. Really cool. As a person, as a tour manager and as a mum." Michael said, beaming at her.

Tears sprang into Eve's eyes. Her emotions overwhelmed her as she danced with her son.

"Can we meet up in England? I really want to get to know you and for us to have a proper relationship," he said. "But no rush. I mean, at your pace, when you're ready..."

"I've been ready for thirty years, Michael."

They looked at each other, stopped dancing and hugged tightly. Now both of them were crying.

"The others are gonna wonder what's up," Michael said, wiping his eyes with the back of his hand. "I'll just have to say I'm overcome at having had such a good holiday!"

"Well, I hope that's true, too," Eve said.

"Too right it is!" he replied as he whirled her around again.

Back at the table desserts were ordered, even though everyone had said they were full.

"I can't believe that I won't be eating rum and raisin ice-cream anymore," Suzanne said. "I've had one every day since we've been here."

"Well, it is yummy!" Natalie said.

"They must sell it back home, surely?" Jo said. "Although it might not be as good as it is here, I grant you."

"And how am I gonna live without my nightly rum punches?" Natalie whined. "I won't be able to sleep!"

"Well, you'll just have to make yourself one as a nightcap every night," Stewart said. "I'm going to!"

"It's been grand, hasn't it?" Donna said, turning to Huw and Jason.

"It's been alright, I suppose," Huw said. Donna and Jason looked at each other and raised their eyebrows.

"Come on! Everyone onto the dance floor!" Natalie shouted, jumping up. "Yes! Even you, Mr McGrass!" she said to Melv taking his hand and pulling him to his feet. "And the love birds!" she added pointing at Deborah and Murray, who laughed and got up to join her.

"And you!" she shouted at Frances. "Or you off for some nookie?"

"I've got time for a couple of dances first!" Frances retorted, samba-ing towards the dance floor.

Only Huw remained in his seat and once they were all dancing he got up and left the table, preferring to stand on his own at the bar. After three energetic songs the band slowed right down to play a medley of ballads and most of the group meandered back to the tables to have a cool-down drink.

"Wanna smooch wiv me?" Dave asked Geri, taking her hand.

"Well, alright," she said, shyly, pleased that he'd asked.

"Dance with me, baby," Melv said to Eve and the two of them held each other, not caring who might see them, their bodies fitting together like a hand in a glove. Smiling and laughing they danced as if they'd never been apart.

Michael sat down at the table and watched his parents moving round the dance floor together, his father leading his mother into a spin that left her giggling and giddy, and a warm, contented glow spread throughout his body. He knew that Natalie was right; he was blessed at having two sets of parents. Each was different from the other yet both couples had made him who he was today. And as he looked at Eve and Melv he recognised his feelings as love. He'd already come to love them and he offered up a silent prayer of thanks and gratitude that he had finally found them both and, he hoped, that they had found each other.

***

Frances had taken a taxi to the standpipe after the Gray's Farm Police Station for the last time. She had mixed feelings about her final date with Neville, if you could call it a date. Frances wasn't sure what to call it. She'd grown fond of him and the amazing sex they'd shared had made her feel young, desirable, beautiful and confident. He had never referred to her scarred breast after that first time, but whenever he made love to her he always caressed and kissed it both gently and passionately as if it were as whole and unmarked as the other one. But, although this intense relationship had made her feel wonderful, she knew she wasn't twenty-five and that she couldn't keep up non-stop, no-holds-barred sex indefinitely; she was exhausted. She felt as if she'd need a holiday to get over this one. In spite of the glow the sex had given her, there were bags under her eyes where she'd gone without sleep. Yet every time she thought about Neville she felt her pussy go wet and start to throb. She giggled to herself again at the word as she lay naked on the bed, while Neville poured out two glasses of wine for them, a joint between his lips.

"I bought this especially for you," he'd said as he opened the bottle. "We gonna get a little drunk together tonight. Get high together 'cos I'm gonna miss you, baby." That had made her snigger like a schoolgirl. He gave her one glass and held onto the other. He took a mouthful of wine from it, but instead of swallowing it, he dribbled it over her breasts and down her belly and pushing her legs apart with his knees, into her pubic hair. He then balanced himself above her and began to drink up the wine again, from her body this time, with long, languid licks that made her tremble with delight. He took another sip and this time dribbled it into her mouth, kissing her as he did so.

"From your lips to your lips," he said, moving down her body.

Frances groaned and squirmed in delight.

***

Murray growled in frustration as Deborah fell back panting against the pillows.

"Sorry," she said, "but I've got to stop for a while, my jaw hurts and my hand's gone numb."

"This has never happened tae me before," he said, indignantly.

400

"Nor to me either!" she retorted, annoyed that he'd make it sound as if it was somehow her fault. "Probably brewer's droop. We've had a lot to drink," she added, thinking she should try to make him feel better, although he didn't deserve it. He was always so defensive about everything and it usually came out as aggression. She didn't like that.

"Aye, but I'm used tae drinking. I'm a Scot."

You're an arrogant bastard!

"Well, perhaps *you'd* like to pleasure *me* for a while, maybe that'll give you a hard-on," Deborah said grabbing his hand and guiding it towards her groin. But embarrassed by what he saw as his failure, Murray wasn't in the mood. He stood up and put his underpants on.

"Mebbe I should go and do some packing," he said.

"Oh, don't behave like a selfish, spoilt little boy!" Deborah said. "You can't get it up tonight, so what? Haven't we enjoyed ourselves the other nights? Hmm? What about last night? Didn't we have fun?"

"Aye, but..."

"But what?"

Murray sighed and sat back down on the bed next to Deborah. She put her hand on his shoulder and massaged it gently.

"I suppose I feel a bit foolish not being able tae do it. I think I'm a bit, you know, emotional. With this being mebbe the last time we'll see each other."

Deborah was taken aback by his honesty. For a moment she saw his vulnerability and it endeared her to him.

"I thought you wanted to see me in London, didn't you?"

"Aye, I did. I do. But you seemed tae be giving me the brush off for that, you know. I thought you wouldnae be keen for us tae carry on when we got back." He looked like a nervous puppy waiting for a stroke.

"Look, Murray. You and I have had a great time together. I'll be honest, I never in a million years thought I'd ever have sex with anyone on this holiday, let alone you. Sorry!" she added hastily, seeing his crestfallen look. "What I mean is, that I didn't come away to have sex with anyone. And you and I didn't exactly get off on the right foot. But I did have sex with you and I've enjoyed myself. But I hope we'll be more than just a holiday screw to each other."

"Really?" His eyes lit up with hope and Deborah felt a lump in her throat.

"Let's just take it a step at a time, shall we? We'll meet up in London and that's a promise. But things will be different back in the real world; we won't be cocooned in the holiday bubble anymore."

"I know that."

"But I'd like to give it a go. I'd really like to see you in London. Okay?"

Murray gave an enormous smile, stood up, kicked his underpants off and jumped back onto the bed. He moved his hand down into Deborah's pubic hair.

"Now, where were we?" he said.

***

Suzanne was inconsolable. She'd started crying after dinner during the dancing when Jo had got them all singing *I've Had the Time of My Life* and she hadn't stopped since. Her mascara had disappeared ages ago and the front of her dress and Stewart's shirt – matching green and purple oleander-patterned they'd bought from Palinda on the beach - were saturated with her tears.

"I've had the best holiday ever and I just don't want it to be over," she sobbed for the tenth time.

"But all good things must come to an end," Stewart said, gently brushing his hand over her hair. "And we'll all keep in touch with each other. Eve's taken a note of everyone's e-mail address and she's going to give us all a copy. And you and me are seeing each other, aren't we? We're together; an item. Or have you changed your mind?" he asked, teasing her.

"No! Of course I haven't! I'm just sad, that's all. Although..."

"What?"

"Well, I just never thought I'd meet someone like you. Someone who'd actually like me."

"Oh, Suzanne!" Stewart threw his arms around her again and pulled her to him. "What's not to like about you? You're a fabulous, gorgeous woman; the most wonderful woman I've ever met. You really are *all-woman*! Just like the mango man said."

"But we'll get back home and you'll forget me!"

"I won't! No I won't!"

"And you certainly won't want to show pictures of me to your friends and family."

"Why won't I? What you talking about?"

"Because I'm fat and ugly! Nobody wants their friends to see they pulled a fat girl!" she hiccoughed, crying hysterically.

Stewart stood up and taking her by the shoulders shook her roughly and raised his voice.

"That's enough, Suzanne! Just stop being so fucking stupid! I'm tired of telling you that I've been with you because I've wanted to be. I like you. I really like you. In fact, I've fallen in love with you! You're a kind, generous, honest, loving woman. But if that isn't enough for you, then that's it! We won't see each other ever again. It's your call. You can either believe what I'm saying and I'll move Heaven and Earth for us to be together permanently, or you can call me a liar and I'll walk away now. It's up to you." He was breathing hard, winded by his outburst. Suzanne stared at him open-mouthed.

"You love me?"

"Yes! Is that good enough for you?"

She nodded and more tears ran down her puce cheeks. Stewart pulled more tissues from the box and dabbed her face.

"Look at you! Stop crying! You're all red and your eyes are puffy," he said, kissing the top of her nose.

"Oh, Stewart, I feel such a fool. Just let me explain..." she gulped. "You see, I've never really had a boyfriend before. Once, a long time ago when I first went to Majorca with Mum and Dad, an English boy started talking to me round the pool. He was from Halifax, on holiday with three friends. We had drinks together and went to the beach together and he kissed me a few times. He'd tried to touch me but I wouldn't let him. Then one afternoon I was sitting on the balcony trying to dry my hair in the sun when I overheard him talking and laughing about me to his friends on their balcony above." She took a gulp and tears welled up in her eyes again. She paused before continuing.

"It turned out he'd tried to get me into bed for a bet."

"What a bastard!" Stewart was seething with indignation against this unknown man who'd upset his girlfriend. He clenched his fists ready to punch him on the nose and knock him out.

"And since then, well, I've stayed away from men and that's why I haven't got much confidence with them. Or in them." She blinked away her tears and looked at Stewart and smiled, making his heart leap. "But I'm really sorry I doubted you, Stewart. And I think... well... I know... I love you, too. I do."

"Oh, Suzanne!" he said pulling her down onto the bed with him. "You're a crazy, wonderful woman!"

They wrapped their arms tightly around each other and tired out and emotionally drained they soon fell sound asleep until morning.

***

The sharp knock on the door as Geri came out of the bathroom surprised her as she wasn't expecting anyone. She padded across the floor in her bare feet to open it and then staggered backwards as Jason forcefully pushed it wider and came into the room.

"What do you want, Jason?" she asked, trying not to show him she was nervous.

"Well, as it's our last night, I thought you and me could have a little bit of an action replay but with a better result. You know, a bit more of what we had the other night," he said walking towards her, hedging her onto the bed.

"Well you thought wrong! Get out!"

"Come on now, Geri, that's not very friendly, is it?" He leaned out and pulled her roughly towards him. She pushed against his chest with her fists but he held her tightly.

"Let go of me! Get out of my room!"

"That's how I like it! That's it! Struggle and fight before you give in. That really gets me going. Remember?"

"You pig! You bastard! You tried to rape me!"

He looked at her in mock horror and then laughed out loud, tightening his grip on her arms and grinding himself against her.

"Tried to rape you? You're kidding me! You were gagging for it, if I remember rightly, Geri. Gagging for it. You just got cold feet at the last minute."

"I'm giving you one last chance to get out of here or I'll scream."

"And with your history, who would believe you? Eh? Who would believe the woman who was fucking the water sports instructor in his little hut while one of her pupils nearly drowned wasn't gagging for it?" He laughed in her face. "You've got previous. It's common knowledge you were the school bike. How many blokes you worked with had you been with? Three? Four? Your reputation's so bad you can't teach any more. So let's just stop playing around and get down to business, shall we?" He pushed her back onto the bed and climbed on top of her and then shouted in pain and surprise as an ice bucket was tipped over his head and then pulled down tight round his ears. He stumbled backwards off the bed, the back of his knees making contact with the stool resulting in him sitting abruptly down on it, the bucket smacking back down onto his head.

"You fucking bitch!" he yelled as he prised the bucket off his head and then gasped in amazement when he saw Dave standing over him.

"Get out, Jason!" Dave said. "Get out before I beat yer to a pulp."

Jason staggered to his feet, shaking ice cubes from his head and then squared up to Dave as Michael appeared through the curtains from the balcony.

"What? You both thought you'd muscle in and take a turn, did you? Being as she's so easy she's probably up for a nice little threesome.

"Foursome, actually," Natalie said, appearing behind Michael.

"Fer the last time, get out!" Dave said.

"You can't blame me for coming back for more, mate. You've seen what she's like. She's been offering it on a plate all holiday. All over me the other night she was."

Jason didn't see the punch coming, just felt a thud against his nose that sent a spurt of blood in the air and made his whole head jolt back and smack against the wall. For a moment or two his head reeled and then his nose began to throb. He put his hand to it in a futile attempt to stop the pain and looked at Dave who stood stock-still in front of him and then at Geri who'd screamed when Dave had hit him and was now crying hysterically and being restrained by Natalie.

"You're welcome to her. She's a fucking prick-tease," he said. Then Michael grabbed him by the scruff of the neck and marched him to the door. Jason gave a half-hearted struggle but he knew that he stood no chance against Michael and he didn't want another punch on the nose. With his free hand Michael opened the door and thrust Jason through into the corridor, then, without saying a word, quietly closed the door behind him.

Geri collapsed onto the bed sobbing. Natalie sat down next to her, took her hand, saying "Sshhhh, sshhhh". Michael went onto the balcony and brought their drinks back in and then sat on the other side of the bed, while Dave righted the overturned stool and made himself comfortable on that. He picked up the ice bucket and then grabbed a melting ice-cube from the floor and held it against his knuckle. Geri's sobbing gradually subsided and she sat up and looked at them with panda eyes as her make-up was everywhere. Natalie went into the bathroom and brought out the tissues and gently wiped Geri's face then handed her the box.

"You must all think I'm a real slag," Geri said.

"We don't fink nuffink," Dave said.

"I want to explain..." Geri began.

"Look, you don't have to explain anything to us, does she?" Natalie said looking at the other two for support.

"Of course not!" Michael said. "Everyone on this holiday's had something going on. I'm just sorry that a bastard like him's upset you."

"But I want to!" Geri shouted in frustration. "I want to get it all off my chest." She took several deep breaths, wiped her eyes one more time and then started to tell them her story.

"You see, I was married to a very successful man... a pilot... and we had a lovely home, two gorgeous kids and a good life style. But I was always in his shadow. He'd been a squadron leader in the RAF and was used to giving orders and everyone jumping... nobody questioning him. And so I did the same. He was the alpha-male and I was the little wife. Oh, I tried to have my own life and career, but nothing I ever did was really good enough for him and his wants and needs always came first. Everything we had was down to him and I was never given the credit for anything. He'd criticise how I was bringing up the kids, how I ran the home, how I wore my hair, my choice of clothes, and he alienated the few friends I had. We always moved in *his* circle, not mine. As time went on he'd even started turning his back on me in bed because he said I was fat. Can you imagine? I weighed under ten stone and he said I was fat! I felt ugly, unappreciated, unloved and unlovable. Then one day a new colleague started at work and he took an interest in me. He was married and he was seven years younger than me, but he was funny and he made me feel as if what I said and did mattered for something. He was, you know, attentive. A few weeks later we went away on a school trip and we ended up in bed together on the first night. Of course, it didn't last. The following term he'd started an affair with a new young teacher who joined the school and I became last term's news. But realising that someone else had found me attractive gave me a real boost. And then I was asked to go away on a trip with the travel and tourism students skiing in the Spanish Pyrenees and while we were there I had a fling with the ski instructor. I should have learned my lesson then really, because one night some of our students got into a fight with some local lads and while they were sorting it all out, the other teachers realised I wasn't around. I was lucky the teacher leading the trip was a friend and although she told me I was out of order, she didn't report me. Maybe she should have done given what happened later. Anyway, after a while sex with a stranger became a regular thing. Whenever I had the chance of a one-night stand, like if I was on a conference, or if he was away on a long-haul trip, I'd leave the children with the au-pair and go to a hotel for the night looking for a pick-up, because it made me feel wanted and it made me feel attractive again. Then I was asked to go on an adventure trip which was part of Year Seven's induction programme. We were met by the instructors and one of them, a guy called Mark made it clear that he fancied me. Or perhaps he'd picked up on the fact that I was indeed *gagging* for it and that I was easy. Anyway, on the first afternoon we'd gone down to the river and the kids had gone kayaking. They all seemed okay and so he lead me into the hut where they kept the equipment and we had sex in there on top of a pile of life jackets. I remember laughing and thinking we were being daring doing it with all the kids and the other instructors and teachers just a couple of yards away, not knowing what we were up to, but really... now I'm talking about it I realise just how sordid the whole thing was. Anyway, it was all over in a couple of minutes. Mark was obviously used to taking women in there; it was his regular haunt for a quick shag. But just as we were getting our breath back I heard shouting and screaming coming from the river. I threw my clothes on and ran out to see two of our kids plunging into the water to try and rescue one of the others, Kevin, who'd fallen in. Mark ran down and threw three life belts in after them but Kevin was unconscious. Mark and a teacher, Steve, went in and managed to bring him out, while Jean, another teacher shouted at me to help her with the other two, but Kevin was in a bad way. He'd knocked his head and he'd swallowed water. One of the other instructors phoned for an ambulance and Mark started resuscitation. Fortunately the paramedics got there in just a few moments and he although he was eventually alright, he spend three days in hospital and his parents came down to take him back. Naturally, they made it their business to find out what had happened and it turned out that a couple of the kids had seen Mark and me coming out of the hut. Anyway, it all came out in the following enquiry and someone took great delight in telling the investigation that I'd had an affair with a colleague and always used school trips as a means of having a fling with someone. Of course, I denied it, but too many people knew the truth. In the end I faced a disciplinary and left the school. I was lucky Kevin recovered or I'd have been facing a negligence, or perhaps even a manslaughter charge. Anyway, when my husband found out the truth he used it as the excuse he'd been waiting for to throw me out. He managed to convince the judge I was an unfit mother and got custody of the children and I ended up in a rented flat working for an estate agent. And three months after our divorce he moved Lucy into our home. Lucy was the stewardess he'd been having an affair with for five years. That was why he'd turned his back on me in bed, not because I'd put weight on. But I played right into his hands. He was the wronged husband and I was the whore. And as it turned out, Jason works with someone who used to work with me and who'd talked about it when the story broke. So Jason knew who I was all along and he followed me the night of the storm. I'd made a fool of myself hanging around Elvis. He was too busy trying to keep the property and the guests safe to bother with me and I was too drunk to realise. He was angry with me and he marched me back to the end of my corridor and then went off. As I was trying to get the card to open the door Jason came up to help and followed me in. He said he'd tell everyone about me if I didn't have sex with him. I said 'no'. I told him I didn't want him. I tried to fight him off, but that just seemed to turn him on even more... but with one last effort I managed to shove him off me and kick him between the legs and he finally left me alone. I've been sort of avoiding him since." Running out of steam, exhausted by the confession, Geri's head fell forward and she started crying again. Natalie put her arms round her.

"That's attempted rape, Geri. We should call the police."

"No! No! I don't want the police. It would be his word against mine and like he said, nobody would believe me. I managed to fight him off the other night. I'm not putting myself through all that. I just want to forget it."

"Okay. Okay, it's over now," she said. "You've been really brave. You've faced what happened, you've told us. And don't worry; Jason won't come near you again. Even he's not that stupid."

"But I feel so ashamed... so dirty... such an idiot..."

"Stop it, Geri! You ain't got nuffink to worry abaht wiv us. We ain't judgin' yer, are we?" Dave said, looking at Michael and Natalie.

"No, we're not," Michael said. "We're your friends, Geri. We won't tell anyone anything. I'm just sorry you went through such a rotten time and sorry that Jason turned out to be such a bastard. I can't believe he thought he'd come back for another pop at you tonight."

"I've been having counselling. Not that it's helped much. The counsellor says I have to build up some self-confidence and self-worth. That's easier said than done, though."

"Yes. And blokes are not worth making yourself ill over," Natalie said. "Bunch of shites. Oh, sorry! Not you two, obviously," she added as Michael and Dave protested. "But you've got loads to offer someone, Geri. I know we all get lonely and it's easy to confuse sex with affection. But I really do think you're better off on your own than being with someone just for the sake of being able to say you've got a boyfriend or a partner. Never settle for Mr Half-OK." Natalie continued. Geri sighed.

"I know you're right. But it is hard and I have been lonely. Very lonely. But... you know... I've looked around the group this week and seen women that I so admire. You know, Jo, for instance. I was really prepared to dislike her..."

"But that was because of Deano." Natalie interrupted.

"Yes. I fancied a man so vain he wore turquoise contact lenses then nearly got swept into the Atlantic, breaking his leg in the process, because he lost one. That just about sums up my ability to pick the right man in a nutshell!"

They all laughed at that; not that they were being unkind about Deano's misfortune, but more as a release of tension after all that had happened.

"And look at Grace," Dave said. "She's a Detective Chief Superintendant. Well cool."

"And you, Natalie. You're so successful..."

"But I've had my ups and downs. Look what an idiot I made of myself over that bloody chav wedding."

"But you're happy and you enjoy your life. Even Dawn and Donna are happy. It's easy to take the piss out of people like them, but they're kind and they're basically nice, decent human beings. The same with Suzanne. I'm ashamed to say I really disliked her just because she was fat. I thought she was a nobody; not worth bothering with. Yet as I've got to know her over the last couple of days, I think she's lovely. I think I should start looking at myself and my values and start seeing the good in people. And I think I should start counting my blessings, too."

The others stood up ready to go to bed. It was after two and they had to be up early to pack and start their homeward journey. And the events of the last hour had given them all something to think about. Especially the bit about counting your blessings.

"Good night, babe," Dave said, giving Geri a kiss on the cheek. Natalie and Michael both gave her a hug and the three of them left. Geri walked back out onto the balcony and looked up at the sky where a thousand stars stared back down at her and she suddenly felt as if a weight had been lifted from her shoulders. She'd told these three people who she barely knew the darkest secrets of her past and they hadn't laughed at her or been disgusted by what she'd done. They'd kissed and hugged her and been nice to her.

I've got to be kinder to myself. I can't change the past but I can change the way I go about the future.

And with that thought she went back inside, to a purging shower and then the best night's sleep she'd had in a long, long time.

***

DAY ELEVEN

The ground engineer took the chocks away and the giant aircraft slowly moved forward, starting its long, laborious journey along the tarmac towards the end of the runway.

In seat 38A Trevor looked out of the window without really registering what he was seeing. His thoughts were taken up with the plans he'd been making to heal the rift with Rose. *With Rose and Sonia,* he corrected himself. He'd scolded himself time and time again during the last few days about his narrow-mindedness and he'd offered up more than one prayer of thanks that Rose, in spite of everything, had been worried about him and had managed to find him to check that he was okay. She was a truly good woman. It was Rose's birthday in a couple of weeks. He knew that she and Sonia both loved the theatre and he was planning to find out what was showing at the Manchester Opera House or the Apollo and send them tickets. He then hoped that any future outings to the theatre would also include him. He smiled to himself and turned to see Dave, who was sitting next to him, lean back in his seat with his eyes tightly closed and his fists clenched. Dave hated flying although he'd never admit it to anyone. He hated the taking off and he hated the landing. The bit in between wasn't too bad, and he'd surprised himself on the way over when he'd actually relaxed enough to watch a film and had then fallen asleep, only to wake up in a panic when they hit a spot of turbulence and had to fasten their seatbelts. Being afraid of flying was the reason why he'd made an excuse not to sit next to Geri on the homeward flight. He'd like to have done because he'd really got quite fond of her over the last twenty-four hours and he'd felt quite close to her after what had happened the previous night. But he didn't want to rush things, either. He didn't want her to think he was jumping in where Jason had left off. He wanted to give her time, so he'd given her his mobile number when they'd been sitting together at breakfast when nobody else was around.

"It's up to you, alrigh'? If you wanna see me ya've got me number. It don't av ter be a romance. I'm appy fer us ter jus' be friends," he'd said, although when he came to think of it, he'd never had a woman just as a friend before. Perhaps it might be quite nice.

She'd seemed pleased and had carefully folded up the piece of paper and put it in her handbag.

"We could sit together on the plane," she'd suggested then and Dave had had to think fast, knowing he couldn't sit with her because he didn't want her to see his fear of flying.

"Nah, babe. Sorry. Trevor's awready asked me to sit wiv im."

So Geri was sitting three rows behind him with Grace, Jo, Natalie and Michael. And Jason, *that bastard Jason,* as Dave now thought of him, was sitting much further forward with Huw. Both men had avoided the rest of the group on the last morning and when they finally joined them to board the minibuses to the airport, Dave saw that Jason had not just a busted nose but a cut and bruise across his cheek which must have been the result of pulling the ice bucket over his head.

Serve im fuckin' righ'!

***

In seats 35A and B, Suzanne and Stewart were tightly clutching each other's hands as if they might be torn apart by some unknown force at any moment. Both of them felt blissfully happy, unable to believe they had found each other. Suzanne had already thought about selling up the shop. They should get a good price for the freehold of the commercial premises and the three-bedroom house next to in spite of the recession, and she could use that to up sticks and move to be with Stewart. He'd already said that house prices where he lived were below the national average. It was true that Mum might need some persuading. After all, she'd lived in Norfolk all her life. But Suzanne would cross that bridge when she came to it. She'd worked tirelessly and without complaint for her family business all her life and now it was *her* time. Mum would just have to understand that.

"From today on I'm going to be really happy," she whispered to herself.

"What, did you say, Suze?" Stewart asked, turning from the window to face her.

"That I love you," she fibbed. She hadn't said it but it was true.

"Me, too," he replied, kissing her gently on the nose. They both gave a deep sigh of contentment and snuggled up against each other.

***

Behind them in 36A and B, Murray took hold of Deborah's hand, but she didn't turn her head; she just kept on looking out of the window, lost in her own thoughts. It had only dawned on her that morning as she was packing her suitcase, putting away clothes, shoes and jewellery that Maurice had bought her that it really was over between them and it felt like someone had thumped her in the solar plexus. All those years of being with him and only him; of buying what he told her to buy; of wearing what he told her to wear; of doing what he told her to do and of being at his complete beck and call were no more. Yet she didn't regret it because she'd loved him with a deep, all-consuming passion that even she couldn't explain to herself.

And now it's over...

After those awful texts, and because his wife knew all about her, there was no going back, only forward; she had her pride and she had her dignity. She hoped that she'd meet a new man soon because she wasn't used to being without a man in her life. She'd have to get out and join clubs and go on a few more Travel Together holidays. She felt Murray squeeze her hand and she turned to look at him, managing a smile. Deep down he was a decent enough man, but she knew he wasn't the man for her. Oh, she'd made the right noises the night before so they could end up friends and she could have some decent sex before she left. A holiday romance had been fine, in fact she'd felt comfortable with him and had enjoyed his company, being able to let her hair down in a way she'd never have envisaged. And she was genuinely looking forward to a few dinners and theatre trips in London with him. But then, she'd already made up her mind that she'd let him down gently. The vital spark was missing. She'd known from the very start that she could never have a future with a man who took his socks off last.

Murray returned Deborah's smile with a beaming one of his own. The holiday had been everything he'd wished for and more. He'd bagged Deborah! Deborah! And she had agreed to carry on seeing him once they were home.

It does nae get any better than this!

***

Geri, sitting between Jo and Natalie in seat 41E, felt a huge sadness that the holiday was over. She couldn't believe it had only been ten days; leaving Gatwick now seemed like a lifetime away. The holiday certainly hadn't turned out the way she'd imagined. Had she really spent so much time and energy preparing to meet the love of her life in Antigua? How could she have been so naive? Tears of shame sprang into her eyes when she thought of what had happened and the way she'd behaved. The incident with Richie; running after Deano; then Elvis and the whole Jason thing. She shuddered inwardly at that. He'd left a voicemail message on her room phone that morning apologising for his behaviour, but it hadn't made her feel any better. She was so lucky that Dave, Michael and Natalie had been having drinks with her on the balcony when he'd turned up last night. And she felt even more fortunate that Dave wanted to see her in spite of everything he'd heard about her. He'd given her his phone number and left it up to her whether she contacted him or not, so that she wouldn't feel pressured into a date. That was nice. She'd really disliked Dave at first, yet now... She gave a contented sigh and began to daydream about the possibility of a future with a used car salesman from St Albans.

***

Next to her in 41D, Jo let her mind finally wander back to Deano and to the ugly scene that morning. She hadn't recognised the woman talking to Eve at first as she'd wandered over to give her the tip money. It was only as she heard the woman raise her voice at Eve that she realised who it was, but it was too late for her to walk away as Rachel had seen her.

"It was sheer negligence! There's no two ways about it and your company or your agents, or whoever, are going to pay for this!" she was shouting at Eve, who was doing a very good job of keeping her cool.

"I really can't discuss it with you, Mrs Dean, other than to tell you, what your husband has already acknowledged, and that is that he suffered an accident because he couldn't see where he was going because he had his sunglasses on. He was attended to swiftly and well. The guide did everything he could, including putting his own life in danger by diving into the Atlantic Ocean and pulling him out. And once the paramedics arrived he was given the best possible medical attention, as you've seen for yourself, in Mount St John's."

"But he should never have been taken where it was slippery and dangerous. Your company knowingly put him in danger and now he's going to be off work for months. And he's self-employed. He'll lose a vast amount of money. My solicitor's going to have a field day with this, I can tell you. And you're supposed to be the one in charge, aren't you? And you weren't even there!"

"Mrs Dean, I'm really sorry your husband had an accident, but it had nothing whatsoever to do with me or whether I was there or not..."

"But you sold him the excursion!"

"Which was *optional* and which he *chose* to go on."

"Well, you needn't think you're getting away with it that easily."

"Excuse me, Mrs Dean. We met the day you arrived at the hospital, I'm Jo Walsh," Jo said, offering her hand, which Rachel ignored, eye-ing her up and down, instead with a sneer.

"Oh, yes. The vicar. I hadn't realised you were part of this set up."

"I'm just a member of the group, like Deano was, except that I'm supposed to be here because I really am single."

"What's that supposed to mean?"

"It means that I think you're angry with your husband, and rightly so, because he's lied to you and to Travel Together by pretending he was single so that he could come away on this holiday. Alone. Not only that, he demonstrated a laughable degree of vanity by wearing turquoise contact lenses and when he lost one he had to take the other one out so that he didn't look like some sort of freak with one hazel eye and one bright turquoise one. Then as he knew everyone would see his eyes had changed colour he decided to wear his sunglasses even though it was dull and overcast. Consequently, he couldn't see where he was going and that resulted in him having an accident. He'd already walked into a planter earlier that morning. So he's the one you should be directing your anger at, not Eve. She did nothing but try to help him. She's even kept his secret; there was no reason for everyone else to know how badly he'd behaved and consequently the only two people who know he's married are Eve and me. So you might want to apologise to her and then leave before anyone else from the group comes over and finds out about him."

Rachel had gone scarlet with fury. She stood with her fists clenched, her eyes boring into Jo's and her body tensed with anger. Then just as suddenly she turned to Eve for one last barb.

"You haven't heard the last of this!" she said, poking Eve in the chest and then turning on her heel she marched away.

"You okay?" Jo asked Eve.

"I'm fine. Thanks." She chuckled. "You think you've seen or heard everything, don't you?" She gave another smile and shrugged. "Sometimes I think you couldn't make it up! And you hit the nail right on the head, Jo. She must be furious with him and so she's taking it out on everyone else."

Reliving it again, Jo was suddenly overcome with a huge urge to get back to her little village in Cornwall; back to sanity and back to reality. She turned and looked at Grace, who'd thrown a fit because she couldn't upgrade and was now sitting sulkily with her eyes closed, shutting out everyone and everything in *Economy*. Jo gave a sigh. She'd loved her holiday and the lovely people she'd met, but she wanted to get back to her parish and her own people. She'd even missed the squabbles with the vicar and she never thought she'd have done that in a million years. She'd never know now what might have happened with Deano and that was probably just as well. She was going home! And Deano was relegated to being another one of life's *What Ifs*.

***

In seats 41 F and G, Natalie and Michael were cracking jokes and just enjoying each other's company. Across the aisle in 41H, Eve looked at them and felt warm and happy. Her gorgeous son turned to her at that moment and smiled.

"You okay?" he asked, reaching across the aisle to touch her arm. She nodded, too overcome with love and joy to speak. He looked so like his father, there was no denying it and she marvelled at the fact that she hadn't noticed from the very first day. She had really liked him as a person, though, from their first meeting at the check-in. And now she had all the time in the world to get to know him. She'd e-mailed Travel Together and told them she wasn't going to be available for two months. They'd have to get someone else to do the China trip. She needed some space, some time to herself to get her head round all that had happened and then she needed some time with her son. At that moment Natalie roared out laughing at something Michael had said.

Don't move in yet, Natalie! I want him to myself for a while!

Eve surprised herself with that thought, afraid she might be turning into a possessive mother already. She hadn't seen Melv since the previous night when he'd told her and Michael that meetings in St John's all day would mean he wouldn't be able to see them before they left. He'd spent a long time with Michael after dinner, chatting and making plans and then he'd come over to give her a hug, whispering "I'll call you in the morning," as he did. And he had called her to wish her a safe journey and to remind her that he'd be over to England in November and they could make more plans then. She was happy to take things slowly with him. She still wasn't sure just how much she believed of his account of his marriage, but she didn't really care. She was happy he was back in her life and that they were going to be together as often as they could. If it turned out that Melv was spinning her a line then she'd deal with him when the time came. And if he wasn't then her conscience would deal with Mary. She smiled and gave a deep sigh. She was due some happiness and today she felt so happy that she thought she'd burst. And not least of all because yet another trip was over. The last day was always a busy one; paperwork to do, packing up, her bill to pay and the tip to be collected and distributed. It had all been much as she had thought. Almost everyone had given the suggested amount except Dave, who'd generously put in thirty pounds and Murray and Ursula who'd only put in five dollars and Huw, who hadn't contributed anything. Eve couldn't help feeling that it was less of an insult to do that than do what Murray and Ursula had done. Plus, she'd had the visit from Rachel Dean. Eve thought that she didn't envy the woman her choice of husband. She yawned. She was emotionally drained as well as physically tired and she was looking forward to having at least a couple of hours' sleep on the flight before landing at Gatwick, a check that everyone's luggage had arrived, the usual round of goodbyes – and she knew today there'd be tears - before the drive home to her lovely little bungalow in Horndon-on-the-Hill. The usual pile of junk mail would be waiting for her, offering her loans she didn't want and credit cards she hadn't asked for; that always went straight in the bin. She'd grab just three hours sleep, before she got up, put on the washing machine, did the Tesco-run and then got herself back into her UK routine.

And she knew she'd be waiting for the e-mails and the phone calls from her two boys.

***

Frances stretched her legs out in seat 38G and yawned. She was so, so tired that she couldn't wait to be able to put the seat back down as far as it would go, put her eye mask on and her ear plugs in and sleep all the way back to Gatwick. She'd had the time of her life, but she was happy to be going home. She wanted to see her son. She coloured a bit at the thought of what she'd been up to and how she'd feel if her son knew about it.

But he doesn't know! And he won't find out!

She knew she'd been foolish; she'd ignored the money that had gone missing from her purse every time she'd been with Neville but she knew he'd been taking it. And on the last night he'd driven her back to the Mango Tree Resort so that she wouldn't have to look into her purse to pay a taxi fare. And when she had finally looked into her purse when she got back to her room, the three hundred US dollars she'd put in there earlier had gone. It hurt her to know for sure that Neville was a thief; that he may only have been with her for the money he could steal from her.

He wouldn't have made love to me without payment.

And although the thought did hurt her, she was able to shrug it off, because she wasn't stupid; that was the way it went the world over when an older female tourist met a younger local man. Instead she thought of the multiple orgasms and the way he'd made her feel: whole, attractive and desirable. Three hundred dollars? It had been worth ten times that! Neville had given her the time of her life. And that was priceless.

***

And in the most important seat on the aircraft, Captain Keith Spires, the Pilot Flying for today, set the thrust levers to the *Take Off* position.

"Thrust set," his First Officer Steve Bettone called and the aircraft started moving down the runway. Keith, one of the company's most experienced pilots, easily kept the aircraft straight as Steve gave the next calls and they gathered speed.

"One hundred!"

"V One!"

"Rotate!"

Keith gently eased back the stick, pitching the nose up sending the plane soaring skyward. They were heading NE across the Atlantic, carrying the Travel Together group back to the real world; on, towards the rest of their lives.

***